THE

HAMMER™

HORROR

OMNIBUS

AF728938

THE
HAMMER™
HORROR
OMNIBUS
JOHN BURKE
TITAN BOOKS

The Hammer Horror Omnibus
Print edition ISBN: 9781835416730
E-book edition ISBN: 9781835416747

Published by Titan Books
A division of Titan Publishing Group Ltd
144 Southwark Street, London SE1 0UP
www.titanbooks.com

First edition: September 2026
10 9 8 7 6 5 4 3 2 1

This is a work of fiction. All of the characters, organizations, and events portrayed in this novel are either products of the author's imagination or are used fictitiously. Any resemblance to actual persons, living or dead (except for satirical purposes), is entirely coincidental.

© 2026 Hammer Film Holdings Ltd.

John Burke asserts the moral right to be identified as the author of this work.

No part of this publication may be reproduced, stored in a retrieval system, or transmitted, in any form or by any means without the prior written permission of the publisher, nor be otherwise circulated in any form of binding or cover other than that in which it is published and without a similar condition being imposed on the subsequent purchaser.

A CIP catalogue record for this title is available from the British Library.

EU RP (for authorities only)
eucomply OÜ, Pärnu mnt. 139b-14, 11317 Tallinn, Estonia
hello@eucompliancepartner.com, +3375690241

Without limiting the exclusive rights of any author, contributor or the publisher of this publication, any unauthorised use of this publication to train generative artificial intelligence (AI) technologies is expressly prohibited. Titan Books also exercise their rights under Article 4(3) of the Digital Single Market Directive 2019/790 and expressly reserve this publication from the text and data mining exception.

Designed and typeset in Albertina MT by Richard Mason.

Printed and bound by CPI Group (UK) Ltd, Croydon, CR0 4YY.

CONTENTS

FOREWORD

Operetta Tenebrae

by Stephen Gallagher

THINGS CHANGED, the way things do.

Where spinoffs, tie-ins and fan fiction have flourished over the past four or five decades, the once-ubiquitous film novelisation entered a fast track to extinction. VHS started it off, DVD picked up the pace, and on it went.

To love a film back in the 1960s meant carrying its memory until it resurfaced in a beaten-up print in some second-run theatre, or waiting five years to catch its appearance on TV. If you were a horror fan you'd be scanning local newspapers for Sunday double bills or, in the ultimate case, acquiring a projector and shelling out serious money for ten minutes' worth of grainy, silent Super 8 in a Walton Films box.

But then there was the book of the film.

For any beloved piece of cinema, the novelisation was the only way to embrace, own, and repeat the experience at will. If the film was an adaptation of a classic you could seek out the source novel and often that would open up a whole new path, one that took you into the world of literature. But that was a different happiness. Valid, of course; life-changing, even. But not the one you'd been seeking.

The film novelisation is almost as old as cinema itself. In my copy of Achmed Abdullah's *The Thief of Bagdad* (1924, Doug Fairbanks on the dustjacket) an editor's note reads, "*Interest in a film is by no means exhausted by merely seeing it… imagination, stimulated by the film, is yet not satisfied until its story is wholly absorbed."*

Which, to be frank, is pushing it a bit. The reality is that for the reader it's a detailed souvenir with a value of its own. For a publisher it's always been a product with a ready market. For the author it's mostly been a rush job done as work-for-hire, an exercise in craft for some fast money to support a writing career.

That's not a put-down, and for the time invested it could be a very worthwhile gig. One writer confided to me that after persuading his publisher to agree to a small royalty on a title that then became a surprise hit, he paid for his house.

That writer published under a pseudonym, as many did to keep the side-hustles distinct from their main body of work. Not so with John Burke, the doyen of British novelisers. Burke did have other writing identities, but he made his own name a marque of assurance for those of us who cared as much for the quality of the read as for the material it was based on.

Burke could write, that was for sure, and he took the job seriously. No other name appeared with greater frequency on such a variety of film-related titles. His work-for-hire ranged from *A Hard Day's Night* to *Chitty Chitty Bang Bang* but his heart and his roots were in supernatural fiction. He was the creator of Dr Alex Caspian, Psychic Investigator in a series of novels and his original screenplay *Terror for Kicks* was filmed as *The Sorcerers* (with his screen credit unjustly downgraded).

In May 1965, Burke signed a contract with Pan Books Limited for *The Hammer Horror Omnibus*, defined as a work comprising four novelisations of thirty thousand words each. Delivery was set for August 30th that year; call that one story a month, an output averaging a thousand words a day. Daunting for many, but doable for a pro. I can imagine him upping the daily figure and taking weekends off—in my cash-strapped early days I turned out two fifty-thousand-word adaptations in a three-week burst, but that's another story.

He'd have been given file copies of the screenplays to work from. Novelisations were routinely written while a film was in production, from a draft of a script that was still a work in progress. The *Omnibus* job would have been unusual, not just for its format but because all four subjects had already been out on release. Photocopying was a new technology and expensive, so I can imagine the Hammer office sending over whichever spare drafts lay to hand. This may go some way to explaining why the Gorgon is Megaera on the screen, but Medusa on the page.

Burke may or may not have seen the films before tackling the work, and I don't think it would have mattered. There's more to an effective novelisation than a simple description of what we can see. The script serves as a trigger for the imagination and the noveliser writes from the movie in their head. There's a certain freedom to add and expand, though not too much; change the character of the intellectual property and you risk both the annoyance of the IP owner and the disappointment of your audience.

Turn to the first page of *The Gorgon* and consider the noveliser's craft. That introduction serves as background, as history, as setup for the story to come. But what's most important is the tone. It's like a declamation from a Victorian actor-manager holding the house in thrall, one hand stretched out to the heavens, features underlit like a demon's in the limelight. Settle in, it says, and know what you're in for.

Then there's a complete change of approach for *The Curse of Frankenstein* with a first-person account from the Baron himself, nailing his intellectual narcissism while seamlessly incorporating the content of scenes in which he hadn't appeared. With barely a pause for breath, the Baron continues the narrative into *Revenge*, making a single tale of the two in a way that's both logical and effective.

(There was an existing book adaptation of Hammer's

Revenge of Frankenstein, penned by original screenwriter Jimmy Sangster under the name 'Hurford Janes' and published by Panther in 1958. That version stands as a separate work.)

Curse was the earliest of the releases, premiering in May 1957. *Revenge* followed a year later, and *The Curse of the Mummy's Tomb* the year after that. *The Gorgon* was the most recent of them, opening to audiences only months before Burke's commissioning. The omnibus was published in 1966, its cover a vivid painted montage by Peter McGinn, for which he was paid £33.

If being a horror fan in the sixties called for dedication, then imagine the challenges for this twelve-year-old. Fortunately, I had options. I couldn't get into the films, but there was Forry Ackerman's joyous *Famous Monsters of Filmland* in the magazine rack with DC and Marvel at the local newsagents. There were the anthologies – with a head in a bucket on the cover, you knew exactly what you were getting with *The Pan Book of Horror Stories*. Then there were Lady Cynthia Asquith's ghost tales, Joseph Payne Brennan's *Nine Horrors and a Dream*, *The Boris Karloff Horror Anthology*...

And then along came *The Hammer Horror Omnibus, A Pan Original*, later to be known as *The First Hammer Horror Film Omnibus* after the arrival of a sibling in 1967.

Both landmark experiences for this reader, it's fair to say. Book-of-the-film took a public pleasure and turned it into a private one, just for me.

So here they are again. Four Hammer classics. Just for you.

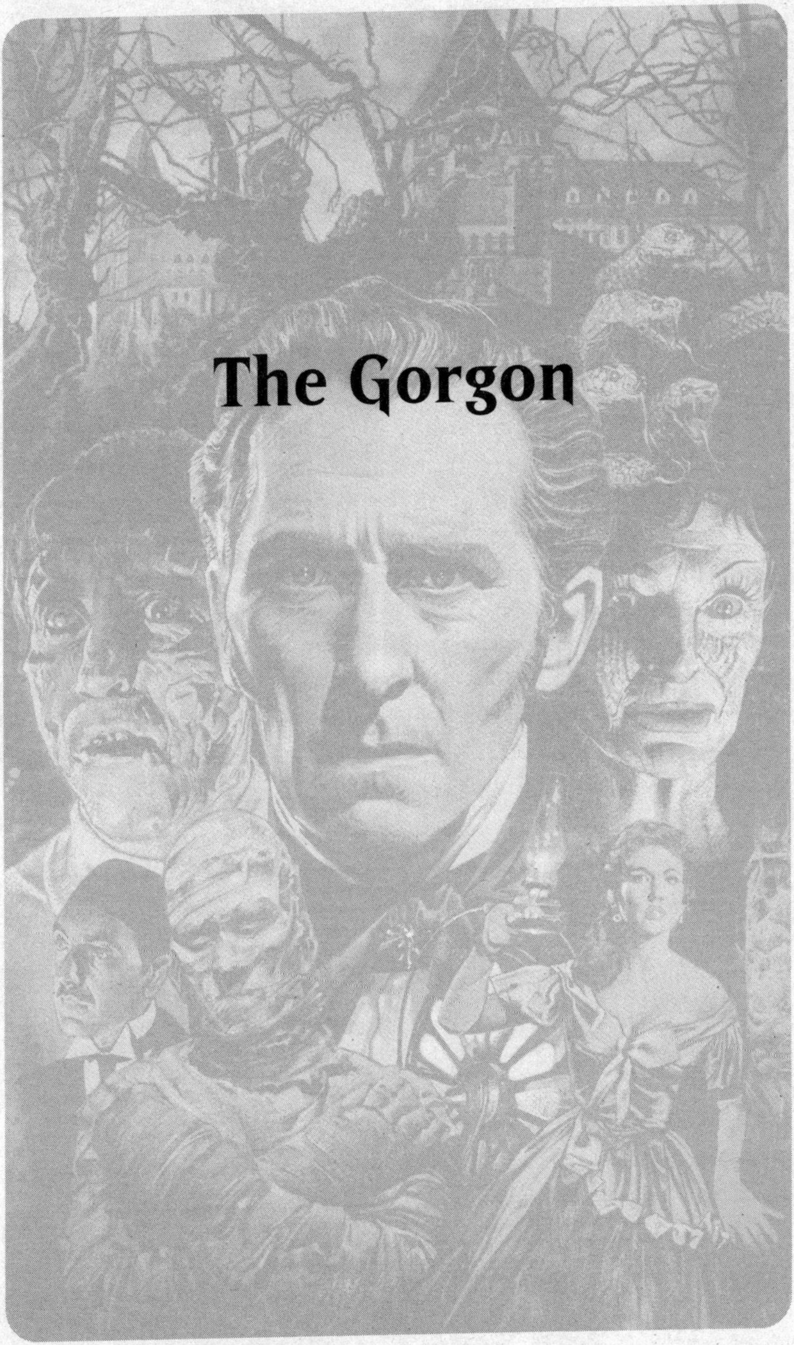
The Gorgon

1

FOR FIVE centuries the frowning Castle Borski had overshadowed the village of Vandorf. Stronghold of a noble Bohemian family, it had always dominated the entrance to the dark valley like a massive stone giant ready to stamp on anyone who tried to creep in or out. Nobody ever did creep in or out without the permission of the knights of Borski. Rumours might drift in on the breeze from the outside world, telling of great political upheavals, of kingdoms toppling and new powers rising, and even of the successful revolt of serfs against their masters. But in this valley there were no revolts. The serfs remained serfs.

Even when the last arrogant scion of the Borski family went to his death in the petty struggles of German nationalism in the nineteenth century, the people of Vandorf were still afraid to raise their heads. They knew nothing and cared nothing of the turmoil of proud new ideas just beyond their frontier. If they lifted their eyes they saw only that huddle of grim towers. The castle had been abandoned long before the end of the century, but to the local families it was still alive, still somehow filled with a superhuman power that must not be defied.

Men from other parts of Europe came into the valley, laughing at it while at the same time admiring it for being so picturesque, so unspoilt, so delightfully sunk in its old superstitions. Collectors of folk song and legend came. Painters came in order to capture on canvas, before it was too late, the sinister hues of this almost sunken land.

Let them come, let them go: the castle might now begin to decay, but its influence would still outlive this and many more generations.

At the turn of the century, when so many new things were setting Europe in a turmoil, something incredibly old came to live in Castle Borski. Nobody admitted it was there, because it was impossible that it should exist. There were seven terrible deaths in the forest, but they were not spoken of above a whisper. In Vandorf Medical Institution, established here by the authorities so that modem knowledge might shed some light into this sombre backwater of the Austro-Hungarian Empire, it was established that each of the victims had turned to stone. The Director of the Institution had been a sceptical man and a forward-looking, outspoken one. Now he was less outspoken. He had no wish to be recalled to Vienna and treated as a man who had lost his reason. Certain incredible suspicions stirred in his mind. They must be verified before he could make an official pronouncement. And he would speak out only when he was sure that it was safe to do so.

The natives of the village and the scattered homesteads in the neighbourhood would never speak out because for them it would never seem safe. The monster which slumbered was too cunning, too terrible, too old in wisdom – perhaps immortal. Safety lay in denying all knowledge of it. If voices were raised in unwelcome questions, those voices must be silenced. To awaken it was wanton folly. To provoke it in any way was a crime – not in the eyes of the police, and not punishable by any imperial law, but a crime that would be dealt with by the villagers themselves.

So the spectre from an ancient land lay in waiting in the vast, dank halls of Castle Borski… waiting until its destructive lusts should drive it forth again to take on human shape – a shape of beauty and yet of grotesque, unimaginable horror.

2

BRUNO HEITZ stood back from his easel and studied the few strokes he had just applied to the canvas.

'Yes,' he said. 'Yes, I think I can start really serious painting in the morning.'

He looked at Sascha and then back at the painting. Already he was absorbed in technical problems. His work was once more what counted. Sascha, staring past the light into his shadowy face, thought ruefully that it hadn't been like this fifteen minutes ago. Then he had not regarded her naked body as merely an academic study in anatomy. The fingers that now toyed with a paintbrush had then been exciting and demanding.

She reached for the clothes that, earlier this evening, she had tossed so eagerly aside. Bruno scowled. She had broken his thread of concentration. She said:

'I think you're one of the most selfish men I've ever met.'

'Dedicated,' he corrected her with a grin.

She took a deep breath. She was trembling, although it was warm here in the old millhouse.

'Bruno… are you going to marry me?'

'I told you, yes,' he said abstractedly. He dabbed a blob of colour into the corner of the canvas and bent forward to examine it. 'As soon as I've got rid of a few debts and seen some money in the bank.'

He had indeed told her this. He had said it more than once. But talking about it was all he had so far managed.

Bruno Heitz had been coming to Vandorf for a few years now. The son of a professor at Berlin University, he had preferred to spend his holidays here rather than in the company of some of his more exuberant, hearty friends. Originally he had stayed at the local inn and painted wildly romantic landscapes, luxuriating in the Gothic extravagance of the scenery. Then he had met Sascha, the innkeeper's daughter, and his interest had turned to a more personal style of painting. He was no longer a guest at the inn: her father disapproved of him and would have banished him from the district if it had been possible. Now he rented the millhouse for the season, and found it better in every way. It was more private, it was quieter, and as it was on the fringe of the dreaded forest there were no busybodies likely to come spying on them.

For Bruno it was ideal. For Sascha there had been hours and days of happiness here, too; but now there must be a reckoning, and he had to be told tonight.

Outside there was utter stillness. Nothing moved in the forest. Even in the daytime no birds sang, and at night there were none of the usual scurryings and rustlings under the trees. The trees themselves seemed petrified.

Sascha said: 'Bruno…'

'Oh, now, for Heaven's sake.' He was like a petulant little boy, hating to be distracted from his game of the moment.

'We can't wait any longer, Bruno.'

'Why not?'

'Because I…' She faltered. Once it was said, everything would be changed. The carefree happiness would be ended. She dreaded what Bruno's expression would be when he knew.

'Well?' he said impatiently. 'Tell me.'

She had meant it to sound cheerful, to give him the chance

of making it a cause for rejoicing, but now she found that she was sobbing. She could not check her tears.

'Oh, come on, now,' protested Bruno, 'it can't be as bad as all that.' He put down his brush and came to her, taking her in his arms. He kissed her bare shoulder. Again he was becoming aware of her; once more she was real to him. 'Just tell me. What's all this about?'

'I'm going to have your baby.'

He stood very still. Sascha buried her face in his jacket so that she wouldn't have to look at him.

He said quietly: 'When did you know?'

'A week ago.'

'I see.'

Slowly he pushed her away from him – but it was not a rejection. He smiled wryly, but behind it all there was an affection that warmed her through. It was somehow going to be all right.

Bruno ran a hand through his hair – the nearest concession he would ever make to smoothing down that unruly mop – and buttoned his jacket. The gesture was an oddly formal one.

He turned towards the door.

'Where are you going?' asked Sascha.

'To see your father.'

'Now? But—'

'I'm not going to evade my obligations. I want him to know that.'

'Your obligations?'

'Isn't that the way he'll consider it?'

The words sounded so dull and hard. This wasn't the way Sascha wanted to think of it. And she had not anticipated Bruno marching straight out into the night. They ought to talk about it, decide what was best, and make plans that would cause the least distress all round. The trouble was that Bruno was so impetuous. Having made a decision, he had no patience: it must be put immediately into effect.

'Don't go to him, Bruno! Not now.'

'It may as well be now as any other time.'

'He'll kill you.'

'I doubt it,' said Bruno. He opened the door.

'You don't have to rush off,' she cried after him. 'We can talk… decide… Bruno, let me come with you. If you're going…'

But already he was striding down the path. The light of the full moon struck across his face as he turned halfway down the slope and made for Vandorf.

Sobbing, Sascha pulled her clothes on hurriedly. She had no time to tidy herself up. Her one thought was to catch up with Bruno and plead with him to return. Tomorrow they could see her father. When they had worked out exactly what they must say and do, they could go to him. It would be better in the daytime. Tonight he would have been drinking with his cronies, the inn would be full of fumes and pipe smoke, and he would be in one of his tetchy moods.

The path which Bruno had taken cut through the lower edge of the woods. It was an old path and had been badly overgrown when Bruno first came to the millhouse, but now he kept it reasonably passable simply by tramping to and fro a great deal.

Sascha ran in under the trees. The moonlight was a broken flicker through the branches, making a ghostly latticework on the ground and the tree trunks.

There was a movement up the slope, away from the path.

Sascha called: 'Bruno!'

Her voice was like the sound of a lonely night creature, the only one daring to raise a plaintive cry in the stillness of the forest.

The shape moved on through the shadows.

Sascha stumbled off the path and emerged into a clearing.

Clouds slid across the moon, obscuring it for a few seconds and then spilling light once more into the gap in the woods. At the end of a long avenue of firs the castle rose sharp-edged against the night sky. Below it, light sparked and shimmered on the surface of a pool that had once been part of the moat. In the silvery glow the scene could have been a tranquil, soothing one but for the craggy harshness of the castle itself.

Bruno could surely not have come up this way. Sascha turned back towards the path.

A featureless shadow stood waiting for her.

Sascha tried to speak, but no words would come. She took a step forward, then glanced desperately to one side. If she ran to her right she could scramble down the slope and meet up with the path farther down the hill.

She began to make a wide, trembling circuit of the unmoving shape.

Then it moved. It came out of the dark shelter of the trees. The moonlight that had been so beautiful was now cruel. It shone with an unearthly radiance on the face of the creature.

Sascha screamed. She knew that she was awake and that this was real, but she tried to claw her way up and out of the nightmare. The creature advanced. Sascha had no strength, no way of escaping. She felt the searing stab of pain in her forehead and put her hands up, but they, too, had lost their strength and fell away again.

She stared full into that mask of terror. The truth was more appalling than any of the tales they muttered in her father's inn. She knew what the truth was, and knew that it was too late. She screamed again and again because it was too late.

3

THE CORPSE was brought down the hillside by pony and trap to the Medical Institution. The staff had heard that it was on its way and were going about their duties in a hushed, wary fashion as though anxious to catch any faint murmur of the details. It was rumoured that it was 'another one of those' – and beyond that nobody cared to speculate.

Carla Hoffmann was filled with dread. When she came here in 1903 as a probationary nurse she had been shocked by the warped nature of many of the local people and by its unsavoury manifestations which so often had to be treated in the clinic. But it had been her job to cope with such problems, and she had learnt that job thoroughly. She had learnt not to be nauseated and not to despise anyone. Even after her own illness, a couple of years after she came here, she had recuperated swiftly and Dr Namaroff had insisted on keeping her on. Physical disgust was something that could be overcome. A physical collapse could be overcome. Fear was not so easy to conquer.

Fear was irrational. Fear was something that came down from the hills and breathed coldly on warm flesh. Fear had no business to exist in a sane, efficient world. Yet it had been settling down into the valley in recent times like a mist that would not disperse. It was not only the superstitious villagers who felt it: it permeated the wards and corridors of the sanatorium. No antiseptic could keep it out, no drugs deaden it.

Carla stood in the entrance hall and waited for the shrouded burden to be lifted from the trap on the drive. The pony whinnied and was difficult to control.

'Ah, Miss Hoffmann!'

She had been so engrossed in the arrival of the corpse that Inspector Kanof's voice came as a complete surprise. She started and turned towards him, trying to keep the distaste out of her eyes. Kanof was a grey little man, always sneering at the peasants of Vandorf yet greasily trying to keep in with them when it suited him to do so. She hated the way he looked her up and down: if it were not known to everyone that Dr Namaroff kept her jealously under his own wing, there would have been trouble from Kanof long before this.

'Inspector Kanof.' She forced a respectful cordiality into her tone. 'You have come to see the doctor, of course.'

'Of course.' The inspector glanced at the two attendants lifting the body on to a trolley. 'Which of us do you think he will wish to see first? I think perhaps his other visitor is in no hurry now, hm?' He snickered and gave her an evil, self-satisfied little grin.

Carla walked briskly away down the corridor. Her own reflection came to meet her from the glass panel of a door at the end – the reflection of a trim, dark-haired girl with brown eyes and a lithe walk. This was how she had always wanted to see herself: a coolly competent young nurse moving skilfully about her business in the setting of a well-appointed modern hospital. But the white walls threatened her with indefinable shadows, and when she entered the laboratory she felt her usual twinge of instinctive distaste. Dr Namaroff's presence had been having this effect on her for many months now. It had been bad to start with, and now it was getting worse. But he had saved her from black despair after her illness and had kept her on here. She owed him a debt of gratitude.

And he intended to exact every penny of it. As he turned to greet her, delicately lifting his scalpel from the fragment of brain tissue in the dish before him, he smiled – the patient smile of a man who intends to get his own way in the end.

'The body's available for you to see, Doctor,' said Carla stiffly. 'And Inspector Kanof's waiting.'

'Better show him in first.'

Carla held the laboratory door open. Kanof came down the corridor with a spry, bumptious stride. Carla wanted to go away and leave them to their discussion, but she could not. Unobtrusively she began to tidy the bench where Namaroff had been working.

Namaroff said: 'Well?'

'The girl is the daughter of Janus Cass, landlord of the Saracen Inn,' said Kanof. He drummed a thoughtful little tattoo on the bench with two fingers. 'This may not be the same as the others.'

'You mean you hope it isn't.'

'Naturally. Another unsolved murder would hardly be good for my prestige in Vandorf.'

'Ah. So you will make sure that this one is solved.'

'Yes,' said Kanof forcefully. 'You may rely on that.'

Namaroff's lips curled into a mocking grimace that stayed frozen on his mouth while his pallid grey eyes stared into and through Kanof. The bleak scrutiny made the policeman shuffle uneasily. Finally Namaroff allowed himself a whimsical nod.

'You think you know who did it?'

'A young man. Staying at the old millhouse and carrying on with the girl. Lovers' quarrel – that's the way I see it.'

'Very plausible.'

'Lovers do quarrel.'

'Of course they do, my dear fellow. Does the young man confirm this theory of yours?'

'He's still missing.'

Namaroff's grave expression retained a hint of the earlier mockery. 'Unfortunate. Most unfortunate. But you know who he is?'

'His name is Bruno Heitz. An artist – the son of some professor at Berlin University.'

The mockery faded. Namaroff whistled softly. 'Professor Jules Heitz,' he said. 'I know him. We were students together. You'll be getting in touch with him?'

'Immediately, Doctor.'

Namaroff pondered, then said: 'I suggest not immediately. Wait until you find the young man.'

'You may be right.'

Namaroff suddenly became aware that Carla was still in the laboratory. He gazed at her with piercing intensity, then softened into a smile which she found even more repulsive than his anger, and said:

'Carla, my dear, perhaps you'll wheel the corpse in. It's time I examined it.'

Carla went halfway along the corridor and waved to the attendant, who began to push the trolley towards her. The attendant was Ratoff, a swarthy little man who belonged to this part of the country, but who had freed himself from his background and become a devoted servant of the institution. He had a streak of callousness that stood him in good stead in this job. His respect for Dr Namaroff bordered on adoration. They steered the trolley into the laboratory. As it turned, it jarred slightly against the door jamb. A hand that protruded from beneath the sheet wavered for a second, and the middle finger dropped off.

There was a scream that rang through the building.

Carla, watching the finger drop to the floor and lie there, unnaturally grey and hard, thought at first that it was her own voice crying out, resounding in her head. But Ratoff had turned and was racing back along the corridor. Namaroff brushed past Carla and followed.

The two men flung themselves through the doors at the end of the corridor. The doors swung to and fro as though in a high wind. The scream came again, and again, rising and falling.

Carla reached the hall as Namaroff started up the main staircase.

Above them a crazed woman was struggling to free herself from two attendants. Ratoff had just joined them, but was in danger of being kicked or elbowed down the stairs again.

It was Martha. Oh, God, poor Martha, thought Carla. This time he won't be lenient. This time it won't be curative treatment for her – it'll be punishment.

The woman's hair hung down over her face. Wildly she tossed her head to free her eyes so that she could see to gouge and kick and spit. Her scream sank to a breathless sob as she doggedly wrestled with her captors. It was an imploring sob, a plea for understanding that was beyond anyone in the universe.

Her struggles weakened. There were three strong, practised men against her now. At last they subdued her and she sank exhausted against the stair rail.

Sister Grethe came out on the landing. She had two gashes down her left cheek, bleeding furiously, as though Martha's nails had struck savagely with the intention of marking her for life. The fury of the attack must have been overwhelming, and Sister Grethe had been glad to leave the final battle to the men.

She cautiously descended a few steps.

Namaroff was white with rage. 'How did this happen?'

'She pounced on me, Doctor. As soon as I got to the door of her cell – her room, that is.'

'This is the second time. Put her in a straitjacket… and keep her in it.'

Martha whimpered and began to sag, her knees giving way until she was a crumpled heap on the stairs. Ratoff stood above her, taking no chances.

Carla felt a sickness that turned her stomach over. She knew all too well what it felt like to be lost. She remembered the bewilderment, the groping uncertainty, the yearning to cry out and beat one's fists against something or somebody. Namaroff had helped her through the worst phase and she had come back to the clean, clear world; but supposing she hadn't been able to respond – supposing she had collapsed into the fog as Martha had done? Would Namaroff have been so patient then, or would he have condemned her to the imprisonment he was now prescribing for Martha? If Namaroff hadn't fallen in love with her he might not have persevered.

She turned to him, wanting to plead with him as he came down the stairs, but Sister Grethe spoke first. As Martha was half led, half carried past her, she shrank back and said:

'It was the full moon again. The same as last time.'

'Sister!' Namaroff's voice cracked like a whip. 'That's quite enough of that. Go and get those cuts of yours attended to.'

'Yes, Doctor.'

Namaroff turned away. He indicated that Carla should accompany him, and they went through the doorway where Kanof had been viewing the proceedings with sadistic interest. The corpse lay in the stillness of death, shrouded and remote from all the agonies and shoutings of life. Carla mutely indicated the finger on the floor. Namaroff made a quick, hissing intake of breath and then twitched the sheet from the body.

Kanof approached. 'You'll perform an autopsy, of course, Doctor?'

Namaroff ran his fingers over the solid, unyielding head of what had once been an eager, vital young woman.

'On a body that's turned to stone?' he said.

4

THE JOURNEY from Berlin had been a long one. The frontier of Bohemia was not impossibly far, but there was no direct route to Vandorf or indeed to any major town in the vicinity. These people had lived in seclusion with their own customs and their own gruff dialect too long to want to make things easy for visitors.

The wretchedness that had clung to Professor Jules Heitz from the moment the news reached him now became worse. He could see why his younger son had been stirred by this sinister countryside and why his youthful romanticism should have brought him back here time and time again. In his creative imagination there might well be a unique splendour to be captured from unique surroundings. But this was no consolation to Professor Heitz. Here there could never be any loveliness. For him this place meant only death: the death of a girl he had never met, and the death of his son Bruno.

It was made very plain to him as soon as he reached Vandorf that he was not welcome. When he had announced his intention of coming to the inquest he was warned that he should not attempt to put up at the local inn, as the dead girl's father was capable of violence. After he had used what influence he had with a local dignitary whose son was studying with him – a remote contact, and one which took some pains to establish – he was found accommodation in a town five miles away, over the ridge and out of sight of Castle Borski. He would have to be driven in for the inquest. And perhaps that was best. Walking down Vandorf's shabby, dispiriting main street, he saw the stunted men of the district nudging each other and pointing him out, and the women twitching back curtains to glare at him. Whatever charm Bruno might have found here, Bruno's father was not one to be charmed by old ways and inbred backwardness.

On arriving at the damp little courtroom in which the inquest was to be held, Heitz was peremptorily told by a wizened little clerk that the coroner was likely to call on him as a witness. Before the professor could protest that he had only just come to the district, the clerk added, 'A character witness, of course,' and fussed away.

The courtroom was crowded. Surrounded by these dour men and women in their dark, shabby clothes, Heitz was reminded of nothing so much as a congregation of ragged vultures. They had come for the pickings. They would scratch over the dead – and drive the living away.

The coroner was a lean-featured man with a pouchy jaw. It was clear from the start that ws mind was made up on the fundamentals of the case. He wanted to hurry it through and be done with it. Heitz had hoped to learn something of what had really happened – something more than the bare, terrible facts which had brought him here from Berlin – but he realized that there was going to be no deep, analytical probe into the truth.

Inspector Kanof was the first witness. He reported the finding of the girl's body by a woodcutter who, skirting the forest in the early morning, had seen a flash of colour in the dark undergrowth and, after a brief fearful inspection, had hurried down to the village to notify the police. There followed a search for the young man who was known to have been spending a lot of his time with the girl.

He was found hanging from a tree not far from the scene of the crime.

Professor Heitz lowered his head. He was a man whose dignity and self-control meant a great deal to him, and he did not wish these people to see the tears in his eyes.

The drone of voices went on – question and answer, perfunctorily exchanged by men who did not want to stir up too many dark elements.

'When I broke the news of the girl's death to her father,' Kanof was saying, 'he said it was no surprise to him.'

'What did you deduce from that?'

'That he had personal reasons for knowing of Bruno Heitz's bad reputation.'

'And had you any such personal experience, Inspector?'

'Yes, sir. There were certain incidents…'

'Describe them, please.'

'Drunkenness, bad behaviour in public. Singing in the streets, starting arguments in the inn – it became so bad that the innkeeper had to throw him out. Many of his opinions verged on blasphemy…'

It was too petty, too dreary. The natural exuberance of youth was something alien to the people of Vandorf. Had any of them, Heitz wondered, ever been young? He looked round the room. The faces were sullen and secretive. All right, Bruno had been a young fool – but he was a generous young fool who gave himself rapturously to life and wanted to share his joy with others. Little they would understand of conviviality and friendship!

Then Heitz started. One face stood out from the rest. It was a face which certainly did not belong here. He recognized it, but for a moment could not visualize it in its proper setting. Then he remembered. Namaroff. An educated man, a surgeon, a scientist. He had visited the Heitz home during his days in

Berlin, and the Professor had been impressed by the range of his mind. A trifle cold, perhaps – undoubtedly ruthless if the need arose – but the detachment of an educated man was what was needed here at this stage.

Heitz felt a flicker of hope. Something was wrong, but one civilized, knowledgeable voice might begin to put it right. The coroner might not find it so easy to rush over the opinions of Dr Namaroff.

'Call Janus Cass…'

The innkeeper was a great barrel of a man, with all the marks of his trade save the essential one of jollity. His heaviness was that of brutality and a limited imagination. In the witness stand he was like a huge animal, lumbering and unapproachable.

'You are the father of the deceased girl, Sascha.'

'Yes, sir.'

'And landlord of the Saracen Inn.'

'Right, sir.'

'Will you please tell the court what you know of the relationship between your daughter and the deceased young man.'

'My girl took to him, unfortunately. Said she loved him,' growled Cass. 'He took advantage of her and then didn't want to face the consequences.'

'When you say "took advantage of her" you mean—'

'It's my belief she was pregnant by him. A thoroughly bad lot. I told Sascha to have nothing to do with him – knew from the time he stayed in my place he was no good – but she wouldn't listen.'

'She disobeyed you.'

'She did. He talked her into it. A sly tongue he had, that one.'

The coroner nodded, accepting, jotting down a few notes. He asked: 'Did you personally observe this man's addiction to alcohol?'

The invitation to confirm the picture of Bruno Heitz as a

drunkard and a wastrel was unmistakable. The coroner was not so much questioning the witness as urging him to say what was required of him. Professor Heitz had difficulty in restraining himself. As a scholar, accustomed to the sifting of evidence and the meticulous checking of every fact before he would even dare to formulate the beginnings of a theory, he was appalled by this perversion of justice. But he knew how little weight his word would carry in this place. They would be glad of the excuse to turn on him.

'Nobody ever had a better chance than I did,' Cass was saying with vicious relish. 'Didn't he stay with me those first few times, before I got on to what he was at? Getting the inn a bad name, he was.'

'A tendency to violence in his cups?' the coroner suggested.

'Well, sir…'

If Cass was baulking at this one, he got no chance to make his meaning clear. The coroner briskly dismissed him without waiting for the answer, and went on to the next witness.

'Call Dr Namaroff.'

Heitz sat up. He looked at the doctor's ascetic, arrogant features and almost begged the man to turn and recognize him. He wanted to convey a plea to him – a plea for decency, for the intellectual honesty that must be shared by men of good-will from the civilized world.

'Will you tell us, Doctor, what in your opinion was the cause of this girl's death.'

'It was undoubtedly the result of violence,' said Namaroff calmly. 'I observed deep abrasions round the forehead as though she had been struck from the front by some sharp instrument. There were indentations in the skull…'

He paused. Heitz willed him to go on. Surely any marks on the skull could have been caused when she fell. How had she fallen – what *sort* of abrasion had there been on the forehead – where was the murder weapon and what was there to ally it with Bruno or with anyone else?

'A violent attack,' the coroner prompted Namaroff.

'Undoubtedly.'

'From the front. Carried out, would you say, by someone she knew and from whom she didn't try to run away?'

'A sound point,' said Namaroff politely.

'Thank you, Doctor. You may step down.'

Again Heitz almost rose from his seat. But even the suggestion of a movement brought a scowl from his neighbour.

Then his name was being called. They were waiting for him to make his way to the witness stand. His hands shook as he took up his position. He was not a short-tempered man but he knew that he was liable to burst out in a rage today; and knew also that it would achieve nothing.

'You are Professor Jules Heitz.'

There was a formal attempt at respect in the coroner's manner, but it was veiled by a more characteristic indifference.

'I am.'

'Father of the deceased man, Bruno Heitz.'

'Yes.'

'You have heard the evidence before this court?'

'If you can call it evidence.'

There was a whisper of indrawn breath. The coroner frowned, and went on sharply:

'Did you know the girl concerned?'

'No, sir.'

'From the evidence before me I have the impression that your son was somewhat of a profligate. Would you agree with that?'

Heitz said: 'He was a talented artist. His life was of his own choosing.'

'The life of a libertine,' the coroner nodded.

'No. Possibly he had a number of young women in his life. That doesn't make him a libertine.'

'There was at any rate one particular girl whom he betrayed.'

'I cannot believe that.'

'You are his father.' The coroner shrugged. If it was meant as a comment on the situation, it was either insulting or meaningless.

Heitz said: 'There is no clear evidence that my son intended to shirk his obligations to the girl. No evidence that he killed her. The medical report' – he glanced reproachfully at Namaroff, who averted his gaze – 'was singularly inadequate. The police findings were no more than—'

'If you have nothing further to contribute to this inquiry,' said the coroner, 'you may stand down.'

'I am not ready to stand down.' Heitz lifted his head so that he did not have to meet the savage eyes of the hunched creatures in the courtroom. 'We are not considering one isolated case – or, rather, we ought not to be considering just one case. I have read the newspapers, and I am a student of human nature. I have read about the unsolved Vandorf murders… and from my brief contact with human beings here I have no doubt at all that everything I have seen and heard has been generated by fear. Particularly what I have heard in this courtroom.'

A bestial snarl rose from the well of the court. The coroner hammered for silence, but his expression made it plain that he sided with his fellow citizens.

He said: 'Professor Heitz, in assessing the evidence before us—'

'Evidence which is circumstantial, prejudiced, and contrived,' said Heitz. 'Evidence which would never be accepted in any civilized community.'

'Professor Heitz, I must ask you to stand down.'

Bruno's name would be stained so that this sinister matter

could be brought speedily to a close. He had been a stranger, so let him be the scapegoat. The verdict was a foregone conclusion: murder followed by suicide.

'I will say no more.' Heitz stepped down. 'But believe me, I shall not rest until I have cleared my son's good name.'

He went back to his seat like a man running the gauntlet between ranks of savages waiting to pounce.

The coroner made a show of sorting out papers. He then picked up his pen and began to write. When he looked up he said:

'I find that the dead woman was murdered by the man Bruno Heitz, who then, in a fit of remorse, took his own life.'

There was a buzz of approval. The courtroom began to empty. Heitz tried to fight his way through towards Namaroff, but others took a malicious pleasure in impeding him. Namaroff had left and was driving away before the professor was anywhere near the door.

A youth with vacant eyes and a fixed, revolting grin jostled against Heitz and wagged his head knowingly.

'You'd better watch out. I'm telling you, you'll be for it.' The local dialect was so thick that the words slurred into one another. 'She'll strike you like she struck the others, eh? *She...*'

An arm grabbed his shoulder, and the drooling, inbred creature of the valley was roughly bundled out of the room.

As Heitz emerged into the open he was faced by a semi-circle of mute, waiting men and women. They made no move to attack him: they simply stood and watched, waiting to make sure that he went away.

He was relieved when the carriage arrived for him and the horses began to strain nobly up the hillside away from Vandorf. The very air seemed clearer over the ridge. Yes, he was relieved to be putting Vandorf behind him at this moment – but he had every intention of returning.

The mutterings of that half-imbecilic youth nagged on in

his mind. *She*... It could have meant anything or nothing. But it stirred a faint memory. Not of Vandorf itself but of places along a route through Europe – a route leading in from Asia Minor, the track of something strange. Or was he trying to make up a theory before he had checked his facts? Professor Heitz had a voluminous memory and was proud of his ability to select relevant details from it when he needed them; but he was also humble enough to admit that he could not retain everything and that for completeness he needed an equally voluminous library. His library was in Berlin. He had access to no books in Vandorf – if they possessed such things. If he could find some way of studying the sources, letting things fall into place, allowing a suspicion to trigger off one idea and then following it up remorselessly until it combined with others, he might have an answer to what was going on in Vandorf. Yet he would be the first to admit that his speculations were wilder than anything that had been said in that dismal little courtroom today.

His friends – for so, in comparison with the people of the village, his hosts seemed – tactfully asked little about the inquest. They lived close enough to the valley to know what its reputation was. They were glad he had come back unscathed.

Their relief changed to dismay when Heitz announced that he was not returning to Berlin immediately. Bruno had paid rent on the millhouse for some weeks in advance, and Heitz proposed to spend some time there. He wished to carry out some research.

And speaking of research, might he have the privilege of looking up one or two points in his host's library? As they knew, his special subject was the influence of myth on the aesthetic development of contemporary poets and novelists, and there were one or two complex cross-references which he wished to clear up. Far from his own cherished collection in Berlin, he was rather at a loss.

He spent another night in the house and devoted most of the following day to intensive reading. Then he thanked his host warmly for the generous hospitality, and went back to Vandorf. He chose a circuitous route, approaching from behind Castle Borski and avoiding the village itself so that he could descend unobserved on the millhouse.

Bruno's paintings were everywhere – a pathetic reminder of his talent and his impulsiveness, and a memorial to the girl his father had never met: a girl living on only in these unfinished sketches and swift portraits, a girl smiling and pouting, stretching out her arms lazily for love and not knowing she was to meet death.

Heitz spent the evening tidying up the place to suit himself and putting away those tragic souvenirs of a shattered happiness.

Next morning he appeared in the village and went to the inn. The innkeeper appeared at the door and said that the place was closed for a few days. He was in mourning – hadn't the professor, of all people, got the grace to leave him alone to his sadness?

An old crone spat at him in the street.

He went to the police headquarters set some distance apart from the village, as though keeping its own counsel. It certainly kept it today: Professor Heitz was refused admittance on the grounds that the officers in charge of the case had nothing to add. A verdict had been delivered in court, and that was the end of it.

In the early afternoon he visited Dr Namaroff and was shown into a spacious sitting room, part of self-contained quarters at the back of the institution. The tense, dark girl who had met him at the door was introduced as Carla Hoffmann and then went away.

'Do sit down, Professor.' Namaroff's voice was at its most rich and soothing. 'I am so sorry about your son. You have my deepest sympathy.'

'Thank you.' Heitz failed to be soothed. When Namaroff offered him a cigarette he shook his head and said bluntly: 'I want you to answer a simple question.'

'Please.'

'You were once a guest at my house in Berlin. You met both my sons. I recall that you talked to Bruno in particular at some length.'

'I… may have done. Yes, I believe I did.'

'What impression did you form of him?'

Namaroff made a great show of lighting a cigarette for himself. He pondered, as though putting on a special act for a difficult patient.

'I thought he was… ah…'

'Normal?' snapped Heitz.

'Why, yes, of course.'

'Yet capable of murder?'

'My dear Heitz' – Namaroff managed a dry laugh – 'that is hardly a fair question. Given a certain set of circumstances, I believe almost everybody is capable of murder. Naturally you are prejudiced.'

'If prejudice means that I am disturbed by the evasiveness of the people of Vandorf, then I am prejudiced. If it means that I utterly discount the so-called findings of that travesty of a court, then I'm prejudiced. I listened to those prevarications and I was sickened. And today when I called at police headquarters I was refused admission. That, you must admit, entitles me to feel biased against the operations of this community. Everywhere I go I sense a conspiracy of silence.'

'I'm sure you exaggerate.'

Namaroff leaned back in his chair and looked out into his garden as though to draw attention to the attractive normality of everything.

He certainly did himself very well. The windows opened

onto a formal garden in which two or three patients were strolling. The hillside beyond provided a dark line of trees as a backdrop which was striking rather than sinister. The room itself was furnished in excellent taste – from Prague and Vienna rather than from local sources, Heitz guessed. All that it lacked was a feminine touch: not that Namaroff had let a bachelor's indifference seep in; rather that it was if anything, too spartan.

Heitz said doggedly: 'There's an explanation somewhere. Do you know what it is, Doctor? Are you a party to this plot?'

Namaroff looked genuinely startled. 'There's no plot, as you call it. I am a party to nothing.'

'You are, then, as puzzled as everyone else by these unexplained deaths in the Vandorf district?'

'Yes,' said Namaroff reluctantly.

'But you do have some information that doesn't leak out to the general public?'

Namaroff was silent.

Heitz went on: 'My son was branded a murderer because he was human and therefore vulnerable. And he wasn't alive to answer back. But behind him, behind the whole story, there is something which the people of Vandorf refuse to mention even behind their own closed doors. Doctor, I need your help.'

'I can add nothing to what I said in court.'

'Let me ask you one more question. Have you heard of Stheno… or Euryale…' He waited, and then flung the last name at the impassive Namaroff: 'Or Medusa?'

'The Gorgons,' said Namaroff. 'Naturally I have heard of them. I may practise one of the physical sciences, Professor, but my education did cover a fair amount of classical material.'

'Two of the Gorgons were supposedly immortal. The third, Medusa, was mortal. She was the most beautiful of the three – a ravishing woman whose magnificent hair was changed into serpents so that her beauty took on an aspect of horror which turned men to stone.'

'A legend,' said Namaroff.

'On what were legends based if not on some truth?' demanded Heitz. 'Distorted they may have been, but somewhere there must have been a foundation for all men's strangest beliefs.'

'An interesting philosophical conjecture,' Namaroff agreed. 'We must debate it some day, Professor. But I fail to see—'

'What happened to Medusa?'

'The figure in fable,' said Namaroff deliberately, 'was killed by Perseus. Her head was chopped off.'

'And her spirit?'

'Professor, we have no reason to suppose any such creature ever existed in the flesh.' Namaroff got up as though to indicate that he wished his visitor to terminate the conversation and leave. 'That being so, I can hardly bother myself with speculations about her spirit.'

'Strange, isn't it,' Heitz went on relentlessly, 'how the story of the woman with snakes in her hair crops up throughout mythology? There were the Eumenides, also – the inexorable Furies, with serpents wreathing round their heads. And long after the period of classical myth there were tales of such creatures in Asia Minor, gradually encroaching on the Europe we know today. Creatures… or one creature?'

'I cannot imagine what—'

'Or one creature?' Heitz insisted. 'The two immortals may be slumbering in the gardens of the Hesperides. But the mortal sister – supposing her longing to survive was so great that she wandered from one land to another… and her restless, vengeful spirit moved from one body to another? She escaped death by feeding on the lives of others.'

'We are men of science,' said Namaroff. 'I don't believe in ghosts or evil spirits.'

'A most unscientific remark. But, as men of science, might we not believe in the symbolic elements of the story? Some dreadful plague, recurring through the centuries, to which men dare not give a name – a disease which fits in with nothing we know and which must therefore be cloaked in myth and symbolism. We might work on that supposition, you and I – proving that my son was not a murderer and at the same time solving some of your problems.'

Namaroff hesitated, then said: 'There is nothing for us to work on.'

'Nothing?' Heitz got up and confronted the doctor. 'Tell me what other symptoms there were – what the condition of those bodies was. All of them, I mean.'

'I don't know what you're talking about.'

'Was that girl in the same condition as all the other victims? Answer me.'

Namaroff went to the door and opened it. He stood with his hand on the knob. 'There is only one way in which I can help you, Professor Heitz. That is by offering a word of advice. Leave Vandorf before it is too late.'

'What is it you're afraid of?'

'I'm afraid for you,' said Namaroff. 'That is all.'

'Or of what I may discover if I remain?'

The doctor did not deign to answer this.

5

It took Professor Heitz a week to get the relevant books from various libraries and friends. Even then he took the precaution of having them delivered to a town ten miles away, where he collected them personally.

During the week of waiting he endeavoured to conciliate the Vandorf villagers. He went for a drink in the inn and studiously refrained from provoking any argument. He tried to get them used to the idea of seeing him in the streets. There were one or two other visitors, including a couple of hearty students, and it was difficult for the local inhabitants to single him out for their malevolent disfavour. But Heitz knew in his heart of hearts that he was making little progress. As soon as he ventured to ask the most cautious, roundabout question they turned away and he was back where he started. If he ever discovered anything it would be not through personal discussions but by the academic methods to which he was fortunately so accustomed.

The books arrived, and he started to plough through them.

There were several references to Castle Borski, but most of them were conventional stuff involving family curses and haunted corridors. Since the castle had been deserted there were only a few passing mentions. A quite recent one in a geographical and historical study of the entire region strongly advised visitors against the castle and the valley, hinting that a dispiriting atmosphere had fallen on the area and that difficulties would be placed in the way of anyone wanting to make a tour of the castle.

This wasn't much to go on. He would have to delve deeper. Another batch of older volumes was on its way, brought this time from his own library by Hans Boehm, who had worked for him these past twenty years and could be trusted with all that the professor held most dear. It would be good to have Hans here to look after him; and perhaps it would be politic to let Hans go into the village to buy all the provisions. With his dour yet amiable manner, Hans might get on speaking terms with the villagers.

On the night of his trusted servant's arrival, Heitz sat up late. Every reference he looked up seemed to start him off on a new track. He was amazed that there should be such a clear trail across the world, leading inevitably in the direction of Vandorf… and then that it should have petered out. But of course it had disappeared for the very good reason that it was now too close in time as well as in space. Those who knew or guessed were unwilling to speak – and so the records were incomplete. They would be completed only when the menace had passed on and gone somewhere else.

Heitz blinked and rubbed his eyes. He was seeing the pages as a blur. And there was a singing in his ears. Time to go to bed. He would pursue his theme in the morning.

Then he realized that the singing was no illusion. Voices surged through the night. Footsteps tramped up to the old millhouse, and now the sound became threatening.

'Get out, Heitz…'

'Go home. Get out of Vandorf…'

Hans came in, apprehensive. He was not a countryman and his first experience of life away from Berlin was not appealing to him.

'Sir, don't you think we should—'

He was cut off by a roar from outside. There was the smash of glass, and fragments of the window spattered across the floor towards the table at which Heitz had been sitting. As he got up and turned, a flaming torch twisted in through the jagged hole, scattering sparks as it came.

Hans dashed out of the room and was back in a minute with a broom. As the flames licked towards the old rugs on the floor he beat at them.

Heitz went to the windows and flung them open. More glass was dislodged, tinkling to the floor.

Three men carrying more torches stepped forward.

'Best get out of this house now,' said the leader.

'Get off this land,' snapped Heitz. 'Go back where you came from.'

'It's you as should…'

'Let's go in… show him…'

They moved forward. There were other shadows behind, spreading out round the house. As Hans went to the door to make sure the fastenings were safe, one man leapt in through the window. Feet pounded along the passage outside, and suddenly the room was filling up. Hans lashed out with his broom. Heitz, pinned against the wall, drove his fist into one seamed, contorted face. But there were too many of them. It would soon be over.

Then someone was cutting a swathe through the intruders. Several of them scrambled out of the window just as they had come, and others scuttled along the walls with their arms up to shield their heads against blows.

Panting, Heitz straightened up. Hans lowered his broom but remained on guard, studying three newcomers mistrustfully.

The first of the three was Inspector Kanof. Two of his men stood like sentinels at the door.

'I hope you're not too badly hurt.' Kanof sounded as though

he would really have appreciated some signs of serious injury.

'Thank you, no.' Heitz tugged at his jacket, which had been wrenched half off his right shoulder. 'It was lucky that you arrived when you did.'

'Next time you may not be so lucky,' said Kanof curtly.

'Inspector, if you think there is likely to be a repetition of this, I shall hold you responsible.'

'My police force is very small.'

'Small or not, it has a duty to protect law-abiding people from the less law-abiding.'

'Its duty is to the local community,' said Kanof, 'not to unwelcome visitors. Your business here is over. Why don't you go?'

'My business is not over,' said Heitz firmly.

'Very well. I've warned you. That's all I can do. If you should change your mind, Professor, I'll see you have safe conduct out of the village.'

Kanof gave Heitz a sardonic little bow and then jerked a thumb at his two men. They left and went off into the night. The brooding silence of the forest crept in again.

Hans contemplated the chaos in the room with a sad shake of the head.

'Leave it until the morning,' said Heitz. 'It may not look so dreadful then.'

His servant's expression of gloomy foreboding said in effect that it would probably look worse and that even if he tidied it up there was a good chance of the ruffians coming back and starting the whole thing over again.

But for the next few days there was peace. Hans stocked up with provisions and found that Bruno had left behind the larger part of a cask of wine. Heitz ate and drank well, and worked without interruption. He could only hope that the appearance of the police would have been enough to frighten would-be intruders off, at least until he had established what he had to establish.

One afternoon he wrote a telegram to Professor Meister at Leipzig University. His son Paul was working with Meister, and although Heitz was reluctant to disturb either his son or his old friend he needed help – not just help in his investigations, but someone to talk to who would understand and reassure him, someone as strong and reliable as Paul was.

He gave Hans instructions not to send the telegram from the village. The town over the ridge was a long way off, but it was essential that the villagers here should not be provoked into fresh hostility or into curiosity about the progress of his discoveries.

Heitz felt a great deal easier in his mind when he was sure the message had gone off. He worked with renewed vigour the following day, and once more was engrossed by the time night had settled on the trees and hills.

The moon swam clear in the sky. Stepping outside for a moment's air before resuming his convoluted trail through. a dozen huge tomes, Heitz saw light glinting on what could only be one of the topmost battlements of Castle Borski. He had not realized that any part of the castle was visible from here. Some swaying of the trees or the fall of a branch must have revealed it for the first time.

It had an oddly hypnotic effect on the professor. He wanted to go back indoors and settle down again, but that pinnacle seemed to be beckoning.

When Paul arrived, the two of them would go up there and explore. He wanted Paul to be with him then. There were things which needed to be verified, and he had no wish to be the only one to return with stories which would be mocked at by others. From here on every step must be carefully planned, every finding confirmed.

He was uneasy. The moon rode high, the trees were splintery black silhouettes against the skyline, and above them all was the one arrogant gleam of the castle.

The answer to it all was in Castle Borski.

Heitz found himself walking down the path and into the trees. He had not been near the castle before, but some force outside himself seemed to be guiding his footsteps. Dry twigs cracked under his feet, but there was no other sound.

The distance was less than he had thought. He emerged from the trees at the foot of a rocky formation on top of which the castle was piled, appearing to thrust up out of the very earth. A rubble-strewn path made a wavering ascent of the rock. Heitz looked back, hesitated, then began to climb.

The path was steeper than one would have guessed from below. Heitz was gasping by the time he reached the top and went in through the crumbling gateway. He crossed a courtyard littered with a soggy accumulation of dead leaves. Here, high above the trees, the wind was stronger. It moaned through the turrets and battlements like a mournful phantom of the valley.

A heavy door stood open ahead of him. Heitz went in and found himself in a shadowy hall. Outside, the moon escaped from the clouds and cast shafts of light through tall windows into the hall. It picked out the treads of a fine sweep of staircase, curving up to a shadowy landing above. Two huge figures blocked the professor's way. He stood quite still until his eyes grew accustomed to the half light, and then saw that they were statues – bad imitations of Greek sculpture, he observed with distaste.

Even in here the wind seemed to be unchecked. It was a sad breath down the staircase and through echoing passages in the depths of the castle.

Tomorrow he must come back in daylight. Or wait for Paul to arrive – if it was late tomorrow, then the next day they would come here. Tomorrow, said one part of his mind. Now, said another.

Professor Heitz began to climb the stairs.

At the top were two stone pillars. Moonlight filtered between them, serving only to emphasize the blackness of the shadows.

One of the shadows moved. Heitz stopped. It must, of course, have been an effect created by clouds touching the edge of the moon. He went on and reached the landing.

Here was a shape more truly classical than the poor imitations below. Splendidly poised, it leaned forward with a grace that was as real and immediate as when it was created. Even in the shifting light the professor marvelled at the tilt of the head and the almost living quality of the coiled hair.

Then the moon was a great blaze upon the face before him. And it was no statue. The lips parted, and a breath stirred the cobwebs festooned between the pillars. The creature stepped forward.

Heitz let out a sob. This was what he had come in search of, and now that he had found it he could have cursed himself for being such a fool; could have cursed if there had been strength in him to produce anything other than a whimper, like a terrified creature of the night waiting to be struck down.

He stared into the blazing eyes of a creature of legend. The mythical horror of an ancient world became real. The Gorgon advanced on him, and as she did so her raven locks writhed and uncoiled, and became a rearing tangle of snakes. A forked tongue flickered, a head struck down like a whip, and Heitz felt the agonizing stab in his forehead. He put up his hands to shield himself, and pain lashed across his fingers.

Suddenly he was able to scream. The madness of it resounded through the corridors and rooms of the accursed building. The sound of his own voice hit back at him, and he turned and lurched perilously down the stairs.

The piled-up leaves in the courtyard tried to slow him down like a quagmire. Rocks spurted from under his feet as he stumbled down the path. Branches scratched his face as he went blindly on through the forest towards the millhouse. They were nothing compared to the agony that was biting deeper and deeper into his brain from that first appalling blow.

He was not sure that he would ever reach the house. When he finally collapsed against the door he could barely summon up the strength to open it. At last he was indoors, groping his way to the sitting room.

A door opened and an oil lamp was lifted high. 'Who's that?'

'Hans…'

Heitz blundered gratefully towards the light. Then he heard his servant's shuddering intake of breath.

'Your face!'

Heitz stopped. He knew that he was carrying death within him. What he didn't know was whether it could contaminate others.

He said: 'Don't come any nearer.' He was stricken by the realization that already it was difficult for him to speak. His vocal chords were stiff and unresponsive. He forced the words out. 'Listen…. carefully. I haven't much time.' He led the way into the sitting room, his legs a great weight so that it was an incredible effort to put one foot in front of the other. 'I have to write a letter to my son, Paul. He should be here – tomorrow, perhaps. Soon. Soon. Take the letter from my table in the morning and give it to him.'

'But, sir, let me fetch—'

'Not much time,' grated the professor. 'Leave me. But make sure that Paul gets the letter – Paul and nobody else. You understand?'

'Yes, sir.'

'Go, then.' Heitz lowered himself into his chair and literally had to order his arm to move so that he could pick up his pen. 'There's nothing you can do.'

When he was alone he began to write. He might have been a child reluctantly learning how to form the characters: his hand moved with intolerable slowness. He would never be finished. All he could hope was that Paul would read as much as could be put down on paper now and would compare it with the other notes he had made during his stay here.

The breath hissed in his throat. If it had not been for the pain he might have derived some ironic, academic interest from the process that was working through his blood and bone – a process of solidification like that of a lava flow settling and hardening until at last it was immutable rock.

The constriction in his chest was stonily crushing the life out of him.

And the Gorgon was in Castle Borski waiting for another victim. There would be more – many more – unless… unless…

He wrote until his arm was a rigid, dead weight across the paper.

6

PAUL HEITZ had begged leave of absence from Professor Meister in Leipzig and made the journey to Vandorf in a fever of impatience. It was unlike his father to send cryptic telegrams. Even through the sparse words Paul had sensed an agitation, an urgency which could only be due to some alarming aspect of Bruno's death. Paul and his younger brother had been very close, in spite of their differences in temperament. If there was something wrong, Paul was in a hurry to be at his father's side.

He arrived to find Hans distraught and his father dead. The body had been removed by the police. Hans could do nothing but babble of 'the professor's face... his terrible face... the *marks*...' and hand over a three-page letter which he assured young Mr Heitz he hadn't mentioned to a living soul.

Paul read the letter and was convinced that his father must have been mad at the end.

He went at once to the police. They were brusque and unhelpful. His appearance was an unwelcome shock to them. He asked to see his father's body. They refused. Paul was incredulous. He repeated that he wished to see his father – demanded to see him. The refusal was adamant.

If his father had been mad, then everybody else seemed to be mad also.

Paul went to the Vandorf Medical Institution. It looked clean and new and healthy. Dr Namaroff looked distinguished and intelligent. Here, surely, he could rely on getting a straight answer.

'Yes,' said Namaroff, 'you may see a copy of the death certificate if you wish.'

He opened a cabinet against the wall of his office and produced a document which he handed to Paul. As Paul read it, the feeling of being caught in a fine mesh of evasions intensified.

He said: 'Why won't the police let me see the body?'

'It might upset you.'

'As his son—'

'There is no need for identification of the body,' said Namaroff smoothly. 'We all knew Professor Heitz. He had been here for a few weeks, as you know.'

'Yes, I know. And I know why, Dr Namaroff. And I don't like any of what I hear. If I insist, as my father's heir, on seeing his body—'

'You are not in your own country, Mr Heitz,' the doctor reminded him. 'We speak the same language here, apart from some stubborn peasants who will not discard their old tribal dialects – but we do not necessarily think the same way. Your father made himself unpopular with the authorities and with the local people, I may tell you. He did not altogether appreciate the hospitality of Vandorf. If you don't wish to be deported without more ado, I advise you to accept the rulings of this land.'

Paul fumed. He looked down at the death certificate and then waved it at Namaroff.

'Doctor, you examined the body?'

'My signature is there to prove it.'

'And in your opinion there was no doubt as to the cause of death?'

'That, too, is there. Heart failure. A violent spasm at the end, I'm afraid. That's why you wouldn't want to see your father. Better to remember him as—'

'How do you account for this?' Paul interrupted. He drew the three pages of his father's last letter from his pocket and read aloud: '"I am agonized by pains in my chest. I am turning to stone."'

Namaroff made an involuntary movement, putting out his right hand. 'May I see that letter?'

'My father gives instructions at the beginning of it that I'm to show it to no one.'

'I see.'

'He knew he was dying when he started to write. He was able to write three pages. That doesn't sound like heart failure. You don't go on working through a heart attack, Doctor: you know that as well as I do.' When Namaroff did not reply, he went on: 'My father refers to a terrible thing stalking among the people of Vandorf. "It turned Sascha to stone and others before her. The conspiracy of silence must be broken before others go the way I am going. If there are cycles of possession by that which was once Medusa…" And there he breaks off, and scrawls those last words about turning to stone. Medusa, Dr Namaroff,' Paul challenged. 'Does that mean anything to you?'

'A character from mythology. Not really my field, Mr Heitz.'

'When my father wrote this letter he knew what was happening to him. He knew how he was dying, and why. And it wasn't heart failure.'

'That is your opinion,' said Namaroff frigidly. 'No doubt you'll have an opportunity of expressing it at the inquest.'

'When will it be held?'

'It has not been decided. But I'll see that you're informed. Goodbye, Mr Heitz.'

Paul had to accept this blunt dismissal. He went back to the millhouse. Hans was anxious that they should leave without delay. He was not surprised by the lack of co-operation being shown to Paul. It had been the same with his father. And look what happened to the professor when he stubbornly lingered!

Paul took his father's letter out of his pocket and began to re-read it for what must have been the tenth time. He strolled out of the cool house into the fitful sunshine and went down the steps to the tangle that had once been a well-kept kitchen garden. At the end of the garden was a fishpond surrounded by a low stone wall. The scene could have been idyllic but for the awareness of evil drifting like a miasma from the forest.

Paul sat on the low wall and turned the sheets of paper over yet again, wondering what terrible experience could have produced such incoherent ramblings from a man normally as precise as his father had been.

This spirit which may be an elemental force or an individual personality of great destructiveness from the past is capable of taking on human form. No other possible explanation. The human envelope itself could not have survived that long. If someone in Vandorf is possessed…

Impatiently he got up and went back into the house, tossing the letter on to the table. But he was restless. His father's books were arrayed on the room's one sagging shelf, but Paul was in no state to settle down to work on them. His father had done too much already. There were scribbled notes everywhere, and innumerable markers jutting out between the pages of the books. But the only result had been death.

Paul shivered. He had to step outside again, into the brightness of day. Again he took a few paces down the steps and looked through the trees towards the castle, demanding an answer.

Hans would be glad if they could pack up those books and go. And what else was there to do?

There was a faint rustle in the room behind him. Paul ignored it for a moment, thinking that Hans had come in. Then something prompted him to turn.

A dark girl with high cheekbones and deep eyes lost in shadow stood by the table.

She said: 'Forgive me for intruding. The door was open – I couldn't make anyone hear...'

'Who are you?'

'I'm Carla Hoffmann.' She came towards the door, and as she moved she gave off a faint musky scent which went well with her graceful, almost animal walk. Yet seen at close quarters she was a trim, modern young woman with an urban self-assurance. 'Dr Namaroff's assistant at the institution,' she added.

'Can I help you?' said Paul with no great enthusiasm. Her attractiveness was undeniable, but if she was Namaroff's assistant he was in no mood to be attracted.

'I'd like to help *you* if I can,' she said.

'Does Namaroff know you're here?'

'He'd be very angry if he did.' When Paul waited non-committally, she burst out: 'Please believe me, I only came here to see if there was anything I could do.'

'Nobody in Vandorf seems very anxious to do anything for me,' said Paul dourly.

Carla looked past him, down the steps, and out into the forest. She said: 'Did Dr Namaroff say anything to you about the local superstitions? About the thing that roams the woods?'

'He didn't want to talk about anything of the kind. He doesn't believe in any of it.'

'Doesn't he?' said Carla softly. 'Perhaps he believes more than he will admit. Your father tried to discuss the fear with him – and although he made a show of brushing it all aside, I know he is beginning to worry about... about...'

'Yes?'

'The creature.'

'Have you seen her?' Paul demanded. Madness, yes; but they were all afflicted by it, and he had a wild moment of debating whether or not this might be the dark curse of the place – an obsessive, contagious madness, a mass hysteria which one puff of sanity might, under the right conditions, dispel.

'Nobody,' said Carla, 'has seen her and lived.'

'Do you really think that Namaroff believes in her?'

'He believes in something that he won't dare to admit; even to himself. But *you*… Mr Heitz, *you* must believe in her.'

Paul was taken aback. 'Why?'

'If you don't, you'll see no reason to leave here at once. And if you stay, you'll be found like the others. Here, you're too great a threat. You won't be allowed to survive.'

A short time ago Paul had been sanely and sensibly planning to leave because there was nothing to be accomplished here. Now it suddenly became imperative that he should stay. In the span of a few weeks he had lost first his brother and then his father. He could not desert them now. Vandorf had defeated them, but there was still another member of the family to carry on the battle.

He said: 'I'm grateful to you, but I can't leave.'

'Please…'

Her concern was so genuine that he felt an impulse to put his arm round her and reassure her. Indeed, he was startled by the force of his own longing to hold her. If things had been different – if he had come to this idyllic setting and met this beautiful girl without any background of menace and hostility – they could have meant something to each other. It was as swift and sure as that.

Bitterly he thought of Bruno, who had loved and died here.

Carla said: 'I must go. I'm on duty in half an hour. But please do as I say. Please, for your own sake, leave Vandorf.'

When she had gone he was drawn back despite himself to that perplexing, insane letter. He picked it up and, denying that it could mean any part of what it said, read it yet again.

7

AT NIGHT the bustle of the institution slackened to the tempo of sleep – a steady, rhythmic breathing in a twilight of shaded lamps. The petulant chatter of the larger wards was hushed. In a private room a sleepless patient tried to read herself into drowsiness. In Namaroff's office, Carla recited from memory:

'"If someone in Vandorf is possessed or subject to periodic fits of possession, that person must be found. In my view it will prove to be a woman. Symbolically and metaphysically this is inevitable. A woman who has become only the slave of this ancient evil, enabling it to satisfy its greed for slaughter. I am trying to find rational terms for a phenomenon which is in fact one of pure terror. Perhaps the old, original terms must stand. The Gorgons – heads crowned with living snakes – anyone who looked on them was petrified. Hence the word 'Gorgonized' – literally meaning turned to stone. Incredible. But our whole history is incredible, filled with monsters and fear."' Carla stopped. 'I'm sorry. He came back into the house just then. That's all I had time to memorize.'

She would have liked to add that she had found even this much of the task unpalatable. She had not enjoyed spying on that young man, whose presence in Vandorf was like an affirmation from another world – a saner, cleaner outside world.

'Hm.' Namaroff had been seated at his bureau. Now he got

up and paced slowly across the room. 'The professor was an expert on the literary aspects of such myths. I am beginning to feel that he was closer to reality than I allowed myself to believe at the time.'

Carla was chilled by this admission. Namaroff had never been one to reveal doubts and hesitations easily.

He turned at the end of a stride and caught her expression. Before she realized what was happening he had put his hands on her shoulders and tried to draw her close to him.

'Carla… you've got to trust me. I want you to stay with me – stay where I know you're safe.'

He tried to kiss her. She twisted aside and freed herself from his grasp. His eyes gleamed with desire, and at last she summoned up the courage to say what had been in her mind for so long. 'I want to leave Vandorf,' she said.

'Leave? You can't. After all I've done for you…'

'I'm grateful to you,' she said in as level a tone as possible, 'but I think I've been here too long. I'm not working as well as I should—'

'I've never made any complaints,' he said quickly. 'After your illness you were afraid of being sent away. I kept you on, looked after you, gave you time to recover your self-confidence, and I thought… I thought…'

It was rare to see him at such a loss. Carla said: 'I know. And it's because of what you've been thinking that I know I must leave. I owe you a lot, Dr Namaroff, and I respect you and your work. But I can't stay in Vandorf any longer, let alone here with you.'

She had tried to make it sound regretful but firm. His face worked. When his answer came it was as savage as a blow across the face.

'You can't leave,' he said. 'That's the truth of it. I won't let you leave. You are not to go out of this building without letting me know.'

'Not… but that's ridiculous.'

'You are in grave danger,' said Namaroff.

'Danger?'

'One thing I can tell you…'

Abruptly the door was flung open and Ratoff stood there, his hair unkempt and a bruise beginning to swell below his left eye.

He panted: 'That devil! She's out.'

'Martha?' gasped Carla.

'Look for her,' snapped Namaroff. 'Don't waste any time. Take who you need. And don't come back here till you've found her.'

'If I do find her,' said Ratoff, 'I'll kill her.'

'You'll bring her back alive.'

Ratoff scowled, but turned away. Namaroff slumped against the edge of his bureau. Tiredness dragged the lines of his face down.

Carla said quietly: 'Perhaps we'd better talk again… settle things… tomorrow.'

Namaroff nodded. Then he seemed to bring her back into focus. He reached out again and seized her arm.

'I was about to tell you that I'm forced to agree with one of Professor Heitz's suppositions. We must assume that the Gorgon has taken on human form.'

'Human?'

Carla glanced instinctively at the window. The curtains were drawn, but she could visualize, beyond the garden and under the black canopy of the trees, poor demented Martha ranging the forest… in search of what?

8

THE WIND had begun to rise in the middle of the evening. A few flecks of rain spattered against the windows of the old millhouse and struck a reverberating note from the section of window that had been boarded up after the assault on Professor Heitz. In the distance thunder muttered over the hills.

Paul Heitz had drunk half a bottle of wine and was staring into the wood fire that crackled fitfully in the iron basket of the grate. The weather was still mild but he found the flames cheering, and Hans had been glad to build the fire for him. It was something useful and normal.

Not that it was proving of much use to Paul. He sought inspiration and found none. The licking flames were soothing, not stimulating.

He had no idea where to begin.

Unless, of course, he explored Castle Borski. He had not dared to approach the villagers too frankly after all that he had heard of their previous behaviour, but even in passing them he could not have failed to notice how they kept their eyes averted from the castle, how the houses themselves were built in such a way that their windows did not face towards the commanding turrets. He had not collated the references to Castle Borski in the various books which his father had left, but its appearance in several scribbled notes left no doubt that in the professor's mind it had played an important part in recent events.

Paul, determined to shake off his languor of frustration, got up and went out on to the garden steps.

The rain had coaxed a fresh, pungent smell from the grasses and the trees. It was still not heavy, and when Paul strolled down towards the fishpond he lifted his face into the cooling shower.

Thunder throbbed again, and the moon edged a turbulent mass of clouds with silver. Somewhere far away, lightning flickered.

Paul looked down into the fishpond. The rain mottled the surface only faintly, not hard enough to distort the reflection of the wall, the edge of the millhouse, and his face.

And that other face…

At first he saw it as curling strands of weed below the surface of the pond. Then, as the moonlight brightened, he knew that it was a reflection of something behind him, looking down from a height – from one of the lower steps.

He almost turned. But when the features swayed gently into their hideous clarity, he was transfixed. There in the water was the face that no painter, no sculptor, no creative madman could ever have conceived. It was a warped, dead thing, drowned in the pond; and yet it was alive. Its lips drew back and those drifting tendrils became serpents. The eyes held Paul's: he tried to look away, but if he looked away he would behold the reality of which this was only the palest reflection.

The snakes appeared to twist upwards in an effort to break the surface like slimy creatures of the pond. Paul could bear it no longer. He put his arm across his eyes and turned to run. But even as he began to lurch towards the house he knew that it… *she*… was waiting for him.

He tottered to one side. There must be a way round this side of the building to the front. He tried to shout for help, to arouse Hans, but then stifled the sound. If Hans were to come out now he might be face to face with the creature without warning.

Paul dared to lower his arm and search for the way along side the millhouse. It came to an end in a jagged wall. He couldn't get over. He pushed himself away from it, and his feet caught in a tangle of tall weeds. The world was going round. A clap of thunder was like some devilish jubilation. Paul felt himself reeling sideways, keeping his balance as he went but waiting to fall, until at last he struck the wall of the fishpond and sagged over it. His head smacked into the staring reflection of abomination and broke it into a swirl of ripples...

Somewhere there was an uncontrollable screaming. He drowned in a nest of weed and serpents, and all the time he was fighting to claw his way back to the surface that screaming went on.

His eyes, strangely, were tightly shut. He tried to open them. The serpents relaxed their grip, but the water still obscured his vision. Then a face began to form in it. Paul recognized the screaming voice as his own, and screamed louder as the face took on substance. If this time he was to see the Gorgon full face, he must die; and he didn't want to die.

Then the fear drained away and he felt the cool sheet over him, the pillow under his head. Carla Hoffmann looked down at him.

'It's all right,' she said gently.

'She was behind me,' he babbled, 'waiting for me to turn. The heads of the snakes were plunging...'

'It was a dream,' she said. 'Only a dream.'

'No.'

A door opened. Dr Namaroff came into the neat, aseptic little room. He stood beside Carla and stared at Paul – not, thought Paul through the blur of returning consciousness, like a doctor concerned about his patient but like a man on the defensive, daring him to speak of what he had seen.

Paul said: 'What happened to me?'

'Miss Hoffmann had some sort of presentiment that something was going to happen to you. We found you lying over the wall of the pool in your garden.'

The memory of a blasphemous monster stirred below the surface, swaying as the surface swayed and then Paul fought it back into the depths where it belonged.

'How long have I been here?' he managed to ask.

'Five days.'

Paul, incredulous, tried to sit up. Carla put a restraining hand on his shoulder.

'Lie still,' said Namaroff. Then he went on, challenging yet reluctant: 'Can you remember what happened before you fell?'

'I… I remember seeing… in the pool…'

'What? What did you see?'

Carla's hand moved down to Paul's and closed on it comfortingly. He said: 'A face. The most horrible thing I've ever seen.'

'In the pool?'

'It must have been there behind me. But all I saw was… No!' It was fearful to think of, impossible to speak of. Paul turned over, burying his face in the pillow.

'You must rest,' said Namaroff in a more conventional, professional tone. 'I'll talk to you again in a day or two.'

'A day or two!'

'You're in a very weak condition. I don't want you to overtax your strength.'

This time Paul succeeded in struggling up to a sitting position.

'For pity's sake, I must know more about this. I'm sorry I wasn't up to it for a moment just then. Look, let's talk about it., We must get to the bottom of this whole thing. I must—'

'You're suffering from shock,' said Namaroff, 'and it's essential that you should rest.'

'I tell you I'll be all right.'

'Miss Hoffmann, please.'

Carla gave Paul a sympathetic glance and went to the door with the doctor. When Namaroff had gone out she stood with the door open for a moment, smiling as though offering a promise – a promise to return, to listen to him, to make things somehow all right.

Paul realized how weak he was. Just the effort of sitting up was a strain. He let himself sink back.

Before Carla closed the door he heard an excited burst of conversation in the corridor outside, dominated by Namaroff's sharp, savage questions.

'Not quite dead when you found her – is that what you're telling me?'

'That's right, sir,' a man's surly voice responded.

'Did she speak? Tell you anything?'

'She'd enough strength left to spit in my face. And then she died.'

Paul groped for some meaning in this, but it didn't fit into the hazy pattern of his own experiences. Some other patient, he supposed. Some other unfortunate trapped in a physical or mental nightmare.

He tried to stay awake. He wanted a clear head in order to sort things out logically. But he was unable to concentrate. Consciousness slipped away and he floundered once more through hideous fantasies before waking again in a sweat. Carla Hoffmann was there. Carla was there whenever he needed her during the next couple of days – or was it weeks, or only interminable minutes? – and when he implored her to stay and talk to him and help him, the touch of her hand on his grew more responsive.

Hans came timidly in to see him. In a fit of clear-cut decisiveness, Paul told him to go back to Berlin. Hans was obviously going to fall ill himself if left alone in that millhouse. Although he tried dutifully to argue, the loyal servant was only too glad to be ordered away.

Dr Namaroff commented approvingly on this.

'And you yourself will be returning to Leipzig when you leave here?'

'No,' said Paul, wiping the approval off the doctor's face. 'I'm staying in Vandorf.'

He found that he had spent three days here since regaining consciousness. It had seemed longer, and he was impatient to be out of the place. His impatience mounted when he heard from Carla that the inquest on his father had been held a week ago, just after he himself had been brought in to the institution. 'I sent a wreath on your behalf,' said Carla. 'I hope that I was right?' He thanked her, but his mind was elsewhere. It was impossible not to wonder whether his protracted coma had to some extent been induced by Namaroff so that the inquest and burial could be over and done with before he was on his feet again.

Yet this would make Namaroff a positive accomplice in some gruesome plan; and Paul was reasonably certain that such was not the case. In some way Namaroff was just as frightened as he was, but for different, inexplicable reasons.

He challenged the doctor with this on the day of his discharge. 'Doctor, I think you'd like to unravel this mystery as much as I. Why can't we work together?'

Namaroff fussed with papers on his desk as though to show that he was a very busy man with no time to spare. But by nature he was not a fussy person, and the effect was unconvincing. 'I don't understand you,' he said. 'What mystery?'

'Don't treat me like one of your neurotic patients. You know perfectly well what I'm talking about.'

'I'm afraid I don't.' Namaroff stacked several sheets of paper meaninglessly into a pile, and then stood up with his hand out. 'Goodbye, Mr Heitz. I recommend a convalescence in your own country.'

'But, Doctor—'

'Good day.'

'You're afraid of her,' Paul accused him, 'just like the rest of them. A man of the twentieth century – as scared as any of the ignorant illiterates of Vandorf. Aren't you?'

Namaroff stood rigidly behind his desk, waiting for Paul to go.

From the door, Paul hurled one last promise. 'I intend to find this creature.'

'Indeed.'

'And destroy it,' said Paul.

He was fuming with impotent rage as he left. That a man of Namaroff's status should be afraid seemed monstrous to him. And there was no doubt that he *was* afraid. But as Paul walked back to the millhouse his first brisk stride faltered. He slowed, trying to analyse the expression that had come into Namaroff's' face during those last few minutes. Certainly it had been fear, but it was not the superstitious fear that warped the minds of the villagers: there was something more complex than that in it.

The millhouse was unnaturally quiet when he reached it. Hans had left everything tidy and had packaged up Professor Heitz's books ready for dispatch when the time came to send them away. There was a disturbing finality about this neatness: it urged Paul to pack up and go, never to return to Vandorf.

He sat in the garden during the late afternoon, regaining his strength. The steps and the fishpond were innocent enough by daylight. He was able without more than a slight tremor to assess the relative positions of himself and the monster by studying the angle of refraction, making a scientific exercise out of it in order not to succumb to fright once more.

When the sky darkened, however, he was glad to go back indoors.

It took a great effort of will to force him out of the house again late that night and through the sleeping village to the cemetery beyond.

He had brought a spade. The earth was still soft and had not been packed down, but even so it was strenuous work digging, and he was certainly not in the best condition. Sweat was pouring off him, while at the same time his arms and legs shivered. When the lid of the coffin was uncovered he had to rest a moment before stooping to lift it off.

In that pause he was sure that he was being watched. He peered round, between the pallid monuments and tilting, neglected gravestones. Nothing moved. He mustn't let the sombre atmosphere affect him too acutely. Once more he bent over the coffin and prised open the lid.

He reached for the lantern that he had set beside the open grave.

There was a rustle of feet between the tombs, and a woman stood above him.

He stared at her ankles, not daring to look up. A violent spasm of trembling attacked him. If he were to raise the lantern and look straight into that face which had so far appeared to him only as a dulled reflection…

Carla said: 'Somehow I knew you'd be here.'

Paul gasped. 'Another of your premonitions?' he managed to blurt out.

They looked at each other for a long moment. Then Carla knelt beside the piled earth and held the lantern for him. Paul turned back to the open coffin and pulled the shroud from his father's face.

The noble features were unexpectedly calm. Whatever pain

and horror there might have been at the end, the lines of the face had somehow settled into a stern tranquillity. Professor Heitz's stoicism had asserted itself in his final agony, and the face was that of a dignified statue.

A statue... Paul touched the head, and his fingers met unyielding stone. He ran them down to the neck. There was no decay here, no dissolution; not even the softness of living flesh.

He looked up at Carla.

'Why did Namaroff issue a false death certificate? Who is he trying to shield?'

While Carla held the lantern high he scrambled out of the grave. She took his arm to steady him, and together they went to sit on the step of a grandiosely columned tombstone.

'"Our whole history is incredible,"' Carla quoted, '"filled with monsters and fear."'

That was exactly what his father had said. All at once Paul realized, too, where they had been said. He stared at Carla.

She nodded sadly. 'Yes. I'm sorry. I read your father's letter. Doctor Namaroff wanted me to memorize as much of it as possible.'

'But why?'

'He was hoping there would be something in it which would throw new light on... on Medusa... the legend...'

The name came out only as a whisper, as though Carla feared that merely to utter it was to bring the Gorgon down upon her.

'Why are you telling me all this now?'

'I'm afraid.'

'Everybody here's afraid.'

'Yes, but this is new. It's not just the castle and the... the creature... that's not all I'm afraid of.'

'Of Namaroff?' he said.

'Yes.' Again it was only a whisper.

'But why?' When her head sank in dejection he commanded: 'Go on – tell me!'

'You asked me just now who he's trying to shield. There is somebody – or something. And I don't know who. He used me to spy on you – he'd use anyone who suited his purpose – and he must want to know more than he does. But he already knows more than anyone ought to. I'm sure of that. There's something in him… something too secretive, too contriving. And possessive…'

The note in her voice struck a resonance in Paul's mind. He said: 'Is Namaroff in love with you?'

'Yes.'

'And jealous?'

'Yes.'

'Then why don't you leave the institution? It can't be very pleasant, working in this atmosphere and with that man coveting you—'

'I can't leave. I owe him a great deal. He plays on my gratitude, and I know he's doing it, but I can't leave.'

It was a grotesque place for it to happen, but suddenly she was in his arms. Paul held her close, and knew that, whatever else happened, when he left Vandorf he would take Carla with him.

Aloud he said: 'You'll come with me. We'll leave Vandorf together.'

'I can't.'

'Don't be afraid. When you're with me there's no need to be afraid.'

She lifted her mouth to his. They kissed, and through her shuddering body he felt both her desire for him and that incommunicable terror which permeated this whole accursed valley.

'Paul,' she breathed.

He forced himself to hold her away from him. 'Carla, there's no need to be afraid,' he repeated firmly. 'You're a free person. You can leave Vandorf – leave Namaroff – whenever you choose.'

She shook her head.

'But why not?' he demanded, exasperated by the defeatism of it all.

'I don't know why.'

In this deathly setting Paul could almost begin to believe in other spells, in a general malaise suffusing the entire district. The whole place was in the grip of a disease, a demoniacal possession which drew people into a marsh, drew them gradually towards the centre where the ultimate horror waited for them. All willpower was sapped; nobody would stand up and defy the powers of darkness.

He said: 'Carla, the two of us… it seems too soon to talk about us, but you know – damn it, you must know—'

'Please… please, no!' She cut him short by getting up and backing away. 'It would all be so simple,' she said, 'loving you.'

'Then make it simple!'

But before he could say any more she had turned and run off into the night. He saw her as a pale wraith flitting between the tombstones, and then she was gone. He could hardly pursue her now. He couldn't leave his father's grave open to the sky and the gaze of any inquisitive villager. He set to work to close it up again.

He was exhausted by the time he got back to the millhouse; so exhausted that sleep was impossible. Thoughts whirled round in his head – thoughts of his father, a stone corpse in the earth, and of Carla, warm and alive and incomprehensible.

A heavy knocking at the door jolted him out of his confused reverie.

Paul looked round for a weapon. No one who called at this

early hour of the morning could mean any good. He seized a poker from the fireplace and went along the passage.

'Who's there?'

'My dear boy, do you propose to keep me standing out here all night?'

Paul slammed back the bolts and opened the door. Professor Meister stood in the doorway, stooping slightly from his great, spindly height so that he could see into the passage. He kept his head lowered as he came in, then straightened up with a sigh.

'I can't tell you' – it came out in a rush from Paul's stammering lips – 'how glad I am to see you.'

Meister was taken aback by this greeting. He studied his young colleague keenly, and his dark features seemed to cloud with even deeper shadows.

'Paul… whatever has happened to you?'

'I've been ill,' said Paul lamely.

'Ill? You look as though you've been in your grave and had to dig your way out.'

It was an unfortunate image. Paul shuddered. To deflect that shrewd, analytical stare he asked: 'How did you get here at this time of night?'

Professor Meister stalked on into the sitting room and looked around. Its apparent cosiness provoked a nod of approval. He let Paul take his coat from him, and sat down by the fireplace.

'Transport in this part of the world is somewhat primitive,' he said. 'I arrived in Vandorf very late. I have the impression' – he glanced slyly at Paul for confirmation – 'that even at the best of times it is not a particularly hospitable village. After dark it does not extend much of a welcome to visitors. It was with the greatest difficulty that I found someone who would direct me to your residence – and then I had to do the journey on foot, taking several wrong turns on the way.' He placed the tips of his fingers together and pursed his lips, as though about to embark on one of his more esoteric philosophical disquisitions. But what came out was a sharp direct question: 'What has been happening?'

'It's a long story.'

'I've come a long way to hear it.'

9

THERE WAS a light on in Namaroff's laboratory as Carla walked round the side of the building. She hesitated. She didn't want to talk to Namaroff or run the risk of being questioned by him. She wanted to go to bed. Even more, she admitted to herself, she wanted to turn and retrace her steps; to go back, to say to Paul that she would leave with him at once. Surely that would solve everything? The intangible fears that surrounded her in Vandorf would be dispelled. She would escape from the miasma of this valley.

Yet she turned and went towards the laboratory. Even while she hated Namaroff and the power he had over her, she could not deny that power. Somehow he made it impossible for her to leave Vandorf. Somehow he drew her to his side now, in the dark hours of the night.

Namaroff did not look up as she entered. He was bent over a table, a scalpel in his hand. Under the scalpel was the head of Martha, her dead mouth twisted as though it had frozen into the grimace made when she spat at Ratoff.

Namaroff lifted the brains from the opened skull and laid them in a dish. Then he said, still without looking round:

'You have been out tonight, Carla?'

'Yes.'

'Where did you go?'

'For a walk.'

'Were you alone?'

'Yes.'

Namaroff carried the dish to a bench along the wall. He began to lay out instruments ready to his hand.

Carla said: 'What are you hoping to find?'

'Hoping?' He shrugged. 'I am merely carrying out a routine examination. Looking for signs of deterioration. Or any special features which may explain the poor creature's illness.'

She noted that, now that Martha was dead, he was prepared to describe her tolerantly as a poor creature.

'What kind of deterioration?' she asked. 'Do you think there'll be something… out of the ordinary?'

When Namaroff did not answer, she went on: 'Do you remember when we found Paul Heitz?'

'I do.'

'It was the night Martha escaped. And the night you told me that the Gorgon had taken on human form.'

'So?'

'Was it… was it Martha?'

'No, Carla,' said Namaroff heavily, 'it wasn't Martha.'

'You suspect somebody?'

'It's too early to say.'

He sighed, as though reproaching her for interrupting him; but she knew him well enough to be able to tell that he was deeply disturbed.

'We work closely together,' said Carla, hating to make such an appeal to him yet driven on by her need to know. 'I think I should know—'

'What you should know' – he swung unexpectedly round to face her – 'is that you are in great danger.'

'Danger?'

'Of your life.'

'But why should there be any—'

'You must believe me,' he said forcefully. 'You must do as I say. Don't go out – alone, or with anyone else. Tell me always what you are doing. Stay close to me, Carla. We will overcome this terrible thing. But you must trust me.'

'I have a right to know. If there's danger, I should know what form it will take.'

'The form it will take?' he said grimly. 'Better that I should not tell you. Not until I'm sure.'

10

MEISTER SAID: 'So you saw only her reflection?'

'It was enough,' said Paul.

They stood looking down on the innocent surface of the pool. With Professor Meister beside him, Paul could almost have felt that the whole thing had been a dream – if his memories had not been so vivid. Even now he could hardly bear to look into the water in case that monstrous face should take on substance and leer hideously up at him.

'Hm.' Meister made a slow circuit of the pool. 'When Perseus beheaded Medusa, he guided his blow by looking at her reflection in the shield he carried. If your story is true, the girl Sascha must have looked directly at the Gorgon – and so did your father. What spared you is the fact that you saw only her reflection.'

'Then you believe me?'

'I'm not saying that the Gorgon exists. Unquestionably you saw something. Hallucination or not, it was real enough for you – and for your less fortunate predecessors.'

'She was not a hallucination.'

'No,' said Meister quickly, 'of course not.'

'Professor, please don't try to humour me. Is the idea of the Gorgon any stranger than the theory of reincarnation, which admits to a dead person's spirit inhabiting a human body?'

'A theory,' came the dry retort, 'which has yet to be proved.'

Meister turned back towards the house. 'Now, as to your own story. Let us start with the assumption that Medusa, whose head is spoken of in legend over many centuries as having never lost its power, has indeed come to this neighbourhood in some form or another. Let us suppose that the true characteristics manifest themselves only at certain intervals, under certain conditions. Have you met many people since you've been here?'

'Very few.'

'Any women?'

'Only the one I told you about – the one in the hospital.'

'Oh, yes. Carla… er…'

'Hoffmann,' said Paul eagerly – so eagerly that he saw Meister smile as they went into the house.

'What's she like?'

'Very beautiful.'

'I see. You're in love with her?'

'I didn't say so.'

'You didn't have to,' said Meister. 'And now' – he yawned – 'I think a good night's sleep is called for. We will follow it by some inquiries at the police station.'

'If they let us in,' said Paul.

Meister looked at him reprovingly. 'They will let me in.'

Paul had his doubts about this. Professor Meister might be a man of consequence at home, but here there was likely to be little respect for his scholarly attainments.

In the morning he discovered his mistake. The professor had no intention of relying merely on his reputation as a scholar.

He loftily talked his way into the presence of Inspector Kanof – or, rather, made his way there by dint of refusing to admit that there could be any possibility of denial. Paul, catching the backwash of Kanof's glare as they entered his office, felt that this was where they came to grief. But Meister, with calculated arrogance, took Kanof's breath away at once.

'I wish to look through the files which you keep on residents of Vandorf – particularly newcomers to the district.'

The inspector gasped. 'How dare you come in with such a request? Such files are confidential, for official use only.'

'I fear they are not used as thoroughly as they ought to be. There are one or two points I wish to check.'

'Under no circumstances will you be permitted to see any of our files. There is no precedent—'

'Don't use long words, Inspector. They don't suit you. I may say that if you don't wish to assist us, I shall go higher up.'

'Higher up?'

'I presume that even you, Inspector, acknowledge the existence of a superior? The Foreign Secretary, for example.'

'I don't believe—'

'A very valued friend of my dear brother.'

'I can check on that.'

'Check on it, by all means,' said Meister savagely. 'But unless you are very quick about it, my good fellow, and unless I am allowed to see your files…'

Kanof writhed and argued, but he stood no chance. Meister was by turns bullying and sardonically reasonable. In the end Kanof agreed that the professor should be given access to the records.

'Starting,' said Meister, 'with those of women aliens registered here within the last ten years.'

When Kanof set his staff bustling down the corridor to collect the files, Meister permitted himself a slight smile in Paul's direction. Kanof, though now obsequious to his older visitor, made a great show of ignoring Paul as though this might in some way restore a balance.

'Visitors to Vandorf,' explained Kanof when files and photographs were piled on the desk before him, 'are required to register only if they wish later to become citizens. Among those still resident here…'

He tried to maintain his dignity by being over-helpful where before he had been uncooperative. Meister paid no attention. He turned over files and photographs quickly, and then held out a picture to Paul.

'Is this her?'

Paul looked at a slightly creased photograph of Carla. Her mouth was too set: she had obviously been uncomfortable before the camera.

'It hardly does her justice, but—'

'But it's her? Mm. How long has she been here?'

'The information's on the back,' said Kanof.

Meister turned the card over. 'Seven years. When did these murders start?'

Kanof jumped. 'Murders?'

'I'm referring to the ones which you failed to solve and which everyone in the community has been at such pains to ignore.'

'Five years ago,' Kanof grunted. 'Thank you.'

Meister put the photograph back and rose. Paul got up, filled with unease. He did not see how Meister's mind was working. As they walked out of the building into the open air, he said:

'I don't see how Carla comes into this.'

'Or you don't *want* to see?' said Meister gently.

11

THE SOUND of Paul Heitz's voice along the crackling, whispering telephone line reinforced Carla's determination. During what remained of the night she had tossed and turned, trying to free herself from a bondage she did not understand. In daylight she had tried to be rational and had found that being rational also meant doing what her heart told her to do. She wanted to cry this down the telephone to Paul, but instead she warmed silently with the fervour of her own resolve, and took his message to Namaroff in the laboratory.

'Mr Heitz is on the telephone. He and Professor Meister want to make an appointment to see you.'

'Meister?'

'From Leipzig University.'

'I can't see them,' said Namaroff. 'Tell them I'm busy.'

'Mr Heitz was very insistent.'

His stony eyes were dull with menace. 'I have told you, Carla, that for your own safety you must do as I say. This is one of those times when obedience is essential. Go and tell Mr Heitz that I do not wish to see him or his friend.'

Carla began to turn away. She would tell Paul that; but she would take the opportunity of telling him many other things.

Abruptly Namaroff said: 'Carla.' When she stopped, he slammed his hand down on the bench. 'When you went for your walk last night, you said you were alone. You lied to me.'

It was all she needed to spark her off. 'Do I have to account to you for everything I do?'

'You were with Paul Heitz, weren't you?'

She needed to hit back, to seize on every opportunity for a break that would be permanent.

'You've been spying on me,' she accused him. 'Who do you use? Ratoff, I suppose. Always Ratoff – spying and watching me, telling you everything I do when I'm out of your sight.'

His expression told her that she was right. In an unexpectedly subdued tone, he said: 'It's only for your own good.'

'And who are you to decide what's good for me?'

'I'm trying to protect you. I told you last night, there are times when you shouldn't be alone.'

He had told her, but not in quite those words. Something about them struck a chill to Carla's heart, which had been filled with such different emotions a few minutes ago. She was afraid of the implications in what he said; yet not so afraid that she was going to evade them.

She said: 'Tell me about those times. Tell me… what happens… what happens to me.'

It was as far as she dared go. And Namaroff simply shook his head. 'I can't. Not yet.'

'Because it's all an invention. You're trying to frighten me.'

'I only want to take care of you.'

The genuine suffering in his voice was the most terrifying thing of all.

'Frighten me!' Carla cried again. 'So that I'll submit to being your prisoner. I've had enough. I'm sick of your jealousy, and sick of these horrors you help to build up around the place – sick of you!'

She turned towards the door and this time he let her go without a word. She would have preferred him to shout abuse after her. It was with a shaking hand that she picked up the telephone earpiece and spoke into the trumpet of the mouthpiece.

'Paul? I'm sorry I was so long. I was trying... but Dr Namaroff won't see you.'

'Won't he? Did he give any reason?'

'He says he's too busy.' There was a sceptical murmur along the wire. Then she said: 'Paul – meet me tomorrow. Tomorrow morning.' She quickly estimated the time she would need, to be able to see him and to be on duty at her usual time.

'Meet me at seven o'clock in the morning,' she said, 'at the Castle Borski.'

Before he could reply she had to hang up. Ratoff was a few yards away, carefully not watching her, and just as carefully appearing not to listen. She was sure he had not been there a moment ago and sure that he could not have overheard her tense, quiet last words. But his mere presence was infuriating. In the morning she would have to take every precaution to shake him off if he had any suspicions of her.

It proved to be a pale, still morning. As she slipped away from the institution buildings she looked back several times, but there was no sign of anyone stirring. Carla felt jubilant. The air was fresh, birds were singing in the trees along the stream, and as she climbed the slope from Vandorf the institution and the village itself looked smaller and smaller, less and less significant.

Then the birdsong grew feebler. By the time she reached the forest there was silence, broken only by her own footsteps and the occasional snap of a dry twig. The castle loomed ahead. In the morning light it could have been imposing, if not beautiful; but it was haunted by invisible shadows, echoing with sounds inaudible to the human ear.

Carla climbed without flagging, crossed the courtyard, and entered the great hall. It was not until she was inside that she asked herself why she had chosen such a meeting-place. Of course she was less likely to be followed here: even Ratoff would be scared of this place. But there had been more to it than that. In this unhallowed, desolate jumble of turrets, statues, and cobwebs she felt strangely safe. At one and the same moment she felt fear and security.

Slowly she climbed the staircase. Between two statues stood a stone chair with the dimensions of a throne. It was spattered with flinty fragments. Carla brushed them aside and sat down facing the balcony rail, waiting.

All was going to be well. Paul was coming and they would make plans and go away. Whatever deep-seated motive it was that had kept her in Vandorf so long, it was going to be dislodged from her mind.

There was a scraping sound from the hall below. A few pieces of stone were kicked across the floor.

Carla rose and went to the edge of the balcony.

Paul looked up at her, and she caught a tremor of apprehension in his face before he recognized her. Then he came hurrying up the stairs.

'Why did you ask me to meet you here?'

'Because nobody else would dare to come.'

'And you knew that nothing would keep me away?'

She ran to him and into his arms as he reached the head of the staircase.

'Paul…'

'Have you changed your mind?' he said.

'Yes.' She burrowed her head beseechingly into his shoulder. 'Paul, I'll come away with you.'

His arms tightened about her. 'You will?'

'I don't feel chained to Vandorf any more. I'm not afraid any longer. I'll go with you, Paul. Now. Can we leave now – today?'

What she was asking was that he should link her arm with

his and hurry her down the stairs, out into the world, sweeping aside Namaroff and the difficulty of getting their luggage to the distant railway station and all the other petty problems. But even as she spoke she sensed his reservations. Something had happened.

He said: 'Yes, we'll leave. But not immediately.'

'Why not?'

'I... I have one or two things to settle before I go.'

'But you were the one who wanted me to turn my back on everything here. You were the one who—'

'Carla, we'll go away together. I promise you that. But remember that my father died here. I came to solve a mystery, and I believe I'm getting closer.'

'Two days ago—'

'Two days ago,' said Paul, 'Professor Meister wasn't here. Now he's helping me.'

'To do what?' she demanded.

'To find the Gorgon.'

Panic took her. There was no safety in Paul's arms. She broke free so that she could see him better, and so that he could see her and be persuaded by her. There was so little time left. Intuitively she knew this. They must leave now or not at all.

'Paul, don't stay! If you love me, take me away from here while there's still time."

'I'll take you away,' he said, 'as soon as I can. I promise.'

'Now, Paul – now.'

'It won't be long.'

He was stubborn. The co-operation of Professor Meister had filled him with new determination. She would not be able to sway him.

Suddenly she felt that she must not stay here for even another minute with him. The impulse that had driven her here now drove her just as frantically away. Unknown forces were closing in on her. She had longed for him to take her away before they struck, but he wouldn't listen. If she was to escape from this place it must be on her own.

She turned and began to run down the stairs.

'Carla!'

His footsteps pounded after her, but he slipped and had to cling to the rail to regain his balance. At the foot of the staircase Carla turned and looked up at him. She made one last, choking plea.

'Now – can we leave now?'

'Carla, I promise that as soon as—'

'Too late!' The echo of her own voice was like an eerie wail from some dungeon in the depths of the castle. 'It will be too late.' She took her last look at him. 'I may never see you again.'

Then she ran across the hall and the courtyard and out onto the precipitous path. Behind her he called her name over and over again, but she knew that if she stopped to listen he would have nothing fresh to say. As she approached the line of dark trees she thought she saw a figure moving in and out of the shadows, and contemptuously she fitted the face of Ratoff to it in her mind. But it didn't matter. It was too late for anyone to do anything. She was herself. She would trust in no one again, be subjugated by no one again.

She sobbed and stumbled towards the freedom and forgetfulness that only she could achieve.

12

THE KNIFE flashed sharply in the morning light. Paul, wretchedly emerging from the trees above the millhouse, turned to look back at the castle and so saw the blade in time. He swayed to one side, and Ratoff blundered into his left arm.

'Paul!'

Professor Meister was scrambling up the slope. Ratoff wavered, then turned and ran before the two men could converge on him. Meister tried to intercept him, but was shaken off with a wild sweep of the knife. Then Ratoff turned and threw the knife viciously and accurately. It whistled past Paul's ear and into a tree.

Ratoff plunged into the undergrowth.

Meister came up to Paul. 'Did you recognize him?'

'It was Ratoff. One of the attendants at the hospital.'

'Perhaps in future you might be good enough to tell me where you're going.'

Paul dodged this one. 'Why did Ratoff try to kill me?'

'Your friend Namaroff probably knows the answer to that one.'

'Doctor Namaroff isn't answering questions these days,' Paul observed.

'Not voluntarily.' They walked down towards the millhouse. Meister reached out and wrenched the knife from the trunk in which it was embedded. 'While you were planning whatever jaunt it was that occupied you this morning, I was doing some research of my own. To be quite candid, while you were snoring the night away I paid a visit to Namaroff's establishment.'

Paul gaped. 'Did he see you?'

'I was not formally announced. I broke in and went through his medical files.'

Paul found it hard to visualize the dignified man striding beside him as a burglar. It was an aspect of Professor Meister's character which would not have been readily credited by most of his fellows or students in Leipzig.

'Did you find anything?' asked Paul, marvelling.

Meister did not reply until they were indoors. Then he produced some folded sheets of paper from inside his coat. They had evidently been torn from a file and stuffed hastily into his pocket. He skimmed them, then looked gravely at Paul and began to read aloud.

'"Carla Hoffmann, probationary nurse. Enrolled Vandorf Medical Institution 1903. Attack of amnesia..."' Thoughtfully the professor skipped a few lines and began to select the relevant items. 'Amnesia – loss of memory – in 1905. That's five years ago. In 1906 she underwent intensive treatment and was apparently cured. Meanwhile she continued to work in her profession. Hmm. That's odd. Now, let's put some of these pieces together.' Paul was possessed by an unreasonable urge to shout Meister down. He didn't want a case built up against Carla. Even if it was a convincing case, he didn't want to hear it. 'The first of the Vandorf murders,' said Meister relentlessly, 'coincided with the beginning of these attacks of amnesia. Namaroff must have been well aware of this. Ordinarily her condition would have put an end to her career as a nurse. Why should Namaroff have kept her on? When you told me your story of events here in Vandorf, you gave me a distinct impression that he was in love with her.'

'That doesn't mean that—'

'Just a minute.' Meister turned over a crumpled page. 'In 1906 Namaroff closed the case and stated that she was cured. But was she cured? I don't think so.' He slapped the paper down. 'She was always being followed – being watched. Didn't she tell you that? And this very morning there was Ratoff, prowling, always following her.'

'Because Namaroff is jealous,' said Paul.

'Possibly. And possibly also because he's afraid of what she may do. Because she still loses her memory around the time of the full moon.'

'How do you know that?'

Meister nodded at the pages before him. 'If we were to check these dates, I'm sure you would find they fitted. The full moon… the occurrence and recurrence of the amnesia… and the murders.'

Paul could stand no more. 'You're seriously suggesting that Carla—'

'Why shouldn't I?' Meister shook his head pityingly. 'I'm not in love with her.'

'Oh, you're mad. A young girl as beautiful as Carla…'

'Medusa was beautiful. According to the legend, it was her beauty that aroused the jealousy of a goddess and resulted in her becoming hideous. There is nothing so hideous as beauty warped. And even if we are talking in symbolic terms – even if the Gorgon myth is something twisted and distorted through the thousands of years in which it has been known – there is still a destructive spirit with which we must contend. It has found a resting place in somebody.'

'Not Carla.'

'In the cemetery you begged her to go away with you,' said Meister. 'That's what you told me, isn't it? She refused. Why?'

'She… she wasn't ready to leave.'

'Why not? Because something stronger than herself held her in thrall.'

'But today,' Paul argued triumphantly, 'she asked me to take her away. She wanted to go immediately. She was even more frightened of staying than she had been of going.'

'Even more frightened,' Meister echoed. Then brutally he said: 'I'll tell you why she was frightened, Paul. Because tonight is the first night of the full moon.'

It was all so neat, so academic. Paul had always admired Professor Meister. He had felt privileged to work with him and to watch his methods. But now he rebelled against the cold, unemotional selecting and arranging of facts and suppositions. Logic and cold reason might be all that counted in purely academic subjects, but Carla was a living, breathing human being. He ought to have taken her away when she entreated him to do so. Whatever had happened here in Vandorf was beyond his understanding. Let Professor Meister stay here for the rest of his life and try to unravel it if he wished. He could regard it as a cultural exercise. He would become a hoary old specialist in the subject.

Paul said: 'What are you trying to do? To destroy Carla – and me?'

Before Meister could reply, there was a scream in the distance. It was a woman's voice. Paul ran to the door and looked along the path into the woods. Meister went to the window.

'This side!'

They rushed into the garden. Beyond the pool, Carla was struggling with Ratoff. She shook him off and made a dash for the house. Ratoff made a move to catch her up, then saw the two men heading for him. He turned and scrambled over the low wall, and was soon lost among the trees. Carla collapsed against Paul, clinging to him.

'I had to see you again.'

'It's all right,' he soothed her. 'It's all right.'

They went back up the garden and into the house. Meister glanced quizzically at Paul, who refused to meet his gaze. Automatically he shielded Carla from the professor, drawing her closer to him and guiding her to a chair facing in towards the fireplace.

Meister said gently: 'I think you'll wish to be left alone together for a little while.'

He made a graceful withdrawal.

Paul drew a chair close to Carla's and took her hands in his. He said again: 'It's all right.' And then he knew that only one thing would make it all right. 'We'll go away,' he said, 'at once. Today.'

'Is there… still time?' It was a plea from the heart of her.

'Of course there's time. There has always been plenty of time,' said Paul bravely, defying the absent professor. 'But if it means so much to you, we'll leave today.'

'I ought not to have come.' Her faith in him died like a candle flame. Her illness and the uncertainties that followed it must have made her subject to these impulsive fits, this swing between confidence and despondency. 'I can't leave. I've always known I couldn't leave. But I came to you…'

'You came to me' – he tried to give her a new, solid assurance – 'because you knew this was the right thing to do.' He willed himself to sound confident enough to overcome all her fears and irresolution. 'You know what life here is like, and what it'll always be like. You've just been attacked by your friend Namaroff's pet jackal – simply because you tried to come and see me, I suppose? There's every reason for leaving and none for staying. I'm sorry I was stupid about it this morning. You're quite right: you have got to leave – and leave immediately.'

After this splendid pronouncement Paul realized that he was a little less sure about the ways and means of getting out of Vandorf in a hurry. The railway station was some distance away, and he had no idea of the timetables in operation here.

Tentatively he said: 'We must get to Leipzig...'

'There is a train at noon.' Carla spoke with all the brightness of a child who had for months been playing a private, secret little game involving just such a journey. 'There is a change at the junction, and then it reaches Leipzig at... oh, it must be about five o'clock. Leipzig' – she repeated the word like a magic incantation.

'That settles it, then.'

The two of them sat back. There was a long silence between them. Now that the decision had been made, there was time for them to look at each other and smile. Paul began to make plans in his head. He would continue at the university – it would be amusing to remind Professor Meister, in years to come, of the fantastic notions he had once had about Frau Heitz, as she would then be – and they would have a son, two sons, perhaps a daughter... He looked at her across the small space between them and tried to communicate all this without putting it too soon and too clumsily into words.

'If I can get away,' she said dreamily, as though answering him.

It was not the answer he wanted. There could be no doubts now. He said: 'You can leave. You're going to leave. After today there'll be no more of Vandorf – for you or for me.'

A fist thundered on the door. There was a brief pause, then another pounding.

Meister came quietly back into the room.

'It seems we have visitors,' he said. 'You had better take her upstairs.'

Paul took hold of Carla's arm and hurried her up the crooked staircase. On the landing he looked into his own room and into Meister's. There were no hiding places.

Below them the door opened and they heard the murmur

of a voice which made Carla tense, like a dog which has been whipped too often, frightened too often.

Then Meister spoke, clearly and directly. 'I've been looking forward to meeting you, Doctor.'

'I'd like to make this brief, if you don't mind,' said Namaroff. 'A short time ago a young woman was seen in the grounds of this house…'

Paul hurried Carla to the far end of the landing, where a narrower and even more twisted flight of stairs led down to a side door.

'You must go.'

'But you…?'

'They'll be searching the house in no time at all. If I'm missing, they'll guess we've made a run for it together. If you go alone—'

'No.' Her whisper was fierce and urgent. 'I can't go alone.'

'I'll be with you as soon as I can. We'll be together – tomorrow at the latest. Even later today perhaps I can manage it.'

'I won't go.'

Up the stairs and along the landing, like a snarling animal, came the growl of Inspector Kanof. 'We have reason to believe she's here now. I have a search warrant. I understand the house is rented by Mr Heitz. If you will call him down…'

Paul said: 'You have got to catch the noon train. Go to the Hotel Kramer in Leipzig. The proprietor is an old friend of mine. Tell him that he is to look after you until I come. I'll be there – you mustn't worry.' He kissed her. 'Now go – while Meister and I keep them occupied!'

She went down the creaking stairs as though going to her execution.

Paul hurried back along the landing and down the staircase which finished by the sitting-room door. He was in time to hear Meister saying smoothly:

'Is she a patient of yours, Doctor?'

'I am responsible for her,' came Namaroff's curt reply.

'An amnesia victim must be a great responsibility.'

There was a pause. Then Namaroff said warily: 'What did you say?'

'One never really knows what they're capable of, does one? They might even commit murder during one of their lapses. And no one would be any the wiser.'

Paul wanted to feel grateful to Meister for stalling like this and giving Carla time to get away, but his gratitude was submerged below a wave of anger against the ideas that the professor was planting in the minds of these ruffians – insidious, grotesque ideas about Carla.

Namaroff said: 'Where is Carla?'

Paul reached the bottom step and walked into the sitting room. 'She's not here.'

Namaroff swung round. 'You're lying.'

Kanof had two policemen behind him. He said: 'Search the house.' Without doing more than wave a slip of paper at Paul, he led the way upstairs.

Namaroff nodded his satisfaction, but was less satisfied when he realized that he had been left alone with Paul and Professor Meister. He eyed them uncertainly.

Heavy footsteps thumped overhead. They went in and out of each room, along the landing, back again…

Namaroff cleared his throat noisily and said: 'Mr Heitz, if this girl is not found I shall charge you with her abduction.'

'On what grounds?' snapped Meister.

'I shall be able to produce the evidence. There will be witnesses.'

'Speaking of evidence,' said Meister, 'perhaps you'll be good enough to return this to your Mr Ratoff with my compliments.' He held out the knife which he had taken from the tree. 'He left it behind when he attempted to kill Mr Heitz in the forest.'

'What kind of tale is this?'

'No tale, Doctor. You sent Ratoff to follow Carla to the Castle Borski where she met Paul. When she left, Ratoff attempted to kill Paul with his knife.' With a sudden, startling violence Professor Meister grabbed Namaroff by his lapel. 'Why do you want Paul Heitz out of the way, Namaroff? Is it because you're afraid he'll take Carla away from you? Or is it because you think he'll find out about the secret that you share with Ratoff? Answer me.'

'Take your hands off me.'

Inspector Kanof was halfway down the stairs. There was a gun in his hand. He said: 'Professor Meister – if you don't release the doctor this instant, I won't hesitate to shoot.'

Meister let his hands fall. Namaroff stepped back and brushed his lapel fussily as though he had been contaminated.

'Well?' he asked Kanof.

'She's not in the house.'

'Have you looked in every room?'

'Everywhere.'

'The attic?' insisted Namaroff. 'Have you searched the attic?'

A policeman coming downstairs said gruffly; 'She's not there.'

Namaroff glared from Meister to Kanof, as though blaming them equally. Then he turned brusquely away and went out. Kanof looked as though there was something he intended to say to Meister; then he changed his mind and gestured to his policemen that they should follow the doctor.

When they had gone, Meister let out a long sigh and said: 'Where is she, Paul? What did you do with her?'

Paul explained briefly what his plan was and how he had put it into action. Meister nodded dubiously. He seemed unimpressed. When Paul had finished, the professor took a small notebook from his pocket and flipped over the pages.

'There's only one other train today that will get you to Leipzig,' he said. 'I took the precaution of noting the times when I arrived in this district. It is a late night train.'

'I'll go on that, then.'

'You should have gone with her in the first place,' said Meister.

'But they'd have been after us at once. As it is, they're baffled. I'll pack at once, and—'

'She won't reach Leipzig,' said Meister dourly. 'She won't even be on the train.'

'Are you still persisting in this preposterous theory?'

'Of course, if the police find her before she reaches the station, then I shall have proved nothing. If, however, she does reach the station and you are right, she will be in Leipzig at five o'clock. Before you do anything further, Paul, I suggest you telephone the Hotel Kramer at about half past five.'

'Yes,' said Paul stiffly. 'I'll do that. And then you'll have to admit that you've been talking rubbish. I hope you'll apologize.'

'I hope I shall be in the position of having to.'

The afternoon dragged interminably. Paul and Meister walked into the village to make the telephone call, and were greeted by the usual resentful stares. One of Kanof's men stood on the steps of police headquarters and unblinkingly watched their progress along the street.

It took several minutes to get the call through to Leipzig. The line was a poor one, but the hotel manager's voice was clear enough for there to be no possibility of mistake: Carla Hoffmann had not arrived. Yes, he was sure that the train had been on time. No, there was no reason why she should not have reached the Hotel Kramer in ten minutes from the station.

As Paul went sombrely back along the street, he said with dogged determination: 'They must have caught her before she got to the station.'

'I doubt it,' said Meister. 'If they'd done that, we'd know about it. Kanof himself would take pleasure in coming out of his office and telling us.'

'They may be questioning her – they've taken her back to Namaroff…'

'I hope for your sake, Paul, that I'm wrong,' said Meister. 'But we're looking for the truth.'

'The fact that she hasn't arrived proves nothing.'

'Nothing at all,' Meister agreed. 'But do we discard my theory simply because it upsets your scheme of things – or do we go on looking for the truth?'

Paul could not reply. They finished the journey back to the millhouse in silence. Twilight was already hazing the trees and the hillside. Paul thought with a sudden nostalgia of his brother Bruno, who had loved the late summer and early autumn here. A cold shadow had fallen on Bruno, just as the cold shadow of winter was reaching out now over the valley, squeezing the days shorter between its fingers.

At the door of the millhouse he looked back. The dark swathes of trees across the hillside were sullen and threatening.

Carla must be somewhere up there, hiding or running like a frightened animal. Namaroff had set the police on her as he would have set tracker dogs on to a wild creature which he wanted trapped – trapped for his own purposes.

Paul made a move to go back down the path. Meister caught his arm.

'She's out there somewhere,' said Paul. 'I'm going to look for her.'

'No. Wait. In an hour's time it will be dark. Wait until the morning.' As Paul fought against the professor's steely grip, Meister implored him: 'Paul, you mustn't look for Carla tonight. Not tonight.'

'Get out of my way.'

Paul tugged himself free. Meister made another grab at him, then swung a hard right at his jaw. Paul staggered sideways. Dazed, he tried to steady himself and make for the gate; but Meister seized him and propelled him into the house. The door slammed behind them. Meister said:

'I'm sorry, Paul, but I can't let you destroy yourself.'

13

IT WAS as humiliating as being a small boy again, locked in his bedroom as a punishment for some petty offence. Paul made no attempt to sleep. He sat on the edge of the bed and watched darkness settle on the landscape. Unless Namaroff had already captured her, Carla must still be out there.

The moon swam slowly out from behind a cloud. On the hilltops thunder rumbled.

Paul went to the door and shook it once more. He shouted Meister's name, but there was no response. The professor had ceased to answer an hour ago: he had no intention of letting Paul out, and Paul had no intention of listening to his well-meant lectures through the intervening door.

A flash of lightning tore the sky, and the thunder redoubled its clamour.

Carla must surely have been captured by now. She might even have given herself up rather than spend a night in the forests. Dragged back to Namaroff by force or by his sinister power over her, she could even now be sitting, defeated, in the institution.

The thought was too much. It goaded Paul into action. He went to the window and raised the sash. It squeaked abominably, but the noise was drowned by the rising wind.

It was a long way down to the ground, but the tangle of ivy would provide a reasonable hold. He waited for the moon to come fully out, and made sure that there were no clouds likely to obscure it too abruptly. Then he put his leg over the windowsill and climbed out into the night.

Ivy tore away from the wall when he was halfway down and he had to make a jump, landing awkwardly but without breaking anything. He walked cautiously round the side of the house.

A light burned in the living-room window. He peered in, and saw Meister slumped in an armchair at the foot of the stairs. The warmth of the room had sent the professor off to sleep.

Paul was just about to move round to the path and make his way into the woods when he heard a muffled thumping. Meister started from his chair. The sound, dulled by the space between and by the fitful wind, must be that of someone at the door.

Paul stayed where he was, waiting.

A moment later Meister backed into the room, with Kanof and two policemen plodding grimly after him. Kanof's voice was faint but distinct through the window.

'I have a warrant for the arrest of Paul Heitz.'

'On what charge?'

'The abduction of Carla Hoffmann.'

'That's ridiculous. You saw for yourself that she wasn't in the house.'

'Will you please inform Mr Heitz,' said Kanof. 'I'll give him five minutes to get dressed.'

Professor Meister spread his arms in a gesture of despair. He realized that argument was futile. He went to the stairs and began to climb slowly.

Paul hugged the wall and made his way round to the path. A police carriage stood in the lane, the driver hunched on his seat, peering apprehensively up into the lowering forest. Paul crept round the back of the carriage and plunged into the sheltering gloom.

The moon lit his way. An occasional stab of lightning threw the trees into vivid relief, giving them a two-dimensional sharpness that added to the unreality of the night.

He had meant to go first to the institution, but now he was sure that Carla would not be there. They would not have sent Kanof to arrest him on a charge of abduction if Carla had already been captured. She must still be loose – still running or hiding, still cowering in terror.

On such a night, with the advancing storm about to break on the hills, there was one place in which she was almost bound to seek refuge. The Castle Borski held no terrors for her. She did not share the village superstitions. She and Paul had met there once; now, he thought resolutely, they would meet again. And this time he wouldn't let her out of his sight until they were free and far from Vandorf.

He half ran through the trees, scrambled up the precipitous path, and felt the stones skidding under his feet as he crossed the courtyard and entered the great hall.

Moonlight was an encroaching tide, lapping in from gaping windows and through tall, narrow embrasures. A cloud scudded across the moon, and there was a swimming, ebbing flux of light and shadow across the vast floor. The face of a statue shone brightly for a moment and then receded into dusky contemplation. Paul lurched into something that leaned away from him and then bumped back against his arm. It was a tall metal candelabrum, thick with rust.

He looked up at the balcony. In the uncertain light it was impossible to make out more than the blurred outlines of the statues at the head of the stairs.

'Carla!'

The wind carried his voice away.

'Carla!'

Lightning flickered into the hall, and a dark, motionless

shape beside one of the statues said: 'I am waiting for Carla, Mr Heitz.'

Paul reached out and his hand closed instinctively on the standard of the candelabrum. He waited for another flash. When it came, he saw Namaroff with an old, heavy-bladed sword in his hand.

Paul began to walk slowly towards him, lifting the candelabrum as though it were a three-pronged spear. Namaroff backed away.

Paul tried to speak, but a cataclysmic roar of thunder drowned him out. It struck Namaroff as a physical blow. He raised the massive sword, and stood his ground. Paul ducked away from the gleam of the murderous blade, and swung at Namaroff with the candelabrum.

They began a grotesque, lumbering duel in the bewildering light. The weight of the candelabrum was enough to throw Paul off balance. When it clashed against the sword, there was a shower of sparks. He began to use it madly like a flail, driving Namaroff backwards by sheer brute force. There was no pause for argument, no appeal for quarter: reason had deserted them once they entered the Castle Borski, and now in this ghostly ruin they battled like madmen. Elemental savagery boiled within them. The unmoving statues looked down placidly on the murderous hatred of two shifting, staggering, demented men.

Then a statue moved.

Paul caught the movement from the corner of his eye. Reeling to one side as Namaroff parried a blow, he knew that something or someone had advanced to the edge of the balcony.

He tried to look up, tried to call out, but Carla's name died on his lips as Namaroff came at him again.

The crash and clang of their weapons was caught up in the swirl of wind and thunder. More important than anything in the world became the need to kill Namaroff. It was Namaroff who had dominated Carla for so long, Namaroff who had imprisoned her, terrified her, driven her out by his sinister influence, and then pursued her and hounded her through the forests. Until Namaroff was dead there would be no peace.

Paul took a mighty swing. Namaroff's sword was torn from his hand and thrown shrieking, grating across the floor. Namaroff went down, grovelling, trying to push himself up again.

Paul turned the candelabrum in his hands and jabbed downwards. In a moment Namaroff would be impaled.

The doctor wriggled desperately to one side. He groped for anything that came to hand, writhed like a serpent across the floor, and reached the sword. By the time he was on his feet Paul was lunging again, panting to draw blood; to see Namaroff in his final agony. They fought across the hall to the foot of the stairs. Namaroff jumped back up two stairs, giving himself the advantage of additional height. But the length of the candelabrum was still the main factor. Paul began to jab him up the stairs. At the top there would be room to swing the candelabrum again. He would finish it; must finish it.

Then Paul slipped. He was down on one knee when Namaroff laughed hysterically and struck back. The sword and the candelabrum locked together. Other shapes seemed to be joining in the struggle, mocking the thrusts and twists of the two men. Forced to one side, Paul found himself staring at his own face: a huge cracked, flyblown mirror was fastened to the wall beside the staircase.

The candelabrum was wrenched from his grasp. He felt the agonizing thud of Namaroff's foot against the side of his head, and then he was turned over and over, kicked down the stairs. He spread his arms, tried to hold on, slithered and bumped down a dozen steps, and came to rest. He could not regain his breath, could not lift his head. He waited for Namaroff to leap down and deliver the finishing stroke.

Then he heard the moan that rose to an inhuman, shuddering cry. He grabbed for the rail and tried to haul himself up, seeing everything at a crazy, tilted angle.

Namaroff had the sword raised as though to defend himself. Or to shield his eyes…

There was a statue where no statue should be. There was a shape that loomed over Namaroff with its arms raised. It was still, yet not still. In the shadows the head was indeterminate, changing shape, alive with a dark life that was best concealed in those shadows.

Exhausted, Paul let his head slump down against the cold marble of the step.

He heard Namaroff scream. There was the clatter as he dropped the sword, and then he was stumbling down the stairs. His foot jarred against Paul's arm. He went helplessly on his way, sobbing what could have been a prayer or a curse. Paul rolled over and looked down. He saw Namaroff stagger against a pillar at the foot of the stairs and then grab for support at a dusty, ragged curtain. It tore, and he sank to his knees and then onto his face.

Paul forced himself up. He groped for the rail and eased his way down the stairs. On the bend of the flight he looked straight into the mirror. And swimming out of it, just as it had once swum up through the weed and shadows of the pool, came the face he dreaded.

'No,' said Paul to himself. 'No.' He swung away from the grinning monstrosity in the glass, and then kept his head down. He reached the bottom of the staircase and refused to look up. The temptation was almost overpowering. He had to see – had to confirm that it was true – had to defy this impossibility from a mythical past. But he made himself look at the floor as he edged away across the hall.

'Paul… where are you?'

It was Professor Meister's voice. And Meister, incredibly, was up on the balcony. He must have found another way into the castle and was approaching the apparition from behind.

Instinctively Paul looked up.

And it was not just because of Meister. Not because of any wish to save the professor, and not because he believed that if he stared straight at the creature it would all prove to be an hallucination. He had to look. There was nothing else for it.

He stared straight into the face of the Gorgon.

It was a classic, beautiful face. The features were those of an alluring woman – but they were only a mask for the evil that festered beneath. Paul Heitz saw what his brother and his father had seen; and the words choked in his mouth, thoughts choked in his mind… and through his body ran a tremor that touched every nerve with ice.

The snakes rose in a seething throng, lashing out as though desperate for something into which to sink their fangs. The Gorgon's head was an abomination of poisonous frenzy. Her mouth stretched in a grimace of fury. If any sound emerged it was part of the savage hissing of the serpents.

Paul covered his eyes with his hands. He knew it was too late: he had chosen to look on that face of dread, and now there was no hope.

There was a faint metallic scrape against the floor of the balcony. Paul's arm fell. Already it was growing heavy. Sluggishly he lifted his head. There was nothing to lose now. The vice was closing on his heart and lungs.

He looked… and saw the Gorgon beginning to turn as Meister rushed along the balcony towards her. She was too late. He had picked up Namaroff's sword, and swung it with all his strength.

The snakes reared in a fury. The Gorgon's mouth opened wider and wider. And suddenly the head was sliced from the body. Streaming blood, it bounced down the stairs and rolled across the floor, coming to rest near Namaroff's corpse.

Paul slipped on the foul slime that was left as a trail. He crawled towards the head. As he did so, the snakes appeared to shrink. They withdrew into the head, retracting into the brain of which the Gorgon had taken possession.

The face itself began to change. Moonlight drifted across it like a silver veil, and it seemed that the skin dissolved. The features sagged, then reshaped themselves.

It was the head of Carla.

Paul let out a last despairing cry. He tried to drag himself over those last few inches, but his strength was failing.

'Carla…'

Behind him, Meister came down the stairs and stood over him.

'She's free now, Paul. She's free.'

Light and shadow, colour and life, hope and despair… all faded and ceased to have meaning. The last thing on which Paul Heitz looked before he died was the severed head of Carla Hoffmann.

'Free,' he murmured.

Free. And dead.

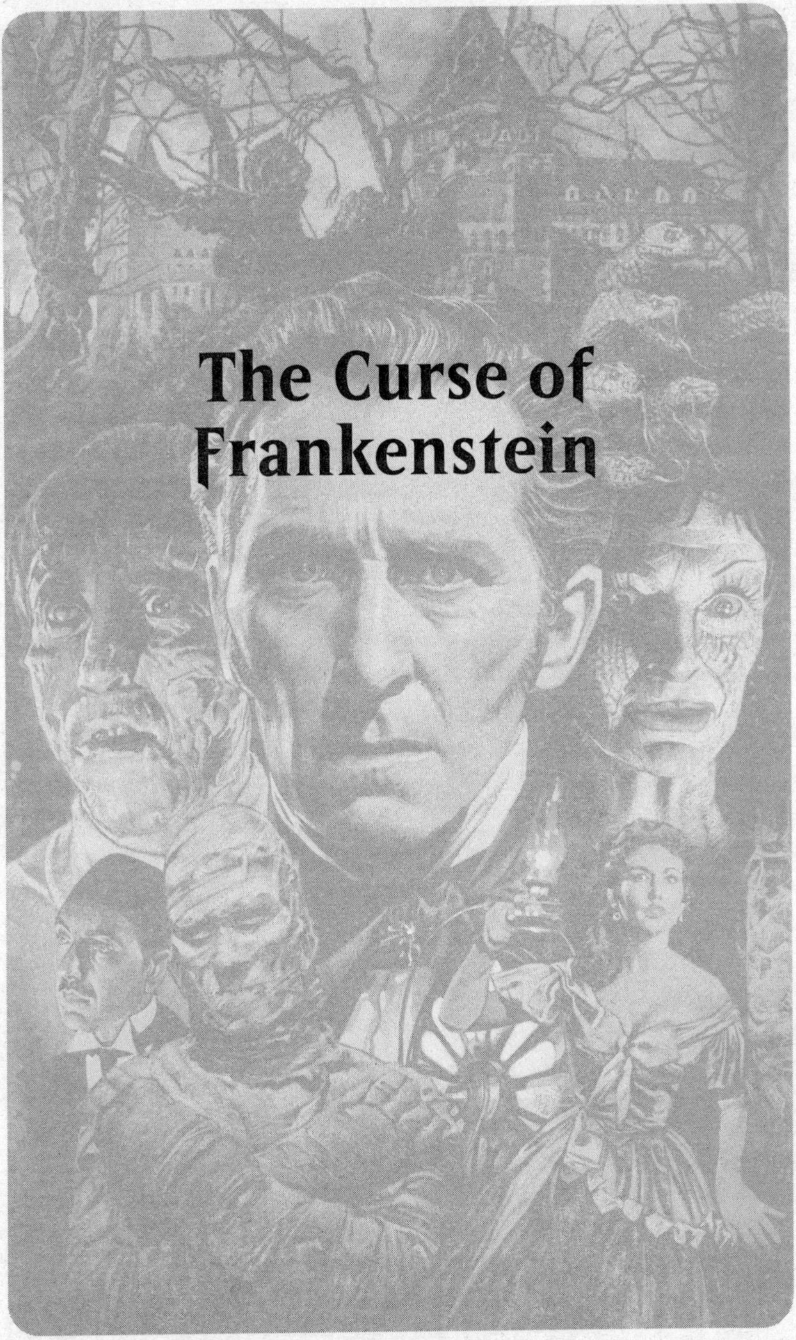
The Curse of
Frankenstein

1

TODAY THE priest came to my cell to offer what he considered comfort and to see if I was in repentant mood. The impertinence of it! Of what should I repent? I was glad to see him, but not because of any hopes he might hold out to me of the next life. It is this life in which I am interested: I am in no hurry to leave it. I wanted understanding and practical help from him, not pious platitudes. To him I would tell the whole story and ask him to pass it on. People trusted him: they listened to what he told them.

He was a drab, unimaginative little man. It was appalling that the survival of a mind such as my own should be at the mercy of a creature like this. Yet I had to try. Tomorrow they propose to execute me. It is monstrous, unthinkable. I am Baron Frankenstein, and there is still so much work which I must do.

'I'm sorry if you think my word will carry any authority,' he bleated at me. 'I'm afraid you're mistaken.'

I insisted that he should listen, and listen most carefully. Unless I could convince him that what I was about to tell him was the absolute truth, in the morning I would die. Yet how could anyone so fixed in his ways understand a word of the complexities for which I and I alone was responsible? He was as limited as the old fool who had been my teacher in Geneva.

Geneva in those early years of the nineteenth century was a lively city, a forum for brilliant debate and philosophical argument. Even as a boy I was a keen student of natural philosophy, and I think I may say without undue pride that I had a bent for research and logical analysis of problems. It was unfortunate that my mother, who knew little of such things, should have sent me for tuition to a bumbling old idiot who knew even less. He had been teaching the same dreary rubbish for thirty years. I doubted whether he had read a new book or considered a new idea for at least twenty of those.

The studies which counted were those I carried out on my own. While my friends – and I had few of them, for I found most of my contemporaries dull – were out carousing, I worked late into the night. With the few resources at my disposal I carried out small experiments which one day would have to be done on a larger scale. I read voraciously. I imbibed scientific theories in the way that my acquaintances imbibed wine. They thought that I was the dull one, and laughed at me for not knowing how to live. But what they meant by life and what I meant were two very different things. If they imagined I was not interested in life, they were absurdly mistaken. Life was just what interested me most – life, and how to create it.

It was something I didn't speak of to others. There were too many sceptics, and too many bigots anxious to suppress every manifestation of true progress.

When my mother died I inherited the Frankenstein fortune. This would enable me to begin the work and life I had always planned. I went back to the great house on the slopes above the pretty, trivial little village which had for centuries provided servants for the Frankenstein family and labourers to work in its fields; and here I endured the irritating formalities of the funeral, the condolences, and the family ritual before I could be left alone to concentrate on things which mattered.

My uncle from Basle commiserated with me and offered his assistance should I ever need it in my financial affairs.

He thought I was rather young to be handling everything myself. If I wished to return to Geneva to continue my studies, he would make himself personally responsible for the estate. I was sure that he would – but I was not too happy about the possible future of the estate in such hands.

My Aunt Sophie had a delicate matter which she wished to broach. It was indeed so delicate that she could not bring herself to speak of it outright, and after some movements on her part as stately as a minuet but less conclusive, I was forced to say bluntly:

'You are concerned about the allowance my mother made you?'

'Oh. Victor, I would not wish to—'

'You need have no fears, Aunt Sophie. I shall continue to pay it.'

'You're a good boy, Victor. Your mother would have been proud of you. The dignity with which you have handled everything...'

'Yes,' I said. I wanted her off the premises so that I could relax and savour my new freedom and the taste of my riches.

But Aunt Sophie had every intention of declaring her over-whelming gratitude and at the same time of insinuating another possibility into my mind. Her daughter Elizabeth had been waiting demurely in the background. Now she was brought forward.

'Elizabeth, thank your cousin.'

'There's really no need,' I said.

She was adamant. 'Come along, Elizabeth, say thank you properly.'

The poor girl curtsied, blushing most becomingly as she did so.

'She's a good girl, Victor,' said Aunt Sophie in what she supposed to be a confidential aside. 'She'll grow into a fine woman one day.'

'I'm sure she will.' This at least I could say with conviction, for Elizabeth already had the makings of that fair, smooth-skinned, graceful woman she was soon to become.

'She'll make someone a fine wife.'

I held out my hand. 'Goodbye.'

Aunt Sophie herself almost contrived a curtsey. It was amazing that so gauche and insensitive a creature should have produced such an attractive daughter.

I was glad when at last they had all gone. The house was mine. The future was mine. All the resources of the Frankenstein estate were mine. At the back of the house were servants who would look after my every need without ever obtruding themselves. In the real sense of the word I was alone; and delighted to be so.

These pleasant musings were interrupted by the deep thud of the knocker on the main door. I was still not accustomed to having a full staff to attend to such matters, and instinctively I rose from my chair and went to the door. A serving girl, little more than a child, was already coming up the steps from the basement. She stopped when she saw me. She had bold dark eyes and a strangely impertinent, inscrutable little smile that was older than her years. I hesitated, not wanting to seem foolish by turning back and leaving her to answer the door. Then I waved her away and went to open it.

A young man stood on the step gazing out over the magnificent panorama of the valley. He turned to face me and made a polite bow in which there was no undue subservience.

'Good morning. My name is Paul Krempe. I have an appointment with Baron Frankenstein.'

I had been ready to dismiss the newcomer without delay, but now I stood back to let him in. He had come more swiftly than I had expected in answer to my summons. This was a good sign. I liked his shrewd, inquiring expression – I needed a man with a mind as relentlessly inquiring as my own – and I approved the speed with which he had got here.

'You must be Victor,' he said as he entered the hall and looked frankly around. 'I'm to be your tutor.'

I led him towards the salon in which my mother had once received visitors in that eternal round of courtesies and conventions which I proposed to abolish. 'Surely it isn't settled yet?' I said. 'I thought this was just an interview to decide whether you were suitable for the position.'

'I have had some correspondence with the Baron, and he seemed quite satisfied with my qualifications.'

'That's right.' I was deriving some amusement from this. 'He did, didn't he?'

Paul Krempe gave me a swift sidelong glance. He was trying to assess just how difficult a charge I was likely to be.

He said: 'Will you tell your father that I'm here.'

'My father is dead.'

This took him aback. 'But that's ridiculous. I had a letter from him…'

'He has been dead for many years. It was I who advertised for a tutor. It was I who wrote to you.'

'You are the Baron?'

'And have been since I was five years old.' I smiled.

'Yet you wrote to me saying that you wanted a tutor for your son.'

I had thought it would save a lot of explanation if I made the man come for a personal interview. In a letter he might have read things awry and been dubious about dealing direct with one as young as myself. He might have decided that the long journey was not worth while merely to satisfy what might be a rich young idler's whim. Now that he was here we could talk frankly.

We did talk, and at great length. I admired the way in

which he reacted to what must at first have been a somewhat disturbing situation. He had a wry sense of humour and a keen appreciation of most of the points I made about my education so far and my requirements for the future. We talked as equals, yet he paid just the appropriate respect to my position, while I found it easy to defer to the wider range of his knowledge.

I had no intention of leaving this house and the estate in the hands of any of my relatives. I had no intention of completing my studies in Geneva, since I was convinced that under such conditions they never would be completed. What I wanted was a man like Krempe, a scientist and a scholar, who would live here and fill in the lamentable gaps in my knowledge. A general education was not what I sought: I was happy enough with my general background, and wished to concentrate now on the specialized work for which I felt I was destined.

'You were engaged as my tutor,' I said at the end of our long discussion, 'subject to the Baron's approval.' We both smiled: it had now become an agreeable joke between us. 'I may tell you that the Baron approves. Do you still want the position?'

'I shall be honoured, Herr Baron,' said Paul with a trace of respectful mockery which I found most refreshing after the hypocrisies and servility of my relatives.

And so we began.

There were times when I grew impatient. Paul turned out to be an admirable tutor, and in two years I had learned all he had to teach. But those two years dragged abominably. Of course, the groundwork was essential; but I wanted to move on to the subjects which really obsessed me.

It was Paul who taught me patience. Now, when he has forsaken me and repudiated all that we worked on together, I wonder if he realizes just how much of my doggedness and unwearying application can be attributed to his personal example? We spent the days, the weeks, the months together, probing into the unknown, investigating, recording, searching… always searching, until gradually the great sweep of our research began to narrow down to a single direction.

To this we finally turned all our energies. We had explored biological byways, had even studied alchemy in the hope of finding grains of truth in the dross; but now we saw how recent discoveries in the field of magnetism opened up possibilities of a stimulus which might provoke the reaction we sought. It took us years of unrelenting work to approach even the fringe of what we longed to find.

During those years Paul lived in the house and rarely went out. We needed no outside distractions. He paid a few visits to some ageing uncle many miles away, but was always eager to return. Sometimes he went down to the village and I refrained from asking what entertainment he found there. For myself, I observed with a by no means dispassionate interest the development of the young serving girl on my staff, and when I fancied some frivolous relaxation I coaxed her into my bed. She required little coaxing. For all the splendid firmness of her body and the burning promise of those restless eyes, there were few in the neighbourhood who could satisfy her, and we spent some rewarding hours together. Justine was her name, and I will confess that there were many times when I murmured the syllables lovingly into her ear in such a way as to persuade her that she meant everything to me. There is little point in pursuing any pleasure, however fleeting it may be and however easily discarded it may later be, unless one is whole-hearted about it at the moment of its consummation. There would come a time when I regretted the romantic glibness of my tongue.

Justine, after all, was merely a diversion. I summoned her when I was in the mood for her, and if she had understood the responsibilities and limitations of her employment in my household there would never have been any trouble. I was Baron Frankenstein, and my life was consecrated to life itself.

Of the activities of Paul and myself she knew nothing. Or so we believed. Our efforts were applied out of sight and sound of the rest of the house. Nobody was allowed into the laboratory. When the place required cleaning we cleaned it ourselves. When there were things to be disposed of – things better concealed from the prying eyes of ignorant servants – we destroyed them in various ways.

And at last, after years of application, we were rewarded.

We had been experimenting on a dog which Paul had lured away from the village. There had been a small outcry about its disappearance as it was a great pet with the family to which it belonged, but nobody suspected that it had found a resting place in the Frankenstein home. They ought to have been honoured. Possibly one day, when the whole story is told, they will indulge themselves in some petty pride: their dog made history, though the history is still to be written for the world to see.

I had killed the animal painlessly and then lowered it into the tank. It floated for two days in the viscous fluid with which we had already dosed or injected some hundreds of rats, mice, and birds. At the end of two days we began to apply the magnetic charges which jolted through the system and beat out an imperious rhythm in the animal's heart. A hundred minor adjustments were necessary. The frequency of the heartbeats and the intensity with which these could be simulated were delicate matters.

We reached the crucial stage late one night. There had been so many failures that I was not unduly optimistic. The most I allowed myself to hope was that we should learn something, some tiny additional piece of knowledge, that would make the next step clearer. I opened the tank and drained it. Paul, as engrossed in the task as myself, was impatient to reach in and take out the dog but I waved him away. The body needed thoroughly washing before we could allow ourselves to touch it. I drew on my gloves and sluiced the dog down until I was sure it was safe to approach the final investigation.

The dog lay as it had lain the day I killed it. Its eyes were open but glazed and unseeing. The paws lay flat and lifeless. There was no sign of breathing.

Paul stood beside me as I applied the stethoscope. He, too, might well have been lifeless: he was afraid to breathe or make a move. I listened, and he watched me.

The throb might be in my own head. I wanted so much to hear it that I could be cheating myself.

But no – there could be no mistake. I stood upright and tried to control my trembling exultation.

'Paul… it's alive!' I scooped the dog up in my arms. It was a limp weight, but I laughed madly over it and felt a wild desire to give it a pet name because it had behaved so well. Good dog… good dog! I said: 'We've done it.'

2

THERE WAS a considerable lag between the cardiac reaction and the first visible signs of life. Paul took the dog from me, wanting to share in my jubilation just as he had so devotedly shared in my work, and carried it downstairs to the sitting room. He laid the dog on the floor, and we drank a glass of brandy while waiting for it to get up on its feet. I was alarmed by its continuing stillness, but Paul pointed out that some time would be necessary for the first heartbeats to circulate life through the body once more.

'In itself,' he said eagerly, 'this opens up magnificent possibilities. Suppose that we could delay or prolong that period in which the body presumably remains dead while the heart is alive – then we'd have a living body with only the barest life spark present. Think what that would mean when it came to performing major surgery! It would save hundreds of lives, reduce shock to a minimum… no loss of blood…' He was beside himself with joy. 'Victor, the medical federation meets in Berne next month. Can we have our paper ready by then?'

At our feet the dog stirred. It shuddered along its whole length and then lazily lifted its head. As we watched, it thumped its tail twice. Then it began to stagger to its feet.

'Do you think we can?' Paul persisted.

'We could,' I said, 'but we're not going to.'

'But why not? There isn't another meeting of this scale for another year. Why wait that long?'

I was conscious of a twinge of disappointment. He had been a faithful ally and had shirked nothing, but now that success was within our grasp he showed himself too naive in his enthusiasm. What we had done so far was nothing to what we could yet do. We had only just started. The door was open: now was the time to go through and find what lay beyond. I had had my own moments of impatience, but these were now conquered. I knew what came next and I knew that it required care and concentration. We had discovered the source of life itself and had used it to restore a creature that was dead. It was a tremendous discovery which was not ready to be shared. We must move on to the next stage.

'It's not enough just to bring a dead animal back to life,' I said. The dog sniffed at me and then went to Paul, who patted it affectionately as though he had owned it for years. 'We must create from the beginning. We must build up our own creature – build it up from nothing, if necessary. Otherwise we have accomplished only half the task we set ourselves.'

'Build?' He was baffled. 'Build what?'

'The most complex thing known to man,' I said. 'Man himself. Let's not concern ourselves with side issues such as operational techniques. We must create a human being.'

'Victor, this has gone to your head. Let's talk tomorrow and—'

'A man with perfect physique,' I said. 'With the mature brain of a genius. Everything planned and perfect. We can do it. Don't you see?'

In all these years I had seen no indication that he was anything but a devoted man of science. Now he revealed unsuspected doubts – the doubts of an ordinary superstitious mortal.

'What you're saying is madness – a revolt against nature. Such a thing can end only in evil.'

'Come now, Paul.' I forced myself to be patient with him. 'You haven't shown any scruples up to now. As for revolting against nature, haven't we done so already and succeeded? Isn't a thing that's dead supposed to be dead for all time? Yet we brought it back to life.'

The dog confirmed this by licking his hand. Paul looked down. The rasp of that rough tongue seemed to convince him more than my words did. He nodded to himself.

I went on: 'We hold in the palms of our hands such secrets as have never been dreamed of. Nature puts up her own barriers to confine the scope of man, but over and over again these barriers have been surmounted or thrust farther back. We have pushed them back. We are in a great tradition, Paul. There's nothing to stop us now.'

With that wry smile I knew so well, admitting rueful defeat, he asked: 'What do you want to do?'

'First,' I said, 'we need the framework – the body. Whatever adaptations may be necessary, that basic material is our starting point. Last week they hanged a man in Inglestadt. He was a highwayman who'd been terrorizing the countryside for months. As a warning to others his body has been left on a gibbet just outside the town. It'll stay there until it rots… or until it's stolen.'

For a moment I thought Paul was about to protest again. Then he raised his glass. We were partners again in our splendid enterprise.

It would have suited me very well to ride out at once and claim the body of the robber, but we had worked deep into the night and were both exhausted. Paul made up a comfortable bed for the dog from an old blanket in the corner of the laboratory, and then we made our own way to bed. I lay awake for a long time, too tired and, at the same time, too ecstatic to sleep.

The following day my thoughts were occupied entirely by the next crucial step. Rising late, I checked that the dog was still alive and healthy, and decided that in a day or two it must be turned loose. Let it go back to its startled owners if it wished! Having a dead dog concealed in my house was no great problem; having a live one padding about the place would certainly arouse some conjecture. I wondered, with excitement rather than apprehension, how we would cope with the problem of a newly created man when that arose.

Justine tried to fondle me as I passed along the first-floor landing during the course of the afternoon. I brushed her off. She was growing much too forward for my liking. She belonged to the darkness and to the hours of my choice: I was disturbed to see signs of a brash familiarity and even arrogance in her manner.

The rebuff brought a dark frown to that usually pert, provocative face. Then she laughed none too agreeably.

'You'll be more friendly tonight, I'll be bound.'

'Tonight I'm busy,' I said.

'Busy?' She was alert at once. 'You and your friend are bringing village girls into the house – is that it?'

'No, Justine,' I said. 'No. We shall be working. And now go and do the same.'

The sulky pout of her lower lip, so entrancing at the right moment, now had the sinister quality of a threat. But she still knew the sound of an order when she heard it in my voice. She flounced away.

She was beautiful – yet not, deplorable as it may seem to some, as beautiful in my eyes as the corpse that swung from the gibbet by the roadside that night.

Paul and I took a horse and cart by a roundabout route to the scene of the execution. We had a ladder in the cart, and it was a matter of minutes to set this up and for me to climb up and cut through the rope from which dangled the robber, twisting gently in the cool night breeze. The body fell neatly into the cart, where Paul straightened it out and covered it with sacking. We drove back to the house.

In the brightness of the laboratory the dead rogue was not an attractive sight. I was delighted to have him, but far from impressed by his appearance. The birds hadn't wasted any time: they had started on his eyes and then demolished one side of his face.

The head was of no use anyway. My idea was to create a perfect human being, and it had never been part of the plan that we should use the defective head and brain of a subnormal personality. I reached for a knife and turned the body over on the table.

'What are you going to do?' asked Paul.

I showed him. Our recent experiments had given me some surgical skill, and it was a comparatively simple matter to cut off the head of the corpse. Once I glanced up to see if Paul was interested in my anatomical knowledge, and caught him with a mixture of horror and amazement on his face.

With the same knife I sheared off a piece of sacking and wrapped the head in it. I held it away from me so that blood would not seep through and drop on to my clothes, and then I crossed the laboratory and dropped the head into the acid tank. The empty eye sockets yawned at me as the head rolled over and settled on the bottom.

It would not take long before skin and bone were eaten away. Less time than it would have taken the birds. In a few minutes there would be no trace.

'Now, Paul' – I had to jar him out of his trance – 'a hand with his clothes, if you please.'

I was eager to see the condition of the rest of the body.

Paul was rather fastidious about it all, and I sensed his reluctance as we stripped the filthy rags from the stinking cadaver. To me this was still a glorious object, not because of its present deplorable state but because of its potentialities.

Together we washed down the body and then wrapped it in bandages from head to toe… or, rather, from neck to toe. As we lifted it into the specially prepared tank, I could not help shuddering. My shudders were different from Paul's: his were those of a squeamish sentimentalist; mine arose from aesthetic considerations. The brute's hands were really too coarse to be contemplated. With such clod-hopping hands he could hardly have been anything other than a robber, except perhaps a gorilla.

We lowered the swathed form into the fluid and I studied the splayed fingers and veinous discoloration with mounting distaste. This was not how I had visualized my creation. But I had been prepared for deformities and the need for alterations. A head, new limbs – carefully chosen, they would contribute to the final unity of which I would be master.

Paul said: 'Victor, I don't think we should continue with this. We should wait and discuss our findings with the federation. If anything—'

'Hands,' I said. I wanted him to concentrate on the essential things and forget his ludicrous scruples. 'Where shall we find the right hands?'

'Listen to me, Victor.'

But I had no intention of listening. I was not to be deterred. After so many frustrations, everything was going well for us now. Only a coward would turn back. I hurried him out of the laboratory and sent him off to bed with instructions to lie awake and think about the difficulties presented to us by this unsuitable corpse. I tried to make a joke of it, but his usual reluctant smile was not forthcoming.

In the morning I still knew that I was right. And among

my correspondence was an item which I could take only as an omen. It was the printed announcement of the death of Bardello, the world's greatest sculptor, in Dresden. He had been a great friend of my father, who had helped him with two or three commissions early in his career. A memorial service was to be held tomorrow. It would undoubtedly be a magnificent affair, complete with florid eulogies, and I decided that I would not go; then, after a brief reflection, I decided that I would go.

It would be a tragedy should the hands of the most gifted sculptor of our time be left to rot below ground.

There was another communication announcing a death. This was less formal. It was a letter from my cousin Elizabeth telling me that her mother, my Aunt Sophie, had passed on. To this funeral ceremony I was also invited. I could not combine the two of them, and I knew which was the more important to me. I therefore wrote to Elizabeth before I set out for Dresden, expressing my grief at my aunt's death and regretting that it would be impossible for me to attend the interment, dearly as I should have loved to do so. I also invited Elizabeth to come and stay with me. It would be a good thing 'to have her in the house: it had been taken for granted from our childhood that we would one day marry, and if this were made tactfully clear to Justine it would go some way to diluting that arrogance of hers. Besides, it was time I married. With so many more absorbing problems in my mind, I devoted little time to the running of the household, and it would be a good thing for the staff to have a woman in the place organizing such matters.

Now I was in a hurry to leave. There was no time to explain every detail to Paul, and in any case I felt it would be wiser not to tell him too much in advance.

'Better not touch our friend in the laboratory while I'm gone,' I said. 'Let him rest in peace while he can.'

And then I left. Paul was bewildered by the speed of all this.

If he thought to ask why I was going to Dresden, it was not until after I had gone.

The business took me longer than I had anticipated. I had to proceed from one little bit of bribery to another – and the more protracted the operation, the more danger there was of someone talking. The pomp surrounding the occasion did not help. One might almost have thought that a reigning monarch had died. At last, however, when the fuss had died down and the attention of the public turned from the dead Bardello to some new fad, I was able to accomplish my mission. At dead of night two men went out and returned with the hands of Bardello.

I hurried back to Switzerland.

I tried to imagine Paul's face when I broke the news to him. But more than that, I tried to imagine the corpse in the tank and how very different it would look when these magnificent, sensitive hands had been grafted to its arms.

The last mile was the longest. I urged the coachman on. With a tiring journey behind me I was nevertheless eager to get to work at once. If it meant staying up all night I wanted to set things in train.

With the precious parcel under my arm I marched across the hall and threw open the door of the salon. I was very nearly tempted to unwrap the parcel and throw the hands down triumphantly before Paul. I was glad I had restrained myself, for he was not alone. A beautiful young woman was sitting by the window. As I burst in she was saying:

'Yes, I've come to live here. This is to be my home.'

'Live here?' gasped Paul. 'But that's…'

Then they both turned towards me.

'Victor.' Elizabeth rose and crossed the room. She was as graceful as I had predicted she would be. Her beauty had the fragile yet firm quality of fine porcelain, but whereas porcelain is fixed, set, hard-surfaced, she was alive and volatile.

'I'm glad you got here safely,' I said. We shook hands very formally. I fancy she expected me to kiss her cheek, but I was already thinking and moving beyond her. 'Paul, you must come and see what I've got. A treasure, I assure you – a real treasure!'

Elizabeth fell back a step, disappointed. I gave her a quick smile and she tried to seem at ease. My social graces had perhaps suffered in the years of seclusion and devotion to the task in hand. With Justine I had needed no social graces. For this reason as well it would be good to have my cousin here. With Elizabeth I could learn again: she would, I flattered myself, find me a charming companion when I chose to be so.

But now there were more urgent demands on my time.

'We'll see you at dinner, my dear,' I said.

Paul glanced at her as though unsure of his own responsibility – whether to stay and provide her with social chit-chat or whether to come with me.

I left him in no doubt. I said: 'Shall we go to the laboratory, Paul?'

With an apologetic smile he left Elizabeth and followed me up the stairs. When we were in the laboratory I indicated that he should lock the door, and then I unwrapped the parcel.

'What about these? Have you ever seen anything so beautiful?'

He started as the long, powerful fingers were revealed. Yet even as he stared at them there was a certain remoteness in his manner. He appeared to have something more important on his mind. But what could be more important than this?

'Where did you get them?' he asked abstractedly.

I told him, without giving too circumstantial an account of the methods I had employed. When I had finished he said:

'Victor, do you realize what this means?'

'It means,' I said, 'that our friend in the tank will be reborn with the finest hands ever possessed by any man.'

'I was referring to the arrival of your cousin. We can't continue with this experiment – not here, anyway.'

'What are you talking about?'

'Elizabeth. She might find out.'

'What if she does?' I could see no cause for alarm in this.

'She's young. Her mind will be incapable of standing up to such a shock. Victor, you don't realize the horror of what you're doing. At first I was blind to it myself.'

'And now?'

'While you were away I decided that I would not continue with this experiment. I hope I can convince you that I'm right, and make you change your mind, too.'

His chance of doing that was small. I tried to make him see reason. 'In six months' time you'll rejoice in the fact that you helped me present this achievement to the world. You'll become as famous as I will.'

'No, Victor,' he said. 'Infamous. I won't help you any more. And I beseech you to give this up – if not for your own sake, then for the sake of that girl.'

It was evident that my delightful cousin had made a strong impression on him. I had not realized that he could be so susceptible. In an endeavour to shake him out of this mood I said:

'Come along, Paul – help me to graft these hands on. It will be fascinating to see how they take.'

He made no move to follow me to the tank. 'Can't you understand, I'm not going to help you any more. And I shall try to make Elizabeth leave here.'

He was really disappointingly naive. With his bourgeois background, he could, of course, not understand how such matters were arranged in families like ours. Elizabeth would listen to me rather than to him, and she would certainly not leave here. There were some explanations which would soon have to be made to Paul; but at this moment I was in no mood for dissertations of that kind. I said:

'If you really mean that you're not going to help me, you'd better leave me alone.'

He went to the door, then hesitated. 'Victor…'

'If I'm to work on my own,' I said, 'I shan't have time to spare for dinner. Every hour that's wasted means a possible deterioration in these hands. Make my excuses to Elizabeth, will you?'

He went out. I took off my jacket and turned towards the bandaged shape in the tank. I half expected Paul to return. How could he possibly resist? But he didn't come back.

I wondered what he and Elizabeth would find to talk about.

3

IT TOOK me the better part of two hours to make the first attachment and submerge it in the tank. The speeded-up revivification of the tissues brought about by the fluid would now establish a firmer growth, and in due course the magnetic process would stimulate the entire organism. But that must wait: there were many faults yet to be corrected in this body.

Letting myself sink on to the laboratory stool after that concentrated effort over the tank, I realized that I was dizzy with exhaustion. If I was to go on working into the night, I needed coffee. I could go for a long time without food, but not without the stimulus of black coffee.

Elizabeth and Paul should have finished dinner by now. If I went down I would be in time to take a cup from the tray. And perhaps when he saw the gleam in my eyes Paul would, after all, find himself making excuses to follow me back to the laboratory.

I went along the landing and down the stairs. The door of the dining room was open and I could hear the murmur of voices as I descended. Suddenly Paul's rose in a plea that brought me to a halt.

'Leave this house at once. It won't be safe here.'

'Not safe?' came Elizabeth's quiet but surprised response. 'But Victor will be here.'

'It's because of Victor I'm asking you to leave. He is

conducting a series of experiments which could be extremely dangerous.'

I was on the verge of hastening down the rest of the flight and into the dining room to cut short this disloyalty. Then I heard Elizabeth's calm voice and noted with approval the tinge of reproach in it.

'I don't think Victor would have invited me here if he had thought I would be in any danger.'

'He doesn't realize himself just what risks he is taking.'

'What are these experiments?'

'You wouldn't understand them.'

'I'm sure I would. I could try, anyway. Please tell me.'

'I can't.'

'Then I shall have to ask Victor. If I am to marry him—'

'Marry him!' Paul's reaction was an absurd shout.

'We are engaged,' said Elizabeth coolly. I foresaw that she was going to make an admirable wife. Her dignity and tranquillity would suit me very well. 'It was agreed years ago between Victor and my mother.'

'But… you've hardly seen him in recent years. You can't know anything about him.'

'It has always been my dearest wish to marry him,' she said, 'and I shall do all that is in my power to be a worthy wife to him.'

There was a silence. Paul broke it with an appeal that had lost all its force. 'I still say that you must leave here…'

He heard footsteps along the passage just as I did. Justine walked into the dining room. I stayed where I was, now more gratified than angered by what I had just overheard.

'Shall I take the master's dinner up, do you think, sir?' Justine asked.

'He may be ready for something by now,' Paul agreed. 'Leave it outside the door.'

'Of course, Herr Krempe. I always do.'

I turned and went swiftly back to the laboratory. When Justine came to the door some minutes later, she rapped twice, but I refused to answer. She stood there for a few minutes. It was not the first time she had done this. Whether she expected me to come out to her or whether she wanted a glimpse into the laboratory I could not tell: whichever it might be, she obtained no satisfaction.

That night I worked until dawn and then stole a few hours' sleep. With some reluctance I forced myself to spend part of the afternoon with Elizabeth discussing our future. The reluctance faded somewhat after I had confirmed my original opinion that she was a serious, intelligent, well-balanced young woman. She made no stickily romantic protestations, and expected none in return. In her face I read both affection and respect, mingled in what I considered the ideal proportions. We had no need to discuss family or financial problems since we were both familiar with all the ramifications of the Frankenstein lineage and estates. We were two sensible adults: it had been established years ago that we should marry – and we had no quarrel with this arrangement. A decent period would be allowed after her mother's death, and then we would have a simple ceremony to which, unfortunately, it would be necessary to invite one senile uncle and two remote cousins. Elizabeth would then be mistress of the household. I made it plain that, so far from objecting to her rehearsing this role before we were married, I would take it as a favour. It would take the weight off my shoulders and enable me to concentrate on my own work.

'This work of yours,' she said tentatively: 'is it very... unusual?'

I knew that, provoked by Paul, she had been about to use another word, but was too noble to do so.

'Very unusual,' I said.

'You are not in any danger?'

I swear that she phrased the question sincerely. It was the possibility of danger to me rather than to herself that concerned her.

'None,' I said. 'And when the work is completed, you shall be the first to share in my triumph.'

She accepted this sweetly, without demur.

Acceptance did not, however, come easily to Justine. In Elizabeth's presence she grew surly, though was never so insolent as to necessitate her dismissal. Elizabeth assumed that the girl had been used to taking many decisions for herself and was finding it difficult to adjust to a new regime. She was patient with her.

But Justine was not patient. One night when I had worked late in the laboratory and was on my way to my bedroom, she materialized suddenly from the shadows in a corner and flung her arms round me. They were strong, demanding arms. She wore only a flimsy shift, and when I touched her I felt a tremor of urgent desire run through that body which I knew so well.

She breathed: 'Victor...'

'How many times must I tell you—'

'Baron, then,' she whispered derisively. 'Herr Baron.'

'That's better.' I had made it a rule that she should always address me this way. The last thing I wanted was for her to fall so much into the habit of using my Christian name that she would one day blurt it out when others were present.

She said: 'How much longer is this to go on?'

Her hands were digging into my neck and yet she was holding herself away from me, not so much tantalizing me as waiting until something essential was said between us.

I was in no mood for her tonight. I said: 'How long is what going on?'

'Meeting like this in dark corridors. Making love in secret.

Treating me as a servant, beneath your notice, in daylight. When are you going to marry me?'

It was an outrageous question. I stifled a contemptuous laugh. She had given me many hours of pleasure and I had no wish to be discourteous. But this was really too absurd.

I tried to free myself from her arms, but she held on. 'What makes you think I would contemplate marrying you?'

'Things you have said to me. In the night. And' – now she pressed herself against me – 'this.'

Only the most strong-willed man could have resisted that woman. Her every movement was so well known to me that it immediately suggested all the following movements, and I knew from experience that my memories of her never lived up to the reality. I was helplessly drawn on. I kissed her. Our mouths fought savagely together, and she laughed. Then, with a typical change of mood, she wrenched her head away and said tartly:

'Herr Baron Victor. This woman – what is she doing here?'

'Are you jealous?' I asked.

'No.' Then she snorted and said: 'Yes, yes, I am jealous. She is not your mistress, that pale creature? No, she could not be. If I thought she was—'

'On the contrary, Justine,' I said, 'she is to be *your* mistress. It is your duty to serve my cousin Elizabeth and see to her every need just as thoroughly as you have mine.'

I expected an explosion, but what I had just said struck her as being funny, and at once she was warm and laughing.

'Oh, no,' she spluttered. 'I think not, Herr Baron.'

'In a different way, of course,' I said, bringing on further laughter.

'Of course,' she said.

And we fumbled our way to my bedroom, where she proved to me that I was not as tired as I had thought.

Elizabeth suspected nothing of this. She had led a formal, somewhat restricted life, and took it for granted that life elsewhere – in her own social circle, at least – followed the same prescribed pattern. Gently and with admirable tact she took over the reins of management. Nothing was said about her eventually ceasing to be merely my cousin and becoming my wife. This was no business of the servants. They would be told when it was appropriate to tell them. For myself, I was not looking forward to breaking the news to Justine. Whatever she might suspect, she was still mercifully conscious enough of her own position to keep her curiosity within bounds. Once or twice she began to edge towards some awkward questions, but I silenced her in the most effective way I knew – which was pleasurable for both of us.

There were no people in our own circle to whom we made any announcement or even gave any hints. This was simply because no such circle existed. Paul had left the house, still firmly refusing to assist me in any further developments, and had settled in the village. This perturbed me slightly. It was amusing that he should have a quixotic desire to watch over Elizabeth, but not so amusing that he should be, as it were, on my doorstep, ready to give away our secrets to others if the mood took him. There was nobody else to pry into my personal or working life. We visited nobody and invited nobody. I could manage happily without company. If Elizabeth felt lonely, she did not complain. Since her mother had never been able to afford to entertain lavishly, the girl was probably used to occupying herself without the need for the chatter of others.

Her only complaint was that she saw so little of me. I spent what time I could with her, but I could not have been a very gay companion. All my thoughts were wrapped up in my experiments, and of these I could not speak to Elizabeth. There must be no false alarms raised at this stage. Only when the creature was complete and I could present it as an accomplished fact, justifying all my labours, would I let her into all my secrets.

I had discovered that the robber had had a defective right ankle, and as his feet were over-large in any case this meant replacing both of them to get a decent result. I made a trip to a charnel house in a canton many miles away: I was taking no chances near home. Then there was the question of the head. It took me several weeks to find a good specimen – and a specimen which was accessible – and then the eyes were in poor condition. A lot of intensive work was still to be done.

Leaving the house for any length of time worried me. I took the most stringent precautions to ensure that no one could get into my laboratory, but at the back of my mind was always the fear that some accident would happen – there would be a fire and someone might break the door down or find traces of my work in the ruins… and the mere idea of a fire destroying all that work was in itself a nightmare.

One day I received word from the keeper of a charnel house – whom I had promised to pay well for such a notification – that if I made haste I could claim a pair of eyes before deterioration set in. I hastily took my small bag and made ready to set out.

'You're going away again?' said Elizabeth wistfully.

'I'll be back tomorrow evening,' I assured her.

'I was hoping you would help me in checking the household accounts.'

'They're your department,' I said, wanting to make it clear that I had complete faith in her. 'I'm sure you'll handle them admirably.'

'But I'd like you to see them. I'd like your assistance with them.'

'You'll be asking soon if you can help me with my experiments.'

It was a rash thing to say. Her face brightened. 'I would,' she said. 'I'd like that more than anything in the world.'

Perhaps one day she would be the helper I needed. It was a fascinating concept. She looked so feminine and so fragile, yet there was a toughness in her loyalty and devotion that could make her worthier than Paul had been.

The mere thought of Paul irritated me. He was a coward. Petty though it might seem, there were times when I felt that above all else I wanted to prove to him that I had been right all along and, furthermore, that I had been able to attain my goal without his assistance.

I went to collect the eyes.

They made a beautiful pair. The man who removed them from the corpse had done so with skill. They were just what I needed.

'Not often we get them perfect in here,' the keeper confided. 'Eyes is generally the first to go.' He looked at me anxiously. 'Well, sir – what do you think?'

'They'll do,' I said. He was still watching as I took coins from my pocket. 'Ten, we said, didn't we?'

'Each,' he nodded.

I was grateful to him for finding these excellent specimens, but not so grateful that I was prepared to be cheated.

'The pair,' I said.

He shrugged. 'The pair, just like you said.'

I packed them very carefully, and headed back to my home and that laboratory under the roof where the miraculous was soon to be made feasible.

It was dark when I arrived. I was glad of this. It made it easier for me to go straight to work without having to make polite excuses or waste time in conventionalities.

Two days later I was unable to resist the impulse to send a message to the village asking Paul Krempe to call.

He came up at once. When he was shown in I saw that he was prepared for some alarming news. There was possibly a trace of disappointment in his expression when he saw that, far from wishing to give him news of a disaster or of a change of mind on my part, I was in a cheerful, confident frame of mind.

'You wanted to see me?' He was curt, immediately on the defensive.

Nothing would have given me greater pleasure than to have us both back on our old footing. 'It's been a long time since you've been to see us, Paul,' I said affably. 'You know you're always welcome here.'

'I told you I wouldn't help you.' He wasn't going to give an inch.

'Then why continue to live in the neighbourhood?' I could not restrain the jibe: 'Do you think you're better qualified than I to keep watch over Elizabeth?'

He refused to rise to this, but said simply: 'What is it you want?'

I suggested that he came upstairs to the laboratory. It was a long time since he had set foot in it. He hesitated, but his curiosity was too great for him. Together we went upstairs.

As I opened the door and waved him in, I said: 'Haven't you found it difficult keeping away, just guessing what I was doing, never knowing how well I was getting on? I've decided to let you see my progress. You can judge for yourself whether I shall succeed or not.'

With obvious trepidation he approached the tank. He was longing to be confronted by a failure. He was scared not of scientific mysteries but of the chance that I was on the right lines. He of all people should have known how little doubt there was of this.

My robber lay in the fluid, no longer as he had been when Paul left but with a head, new hands, and new feet. His head was turned towards our side of the tank, and his eyes, perfect but still sightless, stared fixedly out at us. Soon they would be animated. Soon there would be emotion and recognition in them.

Still Paul said nothing. At last I asked: 'What do you think of him?'

'It's horrible,' he muttered.

I was surprised that he should be so unscientific about the whole affair. I had to admit that my creature's face was not very pretty yet: there had been a great deal of grafting and stitching involved, and the scars were not yet healed. But the features were not important. What mattered was that I had created a being which would live and breathe.

'Victor,' said Paul earnestly, 'I appeal to you once more to stop what you're doing before it's too late.'

'But what am I doing? Nothing wrong.'

He looked at the suspended, floating creature with revulsion. 'You see nothing wrong in that… that *assembly*? That concoction of fragments, culled from God knows where…'

I said: 'I'm harming nobody by robbing a few graves. What scientist or doctor doesn't? How else are we to learn the complexities of the human animal?'

'Doctors rob for the eventual good of mankind. This can end in nothing but evil.'

'Look' – I was patient with him because it was important to me that he above all others should understand and approve – 'I admit he isn't a particularly handsome specimen at present. But the facial expression is conditioned by the character which lies beneath it. A benevolent mind will gradually soften the outlines and show through. An evil mind creates an evil face. What we have here is nothing yet. But it will be something soon: something splendid. For this a brain of genius will be used, and when the brain starts to function within the frame then the features will assume wisdom and nobility. I'm at the last stage but one, Paul – the brain. A brain of superior intellect, with a lifetime of knowledge already behind it. Imagine it – my creature will be born complete with a fund of knowledge such as takes decades of arduous study to acquire.'

'Victor, where's this brain to come from?'

I saw that he was, alas, not to be trusted. At this final stage I would have welcomed his help. But it would not be offered and so I must not say too much of my plans.

I said: 'I'll get it.'

4

ELIZABETH WAS overjoyed when I suggested that we should break our austere routine by inviting a distinguished guest for a few days' stay. She laughed when I went on to say that I was referring to Professor Bernstein, Europe's greatest living physicist, and accused me of offering this hospitality only because I wanted to drag the old man off to my laboratory and pick his brains. I thought this was a singularly unfortunate way of putting it, but did not say so: I merely assured her that I had no intention of asking the professor into the laboratory. We worked in different fields. I wanted to talk to him on general topics, and since I had heard from many mutual friends that he had lost none of the charm and breadth of interests which I remembered from a meeting some years previously, I thought Elizabeth, too, would find him a stimulating visitor.

Professor Bernstein certainly showed no signs of age. He was a spry, twinkling little man with a massive head of spiky white hair. His conversation ranged freely and effortlessly over every subject known to civilized man, and on every topic he was both witty and profound. I also envied him his unforced courtesy: he had a gift for enchanting a woman, and Elizabeth glowed in his presence. Once or twice he shook his head enviously at me. I was pleased by this and by picturing the well-matched couple which Elizabeth and I would make.

I plied the old man with wine until his tongue wagged

more and more animatedly. Elizabeth still enjoyed every word, but I saw that she was a trifle perturbed by the amount I had given our guest.

He began to make rather arch references to the joys which awaited a young couple like us. To my surprise Elizabeth neatly turned these remarks against me. The stimulus of having another man, even an elderly one, being so attentive to her had evidently given her courage.

'I fear,' she said, 'that the only time we spend together will be times like this, when we have a guest.'

'My dear young lady—'

'Your presence at dinner tonight,' said Elizabeth, 'ensures Victor's presence. If you were not here he would be in his laboratory. He stays there for hours on end. Often he doesn't eat, and I'm sure he doesn't sleep. I for one think the world would be a better place without research – at least, my world would.' She took the edge off her words by a gentle smile in my direction, but there was no doubt that she meant them.

Professor Bernstein sat back and looked at me with owlish gravity. 'She may be right, Baron. One can spend too much of one's life locked in stuffy rooms seeking out obscure truths – searching, researching, until one is too old to enjoy life.'

Elizabeth was delighted. 'You see, Victor! The professor is on my side.'

I had to take it in good part. 'You've let me down badly, Professor. Now I shall have Elizabeth quoting you every time she wants me to leave my work and idle away the time with her.'

'Indeed you shall,' vowed Elizabeth. 'I shall say, "Victor, you're only a *little* scientist and I'm not going to listen to you. On the authority of the greatest brain in Europe you must leave your stuffy laboratory and come out into the sunshine with me."'

She, too, was growing somewhat light-headed. I didn't

want this to go too far, but at the same time I had no wish to appear churlish.

'You see, Professor,' I said, 'how women twist our words to suit their own ends. She will be happy only if I give up my work entirely.'

'Is the world ready for the revelations her scientists make?' Seriousness struggled through Bernstein's genial manner. All at once he was very sober and very intense. 'There is a great difference between knowing that a thing is so and knowing how to use that knowledge. To use it for the good of mankind. The trouble with us scientists is that we quickly tire of our discoveries. We hand them over to people who are not ready for them because we are in a hurry to get on to the next thing – which will be mishandled in just the same way, when the time comes.'

This struck me as being an irrationally pessimistic view. Taken to its logical conclusion it would lead to the abandonment of research altogether. I hoped Professor Bernstein wasn't getting senile. I wanted a great mind, not a decaying one…

Gradually the conversation slowed and took on a drowsy note. Elizabeth, playing the part of hostess to perfection, knew exactly when to say: 'I feel we have exhausted the professor.'

'No, no.' It was a sleepy protest. 'I have enjoyed every minute of this delightful evening. But' – he suppressed a yawn – 'I must confess that old age does bring with it an attendant weariness.'

I got up. 'I'll show you to your room.'

The professor said goodnight to Elizabeth. I escorted him out of the room and up the stairs. He went very slowly, holding the banister rail.

'Most enjoyable evening,' he murmured as we mounted the stairs.

'I really am most honoured to have you here, sir.'

'Most grateful to you, my boy.' He stopped for a moment,

breathing hard. 'You know I'm alone in the world. To be a guest in someone's home – especially such a charming home as this... such a wonderful atmosphere... very precious to me.'

'You're too kind, sir.' I took his arm and helped him up the last few steps. Then I halted him, facing the painting at the top of the staircase. It had been bought half a century ago by my father, and illustrated the grisly anguish of a very early operation. I had thought it would interest the old man, and indeed he stooped and blinked to get a better view of it. 'If you step back,' I said, 'you'll see it better.'

He stepped back.

I got him firmly by the arm and flung him against the rail. It was old, and I had ensured that it was none too secure at this point.

Professor Bernstein tried to shout, but I was already yelling. 'Look out, Professor' – my voice rose so that even at the back of the house they must have heard it – 'look out!'

The rail gave way. Bernstein seemed to hang over the drop for an interminable second, and then he plunged to the marble floor below. There was a crack as his head struck, and his arms and legs splayed out like those of a broken doll. He lay quite still as Elizabeth rushed out and moaned with horror.

I hoped the impact had not damaged his brain.

Of course we were desolated by such a ghastly occurrence. I wrote to Bernstein's more distinguished colleagues, who were most sympathetic and fully understood our grief. The least I could do was to arrange a suitably noble funeral for the great man, and as he was the last of his family, with no living relatives, I suggested that his body should find its last resting place in the Frankenstein family vault. It was a gesture which met with great approbation from the visiting mourners.

I ensured that all these famous scholars and lecturers from Dresden should be sent on their homeward way immediately after the ceremony. I spared no expense: they travelled in the greatest comfort in the finest coach my stables could provide. They were overwhelmed, poor penurious pedants. The luxury of it blinded them to the fact that they were being rushed with unbecoming haste off the premises.

That night, when all was still, I made my way to our family vault in the graveyard, complete with the tools I should need. I stood a lantern on a coffin which contained all that was left of my great-grandfather, and began to prise open the newest coffin in the vault. It came away after a couple of minutes with a shriek of nails, and I looked down on the placid face of Professor Bernstein. Whatever contortion of fear might have twisted his face as he fell, it was smoothed away now.

He could not have lived much longer in any case. Better that he should be dead and useful than alive and doddering towards senility.

I would have been able to work more efficiently in my laboratory, but I did not fancy carrying the corpse all that distance. I had come prepared for operations here, on the spot. In the steady light of the lantern I set to work with a scalpel and carefully laid bare the professor's brain.

It was fascinating to speculate how much of the actual personality would carry over with the brain itself. So much of our character is conditioned by outside stimuli and by the limitations, great or small, of our bodies and their functions, that one finds it hard to think of the brain as a detached, separate entity. Yet here it was. I lifted it reverently from the skull – a storehouse of knowledge, a hoard of wisdom from which the body of my creature would draw all that it needed for further development, for developments so far undreamed-of.

In my bag I had brought a jar. I lowered the brain into it. It looked flabby and inanimate; but I knew what brilliant potentialities lay locked in it, and I was confident that I had the key.

As I was putting the jar and my tools back in the bag, there was the faint scrape of a footstep on the stone treads down into the vault. I reached for the lantern, but it was too late. There was nowhere I could run.

Paul Krempe came down the steps.

'I thought I'd find you here.'

'Very intelligent of you,' I said. 'Now you've found me, what do you want?"

He stared at the open coffin. I turned towards the lid and began to settle it back in place. Paul said: 'You killed the old boy, didn't you? You killed him, and now you're mutilating his body.'

'Mutilating?' I scoffed. 'I've removed the brain. There's no question of mutilation.'

'I can't prove you murdered him' – Paul took a menacing step towards me – 'but I can stop you using his brain.'

'Why? He has no further use for it. He'll be proud when—'

Paul made a grab for the bag. 'Give it to me.'

I swung away from him, protecting my precious haul. He tried to hold me with one hand while tugging at the bag with the other. Without dropping the bag I was not free to fight back adequately – and I did not dare to drop such a fragile load.

'Be careful, you fool!' I cried. 'You'll damage it.'

He was a senseless, raving vandal. He forced me back towards the wall of the vault. As I tried to beat him off with my free hand he seized me and shook me to and fro. The bag swung out, and then smacked back against the edge of a stone shelf. There was the sound of breaking glass.

I struck Paul so furiously across the face that he tottered backwards. Then I looked down at the bag. Liquid oozed through it.

'Get away from me,' I shouted. 'Get out! Leave me alone. Get off my land! And if you've damaged this… if you've damaged it…'

The thought was too appalling to contemplate. I let out a

sob of rage. Paul Krempe backed away. He was really frightened. He stared at me fearfully as though I and not he were the irresponsible maniac.

When he had gone I finished nailing down the coffin hurriedly, and then made my way as quickly as possible back to the house. Feverishly I unpacked the bag and lifted the brain from the debris within. It was so soft and malleable that one could hope it had escaped damage. Then I found two slivers of glass embedded in it. The gashes were not deep. All I could do was trust that they had not affected essential tissue.

I worked almost until dawn on the preparatory stages, and then slept for a few hours. I was awakened by voices under my window. One of them was Elizabeth's. I could visualize her strolling as she usually did in the garden, breathing in the morning air and adding a new decorative beauty to the garden. She had ambitious plans for that garden. Perhaps even now she was giving instructions for a major reorganization here, a fresh splash of colour there.

Then I identified the other voice. It belonged to Paul Krempe.

'I've come to appeal to you to leave here.'

The insolence of the man – coming up here from the village to poison the mind of my betrothed! I got out of bed and stood by the window, debating whether to ring for a lackey to throw him off the land.

'Why should I leave here?' asked Elizabeth.

'Now – this very minute, before it's too late.'

'Paul,' she said in a troubled tone, 'we've been through this before.'

I was pleased by the way she so firmly kept him in his place; but a little less pleased by a note of what I could only describe as intimacy in her voice, as though she were fond of the man and had enjoyed many easy, pleasant hours in his company. Perhaps I had neglected her. There had been too many opportunities in the past for them to be together.

'Won't you understand you're in real danger?' the traitor was urging her. 'What Victor is doing is dangerous to everyone in this house – perhaps to the whole neighbourhood.'

'Then why do you stay in this district?' said Elizabeth. 'You're not helping him any longer.'

'I'll tell you why I stay here. I can't bear to think of you in this house with him, unprotected. When something goes wrong—'

'Paul, believe me, you're wrong about Victor.'

'Am I?' he said bleakly.

'You must be. I know him so well—'

'What do you know about his work? Have you ever been in his laboratory? No, you can't possibly conceive the dreadful thing he's proposing to do.'

'What are you trying to say to me?' she challenged him. 'That Victor is wicked… insane?'

I looked down as they emerged from the shadow of the house and stood on the lawn. The slanting sunlight struck flecks of gold from Elizabeth's hair. She was standing very stiffly and proudly.

Paul said: 'He is just so dedicated to his work that he can't see the terrible consequences that must result.' He reached out, and tried to touch her, but she drew herself away. 'I can't bear the thought of any harm coming to you. I'd do anything not to hurt you both – Victor means more to me than perhaps he understands – but he is so wrapped up in his experiments that—'

'Stop it, Paul.' There were tears in her voice. 'Please leave me. I think… I think it would be better for you not to come here again.'

Paul, stricken, looked at her. From where I stood I could not make out his expression, but I had few doubts about what it would show. The presumptuous fool was in love with Elizabeth. His petty slurs on me were all designed to win her away from me. He understood neither Elizabeth nor myself.

Elizabeth stood quite still and watched him as he walked towards the drive and on to the main gates. When he had disappeared, her shoulders sagged and there was a dejection in her whole manner which made me uneasy. She must not let herself feel too ready a sympathy for the absurd man.

Later that morning she asked me in a roundabout way what stage my experiments had reached. I could have been annoyed, knowing what had provoked this curiosity, but she spoke in such a way that there was nothing to which one could take exception. I assured her that all was going well and that I was nearly finished. At the end of the week perhaps she would be able to see what I had been doing. I was, in fact, so exhilarated by the prospect of forthcoming success that my happiness infected her, and she laughed without quite knowing why she was laughing. The morning sunshine and my obvious cheerfulness banished the dark forebodings which Paul had so unscrupulously tried to plant in her mind.

5

IN THE afternoon the skies grew darker. Beyond the peaks there was a slow barrage of thunder. The threat of rain was sufficient to keep Elizabeth indoors. She occupied herself with her embroidery while I, too, did a great deal of stitching – though on somewhat different material.

I worked through most of that night and through the next day, when a sullen greyness lay on the mountains and the valley was sunk in gloom. Lightning flickered pale in the daylight, but took on a new harshness as night began to fall.

Elizabeth and I dined together by candlelight. She was glad that I was in a gay mood: really, it was touching that she should depend so much on my smiles and approval. Her only disappointment came when I said that I proposed to do several hours' work in the laboratory after coffee.

I was tempted to invite her to accompany me. She should have the privilege of watching the final stages. Then I decided against it. Without deferring to any of Paul Krempe's melodramatic accusations, I realized that an ordinary person might be shocked at first by the magnitude of what I was attempting. Better to win the victory before boasting too loudly!

There was a vast difference between those two faces – the gentle face of Elizabeth and the seamed, unresponsive face in the tank. Indeed, the contrast between the rooms themselves was a striking one. Downstairs was the graciousness of a long tradition, the panelled beauty of high craftsmanship from a bygone world; here in my laboratory was a tangle of apparatus under a sloping roof, an accumulation of litter, all the scientific brashness of the new world – but one in which craftsmanship must still count.

There was a set of controls on the side of the tank itself, and a set which governed the magnetic impulses from a sparking wheel against the outer wall of the laboratory. Originally the entire layout had been planned with a view to dual operation, but now that Paul was no longer playing a part I would have to manage on my own. Some of the finer settings would be tricky. However, I had enough confidence in my own alertness to feel that I could cope.

The creature lay there, passive, waiting. The body was strong, the hands and feet admirable, the head splendid in spite of the still unhealed scars. And in that head one of the greatest brains in Europe was about to function again.

I slowly switched on the feed pipes to the tank, and a gentle bubbling began.

There was a flash of lightning. It made me start back, fearing for a moment that there was a fault in the apparatus. A clap of thunder, so far from alarming me, reassured me. I left the tank and set the generator wheel in motion so that the electro-chemical reaction could begin.

I seemed myself to be vibrant with electric forces. Whatever new avenues are opened up in the future, whatever progress is made in the physical sciences, and whatever may come from work which I know is going on in England, for example, at this very moment, history must acclaim me as the true pioneer in the application of magneto-electricity. Without Davy's theories and demonstrations of galvanism I admit I could not have got so far in such a short time; but without my own discoveries of the relationship between the life force and magnetic force, further developments would not be possible.

Now began the delicate business of balancing the various adjustments. I darted to and fro between the tank and the controls of the sparking generator wheel. It was infuriating. A slight increase at one could mean the most minute alteration to the other. The dual controls ought to have been operated by Paul and myself, snapping instructions to and fro. Unless I could maintain a perfect balance, the experiment would not succeed.

The chemical input was surging and bubbling remorselessly now. There was no turning back. At least two hours of intense concentration lay ahead of me. The power pulses had to be injected with unfaltering regularity. I had to turn myself into an automaton – but an automaton capable of checking and rechecking, thinking fast and acting without hesitation, going from one control to the other, studying the body in the tank, pacing to and fro across the laboratory.

The fluid in the tank grew viscous, and the features were blurred. Slowly the body rolled over like a man lazily, contentedly swimming.

But the reaction was not what it ought to have been. From our work on the dog I knew that at this stage there ought to be an appreciable convulsion: there ought to be a sequence of minor jolts, as the body was stimulated by successive punches of power.

The timing was not exact enough. No, that is an unscientific way of expressing it. There was no question of being 'exact enough': it had to be *exact*.

I made a swift, anguished calculation. The process could not be reversed or stopped. But given thirty minutes – forty minutes at the outside – I could cut off the pulses and keep the chemical reaction at its lowest while I went for help. There was no other way: I had to have another pair of hands here. Once more the idea of Elizabeth crossed my mind, this time as an assistant. But even after the preliminary explanations and reassurances, I would still have to teach her the innumerable details. It would be too late. The only man who could fall into the routine with the skill of long practice was Paul Krempe. He had to be persuaded. Faced with a crisis of this kind, surely I could rely on his scientific spirit?

I cut down the input and slowed the wheel to a stop. Then I went swiftly but silently downstairs and out into the night.

The storm was drawing closer. Lightning flickered along the mountain crags, its stabs of brightness as jagged as the peaks themselves. I seized a cape and flung it over my shoulders, then hurried down the footpath to the village.

I pounded on the door of Paul's lodging with a force that should have wakened the dead. I felt that I was hammering life into that creature of mine: I wanted to pick it up and shake it, beat vitality into it.

Paul, swathed in a heavy dressing-gown, opened the door and stared.

Before he could speak, I said: 'You've got to help me.'

'You must be mad.'

'The apparatus was constructed for dual operation. You know that. I thought I could work it myself, but I can't.'

'I'm delighted,' said Paul. A flash of brightness from behind me fell across his face, etching stern lines into it. 'That means your experiment will not succeed.'

'It's got to succeed. Paul, you're going to help me. You must.'

He shook his head.

I kept my voice down although I wanted to shout to the heavens. It was intolerable that my years of application should go to waste now because of the stubbornness of this one man.

'With so much at stake…'

He turned as though to go back into the house. I was desperate. I would have to make whatever terms I could with him.

'Paul,' I implored him, 'if you help me I promise that once I've proved my theories I'll dispose of this creature.'

He stopped. 'How long will that be?'

'A month or two at the outside.'

'And have that thing alive up there all that time? No, Victor.'

'If you don't help me' – I could not suppress my fury, in spite of my need of him – 'then I make no such promise. Somehow I'll manage on my own. However difficult, I'll do it.'

'Very well,' he taunted. 'Go back and do it.'

And then it came to me. It was my last chance. I said: 'Or else I'll train Elizabeth to help.'

'You wouldn't dare. You wouldn't be so—'

'I'll introduce Elizabeth to the world of science,' I said, 'and see how she likes it.'

If he could have killed me with a look he would have done so. 'You wouldn't be so wicked, Victor. Even a fanatic like you… you couldn't.'

'There is nothing – do you hear me, nothing – more important to me than the success of this experiment. I'll do anything to conclude it properly. It's what I've worked for all my life.'

'Very well,' he said bitterly. 'I'll help you.'

'I knew I could rely on you,' I said.

He made an incoherent, contemptuous sound. Then he said: 'I'll get dressed. You go on ahead and set up the preliminaries. I'll be no more than ten minutes behind you.'

'I can trust you to come?' I said.

'Yes, you can trust me to come.'

That was sufficient for me. I walked briskly back up the hillside. It would have been easy to lose one's footing: the fitful lightning illuminated the path in bursts of glaring intensity, followed by a blackness more Stygian than that of an ordinary night. But I knew every inch of the way. This was my home, my property, the scene of my childhood rovings and now to be the scene of my mature triumphs.

The house was abruptly a black silhouette against the sky, and then was lost again.

I quickened my pace, eager to get back to that magic room at the top of the house.

Suddenly there was a stab of lightning so savage that I raised my arm to cover my eyes. It was followed by a crack that was not the crack of thunder. When I dared to look, I saw brightness like a malevolent will-of-the-wisp running along the eaves of my home. The window of the laboratory, high up under the roof, seemed to be lit from inside. It must have been an optical illusion, but it was terrifying in that split second of its occurrence; terrifying because of the uncanny blaze in that square, blank eye, and because of my fears for what lay inside. An electrical disturbance of that magnitude could easily affect the delicate balance of my experiment.

I hurried into the house. The whip-like crack of the lightning still stung my ears, but indoors there was tranquillity. Nobody stirred. Either none of them had heard the sound or they were all cowering in their beds, praying.

For once in my life I was trembling. My knees felt unsteady. I went into the salon and took a bottle of brandy from the wine cupboard. I poured myself a large drink and gulped it down with a haste which was unworthy of the brandy.

Then I went upstairs.

At the first landing I stopped. There was no sound from the direction of Elizabeth's room. I went on my way.

As I approached the door of the laboratory I heard an impossible sound. Faintly, through the heavy door, came the intermittent splutter of the wheel as it turned and sparked. But it had no business to be turning. I had switched it off before leaving. Nobody could have entered the laboratory in my absence.

Filled with foreboding, I thrust the key into the lock. If that lightning had somehow triggered off the process and it was working again, the whole balance could have been wrecked.

I flung open the door.

Standing erect in the middle of the room was my creature. The bandages dripped with fluid. The arms hung slackly, but as I stood there, aghast, they tightened and fought against the bandages. There was a tearing of cloth. The groping hands went up to the face.

In the flickering light cast by the madly rotating wheel, the creature bared its teeth in a snarl. It was a wide, savage grimace such as I had never seen or ever wished to see in my life. It was utter bestiality unleashed.

I still had my hand on the door. The sight had robbed me of all power to move. I could neither go in nor retreat.

Suddenly the creature lurched towards me. Its legs were still impeded by the bandages, which made its shambling gait all the more horrible. I turned to run… and it was too late.

The heavy arm, with torn bandages drooping from it, curled round my neck. I was jerked back into the laboratory. The smell of the chemicals which impregnated the creature and its swathing bit at the back of my throat and in my nostrils. I tried to cry out, but the pressure was tightening. I kicked vainly against the padded, well-protected figure.

The lights in the room began an insane dance. They blazed in and out of a kaleidoscope of other lights, sparking not only before my eyes but somehow inside my head. A great hammer began to pound from within my skull.

I twisted round, trying to get a grip on the creature. Its distorted face was a slavering nightmare, a few inches from my own. I struck out, but the blow was feeble and useless.

To have come so far, and now to be destroyed by what I had created... to be killed by a grotesque mischance, a wayward jest of the elements...!

Then suddenly I was falling sideways. The creature had relinquished its grip. As I went down, I was dimly aware of Paul springing over me and lashing out again and again. I tried to push myself up, to come to his aid, but the roaring in my ears and the pain that ran through me were too much. I saw the feet of the creature trample towards me and then stagger away at a tangent. Paul lifted one of the laboratory stools and beat the creature back into a corner.

As I finally got myself up to my knees, with the floor reeling beneath me, Paul swung the stool against the creature's head. It emitted a croaking, feral sound that rasped hideously through the room; and then it collapsed into a stained, ragged heap.

Paul dropped the stool and hurried to me. He got his arm round my shoulder and helped me to my feet. I leaned against him for a full minute, gasping and vainly retching.

And then, as the pain ebbed away, I was conscious of the most fantastic elation. It was as though, purged of irrational fear, I could see things not just as clearly as before but with an added vividness.

'Paul' – it hurt me to talk, but I was laughing the words out – 'I did it! I did it...'

'Yes.' He was not really listening. He helped me to the only chair in the room – there had never been time for relaxation in this part of the house – and lowered me gently into it.

I put my head back. I had succeeded. The glow of accomplishment warmed me through, driving out the memory of those few terrifying minutes when things had gone wrong. It was not my fault that they had gone wrong. Paul himself was largely to blame. Obviously there had been damage to the brain during that undignified scuffle in my family vault. That could soon be rectified. Also the process had been dangerously speeded up and my equipment had run wild after the lightning stroke. Next time there would be no such mistakes. Next time all my calculations would be strictly observed.

The important thing was that I had done it.

Paul was dragging the creature onto the bench and strapping it securely down. I neither helped him nor interfered. It was undoubtedly a good thing that the creature should be restrained until I could get to work on it.

Paul drew the last strap tight and then turned back to me.

'You must destroy it right away before it regains consciousness.'

I could hardly believe what I heard. Already I was wondering which of the seams in the head to open in order to get at the brain without involving too much further damage to the features.

'Did you hear, Victor?' Paul insisted.

'What did you say?'

'You must destroy this thing now.'

I was grateful for his intervention, but I was not going to be dictated to in this way. I tried to make him see reason. 'Don't you realize, Paul – I've succeeded.'

'You nearly succeeded in getting yourself killed. Another ten seconds and—'

'This is my creation.' I was still marvelling at it. Of course I had known that all would come right, but it was still splendid to have it proved beyond all doubt.

'Your creation,' said Paul: 'a criminal lunatic. It tried to kill you.'

'That was due to the brain damage. When you attacked me,' I reminded him, 'it was damaged. That makes the responsibility very largely yours, Paul. It's your fault that it ran wild. Your fault that it's not what I intended it to be. I can repair the brain. It's what I've done that counts: I've created a living, sentient being.'

'You promised to destroy it, Victor.'

'Never.'

'When you came to ask me for help,' he said, 'you said that once you had proved your theories you would destroy it.'

But the fool could not see that I had many more things to prove, many more things to demonstrate. This was only the beginning. I said: 'When I've finished my research.'

'Don't you see – you've created a monster.'

'I shall operate on the brain tomorrow,' I said. 'It shouldn't take too long.'

The basic principles were sound. From now on the difficulties could only be minor ones.

Paul looked from me to the prone figure strapped to the table. He touched one of the straps to make sure it was secure. Then he shook his head sadly.

'You won't listen to me?'

'When we worked together,' I said, 'I was glad to listen to you. You have contributed a great deal to this discovery, Paul. If you'll continue with me—'

'No,' he said, 'you won't listen. And you're too powerful in this district for me to have any chance of opposing you here.'

'Opposing me?'

'For your own sake, Victor, and for the sake of mankind I think you should be stopped.' He turned away. At the door he said: 'I shall pack my things and leave the village tomorrow. I can see there's nothing I can do here.'

I was sorry that we had to part in this way, but I could not let my resolve be weakened. There have always been opponents of new developments in all science and philosophy. Every great advance has been made in the teeth of ignorant opposition. Even the pioneers themselves, such as Paul might have been, often falter and turn back.

For me there would be no faltering.

It would be foolish to apply myself to the task in hand tonight, though. My body had taken a considerable battering and my fingers would lack the firmness and precision which were essential for the brain examination. I tested the straps holding the unconscious creature to the bench, disconnected the apparatus so that there should be no further mishaps, and went down to bed. I had to lie on my left side, as my right shoulder was heavily bruised, but I slept without difficulty.

The morning was clear and the storm clouds had moved on. I awoke refreshed, and breakfasted with Elizabeth. A dull bruise along the line of my jaw attracted her attention, and I had to improvise some silly little story about walking into a door. She did not know whether to laugh or to reprove me. Once again she referred with mild but genuine disparagement to my cherished laboratory, and threatened to come up and inspect it. 'My rival,' she called it. I did not think that the sight of the creature with its torn bandages strapped to the bench would be the most edifying one to greet her.

As soon as possible I made my excuses and escaped to the top of the house. At the end of the first landing I caught a glimpse of Justine staring at me curiously. She made a move as though to intercept me – to ask me pertly, no doubt, what I was doing with my nights and why I had neglected her charms recently – but I waved her off and hurried up to the laboratory.

I hesitated briefly before opening the door. My experience of the previous night was not one which I would wish repeated.

But it was absurd. The creature could not have burst its bonds. It could not be standing there waiting for me again, ready to strike.

I opened the door.

There was no creature confronting me. There was no creature in the laboratory at all. Straps and bandages lay in a twisted pattern on the bench. The floor was sticky with fluid from a dozen shattered tubes and bottles, and there was broken glass everywhere. The window had been torn open, smashing two of the panes. When I went incredulously to look out of it, I saw a couple more torn strips of bandage caught in the heavy guttering. The way down to the ground was perilous, but the jutting masonry gave enough footholds for anyone determined enough – or mad enough – to choose such a route.

The creature had gone.

6

'He's gone,' I said. 'I've searched the house to make sure, and then gone all over the grounds. Heaven knows where he's got to.'

Once more I was standing at Paul's door. There was a certain grim satisfaction in his manner, as though he saw all his predictions coming true; but at the same time he was truly alarmed.

'We must call out the village – start a thorough search at once.'

'You had better leave that to me,' I said. 'I have the authority here. But I want the two of us to set out at once. We know the creature we are dealing with better than the villagers do. And we've got to pick up his trail before he goes too far. If he gets deep into the woods we'll never find him.'

Paul went indoors to make ready, while I walked away along the village street. I nodded to some of my tenants, and exchanged civilities with two army officers from the garrison down the valley. I did not, however, stir up any unseemly panic. There was no reason why the villagers should know too soon about my experiments. I didn't want their clumsy hands laid on my creation; and I didn't want madly inflated stories about it to go humming along the valley.

I went back to Paul, and handed over to him one of the two rifles I had brought from my small armoury. It had been a long time since there had been any use for them in this peaceful part of the world. I hoped now that we would manage without having to fire them.

We set off into the woods.

In other circumstances it could have been a delightful morning. Working as I did at night and spending so many mornings asleep before resuming this work, I had not strolled through the woods and glades at this hour for some years. As a boy I had known every path through the trees and every clearing. Now it was all strange to me. The fresh morning air had the taste of a sparkling water, cool and tangy from the stream.

When my experiments were concluded and had been acclaimed by the world's leading scientists, I would make a new life for Elizabeth and myself. We would walk here often.

But now there was a grim duty ahead of us. I wanted to find my creature before some stupid peasant stumbled across him. He had to be recaptured and taken back to his birthplace. For that was what my home was for him: his birthplace.

Once the operation had been carried out on his brain, I was sure that I would find him a worthy intellectual companion. He and I might go on to further discoveries, blazing a trail for lesser mortals to follow.

Paul and I exchanged few remarks as we prowled through the trees. A brisk nod was enough to indicate a new direction; one hand held up brought us to a halt when some rustle in the undergrowth or the creak of a branch seemed to indicate another presence.

At the end of half an hour I was growing apprehensive. If we didn't find him soon, others would find him. He would stray into their farms or down lanes which led to other villages.

Or he would lie low in the woods, hidden for as long as he chose to remain still, a constant menace – and perhaps past salvation by the time I found him.

Then we heard a voice. It was some distance away, and came eerily through the trees like the muffled cry of an animal in a trap.

Paul glanced at me. We swung off the path and trampled over leaves and snapping twigs without further concern for the noise we were making. Once again there was a cry, causing us to veer slightly to the left. We broke out, after scratching our faces on a thin but stinging barrier of trailing branches, into a clearing. Through the trees on the far side was a faint glimmer of water, and when we came to a stop we could hear the gentle chatter of a stream.

An old man lay beside a fallen tree trunk in the centre of the glade. For a moment my breath caught in my throat. Then I saw that he was not dead. He stirred and groaned, and reached out blindly with a gnarled hand. He touched the trunk and groped over it. His hand fell back.

Paul hurried forward to help him up.

At the first touch of Paul's hands, the old man flinched and began to moan.

'No… who are you… what are you…?'

Beside him lay two pieces of a stick as gnarled as himself. Clearly it had been his support, but now it was snapped clean in two.

I advanced into the clearing and stood before him. A man of his generation should recognize the Frankenstein face when he saw it. I had hoped to calm him, but he babbled on unintelligibly.

'What is it… what are you…?'

Then I understood his groping and the blindness of his movements. He was indeed blind.

Paul said: 'It's all right. Have no fear. We are friends. What happened to you?'

'My grandson – where is he?'

Trembling fingers clawed at Paul's sleeve.

'Your grandson?' Paul spoke as soothingly as possible, but he glanced at me urgently.

'The stream… he left me sitting here, in the sun… so warm… he went to the stream. Has he wandered away? Or is it after him, too?'

'Is what after him?'

'The stream… my grandson,' the old man raved.

Paul got to his feet. 'Stay with him,' he ordered. It was not his place to give orders, but before I could protest he had moved away and was hurrying towards the stream.

I wanted to follow, but the old man wavered on the tree trunk and once I had tried to hold him steady he gripped me and would not let go. His story came out in fits and starts. His grandson had brought him into the woods as he often did on sunny mornings. It was good to sit here and reflect. The boy was a good boy, very patient with his old grandfather. He would go off and pick mushrooms – sometimes went farther away than he ought to, but he always came back.

Today the grandfather had thought he heard him coming back much more quickly than usual. There had been footsteps – slow footsteps – and then when he had spoken to the boy there had been no reply. Only the footsteps. And all at once he had known that this was not his grandson. He could not tell who it was, and it wasn't right, it wasn't normal.

'When you're blind as I am, you get to know things – to sense things. This thing, it… it wasn't *right*.'

He had groped for his stick and then waved it. He had struck something, and then his stick had been snatched from him and he had heard a crack. In his blind gyrations he must have fallen over the tree trunk and gone down heavily.

'And it went away. I felt it going. Something lost,' he said hesitantly. 'A pathetic thing… a lost soul.' Then his puzzled sympathy was swept away. 'Where's my grandson – my little boy?'

The crack of Paul's rifle resounded through the woods. The old man started against me. I freed myself from that biting grip, and pulled his hands firmly down to the tree trunk so that he would know where he was. Then I raced into the woods in pursuit of Paul.

He had gone some distance along the stream. I caught a flicker of movement between the trees, and charged straight through the undergrowth.

Paul was standing irresolutely with his rifle at the ready. As I came up he said:

'I saw him. Making down that way.'

'Did you have to shoot?'

'Yes,' he snapped. 'I had to shoot. I'm taking no chances.'

'If we can take him back without harming him—'

'The villagers should be on their way by now, surely?' he said. 'Where did you tell them to make for?'

'The south lake shore. I said that if we converged on that we ought to be able to flush him out.'

Paul jerked his rifle towards a gap that had been smashed through some bushes. 'The trail ought to be easy enough to follow. But where's that boy the old man was talking about?'

We went on. The creature had certainly made no attempt to hide its tracks. It seemed to possess no cunning, no intelligence. Or else it simply did not care. In either case it was tragic: had Professor Bernstein's sensitive brain been irreparably damaged?

'There!' breathed Paul suddenly.

We stopped. Through a gap in the trees we saw the stream curling round on itself before disappearing down a shallow slope. A small boy bent over it, plucking at something on the bank. He carried a rough local basket and was filling it with mushrooms.

A larger shape moved across our line of vision. The boy was obscured. The creature, swaying slightly, began to advance through the trees.

Paul raised his rifle.

'No!' I caught at his arm. He tried to shake me off.

Abruptly the boy scuttled away. He had not even noticed the creature plodding towards him. His basket was full and he was on his way back along the winding edge of the stream.

'Grandpa!' There was a cracked note of fright in his voice, but it was not because of what he had seen: it was simply that he had wandered farther than he realized, and was now worried about getting back. He began to run. 'Grandpa...!'

The creature stood still for an instant, then turned slowly as though to retrace its steps. It was facing us. A terrible rictus convulsed its mouth. The fingers flexed.

I had let go of Paul. Before I realized what he was doing, he brought the rifle up again and this time he fired.

The hands – the sculptor's magnificent hands – shot up to the face and clawed at it. The creature took a few helpless steps forward, as erratic as those of the blind man; and then it bent its head piteously back and forth and slowly, in an awful sagging surrender, rolled forward and fell to the ground.

I ran towards it.

'Be careful, Victor!'

Paul's warning was unnecessary. He was a good shot. Too good a shot. My creation, my painstaking handiwork, was dead once more after having been so laboriously brought to life.

Paul stood over me. I gazed up at him accusingly.

He said: 'I did what had to be done. We'll bury him before the villagers arrive.'

'There's no hurry,' I said. 'They won't come.'

'If you told them to meet us—'

'I didn't tell them. I didn't want them prying into my work

and spreading ugly rumours. Better for them not to know.'

'You madman! You risked just two of us against this. We might have been killed.'

'We might. But we weren't.' Did it matter, now that he was dead? In my mind I was blurring the distinction between 'he' and 'it'. I wondered what kind of a man he would have been. 'It's done,' I said, 'and I hope you're satisfied.'

'I'm satisfied we were able to stop this monstrous act before it was too late,' said Paul.

I thought that I would never forgive him. Looking back, I associate all my troubles with Paul Krempe. A loyal assistant turned traitor is more dangerous and more destructive than an enemy whom you know from the start to be an enemy.

We buried the creature there in the peace of the woods. Paul scattered leaves over the newly turned ground and we made our way in silence back to the village. We were dirty and sweating from the labour: digging even a shallow grave is arduous work. Even if we had had the breath to speak, I don't think we would have had much to say to each other.

When we parted I held out my hand. He was reluctant to take it, but finally we shook hands.

He said: 'I shall leave now. You won't see me again.'

'As you wish. If you think I owe you anything in the way of fees for your services over the years…'

I let the remark trail away. He flushed. I could see that the reminder of our relative status hurt him. He replied stiffly: 'I think all the debts have been paid.'

'Where will you go – what are you intending to do?'

'I have no idea. But it's no longer necessary for me to stay here.'

It was on the tip of my tongue to say that his presence had not been necessary for quite some time now. Then I realized what he meant.

'Ah,' I said. 'Of course. Elizabeth – you stayed to protect her. Well, you've done what you set out to do. You can leave with a clear conscience.'

He gave one longing glance towards the path which led away from the village, up to the house. I left him there. He could take his fill. Let him look. The house and its contents were mine, and Elizabeth was mine.

When I reached the entrance hall Elizabeth was waiting for me. She had been troubled by my absence. The sight of the rifles alarmed her. I said that I had been through the woods and had thought of doing some shooting – the second gun was one which I had lent to one of my keepers.

'I like to think of you in the open air,' she said. 'You spend so much time locked away. I would like to walk with you in the woods sometime, if I may.'

I was able to tell her quite honestly that I had been thinking of just this while I was out.

My life could at this stage, I suppose, have taken a different turn. Many a man would have abandoned his researches or at least sought new channels. It was time to make plans for our wedding. Everything else could have been postponed until after the ceremony. To forget the disappointments and frustrations which had ended in tragedy, I could have devoted myself to Elizabeth and shaped a new existence, not just for myself but for the two of us.

It was not to be. I was not a man who could forget. I was not prepared to abandon all that had so far been achieved. Those years could not be discarded: it could not all be allowed to go to waste.

To Elizabeth's delight I spent my next two evenings with her. We made plans for our future. I promised that we would travel and that I would restrict my working hours to reasonable limits. This was a sincere promise. I was convinced that, in spite of all that had happened, there remained very little to do. Soon I would be able to rest on my laurels.

On a night when there was no moon I took a horse through the woods to the place where we had buried my creature. In the gloom the grave was hard to find, but I did not dare to risk going out on too bright a night. At last I found the spot, and took the creature from the earth. I carried him home across the crupper, and over my shoulder up the stairs.

Paul's shot had drilled a hole between the eyes. I foresaw further work on the brain, but that would have been essential in any case.

'I'll give you life again,' I vowed.

7

WE MADE no grand proclamations regarding our forthcoming marriage. I wrote to the few relatives we had, and was relieved when two of them said that due to illness in the family they would be unable to attend the ceremony. The quiet, frugal life which Aunt Sophie had imposed on her daughter meant that Elizabeth had no close friends of her own, and there was a similar lack in my life due to the fact that I had shut myself away with my experiments for so long. We decided upon a simple reception after the wedding, to which we would invite those local dignitaries who would expect it. I called upon the burgomaster, who was overwhelmed to see me: my father had contributed greatly to the social life of the district, and my own seclusion had given rise to a great deal of adverse criticism. The poor man was so transparent: he was sure that my marriage to my charming young cousin would bring me out more into the world and that there would be parties up at the great house, money flowing into the village, and heaven knew what else besides. I did not disillusion him. My wife should be entertained and should build up a circle of friends if she wished, but it would not be to these parochial boors that we would turn.

One evening, two weeks before the date of the wedding, I had been working in my laboratory. The need for absolute precision in the repairs to the brain meant that for practical as well as emotional reasons I was keeping my pledge to Elizabeth. I spent less time in the laboratory because it was possible to maintain such concentration and steadiness of hand for only limited periods. I set myself a target each day, but if I found my vision growing blurred or my hands wavering, I stopped at once. This evening I had decided to finish shortly before dinner. In fact, I made better progress than I had expected, and it was with a renewal of my earlier sense of triumph that I realized the work was complete. I closed up the head. The stitches could be taken out later. I was impatient to see life pulsing through the creature again – to talk to him and explain what had happened, to test the recreated faculties under strict test conditions.

It was with a sense of impending fulfilment that I closed the door of the laboratory behind me and began to descend the stairs.

On the next landing Justine was waiting for me.

'What are you doing here?' I demanded. 'We shall want dinner served in a few minutes' time.'

I made to pass her, but she blocked my way.

She said: 'Is it true?'

'Is what true?'

'About you marrying that… that woman.'

I would not tolerate insolence of this kind. 'You're forgetting yourself.'

'I'm not forgetting that you promised to marry me,' she said.

I looked round. Fortunately Elizabeth was already downstairs. I said: 'That's absurd. It would never have entered my head to make such a promise.'

'The things you said to me…'

I laughed. 'Justine, my dear, we've discussed all this before. I thought you had understood the position.'

'Don't laugh at me!' she blazed. 'Stop it, or I'll… I'll…'

'What will you do?'

'I'll kill you.'

I was really in no mood to deal with a serving wench's hysteria. She needed the sharp slap of reality to bring her to her senses. I said:

'You stupid little fool. Did you imagine for one second that a man of my standing would contemplate marrying you?'

She raised her arm as though to strike me. I gripped it above the elbow and forced her back along the landing, away from the staircase.

'You're hurting,' she whimpered. She could change her tune very quickly, little Justine.

'Get back to your work,' I said.

'You've got to marry me. You've got to.' As I released her she fell back against the wall, panting. 'I'm going to have a child.'

I refused to believe it. It was like a glancing blow – a sudden sting that one instinctively dodges and that ceases to hurt immediately.

'Since when would this be?' I asked.

'It doesn't matter. It's true.'

'Why choose me as the father?' I said sceptically. 'Pick any man in the village. There's a reasonable chance you may select the right one.'

Hatred burned in eyes which I had seen lit with a very different fire. Even when her violence and lack of breeding repelled me as they did now, I could not help but observe what a splendid specimen of womanhood she was. But I was not going to be cajoled or intimidated, whatever variations she might play on her banal theme.

'*She* won't think much of your story about a village man,' hissed Justine. 'Not when I tell her what we've been to each other. And I'll tell her a lot more besides. I'll tell her about what you're doing in that laboratory of yours. And then I'll go to the authorities and tell them, too.'

Her threats might be idle, but I felt a chill of foreboding. She was so silent, Justine, so accustomed to slipping soundlessly along the corridors, entering my room, and leaving it: she could have seen more than she was ever meant to.

'Tell them what?' I said with all the contempt I could muster.

'Oh, I know a lot. If I care to tell.'

'What do you know?'

'You wouldn't like that, would you? Well, if you don't marry me I'll tell.'

'Tell what?' I persisted.

'You know what I'm talking about.'

'No,' I said. 'I don't know. And if you intend to make any accusations against me, you will need proof. Proof, my dear – that's all the authorities would be interested in.'

I turned and left her there. Protracting this conversation could only result in further petty attacks on my self-respect.

She cried after me: 'I'll get proof. Oh, you'll see – there's plenty of proof.'

'I want you out of this house,' I said, 'tomorrow morning.'

After dinner I told Elizabeth that I had dismissed Justine. Fortunately she was relieved. Justine's manner to her had always bordered on the impertinent, and although Elizabeth had tried to run the household smoothly she had been disturbed by this hostility. We would both be happier without the girl.

'Do you think I should have a word with her before she leaves?' she asked anxiously.

'No. I am discharging her because of her slovenliness and insolence, and if you were to speak to her at all I have no doubt that she would take the opportunity to vent her spleen. I have said all that needs to be said.'

Again Elizabeth showed that she was happy about this. She was glad that she had not had to take action and that I had settled the matter of my own accord.

Next morning I resumed work in the laboratory. The routine was a familiar one by now. I had altered the controls so that I could operate them single-handed, and had practised the sequence several times in order to win complete confidence in it. This time I intended that the creature should come gradually to life instead of being rudely jolted into it. I also intended that, whatever happened, it should not have the opportunity of running loose again until I had talked to it, reasoned with it, and, if necessary, trained it.

It or him… in a way I was leaving the decision to the creature. Let him show himself a man, and we would talk as equals; let it be subhuman, and I would train it in whatever way was required.

I adjusted the process so that it spread over the entire day. There were no sudden shocks and no breaks in the procedure. I was confident enough to leave the equipment operating while I went down to have lunch with Elizabeth. The confidence was justified: when I returned to the laboratory, the creature was moving very gently and languidly in the tank. Everything was going according to plan. The head turned, the fingers moved slightly, and the eyes closed against the fluid.

When I lifted the creature from the tank it was like helping a man near to drowning. He appeared to be on the verge of collapse; but in point of fact the opposite was the case – he was on the verge of resuscitation.

I helped him to the one chair and settled him in it. Then, as a precaution, I strapped his arms behind him and put a heavy stick with a solid silver knob against the bench where I could seize it should I need it.

It was now late afternoon. I spent the next hour talking quietly to the creature. I wanted him to feel safe. I wanted him to speak freely – for the two of us to establish a rapport.

At the end of an hour he made a sound. His eyes had been

blankly open all this time, but now I seemed to detect a gleam of understanding, and I saw the lips open and begin to work. They twisted, tried to form syllables, and then produced a long, meaningless groan.

I said: 'If you understand what I'm saying, nod.'

Slowly the head nodded, but slackly, like that of a baby who has not yet learned to control it.

'You know where you are?'

There was a pause, then another top-heavy nod.

'Are you comfortable?'

He shook his head this time and made a jerking motion with his shoulders which clearly signified that the straps were hurting. I studied that unresponsive face. There were no signs of incipient viciousness there. I thought I could risk giving him a bit more freedom. Cautiously, with the stick always in reach, I loosened his bonds. He raised his arms in a parody of a stretch, and then pushed himself to his feet. It was a painful process. I stood well back. It seemed a sensible thing to do, but in fact I would have done better to stay close to him. He took one step forward and then lost control of his legs. He floundered about the laboratory, knocking glasses over and crashing against the benches. I had to leap forward in order to steer him away from a delicate mass of equipment, and his weight almost carried me off my feet.

When I had steadied him he leaned against the wall, panting. He tried once more to speak, but produced only a sickening, gobbling noise.

Of course it would take time. I would have to be patient. The assembly of different limbs, of a new head and a new brain, would take time to settle down as an individual entity. The normal motor skills would have to be relearned, and allowances made in the brain for differences in physical sensation and reaction.

If the brain, that is, had not been so deeply damaged that it would never be able to assume full control...

'Slowly,' I commanded, as the creature made an attempt to move away from the wall. 'Come to me – but slowly.'

I held out my hand. He edged towards me, and the sculptor's hand took mine. At first it was as limp as a shy child's. Then the grip tightened. His hand was like iron. I tried to pull away, and at once he clamped down, in a savage automatic reaction to the sudden movement.

As gently but firmly as possible I said: 'Let go.'

For an instant he was quite still. Then his hand relaxed.

I stood back. He swayed, and once more tottered, blundering against the chair and bringing his arm round in a wide, drunken sweep that could have cleared the bench of beakers and test tubes if he had been a few inches closer.

It was not safe to allow such an uncoordinated creature to roam freely about the laboratory. I did not want to restrict him too much, but obviously he must be kept on a leash until he was able to manage himself in a more civilized fashion.

On a leash, I thought. Yes, that was it. There was, in fact, a length of chain in the store cupboard at the end of the laboratory. It had been used at one stage for hanging dogs in various stages of dismemberment from the rafters, and had been tossed onto a shelf when we advanced beyond those preliminary experiments. Now I took it out.

There was no point in alarming the creature. He looked uncomprehendingly at the chain as I walked casually towards him. I attached one end to a hook in the wall, and hammered the hook closely over the link. He watched, swaying giddily. Then, gauging the distance and the necessary speed, I whipped the chain suddenly round his waist and secured the links behind him. He began to struggle and to beat the air, but as he turned and reached for me I said:

'Down. Keep your arms down.'

Slowly they fell to his side.

With such obedience it would not take long to train him. But to what lengths could I go? Where would I reach a full stop? This was not how I had visualized my creation: not as a massive infant incapable of coherent speech. The thought that the magnificent brain had been damaged beyond redemption nagged at me again and sickened me.

The time had slipped by. Elizabeth would be expecting to see me downstairs. I cleared a space round the creature so that he could roam in comparative freedom without damaging anything, and then went to the door. He watched me like a dog begging to be taken for a walk.

I said: 'I'll come back as soon as I can. We'll soon have you fit to show yourself to the world.' As I was about to open the door, it occurred to me to add: 'You will do as I say. As I say… and nobody else. Is that understood?'

He nodded.

'Nobody else will come here,' I said. 'Nobody else is allowed in here. And you will do nothing until I come back.'

I went out and locked the door. A cloud of depression settled on me as I walked along the creaking boards of the narrow passage. I had a premonition that things were not going to work out as magnificently as I had planned. And there was something else that made me uneasy – something I couldn't define.

It was the slightest of movements that put me on the alert. A wooden beam that rose up the entire stairwell made an alcove, always sunk in shadow, partly obscured at the top by the eccentric slant of the roof. Dust and cobwebs accumulated there, for I allowed nobody up to this floor to clean or to pry. As I passed it on my way to the stairs, my attention was caught by a broken, drifting cobweb. And I realized that the darkness was more substantial than usual. Somebody was hiding behind the beam.

I did not falter. I went straight on, and down a few steps.

Then I paused, flattening myself against the wall, and peered up through the banisters.

Justine emerged from the shadows and scurried along the passage. I went back up the steps, keeping low, until I could see her at the door of the laboratory. From her apron she produced a key. She tried it a few times in the lock, rattling it faintly, and then turned it.

I don't know how she came by such a key. Perhaps there had been a duplicate key in the servants' quarters of which I had never known. Perhaps she had stolen my only key for an hour or so after we had been together and had persuaded one of her young village men to make a copy – though I could not recall ever having missed it or having given her such an opportunity, and I could not believe that she would be so foolish as to put it even for a short time into the hands of some valley yokel.

Wherever the key came from, it worked. The door opened and she tiptoed in.

I returned to the landing and made my way along to the open doorway, treading warily so that the squeak of the boards should not give me away.

Justine was silhouetted against the attic window, through which the twilight cast a faint glow. She bumped against something, and stopped. I saw her grope for the edge of the bench, and then she lit the lantern which stood to one side – the lantern which had accompanied me on most of my more important nocturnal trips.

In the mellow light she looked round the laboratory. I waited for her gaze to reach the creature, but she was distracted by a cage of mice at the end of the room. She went to them and peered down.

The shadow of a hand fell across her back.

I started forward, then restrained myself. She had chosen to go in there. Perhaps this was the answer to many things. She had no business in my house after my clear dismissal, and certainly no business in the laboratory. She intended to be a nuisance to me. Let her pay the price of her threats and this trespass.

There was a heavy thud which I identified as the sound of the creature blundering into some obstruction.

Justine spun round.

In the uncertain light I saw the shadows on her face form a pattern of terror. She rammed a fist into her mouth as though to stifle a scream – very considerate of her, I thought ironically.

The dark bulk of the creature loomed over her. The chain rattled. Justine whimpered and turned to run for the door.

I reached it before her. I pulled it shut and turned the key which she had used and which she had had no right to use.

Now she screamed. Now there was no hand in her mouth – she was shrieking like a soul demented.

She must indeed have been mad. A sane person would have realized that the creature, on his chain, could not operate in more than a restricted area. All the stupid girl had to do was stay out of range. But she must have begun to run to and fro like the mice in the cage. Suddenly there was a gasp, cutting off one of her screams. Her feet beat a tattoo on the floor. And there was a dull muttering, and a crunching sound which I did not wish to identify… and then silence.

8

THE WEDDING invitations, few as they were, had been sent out and the replies were coming in. At breakfast a few days before the ceremony, Elizabeth looked at me with the first sign of awkwardness I had detected in her.

Timidly she said: 'Victor… I've invited Paul to the wedding.

It was alien to her nature to have any secrets, and I was surprised that she should have kept this one; surprised, too, that she should have acted thus without consulting me and that she should in any case have known Paul's new address.

But of course he would have sent word to her somehow. I could imagine the florid missive. It would have been evasive but manly, in Paul's best treacherous style, telling her that if ever she needed help he would be at her service, that he wished us both well but that if she had any doubts she must be sure to consult him and lean on him.

When I said nothing, Elizabeth went on: 'He was a very good friend of yours.'

The past tense was all too appropriate. In recent times he had been anything but a friend.

'I'm sorry if I've done wrong,' she said, her head bowed. 'He hasn't accepted yet, so perhaps he won't come.'

The poor girl was so dejected that I had to reassure her. Although I had no great wish to see the man himself, there was something I wanted to show him. He should see what I had accomplished, and would know what more I could have done if it had not been for his interference.

I said: 'I hope he does come, my dear. I hope he accepts.'

This put her mind at rest. She was able to devote all her energies to the wedding preparations.

On her insistence I invited the burgomaster and his wife to dinner one evening, together with some other local worthies who would be present on the day. She was right, of course: it was better that she should meet these folk now rather than make her first acquaintance with them at the ceremony itself. I had neglected some of my duties as her betrothed. I tried to make up for this in a few sociable hours. Certainly the local dignitaries, becoming rather less dignified and more bucolic as the evening wore on, had no complaints about their treatment. A large meal and a plentiful supply of wine speedily washed away any lingering resentment they might have harboured from the years of indifference which the present Baron Frankenstein had displayed towards them.

Nevertheless, I was glad to be rid of them. I was gracious to their plump wives and took their heavy jocularity in good part, but beneath this surface amiability I was deeply, miserably bored. When at last they had all gone I poured myself a glass of the brandy which had been too good to offer them and smiled over the glass at Elizabeth.

She said: 'Gracious, how quiet it is!' She patted the couch beside her. 'Come and sit with me a moment, Victor.'

She was demure yet alluring – a gracious hostess yet also, I saw, a woman with a latent fire of her own who would be an entrancing wife. I would allocate a reasonable amount of my precious time to her. I would be well repaid. It was good to know that the tattered remains of Justine were safely buried in the woods and that there would never be any fear of her malicious tongue speaking evil of me to Elizabeth.

But I must not allow her to assume that I was going to change into a sentimental courtier and abandon all my more serious occupations.

I said: 'I think I must tidy up some loose ends in the laboratory.'

She came as near to pouting as I had ever seen her. On other women it would have been irritating; on her it was rather charming.

'Victor, I thought that for just one evening—'

'I have to conclude one or two processes before the wedding,' I said. 'I must leave everything tidy – and safe.'

She acknowledged this with a resigned sigh. Then she asked: 'May I come and watch you at work?'

'Not yet, my dear. One day very soon, I promise.'

'You've promised that before. I thought you were going to show me what you had done a few weeks ago.'

'I ran into some difficulties. When they are resolved, you shall see.' I finished my brandy and set the glass down. 'A pity we haven't heard from Paul.'

Elizabeth smiled wryly. 'If Paul were here, you'd show *him*.'

'Because he understands the technical background. He was with me during the earlier stages, remember.'

'And why didn't he want to go on?'

This was taking a turn I had no wish to follow. I said: 'Soon you'll see what it has all been about. Soon.'

I was halfway up the stairs when there was a knock at the main door. I paused on the landing. Elizabeth's new maid, a respectable little girl without pretensions and without undue curiosity, crossed the hall.

Paul Krempe stood in the doorway.

'Are the Baron and Miss Elizabeth at home?'

Elizabeth recognized his voice and came running out with an eagerness which I found unbecoming in a young woman of her station.

'Paul, how wonderful to see you. We were afraid you had forgotten us.'

'You are looking more radiant than ever,' he said.

I thought it was time for me to intervene. I went back down the stairs, saying:

'It is good of you to come, Paul.'

He reluctantly looked away from Elizabeth and up at me.

'How are you, Victor?'

I reached his level and we shook hands.

'Victor has been saying,' Elizabeth chattered gaily, 'how much he wanted to see you. He says he's got something he wants you to see – haven't you, Victor?'

Paul looked earnestly, piercingly into my eyes.

'Have you?'

'Yes.' I took his coat from him and waved towards the stairs. 'Would you like to go up and see?'

'Victor!' Elizabeth protested. 'The very moment Paul arrives…'

'We shall not be long,' I said, moving up behind Paul so that he should not be tempted to turn back.

We went up to the laboratory. Once Paul glanced back inquiringly as though asking for some indication of what he might expect. But I intended that he should see for himself, without preamble.

At the door I took out my key.

'Still keeping the place locked?' said Paul. 'Is that necessary?'

'You can judge for yourself.'

I opened the door and stood back as he entered.

The creature was crouched in a corner, staring at the floor. When it became aware of us it turned its face to the wall.

Paul stared mutely.

'Nothing to say?' I challenged him.

'So it wasn't killed,' he said softly.

'It was. At least, life had passed from its body. But I was the one who put it there in the first place, and it was I who restored it.'

Paul turned away. He headed for the door.

'No, wait,' I said. 'I want to show you something else.'

'I've seen enough.'

'Wait!'

Grudgingly he stayed where he was. He seemed to have difficulty in facing the hunched, huddled body of the creature in the corner. In his face there was no scientific curiosity, no spark of reawakened interest; only loathing.

I stood over the creature. 'Get up.' It shivered slightly and tried to compress itself into an even tighter ball. 'Come on,' I ordered; 'get up.'

Slowly it clambered to its feet. It glanced at Paul and then quickly away at me, waiting for the next command.

I said: 'Now come here.'

It came towards me and stood a few inches away.

'Sit down,' I said.

The creature pondered this, then with an ungainly lurch it lowered itself to the floor with its knees under its chin.

'Is this your creature of superior intellect?' said Paul. 'Your perfect physical being… this animal?' He drew his hand across his brow, and his eyes narrowed in pain. 'Ask it a question in advanced physics. It's got a brain with a lifetime of knowledge behind it. That was the theory, wasn't it? Go on, ask. It should find it simple.'

This sneer was the most monstrous thing of all. I felt anger like a burning poison in my throat.

'Do you know why it looks like that – behaves like that? There you see the result of *your* handiwork, Paul. Yours as well as mine. I gave it life… I put a brain in its head… but I chose a good brain – a brilliant one…' I took a deep, shuddering breath. 'It was you who damaged it, you who put a bullet in it. This is your fault – do you understand? Your fault.'

'Yes,' said Paul sombrely, 'I understand.'

'But you won't stop me, Paul. You won't force me to stop, to despair. I'm going to carry on. I'll try further brain surgery. If that fails then I shall seek another brain—'

'No, Victor.' Abruptly he was shouting. 'No, you will not.'

'And another if necessary,' I said, 'and another and another, until—'

'No!'

He turned and tried to rush through the doorway. I was so accustomed now to anticipating the creature's erratic movements that I acted instinctively. Before Paul could escape I had grasped his shoulder and twisted him back towards me.

'What are you going to do?'

He pushed at me with all his might. I held firm, and we staggered back into the centre of the room. He stopped and I could tell that he was trying to keep his voice steady.

'For your sake and to protect Elizabeth I've kept silent so far,' he said. 'But now I'm going to the authorities. That creature must be destroyed – and you must pay for your atrocities.'

I could have laughed if it had not been for the deadly seriousness of it. Absurdity and tragedy go so often together.

Paul flung me away with a sudden lunge, and my hip jarred nauseatingly against the bench. Before I could get my breath, he was out of the door and running along the passage.

I stumbled after him. As he raced down the stairs, Elizabeth came out into the hall.

'Paul, where are you…'

Her question died on her lips as she saw me in hot pursuit. I followed Paul out into the open, and our feet scuffed up dust from the drive. His pace was slowing. In spite of the pain in my side I forced myself to keep going, and overtook him as he reached the path to the village.

'Paul, wait a minute.'

He swung towards me on the defensive, ready to strike if I tried to grab him.

'Paul,' I pleaded, 'what do you hope to gain by this? You're as much a part of it as I am.'

'I've had nothing to do with it for months.'

'You can't shed all responsibility for the earlier stages. And if you think that by betraying me you'll have Elizabeth for yourself, I can assure you you're mistaken.'

In the evening light it was difficult to make out his features. But he drew himself up stiffly and said: 'I want nothing more than to protect Elizabeth. But I have never tried to win her away from you. If you think that—'

'If you want to protect her,' I broke in, 'you are going the wrong way about it. How will it help her to learn that the man she is about to marry is in danger from meddling officials? How will it help her to know that his old friend and colleague is a traitor who himself worked on the preliminary stages? If we both suffer at the hands of the authorities – and don't imagine, Paul, that I shall accept all blame myself – what will she do? She can't live here alone, the butt of all the malicious tongues in the country. She has nowhere else to go. It is nearly her wedding eve – and you propose to shatter her whole future?'

'You're falsifying it, Victor.'

'Falsifying it?' I said. 'Think of her in that house while the authorities and their booted minions stamp through, examining everything, pulling the place apart, wrecking my laboratory…'

The same thought occurred to us both at the same instant. 'The laboratory,' said Paul. 'When we came out… the door's still open.'

'She wouldn't…'

'Wouldn't she?'

Elizabeth had not followed us out. The main door was still open, shedding light on the steps. She could, of course, have gone back into the salon. Or she could, wondering about our wild chase, have taken the opportunity of going upstairs. And I had undoubtedly left the door wide open.

We stared at the house.

'Victor!' Paul clutched my arm.

High up on the roof a light showed, and there was a flicker of movement. It was impossible to distinguish the outlines of the moving shape at first, but in the stillness of the night we heard the clink and rattle of a chain.

The creature had pulled its chain away from the wall. The light came from the open skylight which led out on to the roof. As we got used to the distance and the darkness, we saw the wavering head and the groping arms unmistakably.

The creature came to the edge of the parapet and looked down.

'We must get up there,' I said.

'Not this time,' said Paul. 'I'm going to the village for help.'

I seemed to have lost the will to restrain him. Everything was going wrong. As he went away down the path to round up helpers and ruin my schemes once and for all, I returned to the house. I did not even bother to hurry. I was in the grip of a bleak fatalism.

But once I was indoors my steps quickened. There was no sign of Elizabeth. She must indeed have gone upstairs.

I went up the first flight two at a time and called her name along the landing. There was no reply. I pounded on my way up to the laboratory. The door was open, and the lights were burning just as we had left them. But the skylight, which came right down to floor level, was pushed open. A faint breeze stirred the sheets of notes which had accumulated on my desk.

A lantern stood on the parapet just outside the skylight.

It must be one which Elizabeth had carried to light her way up the stairs, since I had certainly not put it there. And it meant that Elizabeth had followed the creature out on to the roof.

There was only a low balustrade to save them from the drop to the terrace below.

I opened the desk drawer and took out my pistol. Then I stepped through the open skylight on to the parapet.

Faintly touched with light, almost at the end of the roof, Elizabeth stood looking away from me, looking at something round the corner of the ridge.

'Elizabeth' – I spoke softly, not wanting to alarm her in that precarious position – 'come back.'

She turned and stared at me. It was hardly the face of Elizabeth any longer. Horror was written across it – an incredulous, unconquerable horror that included me as well as the other thing she must have seen. This was not how I had meant her to see the creature for the first time. The shock must have dazed her. Coming into the laboratory just as the creature wrenched its chain free from the wall staple, she must have been hypnotically drawn to follow it, to prove to herself that it was real.

'Elizabeth...'

She shook her head as though to deny that I existed. I took a step out onto the parapet and she waved me back. She might have been trying to ward me off – concerned with keeping me rather than the creature at bay.

And behind her the creature appeared, clawing and rocking its way back from the edge of the roof.

I lifted my pistol. Elizabeth screamed. The creature reached out as though to embrace her, and I fired.

It was a bad, impossible target. Elizabeth jerked as though she had been struck, and even in this light I could see a dark stain begin to spread from her shoulder.

She fell back into the creature's arms.

I had another shot to fire. This time I could not afford to miss. As Elizabeth's head dropped to one side I braced myself and took careful aim. The creature stared stupidly, uncomprehendingly at me.

I fired, and this time it was the creature's turn to flinch. Its arm slid to its side, and Elizabeth crumpled over the edge of the balustrade. She hung there, unconscious, her head swaying over the deadly drop.

The creature touched her once in a puzzled sort of way and then carefully, with a lumbering solemnity, clambered past her and began to come towards me.

'Stay where you are,' I commanded it.

It kept up its slow, steady pace.

'Get back,' I shouted. It must have heard; must know what I was saying. So far its obedience had been unquestioning. 'Get back – get away.'

It was within a few feet of me. I backed away until I was in the skylight opening. Still it did not slacken its advance.

I yelled for help, but there was nobody to hear.

I threw the pistol at the creature. It bounced off, and an eternity later I heard the rattle as it hit the ground far below.

Behind me was the laboratory. If I fled across it I could lock the door from outside and make my escape. The door was solid enough to withstand even the strength of this powerful creature. But to leave Elizabeth out there, trapped with the monster…

I glanced back over my shoulder in search of a suitable weapon. There was none. The silver-knobbed stick was not something I would care to trust against this solid brute force.

At my feet was the lantern. I felt the warmth of the flame against my ankle.

I stooped and picked it up.

The creature plodded towards me and raised its arms. I swung the lantern twice to give it plenty of impetus, and hurled it full at the creature.

As the spurting, flickering light was launched at it, the creature bared its teeth. If it could have sprung at me it would have done so. But it had not yet learnt such co-ordination of movements. It made one further step forward and then the lantern smacked into its chest.

There was a moment when nothing seemed to happen. A faint smear of thick black smoke hung on the air. Then flame blazed up from the lamp.

The creature was on fire. The flames licked up greedily, devouring it at a speed which appalled me. Its eyes stared out at me in agonized entreaty, and then were blotted out by crimson fury. A strangled, hideous voice screamed despairingly. The creature's head jerked back in an effort to dodge the flames, but they were too voracious. Its hands beat vainly on its face. And then, a raging pillar of fire, it came blundering on towards me again.

I stumbled back into the laboratory. The glass of the skylight crashed into splinters, spraying across the parapet and into the laboratory.

And suddenly, rearing up like a living torch, the creature hurled itself forward. In its death throes it sought a respite, something to put an end to the intolerable pain. With one wild, insane leap it plunged into the tank.

The screams went on, reverberating through the laboratory. And the screams were mine. I was yelling like a maniac, trying to stop what had already been done. The tank was no longer full of the fluid in which the creature had once lain. I had recently recharged it with acid. And into that acid plunged the burning creature.

There was an acrid smoke that billowed up and raced like

some elemental fiend about the room. In the tank there was a moment of wild thrashing and churning, and acid splashed out over the floor, driving me back into a safe corner.

Then the noise abated. It died to a sizzling and bubbling that went on for some time before finally fading into utter stillness.

My life's work was destroyed. Destroyed in a moment by the same hand that brought it into existence. Within half an hour there was nothing left of my creature. The acid tank was cloudy, but that, too, would clarify in a short time and there would be no evidence that the creature had ever been in this world at all.

9

THAT IS the true story of what happened. But it is a story which no one will believe. The priest shakes his head and exhorts me to repent. The executioner makes ready, and my hours are numbered.

One man could have saved me. If Paul Krempe had spoken out, then surely the verdict would have gone differently. But Paul had nothing to say. Paul, who was the cause of all that went wrong with the experiment, took Elizabeth away into the quiet countryside and left me to my fate – an undeserved fate.

When Paul brought a dozen villagers to the house that night with the story of a dangerous monster being loose, it was to find no monster. And foolishly, in my desire to suppress any further investigations and any possible scandal, I denounced him as an agitator and trouble-maker. There had been no monster such as he described. I was Baron Frankenstein, and I was shocked that my own villagers should have been seduced by this man's glib inventions. I ordered them to go home and ordered Paul to leave the district before I instituted proceedings against him.

He left the district – and took Elizabeth with him.

I have said that I acted foolishly in so firmly denying the existence of the creature. For a week later some interfering shepherd, who had no business to be on that part of my land in the first place, noticed a peculiar conformation of recently turned earth in the woods, and began to dig into it. Why it should have occurred to him to do so I cannot say: it was but the last in a long series of ironical blows dealt me by fate.

In the grave which he exposed was the mutilated corpse of Justine.

They would not believe that I was innocent of her death. When I told them how the monster of my creation had torn her apart, they shrank away from me and reminded me that I had scorned the notion of any such monster. I tried to explain, but they would not listen. In their eyes *I* was the monster. Justine had been expecting a child, and I had murdered her. The more I cried that it was a terrible accident for which I was not responsible, the more their detestation of me hardened.

I sent out a plea for Paul Krempe to come forward and testify. He did not appear. I implored eminent scientists to inspect the apparatus in my laboratory while I explained how it could be used to create life. I offered to demonstrate the whole sequence of experiments to them. Grimly they said I would not be allowed that much time in this world. And on all sides I was accused not merely of murder but of blasphemy.

The priest to whom I have told the story cannot make up his mind whether I am mad or wicked. He has listened, but none of it means anything to him. He will intercede on my behalf with nobody – and if he did, it would be of little use, for who would make any sense out of his meanderings?

Late today came the worst moment of all. A last hope flickered and began to burn… but I should have known that my trust in old friendships was a vain one.

Paul Krempe came to see me. At last he deigned to show himself. The pathetic little dwarf who is my gaoler, and whom I truly think regards me with respect and a strange affection, showed him in with a flourish. I fancied I detected in the dwarf's sad little eyes the hope that my wishes would be granted and that here at last would be a reprieve.

A great weight was lifted from my heart. Paul, after all, was not going to fail me. He would tell all that he knew. The truth would come out. The rest of the world would have to accept that Justine had been killed not by me but by a creature which, admittedly, I had constructed, but for whose wayward savageries I could hardly be held responsible. Paul knew. His conscience could surely not permit him to remain silent any longer. He must have been trying to hold out, to let me be executed so that Elizabeth would be his; but now he had seen where his duty lay.

I sent for the priest so that he could be a witness to all that was said.

'I knew Paul wouldn't fail me,' I said. 'He will verify everything I've already cold you.'

The priest blinked. He gave every sign of being frightened of learning that what I had said was true. Better, in his eyes, that I should be executed than that these unpalatable facts should be firmly established.

Paul was shown in by the dwarf. I put out my hand, longing to clasp his in mine. But Paul stood sternly aloof.

He said: 'I have come with a message from Elizabeth.'

'She will speak, too?' I said eagerly.

'She wishes you to know that she forgives you and that she will pray for you. I have implored her not to think of the past, but she would not rest content until I promised that I would speak to you before the end.'

'Tell them, Paul. Tell the priest here – and later we will make a declaration to the authorities.'

'Tell them what?'

He was being wilfully obtuse. 'About the creature I made,' I said as patiently as possible. Patience was not easy with the shadow of the scaffold darkening over me. 'Paul, you were the only person ever to see him alive. Elizabeth caught only a glimpse, but you *know*. You and Justine... Justine must have seen him, but she can't help me now, can she?'

'Justine,' he said thoughtfully; 'the girl you murdered.'

It was like a knife in my bowels. I said: 'But I didn't. You must realize that. He was the one. He… it…'

'Who, Victor?' Paul's steely calmness brought fear welling up in me again.

'The creature.' I was trying to maintain my dignity, trying not to shout at him. 'The creature we made together. Don't keep up the pretence any longer. You've got to tell the truth now.'

Paul glanced at the priest and slowly shook his head. As though this had been a signal he was expecting, the priest left the cell.

I clutched Paul's jacket. 'You must tell them! You know what's going to happen to me. Only you can save me. You must tell them. I'll make you speak. I'll make you…'

We fought in the confined space of the cell. It lasted only a few seconds. The guards rushed in and dragged me off him. Paul dusted himself off and gave the guards the same false, regretful look he had given the priest.

This was the only time during these degrading proceedings that I broke down. I began to scream.

'You must tell them, Paul. You've got to save me. You can't let them… can't let me… Paul, I'll promise not to carry out any further experiments, but *tell* them. Tell them now!'

They held me back as he went out of the cell with his head hypocritically bowed.

The priest was waiting outside.

Paul said: 'There's nothing we can do for him now.'

And he left, doubtless to insinuate himself even further into Elizabeth's graces.

I sobbed helplessly. I am ashamed of myself for showing such weakness, but this final betrayal robbed me temporarily of all self-control.

Now I am myself again. They shall not see me flinch. And even at this eleventh hour I feel that somehow there must be an answer. There cannot be such injustice in the world. I am Baron Frankenstein, and I cannot believe that I shall die. I cannot believe that I shall ever die. I who have created life – how can they presume to take life from me?

There must somehow be a way to cheat death.

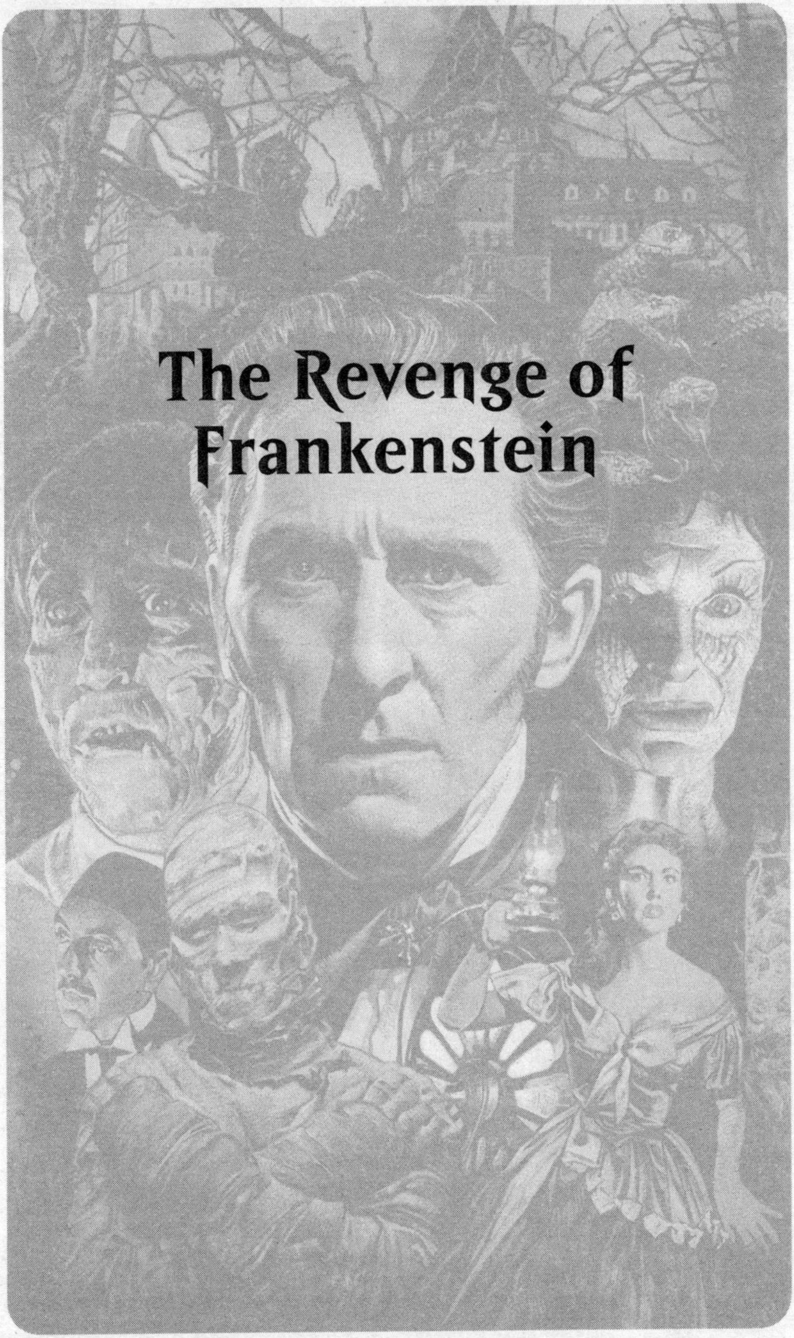
The Revenge of
Frankenstein

1

ON THE morning of my execution I was asked if I had any last statement to make. I replied only that I was innocent of the crime for which I had been sentenced to death. Then I was led by two guards to the yard where the scaffold stood grim and bare in the cold morning light.

One of my guards was a huge ox of a man. The other was a twisted little creature named Werner, a dwarf who was stronger than he looked, but whose strength could not compensate him for the wretchedness of his warped body.

They offered to bind my eyes, but I refused. I was calm. I wanted to see what was happening. When the priest met me at the exit into the yard of death and began to advise repentance, as he had been doing for some considerable time now, I politely rejected his advances.

We walked slowly towards the scaffold. Within the prison I heard the mournful howling that prisoners invariably set up on such occasions. Nobody looked down on the scene, however: that was forbidden. At least in this enlightened country of mine I was, thanks to what little influence I had left – mainly financial, I may add – not to be made a public spectacle.

I glanced down at Werner. He gave me a quick grin. I trusted this meant that all was well.

The dwarf was my last hope. In the middle of the night, sleepless and fretful because there was so much to be done with my talents and so little chance that I would ever be able to do it, I had turned to the dwarf and made a bargain with him. He had always been half inclined to believe my story of a living creature which I had made, and now I set out to convince him of the skills which I had learned during my experiments. If he saved me from the scaffold, I promised to give him a new body. He was very ready to listen to an offer of this kind. His objections were easily overcome. He wanted to believe that I was telling the truth and that I could do what I said. If I was to escape from death and from this prison there would be risks to run – but when the prize was a fine new body, Werner was willing to take such risks.

I had to leave the details to him. He would not or could not tell me how he planned to accomplish the escape. But that sidelong grin was reassuring.

Unless it was all a ghastly joke... I saw myself mounting the scaffold and dying while they laughed at me, laughed at my gullibility in believing that I would be snatched from the jaws of destruction.

Our little cortege stopped at the foot of the steps leading up to the scaffold. The executioner looked down at me appraisingly and then at the priest. The priest began to intone. The dwarf glanced at his massive companion and jerked his head to indicate that the man should go back into the building. They exchanged a knowing wink. I foresaw that this was going to cost me whatever money I could lay my hands on; but I had no intention of complaining or of haggling over terms.

The priest finished. The words he had been offering up to heaven on my behalf were the last he ever uttered. The dwarf leapt suddenly upon him and in a trice had pinioned his arms behind his back. The executioner sprang down from his platform and, while I stood spellbound, the two of them hurried the priest up the steps.

It was all over in a matter of seconds. The rest of the plan was carried out with admirable speed. My little friend Werner might have an inadequate body, but he had a nimble brain. Before the morning was well advanced I found myself a free man in the streets of the city. The dead priest would be buried as Baron Frankenstein and there was no reason why any suspicion should ever arise. I drew in several deep breaths to convince myself that I was indeed alive and my own master again. A heady sense of freedom intoxicated me. Not merely had I put the prison walls behind me: I had shed my old self and carried none of the burden of old mistakes and old hatreds. It was true that I could not touch my riches – but my true wealth had always been in my mind and my creative fingers. I would choose a new name, a new home, and a new future.

I found rooms above a tavern and sent down for a hearty meal and a flagon of rich red wine. After eating and drinking my fill I felt at ease with the world. It had treated me badly, but now I was in a position to fling down a fresh challenge. The revenge I sought was not a vindictive one. All I asked was the admission of the so-called experts in my scientific field that I had been right, that I had gone far beyond them, that Frankenstein had been wronged by his detractors. I would make them bow to me. I would show them up as the doubting fools they were.

Perhaps it would never be possible to claim my full recompense. Having once shed my identity I could not safely resume it. Too many ugly rumours had festered in the valley below my home. But whatever name I might adopt, I would somehow, some day ensure that the credit for those early researches went to the distinguished predecessor who was in fact myself. Whatever triumphs I might achieve, the pioneering successes of Frankenstein should not be kept from the pages of history.

It would take time to build up the necessary finances for further research. As an unknown I would not have access to fully equipped laboratories or to scientific conclaves where new theories were discussed. Working entirely alone, I must somehow find a way of acquiring apparatus and the basic essentials for creation.

I could undoubtedly obtain employment as a doctor. If I chose the right place and built up confidence in me, I could stealthily carry on my own operations under cover of my profession. A slow process – but a practical one.

The noise from the tavern grew clamorous by the middle of the evening. I would have quit the premises and sought a quieter place in which to think out my plans without interruption, but I considered it wiser to lie low for a time. The Frankenstein face was not unknown in this city, and I did not want it to be recognized so soon after my execution!

When I had established myself, I would search once more for cadavers in good preservation so that I could begin painstaking reconstructions once more. First of all I had a promise to fulfil. I had guaranteed that Werner should have a handsome, healthy body, and I intended to see that he was not cheated.

Werner was to call on me this evening. He had remained on duty at the prison to ensure that there was no hitch in the disposal of the priest's corpse, and he was to report to me when everything was settled. Then we would make plans for our next meeting.

There was a gust of bawdy laughter from the tavern. I longed for peace and solitude, but forced myself to reflect that the boisterous noise of life was preferable to the stillness and solitude of the prison cell or, even worse, the grave.

A light tap on my door was almost drowned by the noise. I waited, and the sound came again, louder this time.

I opened the door to reveal the dwarf, hopping impatiently from one foot to the other. When I let him in and offered him a chair he could scarcely stay still. Intelligent as he was, he naively hoped that I could somehow achieve a miracle at this very moment. I had to calm him down and explain that the transformation would take a long time. Even when we had started the actual work, the process would be long and painful; and until I was securely established again, with time and money and materials to spare, we could not even start.

His pathetic clown's face twisted woefully. I feared for an instant that he was about to threaten me or accuse me of going back on my bargain. But he was too anxious for that – too anxious to be made hale and magnificent. If he had to be patient, he would be patient.

I suggested that he continue his work at the prison for a few months at least. It would not do for him to disappear suddenly. When I was ready I would send for him.

He disliked the idea of being left behind. But there was no point in his travelling with me. So far from there being any advantage in it, there was a positive danger: he cut a conspicuous figure, and might draw unwelcome attention to the two of us. He would have to trust me.

He did, in fact, trust me. His faith was so strong that I found myself talking to him as freely as though he had been an equal. After the mistrust and then the growing hatred through which I had floundered these last few months, his frank reliance on me was a great comfort.

I had finished the wine, but suggested that he should fetch more from the tavern and at the same time bring another goblet. He was flattered to be put upon such a footing, and hurried to carry out the errand.

When he returned he was fidgeting with worry.

'My lord Baron—'

'No!' I cut him short. 'Never address me in that way again.'

He quickly nodded his understanding of this; but now he was at a loss. I had observed in the prison that he was a creature of formalities and he had scrupulously used my correct title even though I was, in the eyes of my gaolers, a condemned criminal. Now I had to provide him with a substitute form of address. It had better be one with which we could both become speedily familiar. 'Call me Doctor,' I said.

'Doctor Stein,' he said eagerly.

I laughed. He was delighted. And really, Doctor Stein was a suitable non-committal name. There must be many such. I intended, though, that this one should be more famous than any other.

'Now,' I said, 'what's troubling you?'

'My l— Doctor, they are talking downstairs. About your body.'

'There is always a lot of talk in taverns after an execution,' I said. 'I'd have thought you knew this better than anyone.'

'There are two of them,' said Werner agitatedly, 'who are being paid ten marks to provide a fresh corpse for the medical school. There is not a very plentiful supply of corpses – but the supply of students is plentiful enough.'

I had done a certain amount of grave robbing in my time, as every scientist must. I was neither shocked nor surprised to learn that ten marks would buy a recently buried corpse. But then the significance of what Werner had said sank in.

'*My* body!' I exclaimed.

His head wagged. 'It's a fresh one. The freshest there is. And they've taken a fancy to the notion of digging up a real live baron – I mean a real dead baron.'

There had been times in prison when I had welcomed his grim jocularity. At this moment I would have been happier without it. I am not a squeamish man, but the thought of my corpse – my 'fresh' corpse – being dug up so soon after its interment and being giggled over as that of a real baron was an unsettling one. Of course it was not really my body, but it so easily might have been.

I said: 'To a medical student I imagine one body will be much the same as another.'

'But when they open the coffin they may raise the alarm.'

'Why should they? A corpse is a corpse, no more.'

'We had to work fast, Doctor. We had no time to disrobe the priest.'

I was aghast. 'You mean—'

'We had to bundle him in just as he was.'

Now I saw why he had been so perturbed. I shared his distress. Once it was known that Baron Frankenstein had escaped there would be an immediate inquiry, and heads would roll. I had no wish that mine should be one of them.

'We must go at once.' I got up, reaching for my cloak.

'Not yet, Doctor. They won't go until the town is quiet. And one of them is still nervous. One called Kurt. He'll need a lot more drink inside him before he'll start digging.'

At this the dwarf glanced at the flagon of wine he had brought, and at the empty glass standing beside mine.

'Very well,' I agreed; 'but let us be there in good time.'

Werner did not fail me. He had phenomenally sharp hearing, and did not stir as one group and another staggered from the tavern into the street. But when two distinctive voices rang out under the window, he was on his feet at once.

'There they go!'

We were swiftly downstairs and out on the cobbles, reeking with the smell of spilt wine and vomit. A couple of drunkards slithered over the mess towards a wall and leaned there trying to sing. A more lamentable sound I have rarely heard.

Werner knew a short cut to the graveyard, and we arrived at the new mound of earth before there was any sign of the two robbers. I indicated that the dwarf should remain behind a tree while I took shelter in the heavy shadow of a tilted headstone.

It was an uncanny sensation to stare at the new rectangle of dark earth and know that it was meant to be heaped upon me. I gagged, seeming to feel earth in my throat and nostrils as the lid of the coffin pressed down, cracked, and collapsed.

Footsteps rustled along the path. I tensed. A lantern bobbed between the tombstones like a questing spirit. It came closer, and two crouched figures stooped at last over the mound.

'See?' mumbled one. 'There you are, Kurt. A proper baron under there.'

'Think we could ask a bit more for him?'

They had brought a spade, and took it in turns to dig. In spite of the looseness of the earth they made a slow job of it. The one called Kurt was a bundle of nerves and kept stopping to peer over his shoulder or whisper to his friend Fritz.

At last they scraped away the loam from the coffin. Kurt lowered himself into the hole which Fritz had just cleared, and bent over the coffin. Then he looked up appealingly at his friend. He lacked the courage to rip the lid off. With an oath Fritz sprang down beside him, got the blade of the shovel under the lid, and forced it open with a screech of nails.

They both gasped.

'A priest!' quavered Kurt. 'What's he doing there? What…?'

It was too much for him. Without waiting for his partner he scrambled out of the open grave and dashed across the cemetery. He tripped over the edges of graves, blundered against tombstones, and then crashed into a hedge. Cursing, Fritz hauled himself out and looked as though he might follow. Then avarice got the better of him. He turned to look down at the corpse of the priest. After all, a corpse was a corpse – still worth ten marks to him. And now there would be no need to divide it with the cowardly Kurt.

He was about to venture back into the hole when I stepped out from concealment. He heard the movement and looked fearfully towards me.

I drew my cloak about me and said in the most sepulchral tone I could muster: 'Good evening. I am Baron Frankenstein.'

He let out a moan and swayed on the edge of the grave. Before he could decide whether to run or pray, Werner skipped out and stood on his other side. Fritz let out one last moan and fainted. He pitched backwards into the grave. I took an involuntary step forward to try to save him – I had intended no more than a macabre joke which would drive him away and keep him quiet – but it was too late. Fritz landed on his back on one edge of the coffin. There was a sickening thud.

I stepped down into the grave and moved him so that I could feel for a heartbeat. There was none. Fritz had been most effectively silenced.

Werner lowered himself down beside me and we tipped the second body right into the coffin and squeezed the lid down. I left the dwarf to refill the hole while I stood guard.

A crude wooden board had been kicked to one side. When I picked it up I found that my name had been scrawled on it. I set it up once again, thrust it into the soft earth, and there we left it – the final words on the subject of Baron Victor Frankenstein.

Or so the gullible authorities and public thought.

2

AFTER THE most careful survey of its potentialities I decided to settle in Carlsbruck. Without means or influence, I found the first two years extremely arduous. When I attempted to set up in practice I was met by firm resistance from the Medical Council, which apparently existed purely to eliminate competition. Nevertheless I persevered. I had confidence in my destiny, and after those early trials I began to see this confidence justified. Of my medical skill there could be little question; and unlike so many members of the profession I had the added advantage of good breeding, which was particularly effective when dealing with the impressionable ladies of the community. Among my patients I actually numbered the wife and daughter of one of my most powerful rivals, a committee member of the Medical Council of Carlsbruck. At first he could afford to treat this as a joke and attribute it to the passing whim of silly, susceptible women. As time went on, however, the august members of the council could hardly fail to notice that my patients remained devoted to me and that they themselves were losing more than a few to me.

Sooner or later I knew there would be an approach from the council, conciliatory or aggressive. I had made no application for a place on the council and did not intend to do so. Let them make the first move – and they would discover what reception I had in store for them!

Gradually I was consolidating my position. I started in a shabby quarter of the city, but then was able to move to a more fashionable area. At the same time I volunteered my services to the Workhouse Hospital. When they heard of it, this made some of my more delicate lady patients unhappy. They knew of the squalor in that dismal place – by hearsay, of course, since nothing would have tempted them to venture within its chill grey walls – and feared that I might bring contamination from it. It was admirable of me to give my services to the poor and needy; but were my responsibilities to the rich and fragile not greater? I tried to calm their agitation. Nothing must interfere with my work at the hospital: it provided me with so many things that I needed, though I was not in a position to explain this in detail to those good ladies who equally provided me with necessities – in their case, wealth.

If I had wished to settle down to a prosperous bourgeois life in Carlsbruck it would not have been difficult. Having established myself on my own merits I could have applied to the Medical Council for official recognition, and they would have been relieved to welcome me into the fold. I could have married, and married well. I need lack nothing.

But I had work to do. It was work which had to be carried out in complete secrecy. I had learned my lesson. I would put my trust in no one. Friends were unreliable; a wife in my household would be a danger and an encumbrance.

This, again, was something which could not be explained to the ladies. The shameless ardour of some of them had to be avoided by various stratagems or by a sternly professional concentration on their supposed symptoms. A widowed countess who had clearly decided upon my eventual conquest proved especially persistent: when she could no longer find excuses for visiting me on her own account – perhaps fearing that too long a list of imaginary ailments would detract from her charm in my view – she brought her attractive but somewhat pallid daughter to my consulting rooms day after day. Vera was subject to fainting fits. Vera could hardly walk across a room. Vera needed constant medical attention. And in the end, when the Countess realized that I was not going to fall into her arms, she amazed me by trying to turn my affections upon Vera. Better, she seemed to feel, that I should be in the family as her son-in-law rather than not at all.

The mysteries of creation were my constant study, but even I marvelled at the subtleties and crudities of women. I might create a man in my laboratory; but would I ever dare to create a woman?

'Everything I have goes to Vera when she comes of age,' said the Countess Barscynska one day while I waited for the girl to prepare herself for yet another futile examination. 'It was her father's last wish.' She gave this time to sink in, then went on briskly: 'I am having a musical evening soon, Doctor Stein. If you were free…'

'Much as I like music, I have very little time.'

'You poor man. A life dedicated to the needs of others. No time for a life of your own. But you must *make* time, Doctor.'

I refrained from saying that I made time for really important things when I chose to do so. She might have felt that her musical evenings came into this category.

At that moment Vera emerged demurely from behind the screen. She had not merely undressed for the examination: she had come provided with an alluring négligée. Her mother smiled proudly at her and invitingly at me, as though wanting me to inspect the property which I was being offered.

I used my stethoscope and made the girl jump.

'It's so cold.'

I said: 'Breathe deeply.'

'Last time,' she sighed, 'you used your ear.'

I made a perfunctory examination. There was nothing wrong with the girl. She was in excellent health. Indeed, I cannot deny that she was a most attractive young woman with a complexion which was the envy of her friends and a taut, slim figure which no man other than myself had so far had the privilege of studying at leisure.

I advised a judicious mixture of rest, food, and long walks. The Countess asked meaningly if I ever went riding. I said that I did not. She asked if I would be free on certain occasions to accompany Vera on one of these prescribed walks so that I could observe the effect which this physical exertion had on her. I regretted that other duties compelled me to refuse.

'That dreadful place!' said the Countess as her daughter dressed. 'Such demands on your valuable time!'

That dreadful place…

My office at the Workhouse Hospital was certainly a contrast. Sparsely furnished with the bare necessities of a consulting room, it was only cursorily cleaned by one or other of the shabby inmates, and I knew that if any of my wealthier patients were to see it I would lose them at once. The flotsam and jetsam of human life drifted through here or piled up and stayed here to rot. I did what I could for them; and did what I could for my own purposes. Some of the inmates swore by me; others swore at me. My name was sometimes reviled, sometimes worshipped.

On the very day that I had touched Vera's smooth, silken flesh I sat in my office and looked at another kind of young woman. She was dressed in rags and had dried blood matted in her hair. Yet she, too, could have been beautiful. I had hoped, after the last time I saw her, that she would in fact have a chance of cleaning herself up and acquiring some human dignity. Now I shook my head.

'Inga, not again!'

'I'm sorry, Doctor.' But beneath the apology and beneath the blood and dirt there was an irrepressible pertness that both exasperated and amused me. 'I tried to do what you told me.'

'I thought your husband was still in prison?'

'They let him out for good behaviour.'

I examined the scalp wound. It was not deep, but it went quite a way down behind her ear. She had a tough constitution.

I said: 'Why didn't you tell him what I told you?'

'I did, Doctor. I told him I was finished with him. I didn't want to have anything more to do with him. Just like you said.'

'And…?'

'As soon as I got up in the morning,' she said indignantly, 'he hit me with a bottle again.'

She was a lost cause. She would keep coming back here until one day he dealt her a more serious injury and she either lay permanently in one of the noisome rooms here or was taken off to a pauper's grave. I poured a pitcher of water into a basin and began to clean her up.

'He can't really help it, sir,' she said, flinching as I tried to disentangle the matted hairs. 'He loves me.'

As I worked away at that scabrous head, a grubby little man in an ill-fitting grey uniform which made him look more like a warder than a patient, hobbled in and stood at my left elbow. He was a sufferer from a recurring leg infection which sometimes kept him in bed for weeks and sometimes allowed him to get about, earning a few coins as a ward assistant and general messenger. Now he said:

'There's three men to see you, Doctor Stein. From the Medical Council.'

I had known that sooner or later there would be official representations from that group. It surprised me, however, that they should have chosen to visit me here. My fashionable surgery would have seemed a more appropriate place for such an interview; but possibly they did not wish to have their envy too painfully provoked.

'I can't see them now,' I said. 'They'll have to wait until I've finished my rounds.'

'They seemed impatient.'

I was delighted to hear it. 'I'll see them when I've finished.' As the messenger went away, I called after him: 'Have them wait in the ward.'

That would give them something to think about. The Medical Council of Carlsbruck was not noted for its devotion to the welfare of the poor. Let them learn a little humility while they waited for me!

I allowed them a full fifteen minutes before going along to the ward.

It was not a large room. All the quarters in this grim old building were cramped and inadequate, but they were all that charity could offer. Beds were packed head to tail with only a few inches between them. It was hard to distinguish between the moans of the genuinely sick and the ribald, desperate merriment of those who ought by rights to have been in prison cells. The workhouse attracted all kinds. The only thing they had in common was a putrefying stench. I could see as I entered the ward that my visitors from the council had never encountered quite such a smell before.

'Murdering butcher,' one man was wailing. He tried to seize the arm of one well-dressed doctor, who edged away with a most unprofessional distaste. 'You should come in and watch, you should. There's nothing he won't do to us – nothing.'

'Expects me to do me dance without any legs,' came another lament.

Voices rose from all sides, dinning into the ears of the visitors. I let them savour it for a few more seconds before stepping forward down the narrow centre aisle.

The patients saw me. Silence fell. The two men who had been most vociferous with their complaints shrank down between their filthy blankets. One of them wet his lips and tried an ingratiating smile.

The delegation turned to face me. I ignored them until I had bared the arm of a man in the bed nearest the door. Then I exposed the florid tattoo marks on the forearm and glanced at the three doctors.

'Quite a work of art – don't you think so, gentlemen?'

'Doctor Stein—'

'A great deal of craftsmanship has been expended on this.'

The youngest of the three was staring at me in a way which I found disturbing. He appeared to be trying to remember something, to place me. When he spoke it was slowly and thoughtfully.

'Very picturesque,' he said. He did not take his eyes off me.

'A great pity,' I went on, 'that so much effort should have been wasted.' I turned back to the patient. 'This has poisoned your arm. You must have it off.'

He wrenched his arm away and pushed himself up higher in the bed.

'You're not going to have my arm off – that's for sure!'

'If you'd rather die,' I said, 'it's up to you.'

'Die? After what I spent on it – just back from the Indies, and what money I had—'

'The arm is no use to you,' I said. 'And in a few days' time you will find that the rest of your body is going to be of no use. I'll remove the arm this afternoon.'

'No,' he whimpered. 'Doctor, I won't be able to work. Won't be able to go to sea.'

'Find a trade on land.'

There was a throaty chuckle from the next bed. 'He's already got one.'

'What is it?' I asked.

'Pickpocket.'

'Then he'll have to find another trade – or use his other hand.'

I moved to the next patient. A cloud of foul tobacco smoke blew across my face. One of my visitors coughed in protest. The most pompous of them began:

'Doctor Stein, we didn't come here to—'

'Amazing how dirty these people are, isn't it?' I said. 'I imagine you're not accustomed to it. They tell me it keeps them warm. Do any of you have patients with similar views?'

There was an offended silence, in so far as there could ever be complete silence in this atmosphere of wheezing, coughing, moaning, and spitting.

I decided to be kind to them. I stood up.

'Well, gentlemen? What can I do for you?'

The oldest of them cleared his throat and began what was evidently a prepared speech.

'I am the President of the Medical Council.'

'Congratulations.'

'At our last meeting it was unanimously decided that you should become a member.'

He forced a smile.

I said: 'I'm greatly honoured, gentlemen.'

There was an almost imperceptible sigh of relief from two of them. The third, the watchful young man, continued to study me.

'Then you accept?' said the president.

'No,' I said.

The sound this time was a gasp rather than a sigh. 'I don't understand,' said the president stiffly.

His starchier colleague burst out: 'Every doctor in the faculty regards your attitude as an insult.'

I said: 'When I arrived in Carlsbruck every attempt was made by your organization to prevent my practising medicine. You did not offer to accept me as a member *then*, gentlemen. Now I have built up a successful practice alone and unaided and have grown accustomed to working alone. I prefer it that way. Do I make myself clear?'

'Quite clear,' said the younger man. There was no criticism in his tone. He was still assessing me, and I sensed even that he tended to approve of me. I was not sure that I wanted his approval. What I most wanted was for the three of them to leave.

I said: 'Good day, then.'

They went. At the door of the ward the president turned. He tried to sound and appear stately, but his voice trembled with ill-concealed rage.

'You have not heard the last of this!'

There was faint laughter from the patients – a sycophantic laughter, designed to placate me.

Rid of the delegation, I turned back to my duties. When I had finished and was on my way out of the ward, I was accosted by the man with the tattooed arm. He waved feebly at me, and his voice rose in a whine.

'Doctor, you don't have to take it off – not really, do you?'

'Yes,' I said.

'It doesn't hurt me. I don't feel a thing.'

'That in itself is a dangerous sign,' I said as I went out.

His protests rang despairingly after me along the corridor. They were in vain.

I needed that arm.

3

AT THE end of an exhausting day I had a small roasted chicken sent into my office at the Workhouse Hospital and sat down thankfully at my desk, pausing only to take off my stained overall. A guttering light stood on the desk beside me. The rest of the room was in shadow.

I removed a leg of the chicken with two clean cuts, and was lifting it to my mouth when a voice spoke from the darkened corner.

'A masterly dissection, Doctor Stein.'

The chicken leg almost slipped through my fingers. I peered into the flickering pattern of light and shade. A man sat in the corner – a man who must have come in and settled down to wait for me.

He said: 'You must forgive this intrusion.'

As I grew accustomed to the darkness I saw that it was the youngest of my three visitors earlier in the day.

'I don't recall inviting you to supper,' I said.

To make it clear that I was indifferent to his presence I went on chewing. The chicken was not a very tender one, but after my arduous spell in the crudely equipped operating theatre I was prepared to regard it as a savoury morsel.

'I wished to renew our acquaintance. After a few moments with you this afternoon, I was sure I had seen you before.'

'That's hardly surprising,' I observed. 'I have been practising in Carlsbruck for three years.'

'Before that. A little more than three years ago, in fact.'

My fingers tightened on the chicken bone. I was about to tell him that he must be mistaken, when he went on:

'At the village of Ingstadt, I attended the funeral of one Professor Bernstein. You've heard of him, no doubt?'

'Everyone has heard of Professor Bernstein,' I said non-committally.

'I was in my final year as a student at the university where the professor was lecturing when he… died.'

I removed the other chicken leg and indicated it with the point of my sharp knife. 'May I offer you some chicken, Doctor… er…?'

'Kleve. Hans Kleve. No, thank you.'

He was far too self-possessed for my liking. There could be little doubt that he had recognized me. It was unfortunate. I tried to stave off the moment of accusation.

'Perhaps a little cheese?' I said. 'I can recommend it.'

He paid no attention. 'The professor,' he continued remorselessly, 'was buried in the family vault of Baron Frankenstein.' He paused. 'Need I continue?'

As he had every intention of doing so, I waved affably at him. 'Certainly.'

'I am the first, I suppose, to recognize you?'

'For what I am?' I said. 'Or what you would have me be – this Baron Frankenstein?'

'The resemblance is too striking. That and your present activities lead to only one conclusion.'

I ruminated for a minute or so. The chicken had lost its savour. My past, which I had hoped to dismiss until it suited me to recall it, was coming back like a sour taste in my mouth.

'So?' I said after due reflection. 'What if I am Baron Frankenstein?'

'Are you?'

'Just now you were telling me,' I pointed out equably. 'Now you are asking. Doctor Kleve, what makes you so interested in this gentleman?'

'I am in need of knowledge.'

He spoke so earnestly and with such transparent sincerity that I felt disposed to go some way to meet him. 'Not money?' I said. 'Need of knowledge. So that's it. In that case I admit that my name is Frankenstein.'

He nodded with satisfaction.

'But it's a large family, don't forget,' I hastened to add.

'Remarkable since the Middle Ages for productivity. There are offshoots everywhere – even in the Americas, I'm told. There is a town called Frankenstein in Germany—'

'Are you *the* Baron Frankenstein?' he demanded bluntly.

'Then there are the Frankensteins emanating from the town of that name in Silesia.'

He thrust himself suddenly forward and came full into the light. He was a handsome but rather intense young man, with a tight, impatient mouth and restless hands. I thought he was about to lean over the desk and seize me. I smiled reprovingly and tilted the knife towards him, more as a joke than a threat.

'Are you Baron Frankenstein?' he insisted.

I foresaw that I would be able to turn his fanaticism to good use. I said: 'Yes, Doctor Kleve.'

'I told you I am in need of knowledge.' Now that the admission was out, he rushed on even faster than before. 'I want to learn more than any university can teach me.'

'Highly commendable.' I remembered my own early days – and the private tuition for which I had paid – the gruelling work, the unflagging research, until I knew more than my tutor. I felt a growing warmth towards this young man, seeing myself in him.

'I want to be the pupil of the greatest doctor in the world,' he said. 'I want to be associated with the finest medical brain. To be your pupil, Baron Frankenstein.'

'And if I refuse?'

'You won't.'

Again I looked warningly at the knife. I did not intend to use it on the young man, but I hoped he would put a symbolic interpretation on it. I was not a man who took kindly to threats. I said:

'Either I employ you in my researches or… surely this is blackmail? An ugly failing in a doctor.'

'I see it as an agreement of, shall we say, reciprocal pooling of ideas. Or an exchange of your knowledge for my assistance. My assistance and—'

'And your silence?' I took him up. We faced each other in a mutual appraisal. 'I am not an easy man to work for.'

'Few gifted men are.'

'And when you have learned all I can teach you, then you might change your mind about keeping silent. How can I be sure?'

'You can never be sure.'

I smiled. 'The uncertainty of life is part of its fascination.'

'So I, too, can never be sure.' His gaze fell to the knife in my hand.

'My dear Doctor Kleve, you have put it perfectly.'

'I will take the risk. You accept me as your pupil?'

I kept him at bay for a few more minutes so that he should not consider that his victory had been too easy. I questioned him about his studies so far. His record was an impressive one. He had worked in Edinburgh and Paris, and had studied under Karl Strauss in Vienna. I had made up my mind quite some time before I finally held out my hand to seal the bargain.

As he launched himself into a spate of eager questions, I said sharply: 'Doctor Kleve… Hans… before we go any farther, there is one thing we must establish. You must exercise great caution when addressing me. The name is Stein – Victor Stein.'

'Of course. The Austrian or Swiss branch of that family, Doctor Stein?'

'Let's settle for Switzerland. An exhilarating climate, Hans, if a little heady.'

He sat waiting for me to finish my meal. Although I tried to press a few morsels on him, he was too excited to eat. He wanted to start work at once. He did not know what the work entailed, but was sure that if I was involved in it there must be innumerable fascinating aspects. In this, of course, he was right.

When I was ready, I put him out of his misery. 'Come – I'll show you my laboratory.'

As we walked through the streets towards the city gate I began to feel a prickling of unease. I had taken the admiration in his approach to me as no more than my due; but now I asked myself how he could have known of my reputation in the past. The medical and surgical work of Baron Victor Frankenstein had been a closely guarded secret. My reputation had in fact been no reputation at all until the time of my trial for murder – and at that trial, scorn had been heaped on my claims to have created a living being which had in fact killed the girl of whose death I was accused. Had this ambitious young man somehow led me into a trap?

I asked him what he knew of my work in the days when I still bore the family name. To my stupefaction he told me that already there was a host of legends about me in the valley which had once been mine. Some told of a laboratory in which alchemy and other forbidden arts were practised. Others spoke of monsters created for my sport, of a race of superhuman beings which I had planned to loose upon the world, of sub-human servants whom I kept chained in the rooms of my house.

'Such exaggerations are bound to occur,' said Hans

cheerfully. 'But everyone knows that there is a substratum of truth there. You did make unique discoveries in methods of inducing life into inanimate matter, didn't you?'

The appalling injustice of it made me laugh out loud. My execution had been ordered because no one had believed my story of creating life; yet now that I was supposedly dead, they were all beginning to accept that I had in fact done just what I claimed. The irony of it!

We reached the city gate. I waited until the watchman had paced on his solemn way, and then led Hans to the heavy old door in the city wall – the door beyond which lay a disused wine cellar ideal for my purpose. I had paid a pittance for it two years earlier. It was not the ideal setting for a laboratory, but its remoteness from the fashionable quarter told in its favour. I had been lucky to find it and lucky to be left unmolested for so long.

Inside the door was a small room with several old wine casks ranged along the walls. On these I had placed various specimens of diseased human organs in jars. If anyone by any mischance pried this far, there would be nothing to see but the everyday features of a doctor's research.

On the far side of the chamber another door opened on to a flight of steps down to the cellars proper. An oil lamp burned in a niche in the wall.

I led the way. I was halfway down when Hans, behind me, slipped and came stumbling down. I braced myself and took the impact, steadying him so that he could regain his balance.

'Careful! It would be a shame to lose you so soon.'

We reached the foot of the steps and the third door, the heaviest of them all. This retained its original appearance, but I had taken the precaution of reinforcing it on the other side so that even the most venturesome prowler would be unable to break it down.

I hammered on the door with my closed fist.

A small trap at eye level opened with a click. Hans started back. I laughed, looking into the beady eye of Werner. The dwarf's feet were braced against a support several inches from the ground. When he had assured himself of my identity he skipped down and opened the door. It swung ponderously open.

I stood back to let Hans go in first. Then I caught him up, wanting to see his face. This was the first time I had been able to show my handiwork to a man of roughly my own standing, and it gave me great pleasure to watch his expression.

He was gratifyingly astonished. One could hardly have expected to find anything so complex beneath the old wall of the city.

I had built up the laboratory bit by bit in the maze of vaulted passages which made up the cellars. As I could afford it, I added to the basic equipment. There were benches packed with retorts and piping, a Whimshurst electrical generator, and a sequence of tanks linked in a pattern that made the best use of the convoluted passages. Cages for animals lined two rooms in the depths of the cellars. A furnace burned night and day for the disposal of unwanted material after experiments were finished or abandoned. Near the furnace, where an even temperature was maintained, I had recently installed a chimpanzee in a cage; and on the other side, in an alcove, were Werner's sleeping quarters.

I had sent for the dwarf eighteen months ago. He had grown fretful over the delay, and as I was afraid that in his impatience he might say something rash, I decided to install him in Carlsbruck. He was a good keeper of the catacombs: they were not so very different from the cells of the prison, but were considerably more comfortable, and once he had carried out the various tasks which I assigned to him he was his own master. He followed all my experiments with unwavering concentration. I thought it best to take him into my confidence on every stage, since only in this way would he realize just what a long process his own transformation must inevitably be. The assembly of a perfect new body for him was not easy. I had access to material only from the Workhouse Hospital, and this was rarely in good condition. I found it necessary to discard dozens of items about which I had at first been optimistic. An apparently perfect skull would prove to have some bone defect when I got down to detailed examination. A pair of arms, transported with great difficulty and caution from the mortuary to this underground laboratory, might seem ideal when I started preparing them for a graft, but then begin to rot before I could subject them to preservation treatment.

Now, however, we were drawing close to the time when I felt the important stages of the experiment could be undertaken. I had planned to carry it through on my own, but it would simplify matters considerably if I had the assistance of a man such as Hans Kleve.

His reception from Werner was far from cordial. When I said, 'This is Doctor Hans Kleve – he is to work with us,' the dwarf edged round me and muttered, 'Do we really need him?'

'Yes,' I said firmly. 'Doctor Kleve has presented himself at just the right time.'

The dwarf scowled past me. He was very worried. He was as reluctant as I had so far been to share our secret with anyone else.

Hans said: 'The doctor trusts me; I hope you will, too.'

Werner looked at me. I nodded. He forced a smile, and then, as Hans held out a hand to him, the smile became more natural.

'Good,' I said briskly.

'My name is Werner,' said the dwarf in a precise little voice, as though to draw attention to the fact that I had made no formal introduction. 'Karl Werner.'

'I hope we shall work well together, Karl,' said Hans Kleve.

In all the time I had known him I had not contemplated addressing the dwarf as Karl. I realized that Hans belonged to a younger generation. There were not all that many years between us – but enough to result in a slackening of the conventions.

I mockingly made a formal introduction on behalf of Otto, the chimpanzee, and then turned back to the dwarf.

'You collected the parcel?'

'Over here, Doctor.'

He indicated the side table which I had set up just inside the door. A bundle of sacking had been placed on a surgical dish. A dark stain seeped through, and blood was coagulating in the dish. Werner unwrapped the bundle as we watched, to reveal an arm decorated with tattoo marks.

Hans gulped. 'Isn't that the arm of the man in the workhouse – the one you were examining this morning?'

'It is indeed,' I confirmed. 'I gather that while on land he is a pickpocket. To be a member of that profession you need sensitive fingers. They will be useful to me.'

I moved to another bench and beckoned Hans to follow me. He stood respectfully at my left side and studied the complicated jungle of wires, battery jars, and piping which I had built up.

'What is it, sir?'

'A brain,' I said. As he looked incredulous, I reached towards the glass tank at the end of the bench, covered with a dark cloth. 'Let me demonstrate.' When the cloth was removed, it was to reveal a woman's hand floating in clear liquid. The woman had been a difficult patient, but was difficult no more: a secondary infection had set in, and she had not long survived the operation. Now her hand, severed at the wrist, was connected to a network of flexible tubes and wires.

'If you burn your hand in a flame,' I said, 'what makes you snatch it away?'

'The nerves,' he said like an obedient pupil.

'Exactly. The nerves of the hands send a message to the brain, and the brain activates the muscles for withdrawing the hand. But you don't put your hand too near a fire if you see it first. The eyes recognize fire as a harmful agent before there is any need for the nerves to respond.'

I took him with me to the other end of the bench, and removed the cover from a second tank. Two eyeballs floated on the surface, linked with the first tank through a system of artificial nerves.

'The brain,' I said. 'Observe.'

I left Hans there while I went to start the Whimshurst machine. It rumbled into life with a crackle and shower of sparks. Then I took a taper and carried it to one of the wall niches where an oil lamp burned. I lit the taper from the lamp and, shading it from the draught with one hand, bore it carefully towards the first tank.

I said: 'Watch the eyes.'

I moved the taper towards the hand floating in the tank. From the tank along the bench, the eyes swung to watch the flame. When it approached the side of the tank containing the hand, the hand began to react: it tried to force itself to the far side of the tank, its fingers clenching and twisting. I brought the taper closer. The hand writhed and splashed about the tank in a frenzy. When I brought the taper even closer, so that it almost touched the edge of the tank, the hand went wild and tried to clamber up the far side.

Then I blew out the flame. The hand relaxed and floated gently in the liquid. I went back to the noisy machine, and the electric hum and splutter died away.

'Fascinating, isn't it?'

Hans was staring at the two disembodied eyes as though they were capable of exerting some hypnotic effect on him. 'This is... a brain?'

'All this paraphernalia,' I said, 'and capable of only one simple reaction. Can you imagine the complexity of the human brain? One-tenth the size of all this, and a million times more efficient. It controls every action and reaction, it stores memories, it motivates all life. And this' – I waved towards the tubes and pipes and wires – 'is all I have been able to achieve so far.'

'You should be proud,' said Hans, awed. 'I've never seen anything like it.'

I did not suppose that he would have done. Crude as it was, my contrivance represented an advance on anything that had ever been achieved by other scientists.

I took him farther into my subterranean laboratory. He should see all there was to be seen, and comprehend the tasks that lay ahead. Karl Werner shuffled behind us, his doubts returning as I went to the curtained recess in the farthest cellar and prepared to draw back the curtain.

I said: 'You know that Frankenstein was condemned to death?'

'Yes.'

'You know what for?'

Hans looked uncomfortable. 'It was said that he murdered a girl who had been his mistress.'

'And his defence?'

'You… that is, *he* claimed to have created a being which went berserk.'

'It should have been perfect,' I said. 'I made it to be perfect. If the brain hadn't been damaged, my work would have been hailed as the greatest scientific achievement of all time. Frankenstein would then have been accepted as one of the world's great geniuses instead of branded as a murderer. But I shall have my revenge – the satisfaction of making fools of them all.' I jerked back the curtain. 'This is something I am proud of.'

Set in the recess was a vertical glass tank some fourteen feet high, containing the pale green fluid which I had developed after more than a thousand tests. Suspended in the liquid was the body of a man over six feet in height. Physically he was perfect. I had made sure of that. The lower part of the body from the waist down was still swathed in bandages, while skin and muscle knit more firmly. The upper part was bare. The top of the skull was also bandaged to protect the cavity within until I could lower a suitable brain into position – the brain which had been chosen long ago. At present the face, smooth and without blemish, was utterly devoid of expression.

As the figure rotated gently in the fluid, the arms moved slightly and the head tilted so that the blank, benign face appeared to stare down at the rapt Hans.

'Who is he?' whispered Hans, as though the creature might overhear.

'Nobody,' I said. 'He isn't born yet. But this time he's perfect, except for a few small scars which will soon heal.'

'He's not… alive?'

'Not yet.'

He went closer – to the tank and looked in. I could tell that he was studying the very fine seams round the wrists.

'You made this body from other bodies?'

'My voluntary work at the hospital serves me well,' I said. 'All that is lacking now is the brain. Then I can give it life.'

I sauntered away. Hans followed me slowly, with several backward glances at the large torso that swung gently, lazily in the tank.

'You've seen the result of this' – I indicated the artificial brain which sprawled over so much space – 'and it's by no means my first attempt. I keep this cumbersome thing only to remind me of the impossibility of the task should I think of trying again. No… the brain must be a living one. Unlike the limbs, it is impossible to restore life to the brain once it has been harmed. I learned that – learned it bitterly – years ago. The brain is life… and so a living brain must be used to control that body.'

'That would mean committing murder!'

'Not necessarily,' I said. 'I have a volunteer.' I smiled at Hans, whose head must by now be in a whirl. 'He's here,' I said, 'in the laboratory.'

He was taken aback. Instinctively he moved away from me.

I burst out laughing. 'No, Hans, not you. Your brain is too valuable where it is.' I waved towards the dwarf, who was crouched down by the chimpanzee's cage making friendly noises which made the animal dance happily up and down. 'There he is.'

'Karl Werner?'

I explained the bargain that we had made. The dwarf had saved me from the scaffold, and in return I was committed to finding a new body for him.

'But surely,' said Hans in an undertone, 'that paralysis of his indicates an injury to the brain?'

'I've examined him thoroughly. The paralysis is due to a blood clot. This can be dispersed during the operation. I can't reshape his deformed body – but I can make sure that when the trouble has been cleared his brain will be able to function normally in a normal body. He has a fine brain. He's intelligent… quick… and he has absorbed a great deal of knowledge since working with me. Haven't you… Karl?'

He smiled, and nodded at Hans. 'Doctor Stein is welcome to my brain, so long as he rids me of this.' He struck his sunken chest contemptuously.

'You must have great faith in Doctor Stein,' said Hans.

'I have.'

The dwarf went back to his game with the chimpanzee.

'Are you sure it can be done?' Hans asked me softly.

'The operation,' I assured him, 'will be a complete success.'

4

I WAS NOT unaccustomed to receiving beautiful young women in my consulting room, but when Margaret Conrad was shown in I had to acknowledge that I was face to face with a woman of singular character and attractiveness. She had clear grey eyes which were at the same time kind and ruthless: she had a mind of her own, and in spite of her youth she had made up this mind on most of the important principles of life. Her faintly olive skin spoke of a southern ancestry, but those eyes and her firm mouth were of the cool, practical north.

I invited her to sit down and asked what ailed her. To be frank, she looked the picture of health. It hardly came as a surprise when she said:

'I'm not a patient, Doctor Stein. There's nothing wrong with me.'

'Then…?'

'I come to offer my services.'

I recoiled from the idea of yet another impressionable young woman volunteering to become one of my disciples.

'I'm afraid I don't understand,' I said.

'Your voluntary work at the Workhouse Hospital interests me. I'm not a trained nurse, but there are many jobs I could do there.'

At least this made a change from the usual plea to be allowed to decorate my fashionable surgery. It still did not appeal to me.

'I don't think you quite appreciate the nature of our work there,' I said, 'or the type of people we have to deal with.'

'I have heard all that is necessary,' she said.

'Hearing it and dealing with it in reality are very different things.'

She quivered with annoyance. I could see that she was easily aroused and that she would be passionate about everything that concerned her – personally or philosophically. What she needed was a strong-willed man to distract her.

She said severely: 'It's time we women ceased being purely ornamental. I am sure I could be very useful, and my aunt tells me you have so very little free time. You must need someone to help you.'

'Your aunt?'

'Countess Barscynska.'

It appeared that I was to be for ever the target of the Countess's plans.

I said: 'You live with her?'

'I am staying for a few weeks, and then I may settle in the district. My parents live in the capital.'

It was time I dealt with my patients. They needed me; and I, for my part, needed their fees to subsidize my life's work.

'I'm sure your aunt can find other good works for you to do,' I said, going to the door and waiting for her to accept this dismissal so that I could open it and usher her out. 'Please pay her my respects.'

Margaret Conrad did not move. 'I shall be at the hospital at nine o'clock tomorrow morning.'

'Miss Conrad, I thought I had made it clear: your services are not required.'

She seemed amused. There was not so much a twinkle as an ironic gleam in those disconcertingly direct eyes. 'You have an exaggerated opinion of your own power,' she said lightly.

'My father is the Minister responsible for all hospitals and asylums. He has agreed that I shall work with you. So you see, Doctor Stein, you have no choice. Nine o'clock, Doctor?'

I could have stood up to this and argued it at great length with the Minister, but I did not wish to jeopardize my position. My secret labours in the underground laboratory were what counted: the rest was only a facade, so what did it matter if some over-eager idealist thrust herself upon me?

I said: 'As you say, Miss Conrad, I have no choice.'

She softened a little. 'I shall not interfere with your work, Doctor. I promise you that.'

She had no way of guessing how true this was. Nor would she ever guess what my real work was.

As it happened, I was not visiting the hospital at all the following day. I dealt with the usual group of patients in the morning and drove out on a round of visits in the early afternoon. Then I lay on my bed for two hours, not sleeping but conserving my energies. This evening was to be an important one, and I did not propose to embark on it even mildly tired as a consequence of the day's exertions.

Hans Kleve had asked if he might spend some time in the hospital and I had seen no reason to demur. It would not increase his popularity with his fellow members of the Medical Council, but this was no cause for lamentation: I could imagine the stirrings of alarm when they discovered that one of their number had, as it were, defected to the enemy. Hans took my place on this day. I imagined that he would be more soothing and sympathetic than I was towards the idlers and degenerates who frequented the workhouse. When his day was ended he went home to change, and then after dark called for me at my surgery.

We had a glass of wine before setting out, and while we drank it he told me of the appearance of Margaret Conrad that morning. It had taken him quite by surprise. I apologized for not notifying him of her impending arrival, but I had really had very little time to do so: she had announced her intentions one day, and put them into effect the next.

'She seems a very determined young lady,' he agreed.

'Get her to wash one of the patients,' I advised. 'That should scare her away.'

He then told me with amusement but also with a certain grudging admiration of her resolves on this first day. She had announced that she intended to read to the sick – which prompted me to remark that she would have difficulty making herself heard in that bedlam. She also wished to buy things which they needed, such as writing paper and soap. Hans had told her that the inmates rarely washed and never wrote.

Apparently she had also met Karl Werner. The dwarf had come in with a message for Hans, who had automatically introduced him. Karl had bobbed a grotesque little bow and Margaret had held out her hand, only to realize too late that the dwarf's warped arm could not make the necessary response. It had been an embarrassing moment, but Hans assured me that the young woman had covered it with a warm, sympathetic smile. 'Karl was quite taken with her,' he observed. I was not surprised by this. The dwarf's consciousness of his own ugly frame had, if anything, intensified his appreciation of true beauty when he saw it. Margaret Conrad would have attracted any healthy man; her effect on the dwarf must have been considerable.

When we had finished our drinks I fetched my cloak.

'Ready?'

'I'm ready,' Hans said eagerly.

Tonight we were going to give Karl Werner his new body. The dwarf would disappear and never be seen again.

We made our way quickly through the darkened streets.

Somebody somewhere was singing a plaintive chorale, and in the upper room of a shabby house a man and woman were screaming abuse at each other. Doubtless the customary uproar prevailed in the Workhouse Hospital; and in the fashionable salons of my wealthier patients there would be the usual, shrill, meaningless chatter. It was all remote now. Everything but the task which lay ahead was insignificant to me.

When we entered the cellar, Karl had already removed the cover from the tank. The body floated gently in its sustaining fluid. The wrists were completely healed. As soon as we had been admitted, the dwarf went back to contemplating the body that was soon to be his.

I hung up my cloak and indicated that Hans should do the same. I began to take surgical instruments from the stock which I had built up over these last few years. As I laid them on a clean cloth, I caught an apprehensive glance from the dwarf.

Hans put a sympathetic hand on Karl's shoulder and directed his attention away from the gleaming instruments and back towards the tank.

'Keep looking at him, Karl. In a few hours that will be you.'

Leaving the dwarf, he came to help me with my preparations.

We moved two benches into the centre of the main cellar and cleared them of every scrap of equipment. On each bench I spread a cloth which had been scrubbed white. Then Hans and I climbed up beside the tank and carefully lifted out the dripping body. As Karl watched, willing us not to drop or damage it, we laid it on one of the benches.

Against the wall was a wooden frame on which the dwarf and I had worked for months. He jumped readily to my assistance as I manoeuvred it into position. We then spent a good hour assembling the network of wires and terminals for which the frame had been constructed.

Finally I was ready.

The body lay on one bench. I looked at the other bench, and then at Karl Werner. He stared back at me steadily. He was pale but unfaltering. I nodded once, and like a well-trained animal he scrambled on to the empty bench and stretched himself out to his full length – which was paltry enough.

Hans stood over him and soaked a pad in chloroform. He smiled down encouragingly. The dwarf summoned up an answering grin. Then Hans pressed the pad over his mouth and nostrils.

I waited until Hans had checked the dwarf's breathing and his pulse. Then he stood back without a word.

I selected a scalpel and bent over the still, sleeping head. I had planned the exact incisions so long and had gone over every movement so meticulously in theory that I was able to work swiftly and without hesitation. It was simple and speedy. In a matter of minutes Hans was holding out a jar of fluid into which I gently dropped the brain. It floated for a moment, then sank slowly to the bottom like a bulbous, fissured creature of the sea.

When I had watched Hans place the jar safely to one side, I returned to the mindless body of the dwarf. I bound up the head to prevent the steady drip of blood, and then injected embalming fluid into the veins. The flawed body would be an engrossing study when I could find time to spare.

Together we turned our attention to the business of wiring the framework to the inert body which was to be Karl Werner's. When the main connections had been made I lowered the brain into place and, under the most intense light we could achieve with our limited resources, devoted myself for what seemed an age to the minuscule operation of establishing the nerve connections and fibres.

It was early morning before we were able to enclose the head in a thick band of brass, padded on the inside, with terminals set in at two-inch intervals.

I started up the Whimshurst machine. Energy began to pulse through the wires, dinning in the very walls of the cellars. If it had not been that I had thoroughly tested the equipment at full pressure before committing myself to the further construction of this laboratory, I would have feared that the noise would have brought the authorities down upon us.

After a while, with my watch laid on the bench before me, I signalled to Hans to slow the spinning, flashing wheel down to half speed and keep it there. Then I turned my full attention to the body on the bench.

It was beginning to twitch. Life pulsed into it rhythmically, inexorably. One hand started to beat out a steady tempo on the bench – and then closed, opened again, groped convulsively at the air as though in pain, and pushed itself up like a mad creature dragging the arm after it.

Suddenly the hand grabbed at one of the overhead wires and pulled it down in a shower of crackling sparks.

The body writhed in pain.

'Turn it off!' I yelled at Hans. He slammed the control down, and the machine whined to a halt. I waved him towards the bench. 'Anaesthetic!'

To make way for him, I touched one of the wires with the intention of moving it away from the head. A shock jolted through me. I drew on gloves and managed to clear a space near the head so that Hans could stoop over it with the anaesthetic pad.

The convulsions in the body subsided. When it was quite still I put my ear to the heart and listened.

It was all right. My creation was still alive.

We set to work to clean up the laboratory. I tested the machinery again and established that it was safe. Karl's new body slept peacefully on the bench. Calm settled upon the cellars. The job had been done. There was nothing to do now but wait. Hans helped me to clean my instruments and put them tidily away. Every now and then he glanced at the prone figure.

'How long before he shows any signs of animation?'

'An hour or so,' I said. 'When he regains consciousness, his brain will take some time to adjust itself to his new body. He must have complete rest, and avoid any abrupt or violent movement. As a precaution I shall keep him strapped down for a few days.'

'It was a superb operation, Doctor,' said Hans with heart-warming respect in his voice.

I bowed my thanks. This was only the beginning of our work together, and I felt that I had chosen a worthy assistant – though it was rather a case, I thought ruefully, of his choosing me.

The chimpanzee began to chatter in his corner. We had forgotten all about him for many hours now. Feeding him had been one of Karl's duties, but Karl would not be in a position to carry this out for some time. I took some raw meat on a dish from the store cupboard and fed it in to Otto, who pounced greedily on it.

Otto himself had played a not inconsiderable part in the developments which led up to my final creation of a man. For my first experiment with a live brain I had used reptiles. I removed the brain from a lizard and replaced it with that of a frog. The lizard attempted to jump but this, of course, was physically impossible. It would have been interesting to see whether in the fullness of time it was able to adapt to this; but such a line of research was not my immediate concern. My theory had been proved: the brain continued its normal function regardless of its environment. Eventually I used anthropoids, and gave Otto the brain of an orangutan. The success of the transplanting gave me the courage to go on. Not only was I able to avoid the mistakes that had almost resulted in my death after my first experiments in my home: my dexterity had improved over the years, and I did not see how anything could go wrong this time.

I turned back to Hans.

'We can't leave our new friend here. I want to keep him under constant observation, and I really can't make the journey out here several times a day. We must get him to the hospital. There's an attic room we can use.'

'Won't that be dangerous?'

'I'll ensure that nobody can get in.'

'I was thinking of *him*,' said Hans. 'So soon after the operation...'

'We'll take good care of him.'

Hans, on my instructions, rode swiftly to a nearby private hospital in which I frequently installed some of my wealthier patients. He harnessed a horse to the ambulance and brought it rattling through the streets to the city gate. We transferred Karl on a stretcher from the laboratory to the ambulance, and drove off before the watchman on his rounds could grow too inquisitive.

On one corner a loose cobblestone threw the vehicle to one side and I had difficulty in steadying the stretcher. Hans drove as carefully as possible, but the streets of Carlsbruck had not been designed for the smooth transport of delicate mechanisms – which is what, in his present state, the new Karl Werner was.

I was thankful when we reached the Workhouse Hospital. Dawn was already a chalky smear in the eastern sky. The city would soon be awakening.

We carried Karl in through a side entrance and up a little-used flight of stone steps. Manipulating the stretcher round some of the corners was no simple task. We were breathing hard when we attained the top and laid the stretcher down in a cramped room with one narrow bed against the wall.

Gently we lifted Karl onto the bed. I went down to fetch straps with which to secure him. A bout of coughing came from the ward, and there were the usual moans of protest. As I hastened back to the top of the building I thought I detected a flicker of movement at the end of a corridor, as though someone was watching; but when I paused and waited, there was no repetition. I was tired and my nerves were on edge.

We fastened Karl to the bed so that he could not tear himself free. He might be alarmed when he woke, but I intended to spend as much time with him as I could spare from my routine duties, and would soon set his mind at rest.

Karl had not stirred. We were about to leave him when, without warning, he opened his eyes and stared at the ceiling. Then a stab of pain twisted his face. He let out a wild scream.

I went down beside the bed and gripped his shoulder.

'It's all right,' I said. 'Karl – it's all right.'

He moaned and tried to turn, but the bonds held him fast.

'Gently, Karl,' I went on in a low, soothing tone. 'Relax. You're quite safe. Soon you'll be comfortable. Sleep, Karl… sleep.'

His eyes flickered and then shut again. I waited until I was sure that he would not cry out again. He was bound to have some pain at this stage. I hoped I could keep it to a minimum. But whatever happened, in the end it would surely be worth it.

Hans and I left the hospital as surreptitiously as we had come, and went out into the brightening dawn.

5

ALL THE week I succeeded in maintaining a balance between my medical practice, my work in the hospital, and the constant care which Karl required. Now I was more than ever thankful for Hans Kleve. He took some of the weight from me, particularly in the hospital. I will not say that he did this entirely for scientific or humanitarian reasons: he was by no means indifferent to the presence of Margaret Conrad, and brought her name into the conversation whenever it was possible to do so – as he thought – plausibly. Whatever his motives, however, I welcomed his assistance. If he chose to dally in the grim corridors now and then with Margaret, I had no objections to raise.

By the end of the first week I was able to remove the last bandage from Karl's head. He had suffered great pain and his face had sunk slightly, but once he was on his feet and eating properly it would fill out again quickly enough. The only thing that worried me was his slowness in mastering the use of his vocal chords. I had anticipated some small delay and perhaps a certain amount of incoherence at first, but with nothing to do all day but lie on his back I would have expected a more satisfactory attempt than he seemed capable of making.

Also, each time that I came to give him treatment and encourage him, his eyes showed abject fear rather than gratitude. This could only be attributed to the constant pain. When this slackened, he would be a more rational being.

I was patient with him, trying to coax him on.

'Can you hear me, Karl?'

Ten times a day I started thus. And each time he gurgled in his throat and then, wretchedly, gave up and nodded.

'You're making wonderful progress,' I assured him.

When he strained against the straps I explained how essential they were. In his sleep, or in a moment of itching discomfort, he might move unwisely, and our good work would be undone. At the end of all such explanations he nodded again, but in resignation rather than cheerful acceptance.

I kept his diet severely restricted. It was even necessary to teach him to swallow, and often he dribbled like an infant.

Nevertheless I reiterated that he was making great progress. 'We'll soon have you leading a normal life,' I promised him; and when I persisted, he tried to summon up a pathetic smile.

When there was a lull downstairs, Hans hastened to join me. He was anxious to be present at every crucial stage. I had to assure him that I would fetch him when there was any significant development.

After the first few days, when I realized that Karl's progress was likely to be slower than we had first envisaged, I laid down a programme. While he remained strapped to the bed we would concentrate on speech and on study of his eyes. Hans gave him a regular massage, but I forbade any ambitious movement of the limbs until the time was ripe. When the moment came for the tests on movement, I told Hans to adjust his work in the hospital accordingly.

Karl stared up at the two of us as I unfastened the straps on his left arm.

'Give it a few moments at rest,' I said. 'And while we're waiting, Hans, let's have another look at the eyes.'

Hans had a small mirror with him. He reflected a ray of sunlight into Karl's left eye.

'Now the right,' I said. When Hans obeyed, the reaction of the pupils was good.

Then I gently massaged the left arm. 'Now, Karl – try to move your arm.' I raised my own arm slowly to demonstrate. 'Your left arm.'

Karl raised his arm in the air with very little effort.

'Good!' said Hans. 'Good!'

'Now the right,' I said.

He obeyed when I had loosened the straps, but not quite so well. I had not allowed sufficient time, perhaps, and not given him the requisite massage. But there was very little wrong with him. As I bent over and fastened the straps again, I said: 'Congratulations. At this rate you'll soon be up.'

A glumness settled on him as he was once more bound to the bed. I had work to do in the hospital – I could not entirely neglect my duties there – but I thought it unwise to leave him too abruptly. I suggested that Hans should stay and talk to him for a while, and Hans was only too pleased to do this.

'Except for the movement of the right hand,' I said quietly as we stood together at the door, 'his reactions arc excellent. Even better than I had expected – though it has taken longer than I planned. Don't overtax him, but keep his mind active. We must take it in turns from now on: I want to keep him cheerful and occupied. Talk to him. Keep a record of his progress. When he shows signs of fatigue, you know what to do. Send for me at once if you need me – and when I'm here with him, I'll do the same. We must compare notes every time without fail.'

I left Hans in the room. Perhaps that was a mistake. The first mistake, from which other troubles inevitably flowed. I was trying to do too much; if I had paused to reflect, I would have known better than to take such risks.

Looking back, I see now what went wrong. From various sources I can piece together those events which took place in my absence. And that is where I blundered: I ought not to have been absent. Instead of keeping up a façade of continuing my work in the hospital I would have done better to abandon it at once. There would have been talk, of course – speculation about my motives, criticism of my callousness, and all the titillating gossip which buzzes about the heads of the unorthodox. But what would that have mattered? My work had been purely voluntary, and I could abandon it as arbitrarily as I had taken it up. My real work was the creation of life. I should have clung to that instead of trying to keep up the pattern that I had established over the last three years. I should have been with the new Karl Werner every hour of the day and night, watching over him and not allowing him to be subjected to other influences.

First there was Hans Kleve. Then, in her own way, Margaret Conrad did her share of damage. I was not to know this at the time. Only later did the fragments fall into place.

It might please the susceptible young Hans to see Margaret bustling about the place on her self-appointed tasks. To me the sight gave less pleasure. The girl seemed to be perpetually under my feet. Her manner was respectful and she was quick to obey any order I snapped at her, but her very presence disturbed me. She was too intelligent, too observant: I did not suppose her father, the Minister, had placed her here as a spy, but I felt that if she did chance upon any irregularities she would not hesitate to fall back upon his influence.

Some of the patients resented her presence. Others made up to her and wheedled favours out of her. And the walking patient who acted as messenger and general busybody made a special point of ingratiating himself. He had a craving for tobacco and was continually devising new ruses for getting more than the reasonable allowance which Margaret doled out.

One day in the ward I was trying to concentrate on a man

with a badly torn ear when Margaret and this little wretch began one of their affectedly bantering conversations only a few feet away.

'Soap and tobacco?' she was saying.

'Can I take it all in tobacco, miss?'

'No soap?'

'Never touch it!'

They sniggered together as though they were old friends. I felt that her aunt, the Countess, would hardly approve of this familiarity.

I said: 'Miss Conrad.'

'Yes, Doctor?'

'I must ask you to keep out of the ward when I'm on duty. Treatment is more important than charity.'

She seemed to be framing a retort, then thought better of it and went out into the corridor.

The walking patient turned slyly away and leaned on a broom which had been propped against the wall. It was the most practical use to which I had ever seen the lazy wretch put it.

'Haven't you anything to do?' I demanded.

He started and glanced round. 'Yes, sir.'

'Do it, then.'

He went out by the same door. He must have found Margaret waiting outside, for when I moved across the aisle to another bed I heard him say: 'Cuts 'em up alive, he does! *Alive*!'

Margaret laughed sceptically, and then their voices drifted away. I should have left the ward and followed them. I am sure that this must have been the time when the resentful little man told Margaret what he knew. He was a born spy, a creature of dark corners and grubby curiosity – and he knew what I had wanted to hide from everyone… that there was a most unusual patient in the attic room. This I discovered later: too late.

As far as I can gather, what happened was that the patient fed Margaret with sinister hints until her scepticism turned to doubt and then to the desire to settle the matter to her own satisfaction. It was not her concern, but she could not refrain from meddling. Women are meddlers by instinct. The legend of the inquisitive wife in Bluebeard's castle had its roots in firm reality.

Her informant was able to provide Margaret with the master key. He was also able to wheedle some extra tobacco from her, which was all he really cared about. And so the result of my magnificent experiment hung on the cravings of a degenerate.

He gleefully led her up to the attic and showed her the door. Then he gave her the keys and left her to let herself in, as though by going away at this juncture he could somehow absolve himself from all responsibility.

There are things I shall never know. The exact words of the conversation which Margaret had with Karl Werner are lost, but it is not difficult to reconstruct the general outline of the scene. Margaret's sympathetic manner would have been given full scope. I believe Karl recognized her from the day of her first appearance in the hospital and, in his slow, painful, guttural voice addressed her as Miss Conrad – a recognition which must have baffled her, since she had never seen this man before.

I can visualize her smoothing his pillow and asking him questions to which she would get only fragmentary answers. She probably chatted to him just as she did to the other patients, but in spite of his present impediment she could hardly have failed to realize that he was more intelligent than most of the inmates.

What I know for certain is that she wrote down her home address for him so that he could get in touch with her when he was well, and that when he complained about the straps holding him down she loosened them for him.

At this time both Hans and I were finishing off our routine chores and preparing to leave for my laboratory. There was Otto to be fed, and I had other experiments on which we might now spend a little time. So far as Karl was concerned, all that was required now was patience. By the time we were ready to show him to the world I hoped to be well advanced on other researches.

Hans watched me feeding Otto and, after a brief silence, asked:

'Did Otto eat flesh before you operated?'

'No. I discovered it soon after the operation. He ate his wife.'

'Ate another monkey?'

'What else would he be married to?'

'Do you mean he turned into a cannibal?' The thought seemed to distress Hans.

'Yes. I didn't attempt to correct it. He had been through enough already, and he's perfectly happy and in good health.'

'But suppose… I mean… could the same thing happen to Karl?'

'There's no fear of that,' I assured him. 'So long as his brain is given time to heal and develop its functions gradually. Otto became agitated after his operation. He fractured one of the cells in the brain.'

'Does Karl know about what happened to Otto?'

'He does. It's just as well. He will take no unnecessary risks. Besides, with a less primitive brain than Otto's he can evaluate problems more skilfully. No, I have no fears about Karl.'

In retrospect that might appear as a vainglorious boast, the pride that goes before a fall. Yet I maintain that I was right. The troubles that were brewing were neither Karl's fault nor mine: they were the responsibility of fools and dabblers.

From this distance in time it is as difficult to reconstruct the exact sequence of events as it was to reconstruct the body of a human being, to assemble the torso and limbs and head so that it all made sense. Difficult… but not impossible.

Hans and I stayed on in the laboratory until after nightfall. In this time, Karl had freed himself from the loosened straps and crawled out of bed. I thus missed a crucial stage of his reorientation. It was essential that I should be present to study the working of his limbs, to see how he stood up, how competently he could dress himself in the clothes which we had provided against this day, and how well he carried himself. But I was not present. I do not know to this day what discoveries he made about himself or what strain he put on his nerves and reflexes.

He must have been in good control of his new body, whatever the tensions. He was able to escape through the attic window and make his way over the rooftops. His co-ordination was adequate, if no more. His sense of direction left nothing to be desired: he must have made his way straight to the laboratory, and indeed probably arrived just as Hans and I were leaving.

Once Karl had been removed to the hospital I had decided to appoint a trustworthy janitor. There was now nothing to conceal from him or, for that matter, from anybody else. All traces of our work on Karl had been destroyed in the furnace apart from the dwarf's original body, which was embalmed and locked away in the farthest cellar. The laboratory was situated in an odd place, but if that was to my taste there was no one likely to raise suspicions. The janitor, a surly brute who would do exactly what he was told and no more, took his wage and kept his mouth shut. He maintained the furnace fire, which we might need at any time, and renewed the oil in the lamps. Otherwise he stayed out of the cellars and drowsed in a cubby-hole at the head of the stairs.

He must have been asleep when Karl let himself into the laboratory. Karl knew every inch of the way, and still had his duplicate set of keys.

In view of the struggle that followed, it was difficult to establish his actions when he was alone in the cellars that night. I don't know whether he made direct for the discarded body locked in the cupboard or whether he came across it after a long, inquisitive prowl from one vault to another. In any event, he duly opened the door and took the body out. Proud of his new frame and disgusted by his wretched past, he carried the corpse to the furnace, kicked open the furnace door, and hurled it into the flames.

In that furious heat perished what had once been Karl Werner.

The rattle of the furnace door must have attracted the attention of the janitor. Grumpily jerked into wakefulness, he came down the steps to investigate. He found Karl gathering his few possessions into a small bag. The janitor was a large, well-built man, but the new Karl was his equal in weight. At this time, though, he had not fully learned to control his strength, and if the janitor had only known it he could probably have outmanoeuvred and outfought him. As it was, the sight of this stranger in the place, apparently helping himself to anything he chose to carry off, prompted the man to grab a nearby stool and raise it over his head.

Karl, starting up on the defensive, fell against the switch panel, and started the machinery working. They must have fought their desperate battle in the lurid blaze of the wheel, shattering glass as they fought round the laboratory, overturning the animals' cages and driving the chimpanzee into a frenzy. Karl was at a disadvantage. His first impulse was to protect his head, which was still unbearably sensitive where the covering over the brain was healing. The janitor saw his fear and played on it, making wild swings with the stool.

During the course of that struggle Karl must have slipped and fallen, bringing a bench of flasks and retorts down on top of himself. The janitor moved in for the kill – that, at any rate, is how I see the picture. And I see, as the janitor must have done with terror, the growth of a sudden bestial hate in Karl's face. Karl had come here to collect his belongings and run away. I don't know where he would have gone or what he intended; but certainly he was in flight. Now all that was changed. He was a beast of prey.

The rest of the incident was over in less than a minute. Karl flung himself upon the janitor and strangled him.

I wonder if, watching Otto gnawing raw meat in his cage, Karl felt a hideous temptation creeping over him? The janitor lay motionless on the floor. Perhaps this was a moment of decision – and I ought to have been there to help him, to steer him back towards rationality. But even on his own he was strong enough. Whatever had happened to his head during that fall, whatever corrosive madness might now eat into his brain, he still retained the memory of what was right, of what he must and must not do. If only I could have been with him then, all might still have been well: I could have given him moral support and, if necessary, carried out an emergency operation on the brain. But he was alone. Alone and frightened by what he had done.

He fled from the laboratory.

Hans and I had returned to the hospital intending to make our last inspection of the day. As soon as we entered the attic room we saw the empty bed, the loose straps, and the open window.

'But how could he have undone the straps?' I asked Hans icily. 'He was settled down when I left him. What happened before that?'

Hans moistened his lips. 'Nothing.'

'Pull yourself together, man.' The thought of my creation at large in the streets, perhaps incapable of behaving rationally, and drawing first the curiosity and then the dangerous derision of passers-by upon him, drove me into a fury. 'There must have been some reason. What did you do when I had left?'

'I… I talked to him, as you advised. I told him of your plans for the future—'

'What plans?'

'About the people who would come to see him. Doctors and scientists from all over the world. I told him what an important figure he would be.'

The folly of it was breathtaking, I said, as levelly as I could: 'And his old body… you told him about that?'

'I…'

'Did you?'

'Yes,' he confessed dismally. 'I said you would hold student lectures, showing him in his normal body alongside the embalmed old body. I tried to make him feel how wonderful it would be to play such a part in the advancement of medical science.'

'You fool!' I struck Hans across the face and he reeled backwards. 'You blundering fool! Do you know nothing of human reactions? He has been a curiosity all his life, and now you tell him…' The words choked in my throat. I had to find Karl. Where would he have gone? The answer came to both of us at once. Hans, dropping his hand from his reddened, stinging cheek, said:

'The laboratory!'

We hurried back there, but we were too late. The doors were open, the roar of the machinery was audible from the head of the steps, there was chaos in the main cellar… and the dead body of the janitor lay sprawled where Karl had left it.

And the dwarf's body had gone. He had destroyed this last vestige of his old self. He did not intend it to be displayed to the public.

'Suppose his brain was damaged in the fight?' said Hans timorously.

The same thought was in my mind. I had not wanted to utter it aloud.

It was up to us to find Karl Werner before he laid himself open to danger. If he was still in the city he would reveal himself sooner or later. If he behaved at all oddly or fell sick there was a reasonable chance that he would in any case be brought in to the Workhouse Hospital, when I could immediately take him under my wing, and undo the damage that might have been done. My one fear was that he might have left the city for ever and set out across the countryside. There was no telling what impulses activated that brain of his.

I was unable to sleep, and next day I was unable to concentrate on my work. It was futile to institute a search, I realized in the clear light of day, without having some lead. I was on tenterhooks all morning and afternoon, waiting for some word to come in that would tell me where Karl was and what condition he was in. But there was no whisper, no rumour, no strange stories that would alert Hans and I at once.

My creature was loose. I waited for him to strike – or to be struck down. Whatever happened now, there was a terrible chance that all my work might prove to have been tragically wasted.

6

NOT CONTENT with the havoc he had already provoked, Hans Kleve had still further ineptitudes in store. One would have expected him to have learnt his lesson and to have come straight to me at the first intimation of Karl's whereabouts. But that confounded young woman had more influence over him than I did. The misguided young fool listened to her, obeyed her… and did not turn to me until the thing got out of hand.

Thus it was not until two evenings later that we sat in a coach and headed for the Countess Barscynska's home, set in wooded country some miles outside the city. As we rattled along the country lanes, Hans sheepishly told his story.

'It's my fault,' he said a dozen times, as though by admitting the obvious he would somehow make it less heinous. 'I know I'm to blame for this… but I thought it wiser to go myself. When Miss Conrad told me she had promised…'

'You should have come to me at once! These interfering women…' Then I put my head out of the window. 'Can't we go any faster?'

'We're in the park now, sir,' said the coachman as though he considered this sufficient answer. But he did try to lash the horses on, and the coach swayed as we gathered speed.

There were still three miles to go across the rolling parkland. I gritted my teeth and willed the horses to go faster, to annihilate the distance, even though a few minutes here or there could probably make little difference now.

It appeared that after incinerating his old self, Karl Werner had left the laboratory and made straight for the address which Margaret Conrad had given him – her aunt's stately mansion, almost a castle in its lavish pretensions to turrets and confected battlements. He must have spent most of the night getting there, trudging over the fields and at last concealing himself in the stables. There he lay until morning, when Margaret discovered him.

She had come out to feed a new foal with straw – a cloying love for animals was numbered among her many sentimentalities – and was taken aback when, after a rustling in the hay, Karl emerged.

'What are you doing here?'

'I had to get away. You said you would help me.'

'But does Doctor Stein know you have left the hospital?'

'Don't tell him,' Karl cried frantically. 'Please don't tell him.'

She argued with him. At least she had the wit to realize that he was in need of medical attention. But Karl was stubborn. He refused to return to the hospital and he implored Margaret not to tell me where he was hiding. When I heard this from Hans Kleve, I must confess I was deeply hurt. After all I had done for the man, after the months and years I had worked in order to give him a frame of which he could be proud, this was the way he repaid me! One would have thought I had maltreated him. I could only attribute this bitter change in his feelings to the blows he must have received during the struggle in the laboratory.

The impression he created on Margaret was that of a man slightly unhinged. Deciding not to press the issue of his return into my care, she promised that she would be very tactful, but that in return he must promise to stay in the stables until she returned. She would not be long away.

Karl agreed. Margaret went out and told a trustworthy groom that there was a sick man in the stables who should be closely guarded until she had fetched a doctor.

Then, instead of reporting to me as she should have done, she went to Hans.

Hans Kleve's first impulse was to come to me. We might still have salvaged something from the catastrophe if he had done so. Unfortunately, he was too ready to fall under the young woman's spell. Scrupulously observing her promise, she told him that Karl would not return to me. He needed a doctor – but it must not be that Doctor Stein who had slaved so hard on his behalf!

Hans accompanied her back to the Countess's home.

They went straight to the stables. There was no sign of Karl.

Margaret angrily sought out the groom who had been ordered to keep an eye on Karl. The groom denied all responsibility. He couldn't be everywhere at once, could he? He had looked in at the man once or twice, but then he had been ordered to go and water the horses; and when he came back, the man had gone.

One thing which the fellow said, relayed to me by Hans, struck a chill to my heart. Seeing Karl in the stable, he had noticed there was something wrong with his leg. Those were, according to Hans, his very words: 'Something wrong with his leg... his foot seemed to drag, sort of.' This could mean only one thing. Karl was regressing. His fine new body was in danger of being afflicted by the paralysis which had afflicted the old one. Unless I could get to him without delay it might be too late to stop the decline.

It was not until now that Hans realized there was only one person who could cope with the situation. In spite of Margaret's doubts, he announced that he was going to call me in.

And so we drove through the darkening evening towards

that pompous house, its windows ablaze as the Countess made preparations for yet another of her musical parties. If his leg was betraying him, Karl could not have gone far. He might well be hiding in another part of the grounds, or even in the house itself.

Suddenly the coachman called to his horses and reined them in sharply. The coach bumped to a halt.

I looked out. We were still some distance from the house, its lights now masked from us by a windbreak of trees.

'Why have you stopped?' I demanded.

A cluster of torches moved round the coach, and the light fell on the face and uniform of a police officer.

'It's you, Doctor Stein.'

'It is,' I snapped, 'and I'm in a great hurry.'

'Sorry, sir, but we have to check everyone passing this way. There's been a murder in the vicinity.'

A murder... It didn't have to be Karl; it need have no connection with the wretched, fleeing Karl; but I felt a bleak premonition.

The best way to learn all the details was to offer my services. I opened the door of the coach and got down. 'Can I be of any assistance?' And as Hans descended behind me, I quickly introduced him. 'This is Doctor Kleve.'

The police officer welcomed the assistance. 'We'll need a report on the condition of the body. If you wouldn't mind examining it...'

'Certainly.'

'It's over here.'

He led the way to another ring of torches, set like some funeral observance around a dark, crumpled shape on the grass. To one side a young man, little more than a boy, was huddled up, shivering.

'When did this happen?' I asked.

'About an hour ago, so the boy says.'

I suspected that the boy was in a state of shock. But he would have to wait. I knelt down and turned over the body of the girl. My worst fears were realized. It was no good telling myself that it was a coincidence, that there was no evidence of Karl having been involved. This was Karl's handiwork. The savagely torn face, the arm almost wrenched from its socket, the signs of a bestial, ravening attack… these fitted too well with the certainty of Karl's derangement.

Keeping my head down so that my disturbance would not show too clearly, I said:

'Did he – the boy – see who attacked her?'

The boy got to his feet, still trembling. A man supported him with an arm round his waist.

'All I can get out of him, sir,' said the police officer, 'is that he and the girl had quarrelled. He was walking away when she—'

'She screamed,' the boy panted hoarsely. 'I'd gone a good way – I was well away from her, honestly I was – and then I heard her scream.' He put his hands over his ears as though to shut out an appalling echo. 'There was a man there… and I shouted, and he ran off, and when I went to look…'

He swung away from the man beside him, and vomited on the grass.

'If it *was* a man,' said the policeman.

I got to my feet. 'What do you mean?'

'Well, sir, the boy said he looked like some sort of animal.' He recited what the boy had gabbled out to him some minutes ago: '"A funny shape," he said. Of course, he only got a glimpse of him. "Like some sort of animal – all bent over": that's the way he put it.' The officer lowered his voice so that the boy couldn't hear. 'It looks to me as if it was done by a maniac.' He grimaced at the mangled corpse. 'It's no ordinary murder, sir.'

'Have you searched the park?'

'As thoroughly as we could, sir. Not enough men to do it properly in the dark – but I don't think we missed many of the likely places.'

'Well, there's nothing I can do here.' I was anxious to get on to the house and see if we could pick up a clue there. 'I'll let you have the report by the morning.'

'Thank you, sir.' The officer saluted. 'Sorry to have detained you.'

We went back to the coach. As we climbed in, the group closed around the girl's body and lifted it, ready to be taken away.

The coachman drove on. Hans and I sat in a grim silence.

Where was Karl Werner?

Among all the rumours and melodramatic stories which bred in the lurid imaginations of the local people, there were many which were later sifted by the authorities. An assault some twenty miles away was blamed on 'the mad beast', which was how they came to refer to Karl. At the same time of the night a violent robbery in the city was attributed to this same creature, who must have been able to travel like the wind. The only incident which rang true was quiet rather than dramatic. In a gipsy encampment on the fringe of the Countess's estate, a child saw what she described as a crumpled-up man crouching in the bushes. She was used to meeting strange characters and wayfarers of one kind and another, and was not at all afraid of this huddled shape. She asked the man if he was ill, and he gruffly told her to go away. His leg, she said, was twisted, but when she offered to fetch her grandmother to help him with herbs and spells, he growled at her. He got up, and in the uncertain light she swore that she saw tears glinting in his eyes. When she was asked if he had shown any sign of wanting to attack her, she denied it. He had just looked very sad and very twisted, and he had turned and gone off into the undergrowth.

It could only have been desperation that drove him back towards the house.

Lights from the windows were visible across the parkland. I had seen them from the coach at intervals ever since we entered the estate. Every now and then they were obscured by a clump of trees or a fold in the ground, but each time reappeared with an added brightness.

When we stepped down from the coach and hurried up the steps, the sound of music was audible. The footman asked us our names in a whisper, and indicated that we should wait outside the door of the salon until the conclusion of the work that was being played. This was too much for me. I believe I would have flung the door open and stormed in had it not been for Hans, who put his hand on my arm.

'It's a Mozart quartet,' he said. 'The last movement – only a few bars to go.'

The strings produced a final flurry of sound and a chord which could be nothing but the last chord of the work. A spattering of applause rustled through the closed door. The footman, with a deferential bow, opened the door and ushered us through.

A bewhiskered string quartet sat in the centre of the room. The first violinist was just rising to his feet and acknowledging the applause. Even before it had died away the familiar voice of Countess Barscynska rose unmusically in a characteristic declamation.

'I have nothing against the English composers, Doctor Molke. Nothing, I assure you. But they just won't let themselves go.'

Her neighbour was that senior physician who had led the delegation to question me at the Workhouse Hospital. I sensed Hans flinching as he, too, recognized the man. I had an idea that Hans was not in good favour with his one-time colleagues.

But I was not interested in personal problems of this kind. As the footman announced us, I strode towards the Countess.

'Not even Handel?' Molke was saying.

'Ah, but they stole him… from Germany.'

The Countess rose majestically and turned to greet us. The first violinist had once more raised his bow, but she waved him down. She put out her hand to me, and at the same time contrived to signal her daughter, Vera, to move into full view.

'My dear Doctor Stein – so you finally decided to attend one of my musical evenings?'

'Countess—'

'Vera, do come and greet the doctor.'

Vera, becomingly dressed but harassed by the attention that was now turned on her, dropped me a curtsey and went very pink.

'I wish to speak to your niece,' I said brusquely to the Countess.

She shrugged and turned to signal to the quartet that they should continue. They set to with a will on a graceful dance movement that accorded well with the lavish setting but not with the menace that might even now be creeping up out of the night. The very formality of the music was incongruous.

The Countess drew Vera towards her and tried to bring us together, as though implying that we should sit side by side and listen to the quartet.

I said impatiently: 'Your niece…'

'The night is young,' said the Countess, indicating two vacant chairs and then turning to deal with Hans.

I had no time for sterile courtesies. I looked round the room, and saw Margaret Conrad in a far corner with a group of young friends. Ignoring the hapless Vera, I crossed the salon. Margaret saw me coming and prepared to make some remark – some triviality, no doubt, as though the ritual formalities of so-called good manners were all that counted in this world.

Before she could speak, I seized her by the arm and almost dragged her away from the group. There were hisses of reproach from the devout audience near to the quartet. I saw the Countess's outraged face turned in my direction. Hans hurried over to me and put a restraining hand on my arm. I shook it off. But I made an effort to control myself. It would do no good to provoke too much antagonism here; no good to bluster. I wanted clear answers to clear questions.

I said: 'When you found Karl in the stable – was he the same as when you saw him in the hospital?'

'Yes. But he was very distressed.' She stood back and stared at me accusingly. 'He was terrified of you.'

'Is that the last you saw of him?'

'Yes.'

'Are you certain he hasn't returned here?'

'We have been dressing for this evening's music. He could have crept back into the stables without my knowing – but I see no reason why he should have done so. One of the grooms would have brought word, anyway.'

'He didn't talk to you about his plans, if he had any?'

'I think,' she said compassionately, 'that he was in no state to make plans. If he had waited until I brought Hans—'

'But he didn't,' I said.

I turned away. She had been no help to me in the past and she was no help now. I had no idea what to do. I felt no responsibility for Karl's killings – the blame for those rested squarely on the interfering fools who had released him from my influence – but I wanted to put a stop to his depredations. There had to be a lead, a beginning, a clue somewhere.

Behind me I heard Hans murmuring to Margaret: 'Don't blame yourself. You did what you thought was right.'

'Shall I see you again?'

'I hope so.'

Hans came after me. I was tempted to tell him that the young woman had every reason to blame herself, and that what she had done was criminally wrong. But the infatuated ninny was beyond understanding such things.

The Countess was waiting for me. I might need her influence in the future. She was not a good person to quarrel with. I assumed my best medical manner, and treated her to the smile which she so often and so unashamedly sought.

'You must forgive this intrusion.'

For a second it seemed that she might not succumb. Then she favoured me with a weak smile in response.

'You could never intrude, Doctor Stein.'

She was about to wave me once more towards a suitable chair, while the quartet battled assiduously with a fugal passage, but I was determined to go out into the night and force it to yield up its secrets. I felt that Karl would be drawn to me; that somehow he *must* come back, that our destinies were linked, that only I could save him from the torment which was now closing upon him.

I was on my way towards the door when there was a crash of breaking glass. A woman in the audience screamed, another took her up, and the second violin in the quartet went excruciatingly flat. There was a jangle of notes, and then the music petered out.

I turned. Framed in the tall french windows which opened on to the terrace was Karl.

But this was a travesty of the man I had created. The regression was incredible. His right shoulder had sagged and his arm was twisted against his side. He stood awkwardly, resting part of his weight against the window-frame, his leg dragging. What had seemed pathetic in the dwarf now appeared far worse in this taller, better-made man.

He was staring fixedly into the salon. Nobody dared to

move. I followed the direction of his gaze. He was looking at Margaret. She stood there petrified as he lumbered away from the window and came on into the room, groping as though to clutch her to him. Women in his way scrambled from their chairs. He brushed the chairs aside and went on towards Margaret, who still could not move.

I said sharply: 'Karl!'

It halted him. For an instant he looked puzzled, then turned threateningly towards me. But the threat died. A grimace of anguish racked his face. He began to drag his twisted body towards me. His hands scrabbled imploringly at the air. He mouthed vain, incoherent sounds.

Just as I thought he was about to crash into me, he put his head back and bellowed:

'Frankenstein… help me, Frankenstein! Help me!'

Then he pitched forward on the floor at my feet and lay still.

Hans hurried to my side. I bent over Karl and examined him, while a faint, fearful muttering started up in the salon.

I looked at Hans. Neither of us spoke.

Karl was dead.

7

IN THE confusion which followed it was easy for me to assert my authority. With a minimum of explanations I was able to remove the corpse, implying that the episode had been distressing but not in any way dangerous. Hans made a few hasty remarks to the Countess about an escaped patient in need of special treatment, and there were a few murmurs of 'Poor wretch' mingled with the babble of 'What a dreadful evening' and 'I must go home and lie down – it's too terrible'. The only man I really feared was Molke. He bore me no love, and as Hans and I carried the body out to our carriage he tried to pursue.

'Doctor Stein, I must insist…'

We gave him no chance to insist on anything. We took Karl's body to the laboratory and shut ourselves in.

Hans was very disturbed. When I began at once to open up the head so that I could examine the brain, he tried to stop me.

'Doctor Stein, I beg you to listen to me. Get away from here! We must cross the border… start again, somewhere else.'

'There's no hurry.'

'But everyone heard Karl call you Frankenstein. Molke was there.'

'I'm aware of that, but—'

'He'll report to the Medical Council. They are bound to take action! You know how they feel about you – this is the chance they have been waiting for.'

I was not to be persuaded into taking panic measures. There was nothing that anyone could prove against me. My patients would surely stand by me. My record since I had been in Carlsbruck was impeccable. I had only to stand firm and go on as before. I would deny any ill-founded accusations brought against me. It was unthinkable that my career should be wrecked by the last ravings of a demented patient.

I said: 'I shall be at the surgery in the morning at my usual time.'

But when Hans looked dubiously at Karl's body I had to admit with regret that it would be better not to expose it to examination by Medical Council busybodies. It hurt me to destroy it, but I had had setbacks before and could stand up to yet another.

We thrust Karl Werner into the furnace, and the new body of which he had hoped so much went the same way as his old, warped body.

In the morning I was in my surgery as I had promised.

I was alone. Nobody came. The fashionable ladies, I thought dourly, must be so ill after last night's events that they could not even drag themselves along to my consulting room.

When I heard the click of the outer door I went out to see which faithful patient had come to talk over her latest ailment. But it was not a patient. It was Hans.

He said: 'Your waiting room is deserted.'

'I had already observed that.'

'The whole town knows who you are! Everybody's talking. I have been summoned before the Medical Council. What am I to say?'

The poor boy was out of his depth. I saw that without my guidance he would be utterly unable to cope with what was happening. I said:

'I'll come with you.'

'That would be madness. Let me do what I can. Just give me some idea of what to say.'

'It would be madness for me to hide,' I said, taking up my hat and cloak. 'What can they prove? Let the world see that I am not cowering in the shadows.'

He was almost more frightened by my presence than he would have been if left to face the questioning alone.

The Medical Council conducted the proceedings with all the archaic pomposity I would have expected. We were treated like young upstarts presenting ourselves for a preliminary oral examination – seated in stiff-backed chairs facing a long table at which elderly, bald and grey-bearded pedants nodded in what they believed to be a sagacious manner. Their opinions were beneath contempt; their accusations ill-founded and too hastily prepared.

Thinking that he was showing a forthright courage, the president himself solemnly asked me if I was indeed Baron Frankenstein.

I denied it.

The old fool must have believed that I would crumple at his feet, sobbing with tears of repentance. My bland denial left him with his mouth open, bewildered.

He asked why the name had been hurled at me by the man who blundered into the Countess's salon. I said that I could not imagine. The patient was subject to delusions: there appeared to be no other explanation. So far as I was concerned the whole thing was absurd.

The president tried to resume his lofty manner. 'You deny your name is Frankenstein?'

'Have you ever consulted the street directory, sir?'

'Street directory?' he mumbled.

'If Carlsbruck is still so backward as to have no official publication of this kind,' I said, 'there are doubtless civic records to which you could have access. And other towns in Central Europe – all have *some* record of their citizens.'

'I do not see what bearing—'

'There are dozens of Frankensteins,' I said. 'I am *a* Frankenstein. That I do not deny. Of course I have heard about the Baron whose name has acquired so many legends. Disturbing legends – not the kind of thing a medical practitioner would wish to have associated with him. Naturally, I didn't wish to set up in practice here handicapped by such a name, so I changed it.'

'But the uncanny resemblance…'

'Who claims to have detected such a resemblance?' I asked.

'Two of the ladies who were present last night had a fleeting acquaintance with the Frankenstein family in the old days.'

'A fleeting acquaintance!' I echoed scornfully. 'And in the old days. And there was no word of this until last night, was there? Strange how so much supposed evidence can be fomented in such a short time.'

Emboldened by the way things were going, Hans came to my aid. 'It's a monstrous accusation,' he cried, 'inspired by jealousy.'

A council member at the far end of the table stood up as though to take over from the bumbling president.

'Baron Frankenstein—'

'Doctor Stein,' I corrected him.

He hesitated, then said grudgingly: 'Doctor Stein… how do you explain that wretched fellow calling you Frankenstein?'

'I cannot even be sure that he was doing so,' I said. 'They were his dying words. It was a last outcry – very probably it was not addressed to me at all but to some dying vision. The man had heard the legends, just as you gentlemen seem to have done, and in the confusion of his mind he may have felt that this Frankenstein would in some miraculous way come to his assistance. A very common phenomenon, as I'm sure my colleagues will agree.'

I looked along the line of disapproving faces. One or two of them had the grace to lower their eyes.

It was time to conclude this farce. I said: 'I think a little proof, Mr President, would be more compelling than a lot of gossip. And as there can be no such proof, we are simply wasting time. My own time happens to be valuable.' I turned to Hans. 'I shall see you later, at the hospital, Doctor Kleve?'

Hans gulped and nodded.

'One moment.' The president tried to get round the table to detain me, but as it was so long he had to make a wide circuit, puffing as he did so. By that time I was at the door.

I said: 'Forgive me. I am a busy man.'

'We have not finished.'

'No? But what more is there to say? We all know that Baron Frankenstein was executed. I think that might be regarded as a truly conclusive finish. Good day, gentlemen.'

I left them to their petty squabbles and debates.

The Medical Council would undoubtedly do all they could to make life even more difficult for me from now on. They would not scruple to spread rumours about me even though they had been unable, in my presence, to substantiate any of those rumours. Professional bodies have behaved thus from time immemorial when confronted by a man of independent mind, and there is little likelihood that they will ever change. But gradually the persecution would abate. My patients would. come back to me. I had nothing to fear.

I went straight from the Medical Council assembly to the Workhouse Hospital. My work lay in ruins, but I would rebuild.

There was an unusual hush in the hospital that day. I was conscious of it the second I entered the building. It was as though it were waiting, hardly daring to breathe.

Margaret Conrad had not put in an appearance. This amused me. Apparently the gallant young lady was, after all, a little too squeamish when faced with some of the more stern realities.

The little messenger was halfway along the corridor towards my office when I showed myself. He stopped and backed away. He gave a nervous little snigger.

'Three of 'em gone,' he said.

'What are you prattling about?'

'Three patients upped and left in the night,' he said. 'Weren't going to wait here to be cut up in little pieces – that's what they told me.'

I went on towards the ward. He scuttled ahead of me, keeping a good distance between us. As a rule he would hold the door open for me, bowing and scraping absurdly, but today he let it swing shut.

When I opened the door for myself and strode in, there was utter silence.

I knew most of the faces in here – though in most cases my concern was with other parts of the anatomy rather than faces. The sullen expressions, the fear, the dejection… all were familiar to me. But today there was a change. It did not strike me until I was standing over the first bed, about to make a routine examination. Then I looked round.

They were all watching me. And not one of them was making a sound. There were no bawdy jokes and no groans of terrified anticipation.

Not a sound…

In every face there seemed to be a uniform viciousness which I had not seen before.

I tried to dismiss this impression as I turned back to the first patient. The threatening attitude of the Medical Council must have upset me more than I cared to admit. When I had had a good rest and got over the disappointment of Karl Werner's regression, I would see things in proper perspective.

'How's the head today, Klein?'

I reached out to start undoing the bandages round the man's head, but he jerked away.

'Don't lay your filthy hands on me.'

I could hardly believe my ears. None of them ever dared to speak to me like this. Some of them might grumble, some might plead with me not to operate or not to carry on a certain line of treatment; but defiance of this kind was unheard of.

'Don't be a fool, man,' I said crisply. 'I've got to look at it.'

This time he struck out and knocked my arm aside.

'You heard me. Keep your murdering hands off me... Frankenstein.'

There was still no sound from the rest of the ward, but I sensed a quivering tension. Something was about to snap. I must stay very calm, making it clear that I was still in control of the situation. They would regret this.

'Yes, that's what I said.' Klein was hysterical with his own braveness. 'Frankenstein... fugitive from the gallows... murderer.'

'Murderer,' said a whisper round the ward.

'Murderer,' he yelled at me. 'Mutilator...!'

I turned away. I did not propose to waste time; on this wretch until he was in a more sober frame of mind.

At this moment a bottle flew past my ear and shattered against the wall behind me. As I swung in the direction from which it had come, another one struck my right shoulder a glancing blow and fell on to one of the beds.

I raised my arms to protect myself, and stumbled out into the aisle between the beds, where there was room to move.

Two of the patients nearest the door scrambled out of bed and blocked my way.

Behind me somebody laughed madly.

The wave of vindictiveness that swept through the ward was a physical, pulsating thing. There had been silence: suddenly there was uproar. Screams like those of the damned beat upon me from all sides, and every patient capable of movement was lurching, hobbling, crawling towards me.

One noisome creature, unable to rise from his hands and knees, clawed at my ankles. I kicked out. There was a howl of pain which was taken up by a dozen throats and transformed into a howl of rage.

Then they were upon me. Their claws tore at me. I tried to shield my head, but they tore my hands away and gouged fiendishly at my eyes, ripped flesh from my cheeks with their broken, filthy talons, and spat on me. Pain robbed me of breath. I tried to flinch away as they hammered me down to the floor and kicked me, but there was nowhere to go, nowhere to roll: their feet drove in from every side, into my ribs and my bowels and the side of my head. I tried to cry out, but a noisome fist was thrust into my mouth.

And all the time they howled. Like ravening beasts they shrieked and bellowed triumphantly. Blood ran into my eyes. I could struggle no longer. But even when I had given up all attempt to shield myself from the rain of blows, they kept coming until there was no pain in the impact of each kick or scratch – only one great red, obscene pain raging through my mangled body and screaming in my brain.

I was dead. I was sure that it was over, for the voices began to fade and a numbness crept through the pulpy rawness of my flesh.

From a great, great distance I heard a squeaky voice saying, 'They're killing him in there,' and then Margaret Conrad's voice mixed up inextricably with that of Hans Kleve.

Pain came back when someone tried to lift me. All that prevented me from crying out in agony was lack of strength:

I could not make a sound. It was all over. Beneath the pain, through the bloodshot horror that made thought impossible, there was somehow one little part of me that remained detached and clinical. I was a doctor, I knew what the pain meant and what the growing numbness meant. The brutal messages through my nerves and then their final surrender, their inability to transmit any more pain and any more feeling of any kind… all this spoke of death.

I must have been unconscious for some time. When I became aware of voices again and of faint sensation again, I knew that I was lying on a bench. I tried to move, but nothing would function.

'… the end,' someone was saying. It was an accusation, reaching me through a buzzing sound that would not stop. I strained to hear, but my concentration was defective. There was no meaning in anything. 'The end of a fantastic scheme. The death of the man he talked of benefiting… and now this.'

A woman. Yes, the young woman. Margaret Conrad. Still meddling. I didn't want her here. I wanted her to go away before she caused further damage. But I could not speak. I tried to produce some sound that would tell her I was here, still alive, and that I wanted her to leave at once. But I could not produce even the guttural noises that my recreated Karl Werner had struggled with in his early hours.

'Don't you see?' – she was urging something on someone, demanding agreement – 'Don't you see…?' And through the haze, through the barrier of distortion in my ears, I heard her say: 'Wicked…'

'To transform a dwarf into a normal man – is that so wicked, Miss Conrad?'

I thought it was myself speaking and knew it couldn't be. And then I knew that it was Hans. He spoke clearly and firmly. I wanted to take his hand. He, at least, was still undaunted. He was not to be turned against me.

There was an unexpected sensation of coolness seeping down from my forehead. I tried to open my eyes; but they were not closed. A blurred shape moved over me. I could not bring it into focus.

Then the coolness touched my eyes. For a moment it was excruciating. Then the cool water wiped away the sticky mess from my eyes and from around my nostrils. Hans stood over me, gently dabbing with a moistened towel. When he saw that my eyes were open and that I was trying to keep him steadily in view, he smiled. It was meant to be a professional, reassuring smile; but the poor lad was not very accomplished in such things.

I had to speak. My body and mind cried out for release, pleading that I should let go, slip away… but I had to talk to Hans.

'Try to relax,' he said.

'Hans…'

'Don't talk.'

'It's no good, Hans,' I said. The effort was more extreme than I could ever have conceived. Each word was a huge stone to be hauled up a precipice.

Hans bent over me. A good pupil, he was feeling my pulse, listening to my breathing. And it was no good.

I said: 'Send her away.'

He hesitated, then turned towards where the young woman must be standing. I did not hear a door close, did not hear footsteps; but with some new intuition, some raw exposure of my nerves, I sensed that Margaret Conrad had gone.

I said: 'Hans… you know what to do.'

He stared. His face swam back into the haze that was already creeping in again from all sides. I had very little time left. Desperately I tried to make him understand.

'You know,' I forced it out again. 'You know what to do.'

His face was lost now, but I could still hear his voice.

'You mean…?'

'Everything… is there. The laboratory it's yours… Work… Tell me, Hans… you can…'

It was too much now. I surrendered. I let go and felt a great peace as I slid gently down into the darkness. A last, lingering thought ran round my head like the drowsy piping of a bird at nightfall. Had he understood? And if he had understood, would he have the courage and the technical ability to carry out the long, arduous process?

My fate was in his hands. There was nothing more I could do – nothing but die… and wait.

8

When they came to confront me with the proof which I had tauntingly demanded from the President of the Medical Council, they were too late. Molke, determined to wipe out the insult which he considered I had offered him, had persuaded the authorities to investigate the grave of Baron Frankenstein. The coffin was brought up in great secrecy behind screens – with, on top of it, the crumpled remains of what had been the greedy Fritz. This must have been a shock to the gravediggers and the watching officials; but it was only the first shock. Beneath Fritz were the priest's hat and his rosary, and all that was left of the priest who had so obligingly taken my place.

The president was jubilant. He and his retinue hurried back to Carlsbruck, and the police at once set out to arrest me.

All they found was a corpse beneath a sheet. Hans Kleve sadly lifted the sheet so that they could see what a terrible state the body was in. He explained that the patients at the hospital had gone mad and practically torn Doctor Stein to pieces. Stein… or Frankenstein: it was all one now.

The body was taken away and buried in unhallowed ground. It did not occur to these zealous gentlemen to examine my bruised and battered frame too closely. The terrible beating I had had about the head made a far from pretty sight even in the eyes of experienced medical men, and they were prepared to accept that I was dead. Nobody could have survived with his head so smashed in. There was no reason why they should want to operate on that head and examine the brain.

Which was just as well, since the brain was no longer in it.

Orders were given for the laboratory to be dismantled, but as there was no urgency in this the process dragged on long enough for Hans to remove certain essential items. These included various pieces of equipment whose use the Medical Council reactionaries would not have understood, certain carefully preserved limbs – among them a tattooed arm – and above all a jar full of liquid in which floated a brain. Hans treated this with the utmost care. He had made some serious mistakes in the past, but now he worked to eradicate them.

The task to which he bent all his energies took rather more than a year. He suffered many setbacks and at one stage was near to abandoning the whole thing. I knew none of this. Time passed, but for me there was no time. For me, there had been the pain and then the descent into nothingness. And then I was awake once more. I might have done no more than close my eyes and open them again.

There was still pain, but it was a different order of pain. I suffered internally for many weeks as flesh knit and came to life again. But this I could endure: I knew what was happening, and by not fighting against it I was able to help it along. Hans needed to give me no instructions. I laid down for myself a strict programme of carefully graduated movements. Today I would concentrate on my fingers, tomorrow on gentle exercises with my arms; next week I would walk, and the month after that I would go out into the world and adjust myself to the milieu in which I must now function.

It came as a surprise to me to find what a distance Hans had put between us and Carlsbruck. We were in England. The name of Frankenstein was scarcely known here, and even if someone were to arrive in London from the Continent with grisly stories, there would never be any danger of recognition. The Frankenstein features were gone. The body which I now inhabited could be claimed by no one and recognized by no one, since it was an assembly of so many different items. Hans had done a splendid job. There were one or two minor adjustments I might wish to make to myself in due course, but they could wait. On the whole I was satisfied with my new self.

And as time has gone on, I have remained satisfied. The pains abated, the stiffness and awkwardness of limbs to whose balance I had to adjust soon wore off, and my brain was as clear and efficient as it had always been.

When I looked at myself in a glass this morning, I could detect only the faintest white line of a scar across the forehead. Sometimes my patients have looked at that scar – with curiosity and the admiration which is always aroused by mystery. It has done me no harm: rather the reverse, in fact. Once more the ladies flock to my consulting room. Once more I receive invitations to those musical evenings which seem as common here as they were in my own country.'

But this is my own country now. I am Doctor Frank, a distinguished European physician who has chosen to make London his home. My voice retains enough of an accent to enchant the wealthy ladies. My practice grows more and more prosperous. My valued assistant, Hans, takes some of the weight off my shoulders, and between us we plan great things. I have amassed enough capital to buy the mews stables adjoining those in which I keep my coach. When the doors have been strengthened against prying neighbours and some new equipment installed piece by piece, there are some interesting experiments which we are eager to carry out.

Two of my elderly patients have not long to live. One of them has promised to leave me a small amount of money in her will.

But it is not her money I want. She does not know it, but she is going to donate to me something more valuable than money.

I am impatient to be at work in the laboratory once more…

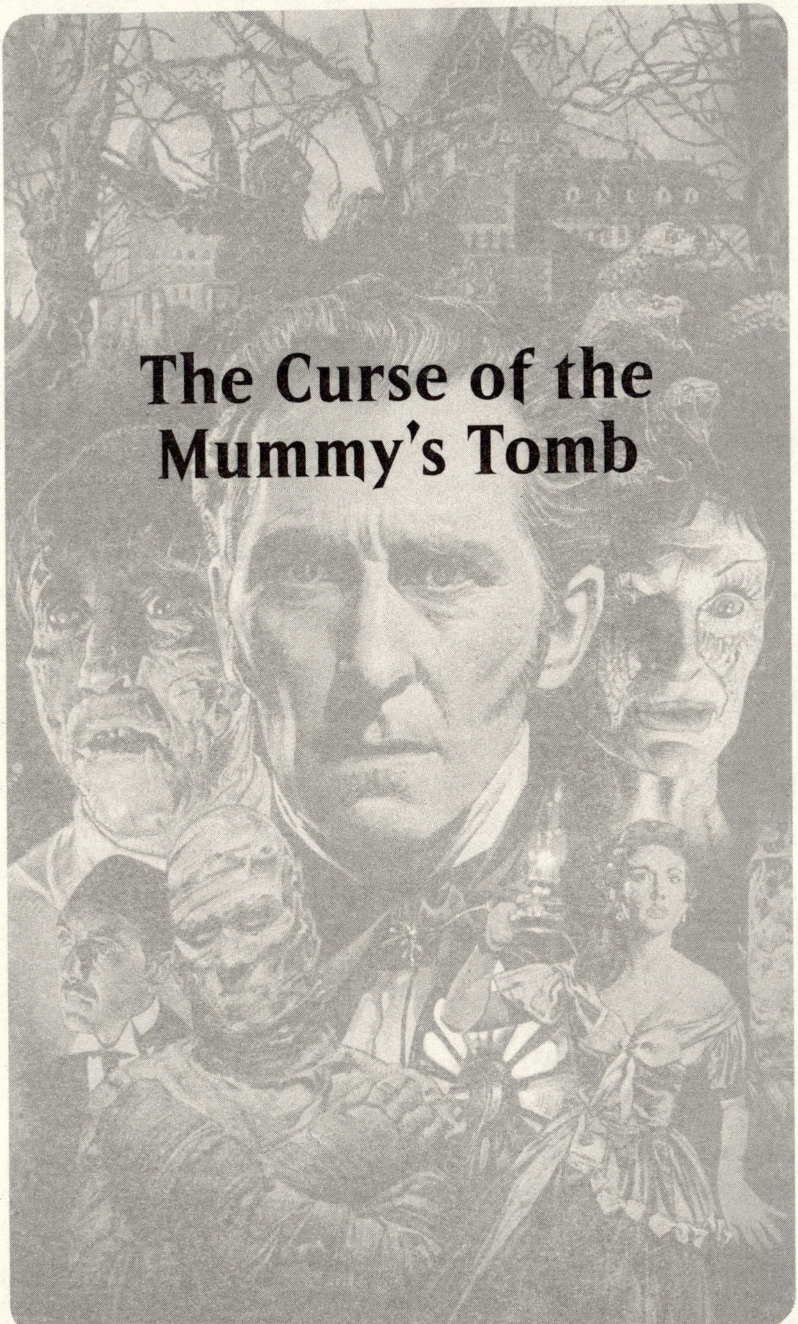
The Curse of the
Mummy's Tomb

1

THEY RODE down upon him out of the desert before he heard even the faintest whisper of their coming. He was crouched over a heap of pottery shards, trying to identify enough of a pattern to make reassembly possible, when a flurry of sand was kicked into his face. Dubois looked up indignantly.

Three Bedouin horsemen had reined in and were staring down at him. Behind him, the three porters who had been working for Dubois closed in without a word. Their silence was a threat. Professor Dubois did not take it too seriously, but as he got to his feet he wondered what demand was going to be made on him. A story about starving families would probably be the next thing, followed by a whining plea for increased wages. The porters were always grumbling, sometimes fawning, sometimes aggressive. Now that they had him on his own he feared they were likely to be aggressive.

'What do you want?' he asked.

There was no reply. The porters ran suddenly round behind him and pinioned his arms behind his back. As he tried to shout a protest, a dark hand struck him across the mouth. He was dragged to the post which marked the corner of the new diggings planned for the following week, and lashed to it.

One of the Bedouins dismounted and drew a knife. Dubois stared incredulously. This could not be real: he had worked with these people, respected their ways, brought them employment and the chance to learn many things about their own history…

The Bedouin stroked Dubois' face with the knife. The touch of the steel made him shiver. The others saw this and laughed savagely. And then the knife swept back, gleamed for a moment in the sun, and plunged into Dubois' stomach.

Dubois choked and sagged forward. He tried to scream, but could produce only a sickening, gagging sound. He was hardly aware of the porter taking his right hand and pulling it out, away from his body. The Bedouin raised his knife again. It no longer gleamed: it was dark with blood. In one swift, forceful movement he chopped off Dubois' hand, watching with grim approval as it fell to the sand.

2

THE KING expedition of 1900 had encountered few difficulties when it first set to work in Egypt. Financed by the wealthy American, Alexander King, and headed by the two greatest Egyptologists which France and England could provide, it had both the wealth and prestige needed to overcome official and personal objections. The French grave robbers and speculators of 1897 had left behind them the ruins of plundered Abydos and the seed of hostility towards all profiteering Europeans. But Flinders Petrie had done something to restore the good name of serious archaeology, and whatever might be thought of the brash, exuberant Alexander King, the reputations of Professor Pierre Dubois and Sir Giles Dalrymple opened the way to the Valley of the Kings. Sceptical observers might suggest renaming it 'The Valley of Alexander King', but while they scoffed and sneered the devoted archaeologists applied themselves to the delicate, careful work of excavating lost tombs and scrupulously recording what they found. Dubois and Dalrymple were not interested in amassing spoils to be sold to the highest bidder or presented as a matter of national pride to some greedy museum. They wanted to fill in the gaps in the world's knowledge of the pharaohs. They sought to find missing links in the dynastic succession. The mummies of many kings and princes of ancient Egypt had disappeared over the centuries, destroyed by vandals; but there must still be many which had simply not been discovered.

King Sekhemre Shedtaui and his consort had been desecrated by grave robbers – but did this also mean that the great Ra Antef, missing from his rightful resting-place in the Valley of the Kings, had long ago been destroyed? Where was Tuthmosis the Fourth, and where the boy king, Tutankhamen? The arduous work of establishing the complicated chronology and of searching for the tombs which would confirm their theories would have worn down lesser men. Under that searing sun, in the parched air that preserved pyramids and inscriptions but could destroy men from another country, only a fanatic would have persevered. But Dubois and Dalrymple were fanatics, and glad to be so. Their life was the study of death and its trappings.

Dubois had as assistant his daughter Annette. Sir Giles took with him John Bray, an eager young man from Cambridge. They endured the intermittent presence of Alexander King with a good grace: he had provided the money, and even if it was hard to treat him with respect it was possible to show gratitude. Fortunately, the climate was too much for the American most of the time. His visits were brief and he was usually glad to return to the comforts of Cairo, leaving the archaeologists to dig and sift, to record and speculate, to brood over the tiniest fragment of potsherd or the chipped remains of what might be a significant inscription.

After ten months of intensive work, the discovery of one small stone step, overlooked by searchers and plunderers for countless generations, led the team to believe that they had found a small burial chamber. It was only as excavations continued that they realized this was no minor discovery. This was not a shallow grave of pre-dynastic times, nor was it the mound of some minor princeling. The deeper they went, the more they uncovered. After six days of unremitting effort, they stood on the threshold of a huge tomb. Below them was the first great door – portals to the past. By the door stood the dog-headed Anubis, patron of embalming and guardian of the tomb.

When they opened the door and went in, the dust of lost centuries filled the air. It was heavy and slumberous, seeming to contain the textures and echoes of a vanished civilization. It clung to the clothes and hair of the intruders and cloyed in their nostrils, as if to lull them into a stupor, to take from them all desire to proceed farther.

But they went on.

At an inner door stood the cat-headed Bubastis, and beyond it a rich collection of grave furniture – the wardrobe and personal belongings of a prince. There were statues of his god, weapons, grain, sumptuous clothing, and jewellery; and set against the farthest wall was the magnificently ornate sarcophagus bearing upon it the moulded likeness of the body which it contained. The painted eyes stared sightlessly yet with terrifying wisdom upon those who had dared to venture into this sanctuary. Around the sarcophagus were set unguent jars and papyrus boat models. All was ready for the dead ruler when he entered the next world.

The intruders were awed by the splendour of what lay before them. They were scholars and accustomed to relating solid objects to the intangible pattern of history; they were overjoyed by the profusion of material now presented to them; but at the same time they were overwhelmed by the sheer emotional weight and dignity of the long-dead ruler. The objects would be catalogued and explained, the hieroglyphics translated – and yet when all the facts and data were added together, they would somehow not amount to the awesome completeness of this burial chamber.

From a dark corner the gilded head of a vulture gleamed on the arm of a chair. There were treasures everywhere – in the corners, on the walls, heaped lavishly on the floor. No comparable find had been made since the days when Bonaparte marched into Egypt and commanded that the doors of the past should be flung open.

Dubois and Dalrymple soon recovered from their first stupefaction. They set to work reconstructing a period of history from the evidence which the earth had yielded up to them. Their academic interest soon dulled the first holy fear which the tomb had provoked.

But Annette Dubois never quite got over those earlier sensations. Standing behind her father when the inner door was opened, she had felt an almost irresistible urge to turn and run. It was as though someone were about to speak – and she did not want to hear the words. A terrible danger lay within, and it was imperative that they should turn their backs on it while there was still time. Her father's training was too strong: Annette did not turn away, but waited as light filtered in where no light had been for more than three thousand years… waited as it fell on the proud mask of the man who had planned to be left here in peace for all eternity. Later she trembled at the recollection. The smell of the place and the clogging dust of the place and the appalling dead silence of the place would remain with her for the rest of her life. It was as though all those who entered the burial chamber had contracted a mortal disease for which there would never be a cure.

Annette was frightened, and went on being frightened. The normal routine of excavation and cataloguing did not absorb her as it absorbed the others. She felt herself shrivelling in the merciless sun. The sun or the mummy's vengeful spirit would turn her to powder, blow her away into the shifting sands of the desert. She pleaded with her father to abandon this site, and saw how disappointed he was in her. Always he had relied on her, treating her as a dependable, clear-headed disciple.

Now she had shown herself to be a typical, unbalanced woman. He brusquely arranged that she should spend as little time as possible at the diggings. Instead, she stayed in the rock caves where they had set up their headquarters and kept all their records: Annette made herself useful as a clerk, sorting out innumerable sheets of notes into coherence and deciphering the scrawled jottings of her father and Sir Giles Dalrymple.

Even though she contributed little to the work on the site itself, the fear remained with her. It was with her that evening in the cave when her father failed to return from the diggings.

Oil lamps shed a warm glow through the cavern. The curtains at the entrance were still: there was no breeze, no sound from the arid expanse of rock and sand outside. This could have been a romantic setting. She had thought of it as romantic when they arrived, but now it was inhospitable and sinister.

John Bray had been washing the grime of the day from his arms and legs. As he came back from the rear of the cave, Annette looked up at him and asked the question which she had already asked too many times.

'What time is it now?'

His freckled, sun-tanned face puckered into a grin of protest. With an exaggerated sigh he took out a large gold pocket watch. 'It's exactly ten minutes since the last time.'

'I'm sorry.' But it was unlike her father to stay on the site after dark. She would not be at ease until he reappeared.

'Perhaps he's found something of special interest,' said John reassuringly.

'That Canopic jar' – she tried to accept his attempt – 'he was going to reassemble. He must have got lost in the work.'

'Darling, I meant something of real interest – such as a beautiful desert maiden.'

Annette forced a smile. 'The only maiden my father is likely to meet would be mummified and at least three thousand years old.'

'Hm.' John nodded. 'I suppose that would be too old even for your father.'

Annette let herself laugh. She wanted to laugh. She wanted everything to be light and pleasurable again.

'That's better,' said John. 'Can I get you a drink?'

Without waiting for an answer he went to the locked cupboard which Sir Giles had installed against one ragged wall of the cave. Dalrymple never travelled without what he called his medicine chest. The lock was his own invention, proof even against the most skilled grave robbers.

'Are you trying to get me drunk?' asked Annette.

John looked round at the stark floor and walls. 'Not here. Not tonight. But I will once we get back to Paris.'

Watching his shadow leaping grotesquely up a wall, and then watching John himself come back towards her with a glass of wine, Annette thought abstractedly that when they got back to Paris, she might well let him. In the twelve months during which they had worked together, making their plans in Europe and then setting to work here, it had somehow come to be taken for granted that they belonged together. If John married her, she knew that her father would be pleased. And Sir Giles would certainly nod a benign blessing on the marriage. John, she trusted, would like it.

And for herself…?

John stooped over her, gave her the glass, and kissed her. Yes, she was very fond of John. They liked the same jokes and the same kind of life. He was dependable, he was creative, he was stimulating to be with; and one day he would be famous in that field of activity which, with her upbringing, she had always regarded as the most important of all.

If her heart sank ever so slightly, dipping just fractionally before she gained control of herself, it was at the prospect of all those years to come which would be the same as the year just gone – digging in gruelling heat, unearthing things best left where they had been hidden, dealing with suspicious natives and uncooperative authorities. Until now she had enjoyed the challenge as much as the others had done. But now some intuition warned her that they had reached a turning point.

Outside the wind rose suddenly and unexpectedly. It brought with it a chatter of Arab voices. They were silenced by the snap of a command in Sir Giles Dalrymple's familiar bluff tone. A moment later the curtain was twitched aside and Sir Giles came in.

He was a plump man who seemed unable to shed even an ounce of his considerable weight even after weeks in the blazing sun. His crisp, curt voice did not go well with his rubicund, almost babyish face. One expected him to squeak; instead, he spoke with military precision. It made him sound cruder and more forceful than he really was. It carried him and his colleagues through many difficulties and apparent impasses. Only when he was actually working on a dig did his basic gentleness come through: then, utterly absorbed, he would sift through sand in search of the minutest fragment of archaeological evidence, and handle everything he touched as though afraid of its dissolving into dust.

Now he looked stern and very tired. His expression heralded some disaster. Annette knew it. She was on her feet before he could reach her.

'Annette, 'my dear…'

'My father,' she said. 'Where is he?'

Sir Giles stood aside. Hashmi, the dark, lean representative of the Egyptian government, who had been with them since the start of their operations, followed him into the cave and held back the curtain. Two stretcher-bearers entered. Annette could not see the face of the body which they carried between them. She did not need to see. She had known all along – in the depths of her had been waiting for just this.

The two men advanced into the middle of the cave and then, as though at a prearranged signal, dropped the stretcher. The covering fell away from the face of Professor Dubois. His mouth was twisted in a grimace of agony that could now never be wiped away. His sightless eyes stared up at the roof.

John Bray gasped. Annette, dazed, felt him brush past her, and then he struck the first stretcher-bearer so violently that the bony little man stumbled backwards and fell to the ground.

'John!' Sir Giles caught his arm.

'He did that deliberately. The leader – I saw him. He meant to drop it… contemptuously.'

Hashmi stepped forward. 'You must be wrong, Mr Bray. It is not our way to be disrespectful to the dead.'

'I know all about your ways,' said John furiously. 'We have had quite a demonstration of them in recent months. The stealing of our stores… inciting our labour force to desert us… Oh, yes' – the anger bubbled out of him – 'you were grateful at first. We had money to spend, and you were happy to get your hands on it. But then we found the tomb of Ra Antef. You took one look inside and decided you wanted it for yourselves. And now…' He obscured Annette's father from her view. He was staring down at the dead face. 'This is what you've done to Professor Dubois. You're trying to frighten us away from here, aren't you?'

'How dare you make such accusations! My government and I have given you every possible co-operation.'

'You've given us no—'

'Gentlemen, gentlemen,' intervened Sir Giles mildly but firmly. 'This is no way to hallow the memory of Professor Dubois.'

He indicated to the porters that they should pick up the stretcher again. Glancing nervously at John, they obeyed, and carried it on into one of the smaller chambers behind the cave. Annette watched it go. All the strength had fled from her limbs. She wanted to follow, to touch her father and tell him to wake up, not to lie there still and mute; but she could not move.

Hashmi said: 'I demand that you withdraw—'

'We'll strike camp tomorrow,' said Sir Giles decisively. 'We are returning to Cairo.'

Hashmi swung away from John, incredulous. 'But your work here is not yet finished.'

'For the safety of the treasures and ourselves, we'll complete the tabulations in the city.'

John snorted. 'It seems that your tactics have worked after all, Hashmi. Now we fold our tents and run away.'

Hashmi's eyes seemed to recede into impenetrable shadow. The flame of the oil lamp on a bench close to him swayed slightly, and runnels of darkness coursed down his sombre features. He said in an undertone that murmured its way into the far, echoing corners of the cave:

'You cannot run away. There is no escape from the curse of the mummy's tomb.'

Annette felt a chill clutch at her heart. Knowing how her father would have derided the mere idea, she had not ventured to say anything about the old legends of the pharaohs who had sealed their tombs not with wax or metal but with an undying curse. But she had sensed the power of that incantation from the very moment of entering the tomb.

'Don't talk nonsense, Hashmi.'

'We are doomed to die.' Hashmi lowered his head and for a moment might have been rapt in prayer. 'I, too – for I have transgressed with you. We are doomed to die for our acts of desecration.'

'If you believe you can pull the wool over my eyes with these old legends—'

'It is not wool that obscures your eyes, Mr Bray, but a lack of vision.'

With a shaking hand Sir Giles opened his cupboard. He poured himself a stiff brandy and gulped it down.

John said slowly: 'The tomb of Ra holds no curses, Hashmi. There are only the bones and the belongings of an ancient prince. Good can come of this discovery, but not evil.'

Annette found herself moving towards the chamber in which her father's body had been laid. The two porters came out and edged round the wall, keeping a good distance between themselves and John Bray.

Annette went in and bent over the bed on which her father had been stretched out.

Then she screamed.

One arm lay by his side, the hand limp. The other arm was at an angle across his body, terminating in a torn, bloody stump. And beside the corpse on the bed was the severed hand with a knife an inch away, caked with blood.

Sir Giles was suddenly behind her, supporting her as she swayed backwards. John hurried in and stood between her and the horror on the bed.

He said: 'The sooner we're away from here, the better.'

3

ALL THAT week they worked feverishly, recording and checking, drawing diagrams of the burial chamber and meticulously marking every treasure that was removed. It would never be said by future scholars that the King Expedition had been slovenly and unscientific at any stage of its excavations. Crates were brought in from Cairo. Hashmi, almost as disturbed as the Europeans by the fate which had befallen Professor Dubois, rode to and fro making arrangements with the government and with the Cairo Museum authorities. John still regarded him with deep suspicion, but was forced to admit that Hashmi was working unflaggingly on their behalf. Perhaps it was simply that the sly, mistrustful Egyptian wanted to see the back of them: he was making the way home smooth for them.

On one of his trips back to the diggings he brought with him two elderly savants from the museum who grumbled at the way in which they had been hustled into making this journey, and then ceased to grumble when they saw what the expedition had brought to the light of day. The immediate result was an offer of seventy thousand pounds from the museum for the treasures of Ra Antef. This would pay all the costs of the expedition and leave a considerable profit for its members.

Sir Giles was delighted. John shared his enthusiasm, but pointed out that the final decision – and the proportions of the shareout – must be left to Alexander King.

'You will persuade Mr King that this is fair, yes?' pleaded Hashmi. 'Then the treasures will remain here, in our own country.'

'I think it is only proper that they should be displayed in your museum,' Sir Giles agreed.

Hashmi sighed with relief. 'Perhaps if it is done so, the curse will be alleviated.'

Sir Giles tactfully made no reply to this. John was tempted to attack this absurdity once more and try to find the real motives behind it, but a warning frown from the older man silenced him.

In the last couple of days there was, in any case, little time for argument. They needed all the willing help they could get to have each precious item crated and labelled. Working their way across the main chamber, taking the treasures out piece by piece, they were at last left only with the lavish sarcophagus itself. They had not dared to carry it out until now: it required all the strength of their porters, and these men could not be allowed to trample across the floor until it had been thoroughly searched for the tiniest relic of grave furniture.

Now the sarcophagus containing the mummified prince was lifted and manoeuvred up the passage to the outside world. Once Ra Antef had lived and feasted under this blazing sun; had hunted the wild geese and, as carvings on his great chair showed, had fished in the Nile and reclined in his barge while musicians played and sang to him. He had been laid in earth, on his way to the feasting and singing of another world; but now he emerged once more, still and resplendent, into the burning intensity of his old world.

Sir Giles supervised the lowering of the sarcophagus into the crate which was ready for it. Sweat streamed down his face. They were nearly at an end and so far there had been no accidents. It was unthinkable that this last and most precious object should be damaged.

John stood with his arm around Annette, some feet up the

slope of the valley, from where he could watch the other end of the crate.

'Steady!' Sir Giles was urging the porters. 'Hassan, your end down…'

There was the creak and scrape of jarring woodwork.

'All clear at your end, John?'

'All clear.'

'Gently, now…'

It was done. The porters began to shriek with laughter, proud that the job was over.

'Well, that's the last. I never thought we'd do it in the time.' John looked down at the sheets of paper he had been carrying. He released Annette, took out a pencil, and added a final tick to the inventory. 'Annette, put these somewhere safe, will you?'

She took the papers gravely from him. Her face was sad and unresponsive. He would be glad when they could take her away from here. He had suggested that she should go on ahead of them, but she had refused to leave until work was completed. She hated the place and all its associations, but she was her father's daughter and could not leave a job unfinished. She worked grimly, without pleasure, and without even the interest she had shown in the earlier stages. Somehow she had closed in on herself. He longed for the time when he could persuade her to venture out again, to smile and relax in his company, to be the Annette he was going to marry.

Sir Giles went round the crate, patting it affectionately as though it were some favourite pet animal, and puffed up the slope. He looked, thought John, five years younger. His mission was accomplished: the tension was slackening already, just as John wished it would slacken in Annette.

'We've made archaeological history,' said Sir Giles. 'We won't be forgotten, my boy. Never! The museum will have the completest collection of royal grave furniture so far discovered, and the finest mummified specimen in history.' He stared down at the crate: he might almost have been able to peer through the wood into the gilded splendour within. 'It's a triumph – for you, for me, for all mankind.'

A dark figure crossed the entrance to the tomb and came up towards them.

'Hashmi,' murmured John. 'I wonder what little schemes he has now.'

'I think you wrong him.' Sir Giles waved and went down to meet Hashmi halfway. 'We're just going to celebrate, Hashmi. Come and join us. Your government must be very pleased with you.'

'Perhaps they'll pay for the champagne,' observed John dourly.

Hashmi looked at the two Englishmen with what seemed a glint of mockery in his dark, secretive eyes: a mockery mingled with some indefinable apprehension.

He said: 'Before you become too full of high spirits, you have a visitor – your benefactor, Mr Alexander King.'

John suppressed a groan. He glanced at Sir Giles, who blandly said: 'Well, this is a surprise! But only fitting that he should be here to join us.'

'He's in the office.'

When they first established their headquarters in the caves, the phrase 'the office' had been a joke; but now it had become so familiar that it had lost all facetiousness and was soberly used even by Hashmi.

They walked towards the rock face and the mouth of the largest cave.

Annette, carrying the papers which John had given her, was already on her way. They saw her go in. Two minutes later they followed her, to find Alexander King booming and laughing in his usual effusive way.

King was a man who liked to be liked. John suspected that if ever he realized someone disliked him he would be immediately vicious. His desire that everything should go the way he wanted it to go was the greedy desire of a child: at the slightest hitch he grew petulant and looked round for someone to blame. But when people and things behaved as he thought they should, he was bluff and generous and back-slapping.

'A little present for you,' he was saying to Annette, quite unaware of her withdrawn, despondent mood. 'A present from Constantinople. Didn't know I'd been there and back while, you were playing with your buckets and spades, did you? Look…

Turkish candy. Try a bit. I want your opinion.'

Annette automatically took a piece. As Sir Giles entered the cave, King swung towards him, beaming.

'And you, Sir Giles. Good to see you. Here – try some.'

Sir Giles took a piece, chewed on it, and nodded. 'Er… yes. Delightful.'

'That's it. Turkish Delight.' King laughed. Then he looked from one to the other. 'How are things going?'

Hashmi was suddenly very still. He appeared not to be listening, but John knew that he was taut with concentration. Sir Giles said: 'I have some splendid news for you, Mr King. As you're the financial backer of the expedition, I'm sure you'll be pleased. Hashmi Bey has obtained a very handsome offer from the Cairo Museum for all our discoveries – more than enough to defray all our expenses and to show… ah… a good return on the investment, if I may put it that way.'

'How handsome is handsome?'

'For the complete contents of the tomb of Ra,' said Sir Giles, 'seventy thousand pounds.'

King's laugh struck a harsh resonance from the dark recesses of the cave. 'Seventy thousand pounds? Seventy thousand? You must be out of your mind.'

Sir Giles stiffened. He was not used to dealing with men who addressed him in this way. A curt protest rose to his lips, and John longed for him to utter it. But Sir Giles remained silent, offended.

'I tell you,' King went on, falling once more into his noisy joviality, 'I'm going to road-show this mummy throughout the whole world. That way we'll make… hell, it couldn't be less than seven hundred thousand pounds.'

'But you can't!' The cry was torn from Hashmi. For the first time John felt sympathy for the Egyptian. There was no questioning the sincerity of that outburst.

'What do you mean, can't? Don't tell me I can't.' King dismissed Hashmi with a derisive wag of his head. 'You stick with me' – he thrust the words at Sir Giles and John – 'and you'll see some real money.'

Sir Giles cleared his throat. 'This is unheard of.'

'It sure is. Never been anything like it before.'

'Relics of this importance and value cannot be treated as a sideshow.'

'It is blatant sacrilege,' said Hashmi.

'Nothing sacrilegious about making money.'

Hashmi's sense of outrage seemed to inspire him with a new dignity. He was a small man compared with the over-powering Alexander King, but he took on a certain stature as he confronted the American.

'If this is your serious. intention and not some form of humour which I do not understand,' he said earnestly, 'then I will be forced to discuss the matter with my superiors.'

'You go right ahead and do that.'

Hashmi turned to Sir Giles, who by now was eyeing the cupboard where he kept his drink. 'Sir Giles, I trust that your integrity and good taste will finally prevail in this matter.'

'Sir Giles works for me,' said Alexander King with an edge

to his voice.

Hashmi nodded slowly and thoughtfully. He began to move to the entrance. 'There are certain steps we must take. If you will excuse me, sir…'

King waved him away. He snorted as Hashmi left the cave. 'Ah, they're all alike. Always getting worked up over something. Well, let him check. He'll find there isn't a thing he can do about it. Now, let's get down to details.'

Sir Giles could resist no longer. He opened the cupboard and poured drinks – a particularly large one for himself. John accepted a glass, but found that all taste seemed to have left him.

'We open in London,' said King, 'on the third of March.'

'You really are serious,' said Sir Giles.

'Like I'm always saying, you got to go where the money is.'

Sir Giles peered morosely into his empty glass and decided that he deserved a refill. After another gulp he said: 'But this…'

'You've been telling me right along what a great discovery this is. Right? One of the greatest things that's happened for centuries.'

'For the good of mankind—'

'Who's in a better position to do them good – you or me?' rasped King. 'You'd let the whole lot go into some stuffy museum in a one-camel town where no one 'ud see it except a few tourists on a wet afternoon. I can show it to the world. If folk want to be educated, I'll educate them… at ten cents a time.'

Sir Giles was flushed with brandy and anger. The two worked and reacted one on the other. His manner grew more pompous and at the same time, pitifully, more ineffectual. John had never seen his superior at such a loss.

'Can't be done,' snapped Sir Giles. He thought around this for a moment and then added: 'Can't be done.' He put his glass down forcefully. 'King… Mr King… if you persist in this childish exhibition, I shall have no alternative. No alternative.

None. Have to withdraw from any further responsibility in this matter.'

'Oh, now, who's being childish?'

'Can't be associated with it,' growled Sir Giles. He turned decisively away; but he really had nowhere to go, and was left clutching the edge of the curtain across the entrance, debating whether or not to march out.

There was a simmering pause. Alexander King stood very still, then turned to John. He raised a sardonic eyebrow, inviting the young man to take a good look at the leader of the expedition – and John had to admit that there was something childishly sullen about Sir Giles Dalrymple's back view. It was even worse when Sir Giles stole a covert glance at the glass which he had melodramatically and rashly slammed down.

King said deliberately: 'Like to change your job, John? Like to take charge of things in London – and see how we go on from there?'

John gasped. He thought of the acclamation there would be, the prestige, the openings there would be for him afterwards. But then he looked at Sir Giles. His loyalties were still to the man who had employed him, who had chosen him out of the dozens of candidates who longed to come on this expedition.

'As far as I'm concerned,' he said, 'Sir Giles is still in charge.'

'Sir Giles leaves the buggy ride right here.'

Dalrymple swung round. Surrender was in his trembling hand as he reached for the glass. He said: 'That's right, John. You heard Mr King. And you heard me – I've resigned.'

'But—'

'In the interests of the expedition,' said Sir Giles bitterly, 'I suggest you accept Mr King's offer. At least the funfair will then be conducted with, at any rate, a modicum of taste.'

'But if you feel like that,' John protested, 'why not retain control yourself?'

'I couldn't.' Sir Giles drank deeply. 'No, I couldn't do it. But you can. I won't stand in your way.'

John directed a mute appeal at Annette. But she had nothing to contribute. She gave him a wan little smile which he might construe as advice to accept. She had heard everything that was said, but it had conveyed no emotional undertones to her. It was unreasonable to think that he should be able to rely on her; if anything, she was the one who needed support.

'Have dinner with me tonight,' said King. He chuckled, ready to be amiable again. 'I know a place where we can sample the local delicacies.'

Local delicacies proved, in Alexander King's view, to be belly dancers and obsequious waiters. The standard of the food meant little to him: he kept the waiters scurrying to and fro, and tossed coins to the dancers accompanied by yells of bawdy appreciation, but the authenticity of the setting and atmosphere aroused as few queries in his mind as the various, courses and side dishes aroused on his palate.

Annette put up as good a show as possible at eating, but she was still remote and uncommunicative. John was more interested in King's plans than in the banalities of a social evening. The man's gross materialism repelled him and yet at the same time fascinated him. All his own instincts were on the side of Hashmi and Sir Giles Dalrymple; but there was something stimulating in this crude, forceful man who knew what he wanted and intended to get it. He provided a challenge. There was something larger than life about him – certainly larger than the restricted academic life which John had lived for so long.

In the middle of a jangling improvisation by three discordant reed instruments and a stringed contrivance which bore some slight resemblance to a decorative figure on Ra Antef's sarcophagus, King abruptly turned his attention to the matter in hand. He switched off one part of his mind and switched on another.

'You've made up your mind to stick with me?'

John was not sure until this instant that he had made his decision. The answer came of its own accord. He said:

'Yes. I'm with you, Mr. King.'

'I'm glad,' said Annette quietly and unexpectedly.

King beamed. 'That's what I like to hear. We're going to get along fine. A pity about Sir Giles, but I suppose you could say he's living in the past. This is 1900. You have to think modern.'

And while we're dealing out platitudes, thought John, why not add that you have to take the rough with the smooth? He was going to have uncomfortable moments with King: he knew that already. But better that he should accept the position he had been offered than that the treasures of Ra Antef should be handed over entirely to showmen and cheapjacks. Whatever lay ahead, he intended to do all he could to exhibit these splendours of the past with suitable dignity. He would be the defender of the dead.

He realized that King was smirking paternally at Annette and himself.

'What do you two kids plan for the future?'

Annette lowered her eyes. A few weeks ago she would have answered swiftly, with a French sparkle that never failed to pluck at John's heart. Now she played at being demure. No... she was not playing.

King waited for a reply.

John said hastily: 'The future? Well... as long as it's a long and happy one... together...'

'Not worried about the curse of the pharaohs, eh?'

It was impossible to tell whether King was probing, testing his reliability, or whether this was just another topic in his bubbling stream of conversation.

'So you know about that,' said John warily.

'Know about it? I wish I'd invented it. Anybody who opens a pharaoh's tomb is doomed to die horribly.' King's pleasure was boyishly naive. 'Hell, there's thousands of dollars' worth of free publicity in that. And don't think I'm not going to use it in my campaign. As my friend Phineas T. Barnum said, there's one born every minute. And they'll love this. The public love to be close to danger as long as that danger isn't real, hey? Say... maybe ten cents isn't enough.'

A dark boy came wriggling through the crowded room towards them. John braced himself for the usual demands for money, the offer of strange pleasures or simply of more food. But the boy said urgently:

'Effendi, I bring urgent message from your master. He says you come quickly.'

'From whom?'

Annette blinked and seemed to come out of a trance. 'He must mean Sir Giles.'

The boy nodded eagerly. 'That is right. Yes. Please, you come quickly.'

John glanced at King. 'He wouldn't have sent this message if it weren't important. Would you mind, sir, if we—'

'I'll come with you.' King was already spilling money lavishly from his fist. 'It'll be quicker. I've got things pretty well organized round here.'

They extricated themselves from the throng. A convoluted dance was just starting. King halted briefly to look back. He had some difficulty in tearing himself away.

'If ever they learn to do that to ragtime,' he observed as they finally went out, 'I could set them up and make a fortune.'

They were driven back through the pale, still night to the caves. Even from a distance lights were visible moving up and down the slope, and the cave entrance was a bright glow on the hillside. Activity of this kind was unusual at this hour. John felt a prickling of alarm.

The alarm was justified. Sir Giles's face when they entered the cave was enough to confirm that. Tight-lipped, flushed, he was examining a case which might have been selected from the litter on the floor – a litter of objects from the grave, scattered around as though by a violent storm.

'What's been going on here?' King strode into the middle of the cave and glared round at the chaos.

'The place has been ransacked,' said Sir Giles. He set the vase down with a sigh. 'Thank heavens, nothing appears to have been broken.'

'Broken, hell. Has anything been *stolen*?'

'Not that I can trace. They were obviously searching for something, but it doesn't look as though they found it.'

'Searching for what?' demanded King.

'If we could answer that question' – Hashmi moved in from the farther chamber – 'we'd know who they were. They have not taken gold or jewels which most men would covet.'

They looked at each other dubiously. It was a relief to learn that none of the treasures had been removed; but disquieting that someone should have been on the prowl and should have been able to wrench open so many of the cases stored here.

'Who was on guard – you did *have* a guard, huh?' snapped King.

'It was Ahmed,' said Hashmi. 'He… he is missing.'

'And I don't suppose we'll be seeing him again.'

'Effendi.' John, nearest to the cave entrance, turned to see the wide, frightened eyes of one of the porters. He went out. Lights swarming to and fro were now all flickering in towards one spot. He stumbled down behind the porter to where a wavering brightness fell on the crumpled form of a man.

It was Ahmed. He was dead. There was a knife in his chest,

and from the condition of his body it seemed likely that he had been thrown or kicked from the cave entrance.

The men who had congregated around him began now to edge backwards. Having seen what had happened to their comrade, they wanted no more to do with him – no more to do with anything that might be going on here.

'John!'

Annette's voice drifted down to him. Silhouetted against the light from the cave, she was beckoning him to return. He indicated that two of the porters should carry Ahmed up behind him as he went, but did not wait to see whether they would summon up the courage to obey him.

When he reached Annette she said: 'John, your lists have gone.'

'Gone?'

'I locked them away, but the container was smashed open. That's what they've taken.'

John groaned. There were no copies of those lists: there had been no time to prepare any. All his work had been wasted.

'But why?' he asked. 'What possible use could they be to anyone else?'

Hashmi stood behind Annette. He said: 'If one wanted to know the complete contents of the tomb, your lists are the quickest way of finding out.'

'This means,' said John, 'that we're not the only people interested in the treasures of Ra.'

4

AT NIGHT the sea was as dark, alien, and limitless as the desert. But from the sea came a refreshing breeze that was like a cool wine after the months in that arid land. Annette felt that she could lean on the ship's rail for ever, day and night, listening to the cleansing splash and hiss of the water as it streamed away from the bows. Thankfully she felt herself begin to unwind. Away from that ancient civilization with its memories of barbarity and its present-day savageries, she would recover from the shock of her father's murder. Nobody had been accused of that killing; nobody had been arrested. It had been accepted almost as an occupational hazard. Perhaps in time she would learn, like the rest, to dismiss it from her mind.

The ship's orchestra played faintly, nostalgically in the distance. A man went past, lazily humming the fragment of a tune. Life on board was leisurely and uncomplicated.

But below decks, in the depths of the ship, far below the laughter and the music and the luxury, the dead relics of the past were laid out. They had not been left behind in their homeland: they travelled with their captors, and Annette felt the great weight of them as a physical burden.

Her hand gripped the rail. A cool, firmer hand covered it. John said: 'It's a beautiful night.'

'I remember a night just like this when we were on our way to Egypt.'

He nodded. 'Do you realize that was almost a year ago?'

It had been a happy voyage. She had felt very close to John and together they had been part of an enthusiastic team, eager to wrest the secrets of the past from the secretive earth. Now the taste of adventure had gone sour. She shivered.

'Cold?' asked John solicitously.

'No, not really.'

'Is there something wrong?'

'I don't quite know. Just that I can't bear to think of that mummy lying down there…'

'You needn't worry about him. Safely locked up and clearly labelled "Not Wanted on Voyage"! You know, the only real danger you may be in – physical danger – is not from the mummy but… from me.'

He tried to put his arm round her. Annette flinched away. She could not explain her reluctance to be touched. Soon she would be ready for John and everything would go as they had planned it. She could not bear to see his hurt expression, yet she was incapable of pretence.

'I'm sorry,' he said sullenly.

'John, I'm not just being silly. There's something… I feel it, but I just can't explain. When we're back in civilization it will all come right. I'm sure it will.'

John forced a laugh. 'A lot of experts would say that what we have just left is civilization – the greatest the world has ever known.'

Annette thought of the brooding atmosphere of the tombs, the obsessive preoccupation with death which made a necropolis more important than a palace and a million times more important than the homes of ordinary men and women, and of the ritual killings which still lingered on as a holy duty despite all the protests of the authorities to the contrary. She tried to make herself think of other things. Soon they would be home. In a different setting the mummy and its accoutrements might seem less fearsome. It would be, literally, what people casually called a museum piece.

Somebody blundered close to them, staggering slightly across the deck although the sea was smooth. It was Sir Giles Dalrymple.

'Good evening, Sir Giles,' said John quietly.

'Hm? Oh. Oh, yes. Good evening. And you, my dear – good evening. You look beautiful. Good… g'night…'

Sir Giles looked puzzled for a moment, then lurched away. When he was out of earshot, making his unsteady way round the promenade, John said:

'If he carries on like this, he'll soon be as pickled as the mummy.'

Annette gazed down into the water. Even through her own sadness she had been conscious of what was happening to Sir Giles. It was a tragedy. At the beginning of the voyage he had stayed in his cabin for a large part of the time, and when at last he emerged it was obvious that he had settled down to steady, heavy drinking. The whole business with King had had a deep effect on him. The unkindest blow of all had been an official communication from the Egyptian government, written in most undiplomatic language, after it had been made clear that Ra Antef and his possessions were not to be handed over to the Cairo Museum but to be removed from the country. The government told Sir Giles, and simultaneously announced to the press, that he had conducted his last expedition anywhere on their territory. Future explorations would have to be carried out under more responsible guidance. This hit Sir Giles hard. It was not in his nature to try to turn the blame where it belonged – on to Alexander King. He remained silent, accepting the thrust without wincing. But he would never be the same man again. His dreams shattered, he sought new dreams in a succession of bottles.

'What will he do?' asked Annette.

'He may have to retire,' said John. 'He's no longer a youngster.'

'But it's such a waste. He knows more about Ancient Egypt than anyone apart from my father. And my father…'

As she lapsed into a bitter silence, there was a sudden cry that rose above the faint music and the steady rush of water below. It was a strangled cry, rising to a cracked note that was abruptly cut off. A man's voice – the voice of Sir Giles.

John pushed himself away from the rail. Annette made to follow, but he stopped her.

'Stay here.'

He ran towards the doors which opened on to a wide companionway. Annette braced herself against the rail for a moment, but she simply could not stand here waiting and wondering. Nobody else appeared to have heard the scream. A tall young man sauntered along the promenade deck towards her, but without haste: he was merely taking an evening stroll.

She went after John.

Just as she reached the door, it was flung open and a man raced out. He cannoned into her, and instinctively she grabbed his arm to save herself from falling. In the uncertain light there was a sudden flash. A knife blade slashed close to her face. Annette gasped and let go. She went reeling off balance against a stanchion, and then collapsed into a chair. The man was poised above her, the knife raised.

There was the thud of an impact, and the rush of breath punched out of him. The young man who had been approaching was suddenly large, purposeful and efficient. He swung two sharp blows to the attacker's stomach, and sent him sprawling across the deck. The knife rattled away.

Annette tried to get up, but she had fallen in an ungainly heap into the chair. As she twisted round, she saw the two figures locked in a struggle, indistinguishable one from the other. Then they were separate again, swinging punches – and her assailant was once more staggering away. He smacked hard against the rail, and in an incredibly slow movement rolled back over it.

All at once the deck seemed crowded with people. They clustered in from every side. A murmur of voices dissolved into shouts.

'Man overboard!'

For most of them it was an exciting experience. They buzzed happily together.

There was the clang of the ship's bell and a sudden blast from its siren.

'Man overboard!'

The man who had saved Annette came towards her, tugging his jacket into shape and dusting his sleeves fastidiously. In the light from the companionway he was, she saw, not as young as she would have thought at a casual glance. He had brooding, almost severe aquiline features – a face that was smooth yet somehow infused with the melancholy of experience. It was strange that he should make such an immediate impression on her: she saw him, as it were, complete and self-sufficient in one vivid instant.

He bowed slightly and said: 'You would appear to have aroused strong emotions in that fellow's bosom.'

'I can't imagine who…' She broke off. 'Where's John?'

She was on her feet again, hurrying down the steps to the cabins and staterooms. Sir Giles's cabin was six doors along. His door was open, and John was crumpled over the threshold. As Annette ran towards him he groaned and tried to get up. She put her arms under his shoulders and helped him. With his eyes still half shut he waved feebly towards the cabin. Sir Giles was in a similar condition – just coming round, and clutching his head in his two hands.

'John, what happened?' she demanded.

He steadied himself on his two feet and leaned against the open door.

'A man attacked Sir Giles. And then me.' He fingered his head gingerly. 'I'm going to have a wonderful lump here. Probably Sir Giles has got a matching piece.'

Sir Giles groped his way towards a cabin trunk which stood open beside his bed. He took out a bottle and took a long swig, then held it out waveringly to John. John shook his head – and immediately regretted it.

'Is there anything I can do?'

The stranger stood behind Annette. She moved to one side so that John could see him. The two men looked at each other: John muzzily and uncomprehendingly, the newcomer in clear, cool appraisal.

'Let me introduce you,' said Annette. 'Er, John Bray… and… er…'

'My name is Adam Beauchamp.'

The two of them shook hands. On the far side of the cabin Sir Giles noisily gulped another mouthful.

John turned to him and said: 'Is there anything missing?'

'Missing?' Sir Giles stared owlishly. 'Couldn't be. Nothing here to steal.' He took out his wallet and tried to count the banknotes, then gave up the task when his fingers refused to separate two notes. 'Money's all right.'

'If it wasn't money he was after,' said Adam Beauchamp, 'do you know what else there might have been?'

John looked uneasy. He was remembering the loss of those all-important lists in Egypt. Before embarking and while on board he had been making an attempt at collating his notes and sketching out the beginnings of a new catalogue. The material was locked away in his own cabin, not with Sir Giles. Would there be another attack there in due course?

Annette said: 'It must be something to do with Ra, mustn't it? It couldn't just be a coincidence.'

'It doesn't seem likely.'

Annette turned to Adam Beauchamp. 'You see, both—'

'You do not need to explain.' He smiled and his slim hands sketched a graceful, deprecatory movement in the air. 'Your recent discovery is far too well known. But surely Sir Giles doesn't keep any of the treasures in his cabin?'

'Certainly not.' John spoke brusquely as though to warn off anyone who might be listening. 'The treasures are in the ship's hold under heavy guard.'

But somebody, thought Annette, intended that those treasures should be returned to Egypt. That basic demand was behind all the difficulties they had encountered while getting away from the country and somehow behind the attack on Sir Giles. The treasures might be safe in the hold, but once they were taken out there would be nothing but trouble again.

'What are your plans?' Beauchamp was asking.

'We're taking everything to London,' said John. 'Originally we planned to spend some time in Paris, but Mr King is anxious to get started with the first exhibition in London. Before we can set it up I have to continue my retabulations.'

And then there would be thousands of visitors, and among them would surely be enemies. Annette's heart sank at the thought of her future with John – of the constant vigilance, the suspense, the dangers into which they could easily walk and from which it might not be so easy to escape. This was not how her father had intended that things should be.

'Where will you stay?'

Adam Beauchamp was in no hurry to leave. Annette could see that John was anxious to be rid of him. John needed to go back to his cabin, satisfy himself that nothing had been stolen from there, and then lie down. She tried to help by moving away from Sir Giles's cabin. Automatically the two men followed her, talking.

'I've booked rooms for us in a Bloomsbury hotel,' said John. 'Annette and I will stay there.'

'Oh, but that's not good enough.'

Annette glanced back, surprised. John frowned. It was an odd comment, coming as it did from a perfect stranger.

John said curtly: 'It's near the British Museum. Useful for reference. It'll suit us very well.'

'I live on my own in a large house in Regent's Park. I wonder if I might ask you to come and stay with me?'

They stopped by the stairs which led up to the restaurant and the bar. Annette felt an absurd quickening of excitement. She could see that John was taken aback by this offer: he had a true Englishman's reticence, and found such directness embarrassing. There was no reason for it – no contact between Beauchamp and himself, no sense behind such a spontaneous invitation. Yet Annette suddenly wanted to accept. She knew it was ridiculous, but Beauchamp's magnetism was irresistible.

John, at any rate, did not find it irresistible. He said: 'I'm sorry. That's quite out of the question.'

'But very kind of you,' said Annette, to soften the blow.

'Your work fascinates me. I've always felt that I should devote more of my time to the arts.'

'Archaeology is a science rather than an art,' said John stiffly.

'I wonder? And surely the treasures you unearth are of artistic rather than scientific value? Or both, perhaps – a wonderful combination such as every philosopher has always sought. You would be of the greatest assistance to me if you would come and stay.'

'I wish I could assist your ambitions, Mr Beauchamp, but I'm afraid we can't alter our plans at this late stage.'

Beauchamp glanced at Annette to assess her reaction.

She tried to look indifferent and to remain loyal to John, while all the time she was hoping that somehow there would be this change, this stimulus… this danger. Yes, she admitted to herself that there was danger in it; danger to John and herself, perhaps, and to all that they meant to each other; and yet a danger she longed to face. She was startled by herself and frightened at what she might learn about herself.

'Join me for a liqueur,' said Adam Beauchamp, 'and we'll discuss it.'

'That would be rather nice,' said Annette.

John scowled at her. 'Look, there isn't anything to discuss.'

'But we could all do with a drink.'

'We've made other arrangements,' said John doggedly.

But Adam Beauchamp and Annette went up to the bar, and after he had been back to his cabin to tidy up John joined them.

5

DURING THE rest of the voyage Adam Beauchamp exerted his considerable charm in a campaign to win John round. Annette shared John's bewilderment, unable to understand why it should be so important to Adam. It had all the signs of being a rich man's whim, but unlike so many whims it did not evaporate overnight. Younger, suaver and more personable than the blustering Alexander King, Adam nevertheless shared the American's determination to make things go the way he wanted them to go. Yet this was an over-simplification. Adam was insistent but without being offensive. He created the impression that he was humbly asking a great favour. The mixture of humility and persistence was a provocative one.

To Annette he described his house with a warmth and pride that endeared him to her. She longed to see the places of which he spoke and to relate him to his background. To John he painted a picture of calm and seclusion where it would be possible to work under ideal conditions. There would be none of the clatter of horse traffic that made Bloomsbury so noisy, and none of the disadvantages of an impersonal hotel. John would make much swifter progress on his cataloguing and on the business of setting up the exhibition.

'But why is he so anxious to have us there?' John asked Annette more than once. 'It has become his ruling obsession. Why should it matter so much to him?'

She had no answer. If she had the glimmerings of an explanation in her own mind, it was too private and personal and disturbing to be confided to John. She was far from admitting the truth – if it were a truth – to herself. But as they approached England she was both exhilarated and alarmed. She found it impossible to meet Adam's gaze, so often fixed on her. She was in the grip of conflicting emotions stronger than any she had ever known.

The confusion at the docks was the cause of John's ultimate surrender. He insisted on supervising the unloading of the precious cargo himself, only to find that the formalities took the larger part of a day, that certain essential papers were missing, and that the transport which had supposedly been arranged was missing. Alexander King stormed and raged. John and Annette doggedly worked at each problem as it came up. But without Adam they would have been lost. His money talked, not as loudly as King's but in a more smoothly commanding tone of voice. As unflagging as John himself, he went up to London and back to straighten out difficulties, and stood by his new friends for a whole night and day. When they were sure that the job was safely completed, they succumbed to exhaustion. And at this stage Adam, laughing, said that there was only one place to go – home, where there would be good food and comfort and decently aired beds to sleep in…

And John grinned and said, 'All right, I give in,' and they all laughed with a sort of hysterical relief.

The house overlooking Regent's Park was all that Adam had promised. Its carved pediment stood out white over the trees as they approached, and in spite of her tiredness Annette felt a thrill of anticipation as they drove in under a noble arch and entered the shaded tranquillity of a courtyard. Here they were, as Adam had assured them they would be, cut off from the bustling world.

John and Annette were shown to their rooms by Jessop, a dignified, unobtrusive manservant who had clearly been given detailed instructions long before the party arrived. Annette thought that Adam must have been confident of luring them here right from the start; but she did not pass on this observation to John.

Her room was small but not cramped. It had a finely grained silk wallpaper which seemed to catch the daylight and glow with it. The window looked down onto the courtyard. After the dust and intolerable heat of Egypt, after the throbbing and rolling of the ship which had brought them to England, and after the irritations of the last day, this quiet little room was all she could have wished for. It was all she could do not to roll onto the bed and go fast asleep.

But they were to have drinks downstairs. She hoped that they would not have to sit up too long making polite conversation; but Adam wanted to make them formally welcome to his home, and it would be ungracious to seem too drowsy and bored.

When she entered the sitting room she found that her desire to yawn was leaving her. The spicy aroma from a bowl of hot punch on a brass table in the middle of the room was both soothing and stimulating. Adam's smile as he rose to greet her was more direct and challenging than any he had ventured while they were still aboard ship. John looked relaxed and uncritical. Whatever reservations he might have about Adam and his insistent hospitality, for the moment he was only too glad of the chance to sink into comfort.

Jessop, the manservant, poured steaming punch into a mug and handed it to Annette. She sipped gratefully at it. The English climate was a great relief after Egypt, but it was capable of provoking the shivers. She laughed. It was so strange to think that in such a short time she should be wanting a warming drink.

Holding the mug between her hands and feeling its prickly warmth seeping into her palms, Annette looked appreciatively round the room. Its gracious proportions induced a certain tranquillity in the occupants. This was a room of which one had to be worthy. Here there could be no haste and no vulgarity.

She was standing by a small glass-topped case with slender beechwood legs. Below the glass there glinted a small arc of jewels, some mounted in silver and one in a florid yet delicate porcelain setting. The collection was an eccentric one – very much one person's unashamed, individual taste – yet perfectly in keeping with the room and its furnishings.

Adam stood at her shoulder. He said: 'You find them interesting.'

'They are so lovely.' Lovelier, she thought, than the over-ornate, overpowering splendour of the Egyptian treasures which by now she almost took for granted.

'Fabergé could sometimes be too extreme,' said Adam, lifting the glass and reaching in. 'But he had some inspired moments. This one…' He removed a small cluster which winked in the light. He held it against Annette's dress and she was sure that he would be aware of her heartbeat quickening. 'This belonged to the Empress of Russia,' he said. 'I've always felt it should again belong to a beautiful woman.'

She lifted her hand and he allowed the jewel to drop into it.

'Beautiful,' she whispered.

'I would like you to have it.'

Annette started and drew back. Vaguely, dazed by tiredness or by the fumes of the punch, she felt that this was forcing the pace too hard… too soon.

'But it's priceless,' she feebly protested.

'It is valueless compared to the pleasure it would give me to think of it in your possession.'

Adam's gravity robbed her of confidence. He was so

weighty, so sure of himself. John, sprawled at ease in an armchair, seemed far away. She wanted to dodge past Adam and appeal to him: it was up to him to save her, to establish normality again. But John, dear hard-working John, was lost in thoughts of his own. Probably he was doing mental calculations regarding the size of the exhibition tent in the park and the placing of the main pieces.

Annette looked into Adam's eyes. Again she had the impression which had been so immediate when they first met: he was older and wiser than a fleeting glance would suggest, and quite sure of himself. Whatever he did, it would be done consciously and purposefully. His offer of a gift was no casual impulse which he would regret later.

'You will take it.' It was not a question, not a command; simply a statement.

'It… it would be ungracious of me not to accept,' she said haltingly.

He touched her hand. She did not withdraw it. With a light pressure between his fingers he lifted her hand and kissed it.

Annette moved away across the room. She was trembling. When she spoke to John she was startled by the loudness of her own voice. Too eagerly, too unsteadily, she said:

'John… look. Isn't it beautiful?'

John looked at the jewel. His mind full of other treasures and an utterly different beauty, he said: 'Hm. Yes.'

His mug was empty. Adam came to take it from him and refill it. He smiled sideways at Annette. The implication was that she and he were in a half joking, half conspiratorial alliance against John. This was not what she wanted.

But was she sure she knew what she did want?

Adam raised his mug of punch. 'May I propose a toast? To the success of the exhibition of Ra.'

John and Annette raised their mugs.

'And,' said Adam, 'may the gods smile down upon our newfound friendship.'

They went to bed early that night. Annette fell asleep before she could fully savour the joy of lying in such blissful comfort in such a room.

The next day she and John started work in earnest.

Alexander King had organized the erection of a huge tent in a corner of Hyde Park. Certain objections had been raised to the questionable commercial elements in this exhibition, but King had ploughed through them. He had made great play with the cultural aspects of his show and enlisted the aid of some eminent savants, largely by hinting that if he did not get his own way in this matter he would transport the whole exhibition at once to the United States without allowing anyone in England so much as a glimpse of the fabulous treasures.

Now the treasures themselves were to be uncrated. King insisted that John should supervise every stage of this. There was no need for such insistence: John could not have borne that anyone else should be responsible. While King took away the breath of contractors in his demands for immediate installation of the tent, the erection of barriers, and the provision of stands and showcases, John concentrated on the careful unpacking of the tomb objects.

Annette knew that John was not happy. He found this rush undignified. There was still a great deal of cataloguing to be done, and in his view it was more important that the exhibition should be scientifically laid out than that it should draw in crowds of the uncritical public. But King was boss. King made that very clear. This was a road show, and if John wanted to preserve certain important elements he would have to do so within the context of that show.

Even before the supports of the tent were safely pegged, King was pacing up and down inside barking orders. The mummy was to be the centrepiece and he knew exactly where he wanted it placed. He wanted lights in such and such a place. A platform here, the panels of hieroglyphics to form a mural along this side of the tent, the unguent jars to be raised on a pedestal just so…

'There you are, John!' The great bellow rang out down the tent, louder even than the crack of the canvas as it flapped and then was stretched tight. 'Come and give me a hand. I'm getting nowhere with these workmen. You'd better try them in their own language.'

'Ancient English,' John murmured ruefully to Annette.

It was John who had to strike a balance between King's pressing demands and the surly slowness of the workmen. He also had to preserve the peace when King changed his mind about some essential part of the display and the carpenters had to be told to start all over again. There was an unrelenting hammering and banging, and in the middle of it all the treasures of the tomb were gradually unveiled.

The dog head of Anubis looked down on this utterly foreign scene. Pert little Cockneys scrambled about under the golden gaze of a prince of Egypt. John was a constant bundle of nerves, waiting for something irreplaceable to be broken, trying to supervise a score of things at once, averting one minor disaster after another and always sure that sooner or later there would be some major catastrophe.

But gradually the pattern established itself. Built around the awe-inspiring centrepiece, the mummiform coffin itself, the grave furniture formed a coherent picture which must evoke dread and an almost religious admiration in even the most materialistic beholder.

King grew expansive and affable again. He slapped John on the shoulder and congratulated him. 'I knew we could do it. Knew we'd get it set up on time.'

Immediately inside the entrance to the tent, shielding the

exhibition from anyone who might peep in, stood the doors of the gilded shrine. Visitors to the exhibition would see the whole story of the life of Ra told on the panels of the doors, and would then turn left to pick out the individual items of rich furnishing.

Annette, tired of stumbling over planks and boxes or of being bumped into by workmen, retreated to the entrance and once more studied the panels. It was the first time she had allowed herself to contemplate the grim but magnificent story since the death of her father. Now she felt herself returning to life; and at the same time it seemed that the golden pictures from the past took on life, the men and women of a vanished age moved from their eternally fixed postures and enacted a story as real now as it had been then, and the world of Ra Antef took on significance once more.

The first panel showed Rameses VIII being presented by obsequious women with his twin sons Ra and Be. Ra was the elder by a matter of minutes. The two boys grew up in the same environment but as very different characters, both physically and mentally. Ra became a thinker, a searcher for truth and the secret of eternal life. But Be was a sensualist who spent his time seeking only the pleasures of the body.

Down the ages there had been writings and poems and tales in Egypt of the legend of the brothers. Here, from their own time, were the pictures which told the story with a dramatic immediacy.

Be was jealous of his elder brother's position and popularity. He jeered at Ra's profound thinking and deep wisdom, and continually conspired to have him branded as a sorcerer. His circle of sycophants did all they could to aid him in this. In the end he was so successful that the ageing Rameses, in an effort to avoid a civil war, was forced to accept the insinuations of his worried advisers and banish his favourite son.

After months of wandering in the desert, Ra and a small band of faithful followers were befriended by an ancient nomadic people in the remote wastes of the Sahara. These wanderers never ventured to the fertile pastures of the Nile. They knew the oases of the deepest desert, and had hardened themselves to the rigorous life which they considered preferable to subservience to an autocratic pharaoh.

As time passed the respect of the nomads for Ra grew. They realized that they had a prince in their midst. His philosophy became their philosophy. Noble in themselves, they recognized in him an even greater nobility. They asked him to become their king and rule over them.

At Ra's coronation he was presented with the most precious object which the nomads possessed. They scorned all valuables save this one. It was a small medallion on which had been inscribed the sacred words of life, a secret which had been in their possession for centuries. It was said that in certain circumstances it had the power to confer immortality, but this power could only be invoked by one blessed by the gods with the awareness of it.

After years with these devoted followers, Ra made plans to return to his homeland so that he could set right the wrongs which had been done to him. He prayed to Bubastis, the powerful cat-headed immortal who would do all things for him. He asked for spiritual guidance and for the strength to use the secrets of the words of life wisely. He then turned towards his own land with the assurance that he would be able to accomplish his mission.

But Be had heard rumours of his brother's plans on the desert wind. None of Ra's followers had betrayed him: there were other nomads, less proud and less courageous, and their jealousy led them to give spiteful warning. Be sent assassins into the desert to find and kill Ra.

The most intricately designed panel on the gilded doors showed an interwoven turmoil of men stabbing and slaying. The stylized emotionless faces conveyed a greater terror than could have been achieved by would-be realistic expressions. Ra kneeled between two priests with his head bowed. The enemy pressed in from all sides, caught for ever on the golden panel in the accursed motion of killing.

They showed no mercy. They killed nomads and priests alike, and at last they reached their main victim. They slew Ra, and as he lay dying they cut off his left hand on which he wore his rings of high birth. This hand they took back to Be, as proof that their cruel work was done.

The burial of Ra Antef was a hurried and unworthy affair. But later, when close to death, Rameses sent for the body to be removed to a magnificent burial chamber and surrounded with all the splendours that were the due of a royal prince.

'And now the mummy has been disinterred once more,' said a voice close beside Annette.

She was transported from the past to the present. Adam Beauchamp stood on her left, scanning the story that unfolded on the magnificent doors.

'Annette…!'

It was John calling. She indicated that Adam should come with her, and together they made their way round the screen formed by the doors. The coffin was in position now, raised so that the wooden head stared out at the audience, its expression one of sorrow but the overall effect one of blazing majesty as a result of the inlays of glass paste and semi-precious stones.

Annette and Adam stopped before this splendid sight. The workmen who had been fussing around it were reduced to silence. Now that it was in place, the sarcophagus dominated not merely the dead relics all round it but the living beings who had brought it here.

'Well' – there was one voice that nothing could still – 'what have you got to say about that, hey?'

'Most impressive.' Adam was lost in contemplation.

'We'll have the whole of London filing through here,' said King jubilantly.

Adam emerged from his brief trance. 'And will you open the coffin?'

'I sure will. Do you want to see what the act is?'

Before they could speak, King snapped his fingers in the air. Lights blazed and then went slowly green and sinister. In a curtained enclosure to one side, pipes and reeds began to play eastern music of dubious origin, interspersed with deep reverberations from a gong.

King snapped his fingers again and held out his hand. A girl handed him a knife. He went towards the mummy case and there was a metallic roar of thunder from an effects sheet behind the curtain.

Annette glanced disconsolately at Adam. His face was inscrutable. With his impeccable good taste he must have been disgusted by this barnstorming crudity; but he gave no sign.

'What's 'appenin', Bert?' came a whisper from behind.

'They're openin' that coffin.'

'Well, they can do without me.'

'Without me an' all.'

The workmen withdrew into the shadows, away from the lurid lights and that dignified, implacable, royal head.

Alexander King bent towards the seal that was meant to protect the dead prince from all harm. He raised the knife. For a moment he hesitated, then turned to wink at John, Adam, and Annette as they watched him.

'Better rehearse it right the way through. Don't want it to go wrong on the opening night.'

He cut the seal. Its two halves parted. King stood back and

made a melodramatic gesture which summoned two Nubians from the shadows. They took hold of the lid and stepped back with it.

Inside lay the mummy, swathed in the bandages of his embalming. He was less impressive than the symbolic carving on the coffin lid – nothing but a white, featureless, dead thing in the middle of all this pomp and brilliance. But this very pomp was a testimony to what he had once been.

King struck the side of the coffin possessively. 'He's worth ten cents of anybody's money!'

Adam remained silent, confronting the mummy as though waiting for some message from beyond the grave. The incongruous music went on, and the metal sheet roared a few more times.

Annette said: 'Mr King, you're… incredible.'

'Well, some of us have got it, and the others ride home in a horse cart.'

Adam touched Annette's arm. He turned away. She took it that he had had enough. He was a decisive man, wasting no time when he had seen or heard his fill. She moved away with him, then waved to John in the background.

'Coming back with us?'

'I've got some tidying up to do. I'll join you later.'

With a twinge of guilt Annette realized that she was not displeased by this. She was glad that Adam had come when he did, and she was not going to ask whether his prime purpose had been to see the exhibition before it opened to the public or to fetch her.

They waited for some time in the expectation of John's putting in an appearance, and then Adam ordered dinner to be served.

Annette had changed into a dress which she had not worn since leaving France. It was a simple, severely cut green velvet dress which her father had liked and which he fondly imagined was in the latest fashion. Annette had refrained from telling him that its main advantage was its practicality and the fact that it did not date too obviously – a very necessary factor, in view of their unsettled, peripatetic life. But it was true that she looked well in it, and she wanted to look well for Adam.

Its simplicity demanded some added ornament. The jewel which Adam had given her was far too striking. Something small and unpretentious, in a colour that would not clash, was what she needed.

At the bottom of her case she found a small disc in a dull ochre hue like sullen gold. She had forgotten its existence since leaving Egypt. Or perhaps, to be frank with herself, she had deliberately buried it under her clothes and made herself repudiate it. It was another memory of her father. He had given it to her the day before he was killed. Neither of them could identify it – it was a humble trifle compared with the treasures they were busily excavating from the tomb – and Professor Dubois had not even got round to telling her its origin. He might have picked it up in a bazaar or among the innumerable shards and battered trinkets which were so easily turned up on the approaches to the Valley of the Kings. Now Annette found that, hung on a chain round her neck so that it lay on the bosom of her dress, it was more striking than she had at first realized. It was far more effective against the green velvet than any brooch could have been.

It caught Adam's attention at once. He put his hands on her arms and drew her close to him.

'This is new?'

'Or very old,' she said.

Then he kissed her bare shoulder so that she was not sure whether he was really interested in the medallion or had merely been using it as an excuse.

At dinner he mentioned it again, and she told him that her father had given it to her. It was a long time since she had spoken of her father. But now it all came out in a rush. The appearance of the grave treasures in their new setting, the dress, and the medallion – all brought back memories, and she found that in Adam's company she was able to face up to them. He seemed to draw confidences from her by a gentle form of hypnotism. She found it easy to talk and easy to put everything that had happened into its true proportions.

She told Adam about her childhood and of how she had adored her father.

'But when my mother died, he went to Paris to lecture at the Museum of Egyptology. It was six years before I saw him again.'

'Why didn't he take you with him?'

'I was a great disappointment to him.'

Adam paused with his fork in mid-air. It stabbed an incredulous question at her.

'Why was that?'

'He always wanted a son.'

'What a very foolish man.'

Annette remembered the bitterness, the shame of rejection by the father she so longed to be near. She had been young and easily wounded. She could not understand; but she had tried to understand. And of one thing she had been determined: she would meet her father on his own ground and show herself worthy of him.

'I studied twice as hard as any son would have done,' she recalled. 'I read everything he wrote and anything relating to his studies that I could get my hands on. In my circle it was regarded as being very unfeminine, but I persevered. By the time I went to Paris I could converse with him on his level.'

'He was surprised?'

At this point memory became a joy. This she would never

forget. 'He was delighted,' she said. 'He insisted I should join him as his assistant.'

'So the story has a happy ending.'

'Until that night in the desert,' said Annette soberly.

Adam nodded. He did not speak again until coffee was served. Again he had fallen in with an uncanny responsiveness to her mood. She had wanted to talk of her father, to break the spell as it were; and now she wanted to think for a little while rather than talk, giving herself time to readjust. And Adam understood. Adam was as sensitive to the subtlest change as though he had been reading her mind.

When they were drinking a glass of brandy he looked across at her and said lightly, to free her from her reverie:

'A perfect distillation of the most admirable ingredients. Like the blend of beauty and intelligence in a woman.'

They moved away from the table and Annette sat down while Adam stood thoughtfully above her.

'But it often disturbs me,' he went on abruptly, 'when women use their intelligence only for academic pursuits.'

She felt a stab of disappointment. It was unthinkable that he should be numbered among those who shook their heads over her and said that a woman's place was in the home. Sadly she prompted him:

'You think we should sit in seclusion with our embroidery?'

Adam smiled. 'You mistake me. I mean only that intelligence can be as gainfully employed in the home as in the academy. A man should ask not merely the obvious marital duties from his wife: he should be able to expect wit and intellect. She should have a grasp of his work, and at the same time keep her mind fresh by interests of her own. And, of course, the husband must respect these interests. They will be better companions that way – happier, more rewarding… and well rewarded.'

To hear her ideals put into words in this way was too much

for Annette. She put her glass down on the low table beside her chair. There had been no hint of superiority in Adam's voice: he had been talking, she realized, to an equal, and talking about a relationship that must be based on equality.

Sharply, as though seized by a desire to wreck what he had just done, he said:

'John understands this, I'm sure.'

'Not… not completely.'

'You must have talked this over. You work in the same field. It must mean a lot to you.'

'He's prepared to allow me to continue my career when we are married.'

'You make it sound like a concession rather than a positive encouragement,' said Adam. He cupped the brandy glass in his hand and swirled the amber liquid gently. 'But you will marry him?'

Annette heard herself say: 'I'm not sure.' This was treachery and she was appalled by it, yet nothing could have held the words back. It was settled that she and John would marry. She had been sure until… until when? It was impossible now to look back and decide at what point she had become aware of the first doubts, the tentative sidestep which had led to this admission.

'Not sure?' said Adam. 'Then I implore you to be certain before you go any farther. A wasted life is tragedy enough, but for someone like you to throw away the years on a compromise would be doubly tragic.'

'You're very… disturbing, Adam.'

He said: 'And you're very beautiful, Annette.'

She waited for him to come towards her. When he did she knew she would be unable to resist him. Her world was spinning insanely, but she didn't want it to stop.

6

JOHN BRAY crossed the hall and Jessop opened the sitting-room door for him. Adam and Annette turned to face him. They looked strangely frozen, like two actors interrupted in mid-sentence and waiting for a cue to set them off again. He paused, feeling that he did not belong here. Strictly speaking, neither he nor Annette belonged; yet she had the air of one who was settling down, accepting and being accepted.

He was too tired to sort this out. 'I'm sorry I'm late,' he said, and thankfully accepted the glass which Adam put in his hand.

'Are you very tired?' asked his host solicitously. 'Would you like to eat in your room? I'll get Jessop to—'

'Thank you, I've eaten.' He remembered with distaste the sandwiches sent in to the tent while he and King added the finishing touches to the exhibition. They had not exactly satisfied his hunger but they had certainly taken away his appetite. 'I'm afraid Mr King's New World charm is beginning to wear thin. If he continues to work me as hard as he is doing now, I'll soon be as… well, as moribund as the mummy.'

He moved towards a chair facing Annette. On the way he stooped to kiss her. She sat quite rigid. Even through his weariness he began to feel the gnawing of suspicion. Adam Beauchamp was just too smooth; and was contriving to spend too much time with Annette; and was just too inexplicably lavish with his hospitality. John sensed that he was being edged out.

He looked accusingly at Annette. She lowered her eyes. The movement drew his attention to the small medallion which she wore around her neck.

He said: 'What's that? I don't believe I've seen it before.'

Reluctantly Annette lifted it for him to see. John blinked. He had been concentrating so intently for the entire day that his vision was blurred. On the small surface of the medallion it was difficult to make out the design, which might be purely ornamental or an extremely fine-etched form of cuneiform writing. One thing was certain: this was an example of very ancient craftsmanship.

John looked past Annette to Adam. 'Did he give it to you?'

'My father did,' she said, 'the day before he died.'

Adam came closer and held out his hand. As though there were some rapport between them which did away with the need for words, Annette took the chain from round her neck and passed the medallion to him.

'Is it from the tomb?' asked John.

'Of course not.'

Her indignation was immediate and unforced. But he wondered how she could be so sure. It was strange that she should be in possession of something so unusual, passed to her by her father of all people.

He said: 'It's very odd. All discoveries made on the expedition should have been verified by—'

'John, you're not suggesting my father would have—'

'It can't be from the tomb,' Adam interrupted, turning the medallion over in his hand. 'Both the stone and the hieroglyphs are at least two thousand years older than that. These are Early Old Kingdom.'

John bristled. He had had about enough of this languidly self-assured fellow, and now that they were on his own territory he proposed to put a stop to these pretensions.

'How would you know that?' he demanded.

'My interest in your work is not an entirely amateur one.'

'It's the first time you've mentioned this.' John glanced scornfully at Annette, inviting her to share his scepticism. But she would not look up.

'I did not wish to be too brash on subjects which are so much more your province than mine,' said Adam. The tone was courteous and even deferential, but John would have sworn that there was an edge of irony to it. 'My studies,' he added with a disparaging shrug, 'were of an earlier period.' He held out the medallion to John.

There was certainly little in this rather dull little piece to suggest kinship with the richly decorated funerary splendours of Ra Antef. Yet John felt sure that somehow this was a keystone. Somewhere it fitted into the scheme of things, and its very insignificance was relevant.

He said stubbornly: 'I still believe it could be from the tomb.'

Adam's eyes hardened. John was glad that he had been able to sting the usually imperturbable host into a display of open hostility. 'Let me assure you, Mr Bray, it is Old Kingdom.'

'Nobody could be as certain as you are, Mr Beauchamp, without extensive examination.'

'Then why don't you reserve judgement until you have made an extensive examination?'

'Very well,' said John. Adam was making an untypically fidgety movement with his right hand, as though wanting to reach out and reclaim the medallion. John held on to it and said to Annette: 'With your permission…?'

'What is it?' She was as uncertain as Adam. Before either of them could gain control of the situation, John said quickly:

'There's only one person I know who has the full references to this period, and that's Sir Giles. He knows more about the subject than any of us. I'd like to see him now.'

'Now?' Adam did his best to be the courteous host again. 'John, it's getting late. Another drink, and then tomorrow—'

'Now,' John insisted. 'He won't be in bed yet. If you'll both excuse me, I'll start right away.'

Again they turned to watch him. As he left the room he had the satisfaction of knowing that they were both disturbed and that the pleasure they might derive from each other's company would not be as unruffled as it might have been earlier in the evening.

Sir Giles was, as he had predicted, still awake. If one could call it that. As soon as he entered the library John knew that the archaeologist had been drinking. Even in the few days since they last met there had been a deterioration. Sir Giles's military crispness was crumbling, his voice slurring into plaintive incoherence.

John, without preamble, gave him the medallion and waited for a verdict. Sir Giles shook his head muzzily over it and then began to recite his woes. His old friend Dubois was dead, King had cheated him, he would never be able to work again… the self-pitying stream flowed without cease.

'I want you,' said John at last, brutally emphasizing the words and driving them home through Sir Giles's mutterings, 'to identify that medallion for me. Its period. Its significance.'

Sir Giles pouted reproachfully at him. He tried to focus on the medallion. Then he waved a hand towards the bookshelves.

'Try over there. Third shelf. No, fourth. Try Belzoni. And de Morgan.' As John began to explore the shelves, Sir Giles poured himself another drink, splashing a fair quantity down the side of his glass, and rambled on: 'If money is to be the yardstick by which the value of education is to be ass'd… assessed… then I fear for the future. The past isn't inviolable – we've discovered that, haven't we, hey, my boy? – but the future… oh, think of the future! Let's make the redoubtable Mr King headmaster of Eton and be done with it. Huh. In six months he'd turn the playing fields into a fairground, with each boy a barker on a percentage share of the profits.'

John, turning over the yellowing pages of a musty book, commented: 'Well, at least their arithmetic would have to be good, if only to make sure of them getting their fair share.'

This appealed to Sir Giles. He chuckled. He couldn't stop chuckling. He began to rock to and fro in his chair. Then the noise changed in a split second to lamentation again.

'Think of me! Whoever heard of an Egyptologist who wasn't allowed into Egypt? Forbidden. Undesirable – that's what I am. And there's no court of appeal, you know.'

'What page will it be – what section, anyway?' asked John, picking his way through a complicated index.

'Oh, that damned Hashmi! Why couldn't he have told the authorities it was King who was responsible for removing the relics, not I?'

'What page, Sir Giles?'

'Mm? Oh, that book. Yes, there ought to be something. Somewhere in the three hundreds, I think. A couple of sketches. Might help.'

'I was wondering…'

John let the question die. It was no use. Whatever knowledge Sir Giles might have stored away in that podgy head of his, he would be incapable of extracting any of it now. Or perhaps ever again. When a man drank himself into this kind of stupor and wilfully kept himself there, it meant that he had abandoned all his previous values.

Sir Giles became aware of John's gaze. He produced a feebly ingratiating smile. To show how willing he was to offer his advice, he groped for the medallion on the table at his elbow. His glass went flying and the table rocked perilously.

To see one of his old idols crumbling like this was too

much for John's self-control. He burst out: 'Oh, you clumsy, drunken old...'

He checked himself. But it was too late. An incongruous, shameful tear welled in Sir Giles's left eye. 'I see I've lost your respect now, too.' He forced himself up, wavered, and steadied himself. 'You are undoubtedly better left alone to your studies,' he said with a pathetic attempt at dignity.

'I'm sorry, Sir Giles. It's only that—'

'Goodnight,' said Sir Giles. He made his unsteady way to the door. 'When you have finished, no doubt you can find your own way out.'

John perched on the arm of a chair for a moment, unable to continue his researches. He was ashamed of his outburst. Yet it had been justified. Whatever the pressures on him, Sir Giles ought to have been capable of standing up to adversity. If he had remained sober and determined, he would have been able to reinstate himself without too great a struggle. Now he could only sink.

John sighed and turned his attention to the medallion. He found a magnifying glass on Sir Giles's littered desk, and pored over the convoluted signs.

An incredible theory formed in his mind. He saw that both he and Adam could be right. This medallion could be Old Kingdom, yet could have been in or near the tomb of Ra Antef. Perhaps it had been hidden close to the tomb after the burial chamber had been sealed – hidden by a devoted follower who knew that no ordinary mortal must be allowed to interpret the words on the face of the stone.

He turned back to the bookshelves. A faint breeze stirred as though a window had been opened and closed. He looked over his shoulder. The curtains billowed faintly and then subsided. John carried a book to the desk, and went through it in search of a detailed examination of the story of Ra and Be. But there was no solid foundation from which to work. All that was most significant in the story was yet to be written down, since it would have to be based on the discoveries so recently made by the King expedition. There were hints and speculations, wary references… no more.

But by assembling various references, he might be able to arrive at a rough interpretation of the minuscule writing. He picked up the magnifying glass again, and settled at the desk.

When footsteps rustled swiftly across the floor towards him he tried to get up and turn; but he was too late. He was aware of an arm raised, of a flurry of movement, and then he was struck on the head and beaten down into oblivion.

7

TEN MINUTES before the opening of the exhibition to the press and selected dignitaries, Hashmi Bey entered the tent.

Annette was the first to see him. She and Adam were standing by a table laden with food and wineglasses. Alexander King knew the best way to win the goodwill of gentlemen of the press. King himself was fussing to and fro making a number of unnecessary last-minute alterations. He was dressed in a garish garment which a theatrical costumier had assured him was a genuine Egyptian ceremonial robe. 'Atmosphere,' he had explained to the bemused Annette. 'Got to get the atmosphere just right.'

Annette thought that Hashmi's expression when he saw this apparition would have been funny if it had not been so grim. She drew Adam's attention to the newcomer, who made straight for King and began to talk forcefully and earnestly. King shook his head. Hashmi's eyes widened, and he began to pound his fist on a table.

'I think we'd better go and protect Mr King,' said Adam.

Annette doubted whether King needed protection, but she was glad to cross the tent and find out what was happening.

Hashmi acknowledged her presence with a curt nod. He was not to be distracted by the need for an exchange of formal greetings.

'This is not a joking matter, Mr King,' he was saying into

that complacent, self-satisfied face. 'I would have thought the sum of one hundred and twenty thousand English pounds would have made even you reconsider.'

'Chicken feed,' said King blandly. 'You seriously expect me to pack up this whole kit and ship it back—'

'My government would gladly accept the responsibility for the transportation charges.'

'More chicken feed.' King patted Hashmi condescendingly on the shoulder. 'My show is advertised clear across the United States already. Or if it isn't, someone's going to get fired the minute I arrive. You don't want me to disappoint all those little Middle Western people, do you? Do you know what a circus means to them?'

'A circus!'

'An outing for the whole family,' said King with a cloyingly sentimental smile; 'a day to remember.'

'For the last time I beg of you to accept my government's offer.'

King laughed.

'Then,' said Hashmi, 'the consequences of the actions you contemplate must rest upon your own head.'

'Well, let the consequences commence.'

King waved Hashmi aside and spread his arms before Annette. He was obviously waiting for her reaction to his flamboyant garb.

She said: 'You'd put Ra to shame.'

He beamed, then assumed an unconvincingly regretful mien. 'Say, I'm sorry John can't be here. After all he's done to make it a success, it's just too bad. How is he?'

Adam and Annette had left John only just before arriving here. He had still not regained consciousness and the doctor would not let him be moved from Sir Giles Dalrymple's house. Shocked into sobriety, Sir Giles was being an attentive companion, but so far John had been unable to give any idea of what had happened to him or who his attacker could have been. It was Sir Giles who pointed out that the medallion had disappeared. He wished now that he had been in a better condition to examine it when John showed it to him. Remembering Sir Giles's distress and realizing how much of it was due to the arrogance of Alexander King, Annette found it difficult to be amiable to the organizer of the exhibition.

'John's very ill,' she said tersely, and left it at that.

King shook his head. But nothing could depress him this evening. His cherished schemes were coming to fruition. At any moment he would be the centre of attention – he and the mummy, really, but he wasn't anticipating any interruptions from the dead prince.

Adam looked round as a buzz of voices filtered in from the entrance.

'I see the press are arriving.'

'And all their friends,' said King. 'They all show up when they know it's for free. If you'll excuse me, I... er... I have a show to put on.'

They watched him go to greet the new arrivals effusively. As more and more flocked in, the chatter of conversation surged up under the roof of the tent. There was a clink of glasses. Through it all King's voice went on insistently, talking and explaining and boasting. His boyish naivety could have been almost likeable, thought Annette, if only he had possessed just one grain of good taste.

Yet as some of the reporters and critics gathered round the items on display, she wondered if perhaps King was not right. Taking culture to the masses, in however brazen a way, might be better than shutting it away and hoping that the masses would somehow find their way to it of their own volition.

In the crowd she saw Sir Giles. He was shockingly haggard,

but he was clearly in full possession of his faculties. It might have been better if he had stayed at home and spared himself the pain of what he was about to witness. But she realized that he would not have been able to keep himself away.

There was a throbbing roll on timpani behind a curtain, and the long resonant boom of a gong. Voices babbled on for a few seconds and then died away.

King stepped out on to the stage at the end of the tent and raised his arms. Trumpets played a fanfare.

Reporters, several of them still clutching their glasses, edged into seats. Sir Giles settled himself at one side. Adam guided Annette to a chair and put his hand briefly on hers as they sat down. She wanted to think of John and to will him back to health and consciousness, but her mind was full of Adam. In every fibre of her being she sensed that things were coming to a climax. Soon she would be faced with a decision.

'Distinguished guests, ladies and gentlemen of the press' – it was King in full-throated joviality – 'this is an historic moment. Today we are to open the three-thousand-year-old coffin of Ra Antef, royal prince of Egypt.' He waited for the echoes of another fanfare to ebb away, then went on: 'But first I want you to absorb some of the atmosphere, much as it must have been to those intrepid explorers...'

He stepped slightly to one side, and a beam of light fell upon a screen at the back of a stage. To her surprise Annette saw the face of Sir Giles Dalrymple on the screen. She had forgotten that King had taken a great many pictures during the early stages of the expedition, evidently with the intention even then of turning them into lantern slides. She wondered what Sir Giles was thinking. Probably the same thing as she was. Right from the start the whole expedition had been, in King's view, a stunt. All of it had led inevitably to this exhibition tent.

'A leading member of our team,' King was saying, 'was

Professor Dubois from the Paris Museum of Egyptology.' On the screen appeared Annette's father examining a rock formation with John. He was caught for ever, petrified in a characteristic stance, just as Ra Antef was caught in the panels depicting his life. Caught, preserved… but dead. 'The youngest, and by far the prettiest, of our team' – King was playing to his audience without any concern for the susceptibilities of certain members of it – 'was Annette Dubois, a breath of Parisian charm who did much to help cool the hot winds of the desert. In addition to being decorative, she was an able personal assistant to her father, the late Professor, who unfortunately…' He paused histrionically, then lowered his head. 'Who unfortunately lost his life at the hands of superstitious natives.' He allowed it full value, then brightened immediately. 'The guiding light of the expedition…'

A slide of a painting of Rameses VIII appeared on the screen.

'No, not him,' bellowed King. 'Myself!'

There was a ripple of laughter.

King ploughed on with what he supposed to be a dazzling technical description of the methods used in the excavation and the collating of the team's findings. Annette wondered whether he would have allowed John to handle this if John had been well enough to attend. Behind and to one side of her she heard a chair creak and guessed that it was Sir Giles squirming.

Some of the newspapermen were jotting down notes. Others looked around, sizing up the exhibits.

King reached the end of his talk and loudly reclaimed their attention. 'And now… ladies and gentlemen, please… before this great historic moment I must take you into my confidence. I must warn you. There is a curse which says that all persons present at the opening of a pharaoh's coffin and who gaze on the face of the mummy therein… shall die.'

The audience murmured. King smirked with gratification, then tried to look imposing. 'They will be struck down,' he cried melodramatically, 'by the wrath of the Egyptian gods. So any of you of a nervous disposition who wish to leave now may do so.'

He looked challengingly over the audience. A woman giggled nervously. Sir Giles grunted with disgust and shifted in his chair. Annette glanced along the row and at the end of it saw Hashmi, utterly still, expressionless but watching, always watching.

King said: 'Well, you have been warned!'

Again there was a gong, again a roll of drums, again a florid fanfare. The lights dimmed.

'Ladies and gentlemen… for the first time, and before your very eyes, I will cut the royal seal.'

Adam glanced sardonically at Annette. She wondered whether it would be 'the first time' every time the show was put on.

A spotlight settled on the gleaming head of the sarcophagus and then spread to take in the seal. Knife in hand, King stepped towards it. He sliced through the seal and waved the two well-rehearsed Nubians into position on either side of the coffin. They lifted away the lid.

'Alexander King is very proud to present to you the mummy of the royal prince, Ra Antef.'

There was a murmur of anticipation. Then someone laughed. A reporter looked up from his notebook and said, 'Now wait a minute…' And there was the scrape of chairs being pushed back as a few men stood up and began to jeer.

The mummy case was empty.

Annette began to get to her feet. King, his arm raised in a histrionic gesture, was puzzled by the reactions of his audience. He turned to stare into the coffin. His arm fell to his side.

It was left to Annette to rush outside and fetch the police

inspector in charge of the small contingent which had been on duty here since work began on the erection of the tent. The inspector was more skilled at directing traffic and keeping crowds of curious sightseers in check than in detective work; but he welcomed the change in routine and set to work with a will.

Several disgruntled reporters and guests had already left the tent. The inspector ordered his men to stop any further escapes. It was unlikely that anyone could walk past a police guard carrying a swathed mummy, but until he had asked certain questions he did not want the audience to disperse too quickly.

The questions were not very rewarding. They kept coming back to the same thing:

'Who would want to steal a mummy?'

'A competitor,' raged King. 'Somebody who wants to ruin me.'

'You have enemies, Mr King?'

'Of course I've got enemies. I'm in show business. Any one of my so-called friends could be an enemy.' King pointed at Hashmi, who was standing close to the empty coffin. 'He threatened me tonight, for one.'

The inspector turned to Hashmi. 'Is that correct, sir?'

'Threaten him? No. I merely warned him of what might happen.'

'That the mummy would be stolen?' said the policeman keenly.

'That is the last thing I would have wanted.' Hashmi spoke with heartfelt intensity.

'Ha! It made his day for him,' King snarled.

'Why would that be, sir?'

'He wants it tucked away in some stuffy old museum.'

Sir Giles Dalrymple stepped forward. 'And if that's where it had been,' he said, 'none of this would have happened.'

The inspector tried to look masterful, but was clearly at a

loss. He examined the mummy case and the ground below the stand on which the case had been placed. But reporters and others had been milling about there even before the revelation of the empty coffin, and there was nothing that would help to identify the robber.

One or two of the newspapermen were getting restless. They hinted that there might be some comments about police methods – or lack of method – in their columns the next day if they were kept here too long. It might have occurred to the Inspector to keep them here until it was too late for them to meet the morning editions; but that would only have been postponing the day of battle, and discretion won. He allowed the audience to disperse after leaving names and addresses with two of his men at the entrance to the tent.

'Is that all you're going to do?' spluttered King.

'I'll get word sent out, sir, and any information we pick up that might give us a lead—'

'The mummy could be out of the country by tomorrow!'

'I wouldn't worry too much, sir. He'd never get past the customs.' The inspector took out his watch and consulted it as though it might hold the key to all his problems. 'What I'll do, sir, is leave two of my men on guard here while I go to Scotland Yard and get some of our scientific chaps to examine the coffin. As soon as there's anything to report, we'll be in touch with you. Well… goodnight, sir.'

Speechless, King watched the inspector leave the tent. At last he moaned to himself. 'If that's an English policeman, I should have asked him what time it was – I'd have got more out of him.'

Much as she detested the man, Annette could not repress a sympathetic smile. This presentation had meant a lot to him. It was to have been the big moment, the culmination of the time and money he had spent – and it had all gone wrong.

'Don't you think you should go home and get some rest?' she suggested.

'Home? That hotel… And how can I rest? I've got a show – with no star.'

Adam stood beside Annette and added his voice to hers. 'If there's anything I can do… '

'Yes,' said King with a return of his old derisive vigour, 'you can wrap yourself up in some dirty bandages and get in that box.'

Adam took Annette's arm. 'Goodnight, Mr King.'

'Goodnight.'

They went down the tent, leaving the furious tycoon pacing round the sarcophagus as though in search of magic doors or a cuneiform incantation which would miraculously put everything right.

8

THERE WERE lights still on within the tent when John Bray arrived. He walked slowly up to the entrance, fighting off pain and dizziness. Sir Giles had tried to make him stay in bed, but after what the Egyptologist himself had told him, John had known that he must get here and contribute what he could while there was still time. On the way here he had been trying to concentrate, to sort out the muddled memories and tangled theories which had been pounding in his brain while he lay half conscious in bed.

A policeman stepped from the shadows and challenged him. 'Must see Mr King,' John muttered. He was swaying so badly that the policeman obviously suspected him of being drunk.

'There's nobody here, sir.'

'Are you sure that Mr King—'

'John! John – is that you?'

Warily the policeman shepherded John into the tent. King was on the platform, erect beside the empty sarcophagus. It was true, then: the mummy really had gone. The sight of the empty coffin was somehow more appalling than John had expected.

'So it's really gone!'

'I wanted publicity, I sure got it.' King jumped from the platform. 'Say, shouldn't you be in bed?'

John said: 'I think I know why it happened.'

King stared. 'What?'

'I found out the meaning of "the sacred words of life". The medallion. The old powers of Ra Antef. But they were stolen from me – hadn't finished, and they were stolen from me.'

King's blank face was infuriating. The man had put all that money into the expedition, but knew nothing of the truly important findings. He was a showman to whom the treasures of ancient Egypt were about on the same level as a modern freak from some Indian backwater. He would have been happy with a flea circus if there had been something saleable about the fleas.

'Whoever has stolen the mummy,' cried John, 'may be trying to bring it back to life.'

Again he felt dizzy. King's face blurred. And King's voice rasped in his ears. 'That must have been some wallop on the head.'

'You don't believe me, do you?'

'Oh, you're real sick, boy. I'm going to get you a cab.'

'Look, Mr King...'

But without a background of historical knowledge, how could King be expected to understand the significance of the medallion and its probable message? To take him step by step through the story of Ra Antef at this time of night was impossible. John was simply not up to it. But he wanted to impress on someone the need to act now. He was haunted by the vision of ancient sorcery doing its work, of an ageless terror being released into the modern world – of the blasphemous restoration of life to someone... something... which should have been allowed to rest throughout eternity.

'Officer, do you think you could call a cab for this gentleman?'

King was steering John towards the tent flap.

'If someone really wanted revenge,' John persisted, 'what better instrument to use than the mummy brought back to life?'

'Sure. Now come on.'

'What better way to cover the real motive than to blame the legend?'

'Sleep on it,' said King solicitously. 'I'll see you in the morning.'

'You don't want to listen to me, do you, Mr King?'

'Not right now. What I want to figure out,' King confided, 'is how Hashmi did it.'

'Hashmi?'

'It must have been him. It's *got* to be him. That's the only thing that makes sense. You only had to look at his face tonight—'

'He was here tonight?'

'Don't ask me how he did it. But the police have got his address. Once I can figure out how he pulled this off, it won't take long to break him down.'

The policeman who had brought John in now escorted him along the path to the road, where a hansom was waiting. Before they reached the gate, John said:

'Did you take Hashmi Bey's address?'

'Which one would he be, sir?'

'Hashmi Bey. Mr King says you've got his address – I want to drive round there and see him at once.'

The policeman stopped under the flickering gas lamp above the gate, and took out his notebook. He fingered his way down a scribbled list of addresses.

'May have been my mate, sir. We had a job getting them all down, I can tell you. No… here it is.'

He turned the page towards John. John read the address and nodded his thanks. Then he turned to the hansom cab and got in.

9

ALEXANDER KING was very tired. He was also very angry. But the tiredness was winning. There was nothing more he could do tonight. The mummy had gone, and no matter how much he fumed and paced round the exhibition tent he wouldn't be able to bring it back. Tomorrow he would start afresh. Tomorrow he would stand over the London police and lash them into some kind of activity.

As he went out of the tent, the policeman near the entrance stepped forward.

'Want a cab, sir?'

'Thanks, no.' A brisk walk through the quiet streets might help to calm him down. He needed calming if he was to get a good night's sleep.

King set out.

A wispy fog swirled up from gratings in the street and clung to the walls. Gas lamps became blotches of fuzzy yellow light through the drifting tendrils. A clock struck, its note oddly muted by the fog.

A woman stepped from a doorway into King's path. 'You in a hurry, guv?'

'What can I do for you?'

'Nothing, dearie. I wondered if there was anything I could do for *you*?'

King shook himself out of his trance. 'No. No, thanks.'

He walked round the woman and went on his way. It took him another ten minutes to realize that he was lost. He thought he knew London pretty well, but his mind had been so occupied with thoughts about the mummy and about the ridicule that was likely to be heaped on him in the newspapers that he had not been paying much attention to the streets down which he walked.

He stopped on a corner, baffled.

Still doubts and speculations jangled in his mind. Maybe the publicity would be a good thing. Crowds would flock in to the exhibition. If the mummy came back…

He had to find the mummy. Without it, the exhibition was just not good enough.

When it came back… if it came back…

He tried to make himself concentrate on his route. There was no street name on the wall above him. He crossed the road, to where an archway opened onto what might be a mews. But as he came closer he heard the faint lapping of water, and there was a sudden mournful groan from a ship's foghorn.

He must be close to the river. It was incredible that he should have walked so far in the wrong direction.

King hesitated, then turned back.

Another archway swam out of the fog. It was growing thicker here, mingling with a river mist and producing strange shapes in the shifting darkness. There was an almost solid shape framed in the archway.

As he drew level, King found that the shape did not dissolve into wisps of fog. It remained substantial – the figure of a man, motionless, apparently waiting for him.

He cleared his throat from the prickling discomfort of the fog. 'I reckon I've lost my way. Where would I be right now?'

There was no reply.

'Look' – King was in no mood for further difficulties after

what had happened tonight – 'I don't know who the hell you are, but don't just...'

The figure stepped out of the archway. The diffuse light gave it features which had been concealed in the shadows. King saw the bandages strain as the arms were raised, looked into the travesty of a face – and was utterly unable to accept what he saw.

A cracked laugh burst from his throat. 'If you think this is a joke...'

But the mummy was no joke. The mummy was real and powerful and relentless. It was a solid, vengeful ghost from remote ages; something which ought to have been dead but was alive with a fearful supernatural force.

The arms closed on Alexander King. They lifted him high from the pavement, and he spun round until he was staring into the eye sockets of what had once been a prince of Egypt.

He screamed.

The buildings seemed to reel past him. The archway spun dizzily, a flight of steps fell away from him at an angle. The mummy threw him... threw him so that he fell in a vertiginous arc without end... until he crashed with a sickening final agony against solid stone, rebounded from it, and sank into the river without another sound.

The waters closed over his head.

10

JOHN BRAY said: 'I believe you have a foreign gentleman staying here?'

The unshaven man who had opened the door to him peered round it and grunted suspiciously: 'And what business is that of yours?'

John took a handful of coins from his pocket and jangled them slightly. Behind the man he caught a glimpse of a woman with stringy hair and a sallow face. The only gleam of hope or happiness in that face was in her eyes as she heard the rattle of money. She stepped past the man and elbowed him so that he had to open the door wider.

'An Egyptian gentleman,' John prompted her.

She held out her hand. He dropped money into it. She said: 'Yes, that'll be him on the first-floor back.'

'Thank you.'

John went past her and up the narrow stairs, stubbing his toes against the torn linoleum. Behind him he heard an argument break out between the man and woman over the money. There was the slam of a door as they shut themselves away to thrash it out.

John walked along the first-floor landing to the back of the house. Fog clawed at the grimy window. There was only one door at this end of the passage. He tapped on it with his knuckles, then hammered louder.

'Hashmi! Open the door.'

There was no reply. John looked back towards the stairs. If he made too much noise, the couple below might call a truce to their bickering until they had got him out of the house. He listened. There was no sound now from downstairs, and no sound from within the room.

He banged again, then tried the door handle. The handle and the lock itself shifted. The house was shabby, the door fitted badly, the lock was loose. John applied his shoulder gently to one of the panels and increased the pressure.

At the second attempt he pushed the door open and staggered into the room.

It was empty. He struck a match and lit the gas jet. It sighed mournfully as he began to search the room.

Hashmi had brought very little with him. His battered case contained only a few clothes, and one suit hung in the musty wardrobe. The furniture here was sparse and there were few places of concealment. John was tipping back the mattress on the bed when Hashmi came softly, cat-footedly into the room and drew a knife.

'Have you found what you're looking for, Mr Bray?'

John straightened up. The mattress fell back on to the frame of the bed with a dull thump.

He said: 'Where is it?'

Hashmi advanced, the blade of the knife jutting towards John. 'If I knew what you sought—'

'You know very well. The medallion. Where is it?'

Hashmi drew in breath with a hiss grotesquely like that of the gas jet.

'So…! It does exist.'

'And you stole it from me,' said John.

Hashmi studied him for a moment, then tossed the knife onto the washstand. He closed the door.

'We are speaking of the same thing, are we? The sacred medallion of Ra Antef, conferrer of life, presented to him by his nomad people? The medallion which never fell into the hands of his brother Be… Be, whose hired assassins did their foul work and brought back proof, but who knew nothing of the greatest of all Ra Antef's possessions…'

John said: 'As I suspected, you know all about it. You have known about it from the start. And when I began to get too close to the truth—'

'You fool!' snapped Hashmi. 'If I possessed the secret of reviving the dead do you think I would have misused it in such a stupid way?'

John did not know what to think. Without knowing the purpose behind this baffling sequence of events, he could not fit Hashmi or anyone else into the pattern. There was a burning integrity in the man which seemed to rule him out as a thief, particularly where it was a matter of stealing a holy relic of his country's past; yet the integrity could be that of a fanatic, capable of taking any violent steps which would lead to the mysterious end.

John said abruptly: 'Will you come with me to the police?'

'I shall be happy to co-operate in any attempt to stop further useless violence.'

At the door John could not resist asking: 'Do you know who is behind this whole weird business?'

'I know there are forces at work,' said Hashmi solemnly, 'which the most highly developed scientific mind in this country could not hope to comprehend.'

11

SIR GILES Dalrymple took the stopper from the brandy decanter and reached for a glass. Then he replaced the stopper. He pushed the glass away from him. It was important that his head should stay clear. He had a lot of work to do. He ought to have started on it the moment young John Bray came here with his suspicions. The young man had been on the right track. It was up to the older one, now, to follow that track wherever it led.

John had left a few scraps of paper on the desk when he was struck down. Sir Giles recognized the outlines of certain hieroglyphics, but was not so sure of others. There were, however, resemblances to sketches which he had once seen – sketches to which he had referred John.

These scrawls here, in the corner – from the medallion? Sir Giles pored over them. The sacred words of legend… No, that was absurd. The sacred words of life.

Absurd, said one part of his mind. But in another part there was a growing sense of awe.

Sir Giles sat back. He badly needed a brandy. But he was still strong. Temptation of that kind must be resisted. He would show them all that he was still what he had always been – the great interpreter of ancient Egypt, the man who could solve every riddle of the past.

He began to write with laborious precision a line of

hieroglyphs that would make sense of John Bray's scattered jottings. As he wrote, he murmured over them, caught in a strange spell which grew more vibrant minute by minute.

It was broken by a crash of shattered glass. Sir Giles sprang to his feet as the window disintegrated and the mummy shambled into the room.

There was a gun in the top right-hand drawer of the desk. It was a ludicrous weapon to use against this monstrous apparition, but instinctively Sir Giles grabbed at it. The mummy came on. He fired, then fired again. The mummy shook, jolted by the impact, but its portentous tread did not falter. Sir Giles fired a third time. Then the mummy raised its arm and scooped him up.

Sir Giles uttered a choking cry. It was stifled as the arm tightened.

He was smacked down across the desk, hearing the crunch of his own bones and feeling stabs of pain as though he had been knifed from every side simultaneously. The arm round his throat grew tighter. He flailed out, but met only the thick wadding of the bandages. Then, as his eyes filmed over, the last thing he saw was a china cat which the mummy had lifted from the desk. It was poised over Sir Giles for an instant before coming down. Three times it struck his forehead before smashing; but by the third time Sir Giles Dalrymple was unaware of its savage impact.

12

A BOOK LAY open on Adam's lap. He read from it in his meditative, musical voice, occasionally glancing across the glow of firelight at Annette:

'How do I love thee? Let me count the ways.
I love thee to the depth and breadth and height
My soul can reach, when feeling out of sight
For the ends of Being and ideal Grace.
I love thee to the level of every day's
Most quiet need, by sun and candle light…'

Annette was lulled by the rhythmic beauty of it and by the drowsy contentment induced by the fire. She recognized Adam's motives: he had every intention of coaxing her away from John; but she had no power to resist.

'I love thee freely, as men strive for Right;
I love thee purely, as they turn from Praise.
I love thee with the passion put to use
In my old griefs, and with my childhood's faith.
I love thee with a love I seemed to lose
With my lost saints – I love thee with the breath,
Smiles, tears, of all my life! – and if God choose,
I shall love thee better after death.'

The last line went on reverberating through the room. Adam sat contemplating the page for what seemed an eternity, then looked up at Annette.

'"Better,"' he repeated, '"after death."'

Annette tried to find some flippant rejoinder, but now was no time for flippancy. Now was the time for truth, unequivocal and unavoidable.

Adam closed the book. He said: 'I have to leave London.'

'Oh, no.' The protest was drawn from her like a cry of despair.

'I could make arrangements for you and John to stay on while the exhibition remains here.'

'Without you?'

'You would be quite comfortable. You wouldn't want for anything.'

She said: 'I couldn't bear it.'

He put the book down and got up, putting out his hands to her. She took them and he drew her to her feet.

'Or,' he said, 'you could come with me. I want you to come. Dare I ask it of you?'

It did not occur to her to ask him where they would go or how long they would be away. She made no protestations. There was no coyness and no doubt in her. She simply said:

'When?'

'Tomorrow morning. Early.'

'How do we tell John?' There was no need for them even to discuss the complications of the present or the future. It was not a matter of her having to decide that she was not meant for John: the decision had been made deeply and secretly without her having to wrestle with it. The only question was that of the kindest and least evasive way of breaking the news.

Adam said: 'You won't want to upset him by a harrowing scene while he's ill. I suggest you leave him a note.'

'I don't like to, but…'

'Write it now.' Adam spoke quietly but authoritatively.

Annette felt that her life was passing into his hands. She was left with no initiative of her own. Somehow she could have predicted that it would be like this and that she would accept it. There was a lifetime of authority in Adam's voice and manner. She realized that she knew almost nothing about him – about the source of his wealth, the career that had given him his aristocratic self-possession, the ability to command and to compel immediate obedience…

She freed her hands from his and went up to her room. In the white stillness of this bedroom she was farther away from Adam and farther from his influence, and for the first time she felt a flicker of revolt. It was too easy for him. He snapped his fingers and she jumped through the hoop. He told her to cast John aside, and she was about to do so without a murmur.

But stronger than this belated doubt was the anxiety to get back to Adam. The sooner she finished the letter, the sooner she could be with him again.

She began to write to John.

Immediately in front of her was her dressing-table mirror. When she paused to think of the right phrase, she saw her own pale, reproachful face staring back at her. It was cruel to do this to John, and cowardly not to wait until she could talk to him face to face. But she was a woman possessed. None of the normal values prevailed any longer.

'I can only hope that some day you will forgive me…'

She said the words aloud as though to test them. Then, as she was about to put them on paper, there was a crash from below. It shook the house. It was no commonplace sound – not just the accidental overturning of a table, or somebody dropping a tray. A dull thumping followed, like the noise of a struggle.

Annette got up and went to the door. She hurried along to the head of the stairs and looked down.

And she screamed.

In the hall below, Adam was fighting desperately with the mummy. Some of the creature's bandages were torn and flapped about it like the trappings of a scarecrow. Its arms were crushing the breath out of Adam, who beat savagely but unavailingly against the swathed head.

Annette's scream cut through the sound of the struggle. The mummy paused. Adam went slack. The mummy suddenly hurled him aside so that he fell in a crumpled heap at the foot of the stairs.

The mummy stepped ponderously over him and began to mount the stairs.

Annette leaned against the wall, whimpering to herself. She wanted to turn and run, but was rooted to the spot. If she tried to shut herself in her room, this creature would surely smash down the door. There must be another flight of stairs, another way out, some way of escaping from the house and raising the alarm… but all her willpower was sapped by the sheer horror of this impossible, implacable thing plodding up towards her.

And suddenly she realized the worst thing of all. Her own breath rasped in her throat, but it was drowned by the noise of other breathing. The mummy was steadily, hoarsely *breathing.*

It had almost reached her. One arm was raised. Annette knew that her knees were going to give way. She was going to collapse abjectly, right in its path.

Then Adam, at the foot of the stairs, forced himself up to his knees. Shakily but commandingly he mouthed:

'Hoom a Ra.'

The mummy halted.

Adam came up two steps. 'Arrer as… Nek hebet!'

The mummy seemed undecided. The head turned, shaking solemnly. Annette tried to back away, to hide round the corner of the landing. The movement attracted the mummy's attention, and it reached out for her. The slow, relentless movement of that arm was too much for Annette: she slid down the wall into a sobbing heap on the floor.

She was aware of Adam rhythmically, desperately calling. In her waking nightmare the sounds were jumbled and nonsensical. Again the mummy shook its head as though to dismiss the petty sting of the words. It loomed over Annette. She did not know how much was reality and how much distorted fantasy. It seemed to her that the mummy bent over her for an age and that it then touched her limp hand almost tenderly, regretfully. There was a stale, sickly sweet grave smell; and all the time the heavy breathing.

The smell drifted away. The sound of breathing receded. Lying with her cheek on the floor, she was vaguely aware of the shrouded feet turning and pacing back down the stairs. She tried to pull herself round. Adam swam into view, facing up as the mummy descended, challenging the creature.

An arm swung like a slow, weighty hammer; and Adam went down again.

There was noise. More noise. Annette seemed still to hear that painful breathing and at the same time to be assailed by a hammering on wood, the racket of a doorbell swinging and clanking, and men shouting.

The mummy had gone. Adam lay still. And suddenly the place was full. Men crashed into the hall, and one came racing up the stairs towards her.

Firm hands took her gently by the shoulders and turned her over.

'Darling… darling, what's happened?'

It was John. Even through her fading nightmare she was sorry that it should be John.

She whispered: 'Adam – how's Adam?'

Two police uniforms struck an incongruous note in the delicate green and white colour scheme of the hall.

'All right, sir?' growled a voice below her.

'Adam,' she said again, struggling up.

'He's all right, miss.'

'Thank God.'

With John supporting her, Annette went downstairs to join the group at the foot of the flight.

'You remember me, Miss – Inspector Mackenzie.' Yes, she remembered, though it seemed a lifetime since the mummy disappeared. So much had happened, so many things had altered since then. She was scared – torn between wanting it all to have been a terrible dream, and wanting part of it not to have been a dream. 'Miss' – it was the inspector, urgent and insistent – 'can you tell me what happened?'

'The mummy,' she said.

The thought of it made her feel faint once more. John's arm tightened across her shoulders. Hashmi Bey – whatever was he doing here? – stepped forward, intent on what she had just said.

'Yes?' he prompted her. 'It was here, yes?'

'It was here,' she said. 'It's alive.'

'You actually saw it?' said Inspector Mackenzie.

'Yes. It… it attacked Adam.'

'Attacked Adam?' The incredulity in John's voice was not, she somehow knew, directed against the mere idea of the mummy being alive. There was something deeper and stranger than that.

Hashmi and John exchanged glances.

Hashmi said, puzzled: 'But why should it do that?'

The inspector tugged thoughtfully at his lower lip. He was on utterly foreign ground. John said: 'It looks as though the theory we brought to you, Inspector, has been proved wrong.'

'That's often the trouble with theories, sir.'

The baize door on the far side of the hall opened quietly and Jessop came in. His eyes widened as he saw his master lying on the lower steps of the staircase. The police sergeant with Inspector Mackenzie gave him a hand to carry Adam up to his room. When they had gone, the group of people in the hall stayed together, waiting for someone to give a lead, to say something that would make sense.

John broke the baffled silence. 'And yet, you know, it's the only theory that works. Unless… well, of course, it could be that something else has gone wrong. Just could be.'

Annette could not follow what he was talking about. She doubted whether the inspector was doing any better.

'Look' – John turned to Inspector Mackenzie – 'will you give us another chance to prove that we're right?'

'That's one advantage the amateur detective has over the professional: a second chance.'

John was too preoccupied with this new opportunity to notice when Annette slipped gently away from him and hurried to Adam's room.

Jessop and the police sergeant had laid him on the wide bed. A lesser man would have been swamped by the airy proportions of the room with its spartan furnishing and lack of clutter; but Adam, even struggling up from unconsciousness, dominated his setting. He waved Jessop away and continued the gesture to include the policeman.

The sergeant hesitated at the door.

'I think the inspector will be requiring a statement from you, sir.'

'Not now,' said Adam imperiously.

'When you're quite recovered, sir, of course.'

'I'll notify you when that is.'

Dubiously the sergeant went away to report. Adam sank back on the bed and put out his hand. Annette took it.

She said: 'I still don't understand. I… it makes no sense.'

'It will.' Adam stared at the ceiling. 'It will all make sense when you know the truth.'

'The truth? But why should the mummy attack you? If all the old legends are true, it should be seeking out the… the desecrators of the tomb… meaning Sir Giles and John and myself.' Annette shivered. 'But you had nothing to do with it. You weren't there. Just because you offered us hospitality when we got to England…'

She was bewildered by his calmness. In spite of that terrible attack on him he showed no fear, not even a trace of resentment that his generosity should have had such results. As he lay there tranquilly with his eyes open, gazing at something remote which she could not share with him, he seemed almost to be welcoming what had happened and would happen. He might have been waiting a lifetime for it – a lifetime of incredible length.

He said: 'When those people downstairs have gone, we will talk.'

'They'll be here for ages yet.'

'No,' he said softly, 'I don't think so.'

As though to confirm this, there was a tap at the door and John came in. His eyes took in the scene – Adam with his hand in Annette's, the two of them caught in a world of their own – but his voice was steady as he said:

'We've got to lure it out into the open. If I was right about the incantation, that's the best way. We've got to go and see Sir Giles – got to make him work with us, if we have to pump the alcohol out of him first!'

Adam continued to stare upwards. 'You're very… determined,' he said abstractedly.

'Yes,' said John with unusual vigour. 'I am. And when you've quite recovered,' he added ironically, deliberately setting out to bring a flush to Annette's cheeks, 'perhaps you'll contribute your little bit by making a detailed statement to the policeman downstairs. He'll stay there on guard until you're ready.'

Annette recognized the threat in the words. It made no impression on Adam, but she was suffused with a sudden misery, like a child deprived of a promised holiday. Something menaced their happiness. They would not be allowed to leave early in the morning. They were involved in this horror and would not be able to flee from it until the whole affair was cleared up. John could hardly conceal his gratification: in his view the policeman would be a gaoler rather than a protector.

She said: 'I think Adam should rest.'

'See that he does, then.'

John turned and left them. They heard his footsteps die away, and a little while later the front door slammed.

After a long pause Adam said: 'They must be very foolish if they think I cannot get past a policeman in my own house.'

'Shall we…' Annette fumbled, hardly daring to put it to the test. 'Are we going to leave, as we planned? Will we be able to go after all?'

'First,' he said, 'I think you should know the truth.'

He turned over to face her. She was shocked by the impression of age communicated by his eyes. He was not the Adam she had thought she knew: there was someone else there, someone who must always have been waiting.

'You're tired,' she said, trying to put off the moment when irrevocable things might be said. 'We can talk later.'

He said: 'I have so much to tell you. Think back first to the legend of Ra. Even there, there are facts which none of you could see when you tried to interpret the writings. And some details of the story are lost in the mists of antiquity. How much simpler for all your earnest scholars and interpreters if they had had access to the missing fragments! You see, when Rameses heard the news of the death of Ra, his favourite son, he suffered a stroke which was finally to kill him. Before he died he sent emissaries to ensure that Ra should have a worthy burial. This much you know. But you do not know that on his deathbed he sent for the person who had been responsible for the death of Ra and, truly, for his own impending death. He cursed that person – cursed him to everlasting life, unless he could die by the hand of his own brother.'

'How would you know this?' Annette whispered.

'Because I am that person.' Adam sat up, swung his legs off the bed, and stood in the middle of the room. He lifted his head arrogantly, once more staring beyond her into the infinite. 'I am Be, younger son of Rameses the Eighth, Pharaoh of Pharaohs.'

The house was still. The walls of the spacious room seemed to contract and close in on Annette. She wanted to believe that she was listening to a madman, but knew that she was not. He had promised her the truth and this was it.

'Cursed to eternal wandering,' he brooded, 'for I could never die. The only person who could release me from the curse had already been destroyed at the hands of my hired assassins. My father had knowingly burdened me with this grotesque fate. No escape for me unless I could be killed by one already dead – a mockery, an impossibility…' He was convulsed by a groan of despair, echoing with the memories of thousands of years. And then he said almost inaudibly: 'Until now.'

13

The corpse of Sir Giles Dalrymple lay in ghastly ruin in his library. When his housekeeper had tapped several times on the door and then opened it to admit John, Hashmi, and Inspector Mackenzie, she collapsed.

The inspector sent for more men, and while John and Hashmi ploughed their way through books from Sir Giles's shelves, policemen examined the body and the floor, the shattered window and the debris around the desk. Finally the corpse was removed. Whatever doubts his superiors might cast on his reports, the inspector was beginning to believe the gruesome story advanced by John Bray and the Egyptian.

The curtains stirred in the draught through the broken window. The inspector suggested that he should try to have it boarded up without delay, but John was firm about this.

'I have a feeling in my bones' – the phrase made the inspector shudder – 'that we may be disturbed. And I think it's best to make things easy. Leave the window as it is. We won't be too cold. But if you could deploy your men…'

Inspector Mackenzie guaranteed to take the necessary precautions and then left the two men to their studies.

The reference books proved unhelpful. They said what John had expected them to say, confirming all that he and Hashmi had based their suspicions on. Every solitary reference to the curse agreed that only those directly involved in opening the tomb were in mortal danger. There must be some other element, something which had never been told and never written down.

It was inconceivable that the mummy, restored to its grim semblance of life, should be simply a mindless killer. Yet where would it stop; how could one tell who was in danger and who might be next; what ancient ritual governed its murderous actions?

John half hoped that tonight he would have to face the terror himself. If it must come, then let it come soon. He and Hashmi had both been concerned in the desecration of the tomb: they were here together now, and whatever psychic force drove the mummy to seek out its victims must surely guide it to where these two were waiting.

The curtains lifted gently inwards, then fell back like the slowly billowing skirts of a woman.

Hashmi looked up.

'Found anything?' asked John.

'There is nothing.' Hashmi closed another huge tome.

Again the curtains moved. John was directly facing them. He saw the bandaged hand gripping the edge of the velvet. The outlines of the fingers forced through, straining against the bonds, trying to become flexible and free.

Hashmi looked into John's face and understood. He slid from his chair and edged round the desk.

Suddenly the curtains crashed down. The mummy was framed in the broken window. Its breathing was laboured, its movements slow yet as inexorable as a juggernaut.

John groped behind him for the door handle and opened it.

'Inspector...!'

Mackenzie moved fast. As John and Hashmi stood aside, two policemen rushed into the room with a huge net. The inspector followed them in, and watched approvingly as they flung the net. It settled over the mummy's head and shoulders.

The inspector darted forward and tugged it down. The mummy struck out, but already the net was tightening around it. The policemen held firm as the creature strained against the trap; then, as they pulled on the ropes, it toppled forward with agonizing slowness and hit the floor. There it writhed impotently while John and Hashmi watched.

Hashmi stepped towards the imprisoned creature. Contrition came into his face. A cry of protest was torn from him.

'Stop it!'

Inspector Mackenzie glanced at him in surprise. John put out a hand, but Hashmi was sinking to his knees beside the mummy.

'O Ra Antef…'

The mummy stopped struggling and lay still. It ceased to breathe.

'Thou mighty prince of Egypt, son of the Pharaoh of Pharaohs, gaze upon the humblest of thy humble servants, who has transgressed against thee and heaped ridicule on thy head.'

'Hashmi!' John wanted to seize the Egyptian and drag him back, but something prevented him – something nameless and all-powerful, something which demanded that the scales of justice should balance.

'May the memory of my ancestors be erased for ever,' Hashmi sobbed, 'and the memory of my unworthy self remain only in the minds of vermin and the deceased creatures of the earth. I, who have committed the unforgivable and allied myself with desecrators and non-believers, implore thee to destroy my body painfully, and my soul shall pay penance through all eternity.'

The mummy's breathing began again, harsh and purposeful. The two policemen, who had been gaping at Hashmi, had let their grip on the ropes slacken. Before they could resist, the mummy had reared up and thrust its arms away from its side.

The ropes strained across its chest and then broke.

One of the constables lost his nerve and scrabbled away like an ungainly crab.

The mummy stepped towards Hashmi.

Hashmi's head sagged to the floor. The mummy raised one foot and set it on Hashmi's ear, lightly, as though to gauge the distance. Then the foot came up again… and down. Hashmi uttered one inhuman sound that was neither a scream nor a plea. The mummy stamped; and stamped again. Hashmi's head was left as a pulp of blood, brains, and splintered bone.

One of the policemen retched. The other grabbed a heavy inkstand from the desk and nerved himself to creep towards the mummy.

John waited for his turn to come – for the mummy to advance on him and crush him as it had crushed Hashmi. But Inspector Mackenzie and his two men formed a barrier between them. The mummy retreated before their shaky but courageous attack. As they grabbed for the ends of the net, it was twitched from their grasp. The mummy turned and blundered out of the window.

The inspector followed it out, then stopped. He snapped orders over his shoulder.

'Get Sergeant Walters. Follow that thing – but keep your distance. Smith, find something to cover him up.' He nodded towards the corpse on the floor, then looked questioningly at John in search of inspiration. 'Any idea where it could have gone?'

'Apart from the attack on Adam Beauchamp,' said John, 'it appears to be revenging itself only on those who disturbed its peace.'

'Then that leaves you and Miss Dubois in danger. It's left you for the time being. So…'

'I'm going after your sergeant.'

'Not on your own,' said Inspector Mackenzie dourly. 'I want to be in at…' He faltered.

'At what?' demanded John.

'I nearly said… "at the kill!"'

14

THE BASEMENT was more extensive than even the spaciousness of the house above would have led her to expect. Annette stared into the dim recesses and marvelled at the world she had entered. For it was not just the space that took her breath away: there was, above all, the way in which the space had been filled. At the foot of the basement steps crouched a black statue of the jackal god, Anubis, with eyes of obsidian and alabaster. Erect and splendid beyond it, with a lamp burning at its feet, was a gilded figure of Osiris. The walls were obscured by shelves, laden with precious objects. Many of them were familiar to Annette, though she had never seen so many perfect specimens assembled in one place.

She said: 'I… I can't believe it. Everything's in such wonderful condition.'

Adam was beside her as she stopped at one shelf and picked up a magnificent crown. It carried the head of the vulture goddess Nekhabet, picked out in turquoise and lapis-lazuli.

'A pharaoh's crown,' breathed Annette.

'It has always been mine.'

Annette replaced it and steeled herself to face him. In this incredible setting she saw the true Adam – or was he now the true Be?

'What is going to happen? You… and I… what does it all mean?'

He said: 'It means that I can die.'

'Adam!' It was the name of a human being, a man of her own day and age, that was torn from her. But now, calm and implacable, he was no longer Adam.

'When your father found the tomb of my brother,' he said, 'he provided the means. But it was lifeless. It was left to you – you, my dear Annette – to provide the words that would revive it.'

'To me?'

From his pocket he took the medallion. Before she could ask how it had come into his possession he was gently fastening the chain round her neck.

'While the hand of my brother lives, I must use it. And then we can be together as I wanted. You and I, Annette, together. You said you would come, didn't you?'

'Yes,' she said without knowing what she meant.

'Now.' He took her arm and led her to the centre of the cellar, where they were looked down on by the bland animal heads of gods aligned on every shelf. The place, thought Annette hysterically, was like some supernatural toy shop. She wanted to draw Adam's attention to this; but Adam was no longer the man she had known. He knelt and indicated that she should do the same. His spell was still strong. She obeyed, while all the time her whole nature was trying to rebel. He said: 'Repeat after me… "Awaken, O Silent One, thou who hast slept…"'

Annette's lips were tightly shut. Her throat was dry. She clasped her hands together, but made no sound.

'Say it!' he shouted.

The words began to come from her, forced out one at a time without coherence. '"Awaken, O Silent One, thou who hast slept…"'

'"Appear!"' intoned Adam. '"Thou art justified against those who sought to harm thee and thy resting place."'

'"Appear! Thou art justified…"'

Annette gasped. A panel at the far end of the cellar creaked open. Framed in the dark opening was the mummy. It stepped onto the stone floor.

Adam, his hands clasped in prayer, looked up. A wave of tenderness flowed into his face. The colour ebbed and returned. A fearful joy throbbed in his voice.

'Osiris, father of all, give this thy servant that which you bestow upon the unborn bird in the egg. Give it life and the powers of death.' Adam held out his arms imploringly towards the mummy. 'Osiris, set the time that it may come forth and loudly raise up its voice to praise thee. And may it do thy will. Grant me release.' On his knees he edged towards the mummy, a supplicant with his arms still outstretched. 'Awake, O Ra, my brother. Awake, son of the Pharaoh of Pharaohs. Awake, Ra, Prince of the Desert.'

Annette heard what she had not heard until now – the sound of the mummy's breathing, quickening and intensifying. It took three steps towards Adam.

Adam rose. 'Welcome, my brother. The time is now at hand for you to complete your earthly mission, that you may rest in peace again for all eternity. I plead for your mercy on me. And first' – without looking at her he reached out and seized Annette's arm – 'I humbly offer you one whom you have been seeking. Destroy this miserable desecrator!'

Annette tried to free herself, but she was held in the grip of a madman. Desperately she writhed, while Adam stood holding her and grinning in sadistic triumph.

The mummy came closer, its right arm raised. Annette screamed. Adam wrenched her forward, offering her as a sacrifice. This was his love, this his purpose for her – to be given up into the ritual killing which his ancient tradition demanded.

'Before we brothers pass into the shades,' cried Adam, 'let this creature be obliterated. She is not fit to look on our final rites. Deliver me, Ra – but do not defile us by suffering the presence of another.'

Somewhere overhead there was a faint thud. A faint patter of footsteps went across the floor like distant rats scurrying for cover.

Faintly the voice of Inspector Mackenzie called: 'Search the house. The whole lot. Don't miss anything.'

Annette screamed and screamed again. Adam tried to stop her, but she yelled until her voice cracked. A door rattled, not far away. Voices were suddenly loud down the echoing basement steps. And as she reeled away from Adam, strong arms were folded round her. The foetid grave stench enveloped her. The mummy lifted her and floundered away through the panel.

'Adam!' She heard John's cry and then, more faintly, 'Annette... where is she?'

The panel must have closed behind them, for now there was nothing but darkness. The cloying smell which seeped out of the mummy's ancient wrappings grew more oppressive, and somehow there was a stronger, different stench of corruption. In the hellish darkness Annette had no idea where they were going, but she felt that they were bumping down further steps into the very bowels of the earth.

From behind them there was a crash, and light filtered down the steps. It reflected from the surface of dark water below.

They were in the sewers. And Adam was scrambling down behind them. John shouted after him. Dark shapes jostled through the opening.

The mummy reached the bottom of the steps and turned along a narrow walk beside the noisome, steadily murmuring water. It went from one low-roofed tunnel to another through a grating which swung open. Adam hurried after, with John and Inspector Mackenzie in hot pursuit. As Adam ducked and came through the grating, John plunged madly forward and caught hold of it. He dragged the grill back… and it sliced through Adam's hand. Trapped for a second, the hand seemed to clench and then let the fingers splay out; and then it drooped and fell.

Adam was howling like a wounded beast. He stumbled, clutching the stump of his arm, and splashed into the foul channel of the sewer.

Still the mummy did not falter. It trod on its way, clutching Annette and stooping below the slimy roof. Annette tried to look back, but could see only the edge of the water.

The surface rippled and broke. Adam pushed himself up and groped hideously back onto the walk. He was beside the mummy as they reached a wider chamber in these rustling catacombs.

'In there!' he said.

The mummy lowered Annette and gently but firmly set her against the rear wall of the chamber. The mummy and Adam blocked the exit.

Adam was almost doubled up with pain. Blood dripped to the floor. Soon he would be too weak to walk or think. But he was immortal, thought Annette wildly: he would go on living, he would recover, there was nothing that could happen to him which would kill him. Unless…

The mummy, having stood back as though to contemplate her, now moved forward again.

'Adam… please.' She could not bear to die: not here, in this awful place, at the hands of this monster. 'Stop him. Please stop him.'

'Don't be frightened of death.' In spite of his agony, Adam's voice was as level and persuasive as ever. 'Welcome it as a release. Turn away gladly from the torture and torment which fools call life.'

'No. No… I want to live.'

'There will be no suffering. Death will be brief. It is nothing compared to the pain I have seen, wandering this earth for three thousand years. Plagues, famine, pestilence, wars, and man's daily inhumanity to his fellow men.' Adam raised the mangled, dripping stump of his arm. 'The pain of this is nothing, set beside what I have seen. Life without end is the only thing we should not be asked to suffer. You are so fortunate, Annette. So fortunate, my dear.' He watched the mummy and smiled, urging it on. 'Now, Ra – now!'

The mummy's hand reached for Annette's throat. She felt the coarse clumsiness of the groping fingers. Yet they were gentle. Suddenly there was a sharp tug. She felt the chain of the medallion snap.

The mummy stepped back again, the medallion dangling from its hand.

Adam stared.

'Kill her!' The shriek, so different from his measured tones of a few seconds ago, echoed along the sewers.

The mummy stood quite still. The medallion swayed and turned slowly, revolving in the faint, pallid light.

'Kill her!'

There was a knife in Adam's hand. He stepped past the mummy, his face contorted as he approached Annette. All the evil of his past throbbed through him and transfigured him.

'Ra,' he cried scornfully. 'Must I do this for you? My poor, aesthetic, beauty-loving brother!'

The knife was raised. Annette let out a sob. The knife did not descend. It was held in mid-air as the mummy's hand closed on Adam's wrist. There was an instant in which the two stood still. Then Adam, with one arm useless at his side and the other stretched to its limit, began to sag.

The mummy turned once. It was enough to drag Adam round and pitch him over the edge into the water. The mummy held on to his wrist until the last moment. Adam's hand thrust out above the surface, the fingers suddenly limp, the knife gone. It was a picture which would be burned onto Annette's mind until her dying day. Then the hand seemed to float away, turning in on itself and at last disappearing.

The mummy straightened up and looked back at Annette. She tensed. It must end soon. She could bear no more. She would sooner throw herself into that foul channel and be carried away than endure another minute of this. But the mummy blocked her way. She could not spring past it.

There was a faint chinking sound as the medallion rotated. The mummy appeared to look down.

Here, surely, the story must finish. Annette offered up a silent prayer. The ancient curse had been wiped out. Did there have to be more killing: had their crime in opening the tomb of Ra Antef to be expiated right to the last breath of their lives?

Abruptly the mummy was no longer standing across the mouth of the recess. It stepped out along the walk and stopped at the junction of two sewer channels. Annette crept forward, not daring to run yet, and not knowing which way to run if she had the chance.

The mummy raised its head and reached up to touch the ceiling, curving down over the tunnel. The roof blocks were ragged, with gaps between many of them where the filling had rotted away. The mummy's hand probed into a crack. A shower of fragments fell into the water, followed by the splash of a large stone.

Annette backed away and flattened herself against the wall. The mummy lifted both hands and pulled with inhuman strength at the roof.

It began to collapse. A huge slab fell sideways across the mummy's shoulder. Stones and dust seethed down in a growing avalanche. The mummy remained erect in the middle of the chaos, staggering under the impact of repeated blows but keeping its arms uplifted. The medallion swung and danced in the dust cloud.

'There she is!' It was Inspector Mackenzie, somewhere not far away. 'I can't see anyone else.'

'Annette!' John was calling.

She turned her head away as a few jagged splinters of stone were tossed against her cheek. But she had to look back, to watch the mummy as the world collapsed around it. She saw the medallion fall at last, to be lost in the water, swept away or buried in a jumble of masonry. She saw the mummy's arms drop to its sides. The head bowed at last, the shoulders bent and succumbed, and the tattered bandages disappeared into the dust and darkness.

Light stabbed in through a great gap in the walls. John was scrambling over the rubble towards her.

And a resonant voice cried once along the tunnels: 'It is ended, my father. Rest. Rest…'

AFTERWORD

Hammered by Burke

by Ramsey Campbell

THERE'S NO reason why a novel based on a film or screenplay should be created with any less care than a film based on either of the other two or both. At its best it's an art in itself, whether the book seeks to cleave to its source or develop elements or unite these approaches. The prolific John Burke produced many such books, numbering screen versions of John Osborne plays and the Beatles' first film among the sources he adapted, but he had a special feeling for horror and the macabre, variously represented by the *Tales of Unease* trilogy of anthologies he compiled and by his uncredited screenplay for the Michael Reeves film *The Sorcerers*. Here are four of his novels based on Hammer films (a second volume is uniform with this one).

The Gorgon preserves much of the dialogue of the film but inflects it with (in some cases) significantly different characterisations; thus Dr Vandorff's concern for Carla Hoffman hints at lechery absent from Peter Cushing's civilised portrayal. Where the film gives Megaera a siren song to lure her victims, she's mute in the novel, which contents itself with psychic enticement. Both accounts deny the victim of possession any overt awareness of her state, an approach that risks wasting the splendid Barbara Shelley in the film, but Burke multiplies eloquent hints. He adopts the film's uncommon lunar cycle, perhaps peculiar to that part of the world.

For his two tales of Frankenstein he looks back to the original creator, Mary Shelley, in making the scientist the narrator. *The Curse of Frankenstein* distils the Baron's character in the opening paragraph and continues to scrutinise his inexorable progress into hubris. Like the film, the novel involves variations on elements from the original source (the blind man) and the Universal movie (the child by the lake). To what extent is the reader of such a novel expected to have seen the film on which it's based? The creature's face is barely described (though perhaps this lack conveys the scientist's indifference). By contrast, Burke inserts crucial scenes showing how the creature's limited intelligence is consolidated. He ends the novel with a witty Hammerish allusion, prefiguring a sequel.

In a sense *The Revenge of Frankenstein* returns to Mary Shelley by according the creature a voice. More precisely, Karl already has one, having started off as human before a violent encounter turns him monstrous, reversing and distorting Frankenstein's benign corrective surgery. Burke's account establishes how Karl and his benefactor became mutually dependent and knits the plot together in the process, explaining Frankenstein's mysterious survival of the guillotine, but the first-person viewpoint reduces several key events to hearsay or speculation.

Burke's book is one of three that adapt the film. From 1958, the first is uncredited but "based on a screenplay by Jimmy Sangster with additional dialogue by Hurford Janes" (a mysterious writer born in Fulham in 1909, according to IMDb). It introduces an extended interlude in which Karl takes refuge in a Romany camp, recalling Larry Talbot's encounter with one in *The Wolf Man*, but denies Karl the least taint of cannibalism, surely a crucial element. Shaun Hutson's novel is the most recent and most personal. It emphasises both the horror and the tragedy in a bid to summon the spirit of the film.

Whereas the Universal mummy cycle kept resurrecting the

original cadaver, the Hammer series offers a variety of them. *The Curse of the Mummy's Tomb* adds an American showman to the roster of the cursed, and we may think he deserves his deserts from the desert for claiming to name Turkish Delight, even before he proposes not just to put the mummy on the road but to make the curse a selling point. Although the Universal and Hammer originals set their mummies in motion early in the tale, this entry in the series withholds all sight of him until the halfway mark. The story incorporates variations on previous Hammer tropes (the mysterious saturnine Egyptian, played in the film—as in the studio's first *Mummy*—by George Pastell; the reading of the words of resurrection; a romantic relationship rooted in ancient Egypt, a state of affairs wittily epitomised by the last line of Elizabeth Barrett Browning's celebrated poem), so that it often feels like a reminiscence addressed to Hammer fans. Even the name of our hero—John Bray—incorporates an in-joke for the aficionado, while the preoccupation with severed hands seems to prefigure Hammer's subsequent mummy movie, *Blood from the Mummy's Tomb*. Despite all this, *Curse* achieves coherence and evokes the old magic.

On their original British release these films bore an X certificate, which meant audiences had to be or feign to be at least sixteen years old. These days all four films adapted in the present book are deemed suitable for preteens, but back then this volume (along with magazines such as *Famous Monsters of Filmland*) functioned as an extended trailer for those forbidden delights as well as a memento for folk who had seen the films. This book may stand as a monument to that Hammer era and a reminder of their great days of the Gothic, but it isn't merely nostalgic. The studio has risen from its grave, having cheated death, and now it rides out, helped by the spell of our book.

About the Author

JOHN FREDERICK Burke was an English writer of novels and short stories, specializing in film and tv tie-ins, including *A Hard Day's Night* (1964), *Ian Fleming's Chitty Chitty Bang Bang* (1968) and *King and Castle* (1986) Writing as Jonathan Burke, J. F. Burke and John Burke, he produced several suspense stories and psychological thrillers, including *Swift Summer*, for which he won the Atlantic Award in Literature, *These Haunted Streets* and *Echo of Barbara*, which was later adapted into a film. He achieved equal popularity with his science fiction short stories in magazines like *New Worlds* and *New Frontiers*, and the best of these were collected in *Alien Landscapes*.

For more fantastic fiction, author events,
exclusive excerpts, competitions, limited editions and more

VISIT OUR WEBSITE
titanbooks.com

LIKE US ON FACEBOOK
facebook.com/titanbooks

FOLLOW US ON TWITTER AND INSTAGRAM
@TitanBooks

EMAIL US
readerfeedback@titanemail.com